T0271511

Clare Mackintosh

OTHER PEOPLE'S HOUSES

Signed by the author

SPHERE

OTHER
PEOPLE'S
HOUSES

Clare Mackintosh is a police officer turned crime writer, and the multi-award-winning author of seven *Sunday Times* bestselling novels. Translated into forty languages, her books have sold more than two million copies worldwide, and have spent a combined total of sixty-eight weeks in the *Sunday Times* bestseller chart. Clare lives in North Wales with her husband and their three children.

For more information visit Clare's website claremackintosh.com or find her on Facebook, Instagram and TikTok as @ClareMackWrites

Also by Clare Mackintosh

DC Ffion Morgan
The Last Party
A Game of Lies

I Let You Go
I See You
Let Me Lie
After the End
Hostage

Non-fiction
I Promise It Won't Always Hurt Like This
A Cotswold Family Life

Clare Mackintosh

OTHER PEOPLE'S PEOPLE'S HOUSES

SPHERE

SPHERE

First published in Great Britain in 2025 by Sphere

1 3 5 7 9 10 8 6 4 2

Copyright © Clare Mackintosh Ltd, 2025

Map illustration © Viv Mullett, The Flying Fish Studios

The moral right of the author has been asserted.

A CIP catalogue record for this book is available from the British Library.

Hardback ISBN 978-1-4087-2600-6
Trade paperback ISBN 978-1-4087-2601-3

Typeset in Sabon by Palimpsest Book Production Limited, Falkirk, Stirlingshire
Printed and bound in Great Britain by Clays Ltd, Elcograf S.p.A.

Papers used by Sphere are from well-managed forests and other responsible sources.

Sphere
An imprint of
Little, Brown Book Group
Carmelite House
50 Victoria Embankment
London EC4Y 0DZ

The authorised representative
in the EEA is
Hachette Ireland
8 Castlecourt Centre
Dublin 15, D15 XTP3, Ireland
(email: info@hbgi.ie)

An Hachette UK Company
www.hachette.co.uk

www.littlebrown.co.uk

For Lucy Malagoni

Thank you for taking a chance on me

The Hill, Tattenbrook, Cheshire

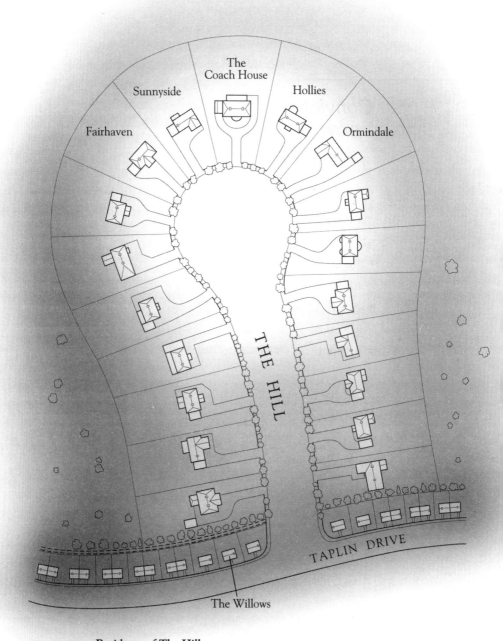

Residents of The Hill

The Coach House	Bianca Dixon, Scarlett Dixon, Grandad Dixon
Fairhaven	Philip and Suki Makepeace
Sunnyside	JP and Camilla Lennox
Hollies	Mikaela, Cara and Alex Jefferson
Ormindale	Warren and Emily Irvine

Residents of Taplin Drive

The Willows	Allie and Dominic Green, Haris Brady

Without Conviction:
Season 4 now available

You asked . . . and we delivered! The new season of *Without Conviction* has finally dropped, and there is TEA! We've all been celebrating the posthumous pardoning of Karl Munson, but the story doesn't end there. Season 4 of *Without Conviction* lifts the lid on the flawed police investigation into the Carmichael killings on Valentine's Day 2014. We've passed everything we've found to the police, in the hope that – this time – they'll do their job properly.

Ten years ago, Peter and Stephanie Carmichael were murdered in their own home. And the killer's still out there.

Subscribe now on Spotify

PROLOGUE

SUNDAY

The weather broke overnight, rain drumming on to baked earth and swirling along the pavements. There were few awake to see it, and, by the morning, summer was restored. Now the sun is hot and high, despite the early hour. Water has drained into gutters and soaked into the cracked earth, and all that's left of the night's sudden storm is a welcome freshness in the air and the swollen banks of the Awen. The river tumbles over itself in its effort to reach the lake, rushing over rocks and tree roots in a torrent of white foam. Every now and then, the force of the water dislodges a stick or a handful of moss from the bank and whips it downstream too fast for the eye to follow.

Fifteen-year-old Ed Clough is walking along the southern bank, away from the rafting centre. He has been sent to look for a missing kayak, and he is taking his time over it. Ed is supposed to be on kitchen duties this morning, but he spent yesterday evening at a Young Farmers rally and the thought of greasy bacon pans is making his stomach churn. He draws deep lungfuls of clean air and wonders how long he can string out his search.

Most of the rafts and canoes are locked in a secure unit at night, but there are a few old yellow kayaks on a rack at the back of the centre, and they occasionally go missing. They are carried aloft by drunk stags and abandoned in the road once enough fun's been had, or they're launched into the river by bored kids. Before Ed started working at the rafting centre, he'd once done exactly that with his best mate, the two of them sprinting down the banks to try and beat the empty vessel to the lake. They had lost by a country mile, as they'd known they would. White water won't be beaten.

Just as Ed is about to turn around, he sees a glimmer of yellow through the trees. He brightens. Donna can't give him a row about how long he's been away from the kitchen if he finds the missing kayak. She might even let him off bacon duty.

The vessel is upside down between rocks, stern pushed under water and bow in the air. Ed tugs at it, but it's hard to get a purchase on the resin hull. The bank is steep and slippery, and he grips a tree root with his left hand to stop himself from sliding into the water. He pushes his foot against the kayak, but it won't budge. Ed sighs, then he kicks off his trainers and strips to his underpants. Donna better put something extra in his pay packet this month; this is above and beyond a minimum wage weekend job.

Despite the heatwave, the river is freezing. Mud squelches beneath his toes; something flits, tiny and fast, between his legs. Ed squeals involuntarily and immediately looks around, relieved to confirm there was no one to hear it. Waist-deep, he reaches over the kayak to grab the opposite side of it, so he can use his full force to yank it out from between the rocks and flip it back over. It's stuck fast, and Ed pulls and pulls and suddenly it comes free. And now the kayak is right-side-up and it's Ed who's upside down, thrown off balance and clinging on to the kayak as he flails for a footing.

It's barely a second (although it feels like longer) before he resurfaces, cursing this stupid job, his stupid boss, the stupid kids who stole a kayak and let it float downriver to lodge itself in these rocks and . . . and . . .

Ed stops thinking. He stops breathing. His entire body is trembling, goosebumps covering his skinny frame, from his ice-cold feet to the white-knuckled hand still gripping the kayak. The kayak that had been so hard to turn over not only because it was trapped but also because it was heavy.

Because there was someone in it.

Ed's stomach gives a sharp, painful spasm. The kayaker is dead, that much is obvious, and yet the face is . . . the face is *moving*. Ed cries out, and this time he doesn't care who hears him.

It's only river water, he tells himself, that's why it looks as though the skin is sliding off the skull. River water seeping from the eyes and nostrils. River water trickling from the corners of those deep-blue lips . . .

Ed's throat fills with bile. He staggers backwards, then he turns and vomits into the foaming waters of the Awen.

ONE

SUNDAY | DC FFION MORGAN

'What do you mean, "he let it go"?'

Five minutes ago, Detective Constable Ffion Morgan had been in the perfect state between sleep and wakefulness, with every intention of having another snooze once she'd let Dave out for a wee. The call from her boss has ruined her lie-in, not least because Dave has lately begun taking Ffion's ringtone as a cue to bark furiously. He jumps on the bed, one heavy foot on Ffion's stomach, and yowls at the phone.

'Just that,' Detective Inspector Malik says. 'By the time the lad finished puking his guts up, the kayak was sailing merrily on its way.'

'Will you shut UP?'

'I beg your pardon?'

'Sorry, boss, I was talking to the dog.' Ffion swings her legs out of bed and grabs Dave's collar, marching him out of the bedroom and shutting the door. Cardboard boxes form teetering pillars on either side of it, labels identifying the contents as *Clothes*, *Books*, or *Misc.* 'Are you telling me we have an AWOL corpse in a kayak?'

'That's pretty much the size of it. Air Support are looking for it now, and a couple of local units are on the ground, but I'd like you on hand when the body's recovered. Call me once you know what's what. And let Cheshire CID know, in case it floats into their waters.'

'But it's my weekend off.'

'Not any more.'

Malik ends the call and Ffion heads downstairs, only for Dave to hurl himself after her, barrelling into the back of her knees. She grabs the banister just in time to stop herself going arse over tit.

'You are such a dick,' she says.

'For bringing you tea in bed?' Leo is standing at the bottom of the stairs, fully dressed and with a mug in each hand. 'Seems harsh.'

'Not you. Although you can be a dick too.' Ffion grins and takes one of the mugs. '*Diolch.*' She steps down to the bottom step, so her face is level with Leo's, and kisses him, feeling his smile match hers. Leo's hand slides over her naked hip; Ffion responds by pressing her own against his crotch. 'I think you're overdressed for the occasion, DS Brady,' she murmurs.

'Some of us have to go to work.'

'Shit!' Ffion breaks away. 'Good save – I need to get dressed. Turns out I have to go in too – there's a dead body making off down the Awen in a kayak.' She wriggles past him, taking a slurp of tea as she does. 'God, you make a good *paned.*'

'A dead body in a kayak?' Leo follows her into the kitchen, where more boxes wait on the counter to be packed. 'Does that make it a canoe-dunnit?'

Ffion groans. 'Don't give up the day job.' She opens the washer-dryer and drags the contents on to the floor. 'That's the third time this month Malik's called me in on my day off. It's almost like he does it deliberately.'

'Good job you hadn't made any plans, I guess.'

Ffion stares at him. 'I had plans.'

'You said you were going to spend the day in bed.'

'How is that not a plan? I have a tub of Ben & Jerry's in the freezer and the new season of *Without Conviction* to binge.'

'You are obsessed.'

'With ice cream or the podcast?'

'Both, but especially the latter.' Leo tips the dregs of his tea into the sink and puts his mug in the dishwasher.

'You say that like it's a bad thing.' Ffion rootles through the pile of laundry. 'Anyway, I wouldn't need to be obsessed with the Carmichael case if my boyfriend would only give up the goods.'

'I don't *have* any goods! The cold case review team isn't even in the same building as me. I literally know as much as you do.' Leo considers this. 'Less, probably.'

Leo's phone is on the counter on top of the washing machine. It flashes a notification and Ffion reaches to hand it to him, but Leo gets there first. He glances at it, then puts it in his pocket. 'BBC app,' he says. 'Breaking news.'

'What's happened?'

'What?'

Ffion stares at him. 'The news?'

'Oh. I didn't really read it.'

'Right.' Ffion leaves a beat. 'Can you give your lot the heads-up we've got a body heading towards Llyn Drych? Just in case they get a call on the nines.'

'Sure.'

Llyn Drych (or Mirror Lake, to give it its English name, which Ffion concedes they occasionally must) straddles the border between England and Wales, making it pot luck as to whether a call from a concerned bystander finds its way to Cheshire Constabulary or North Wales Police.

Ffion tugs on her underwear and grimaces. 'These are still damp.'

'Stick them back in the dryer.'

'I don't have time.'

'Eat something, at least.' Leo is spreading jam on a cut bagel.

'I don't have—'

'Eat.' He slaps the two halves together and closes Ffion's hand around it.

'Very Michelin star,' she says, but she kisses him again. 'Thanks, *calon*.' Her eyes widen. 'Fuck!'

'If you don't have time to put the dryer on, we definitely don't have time to—'

'Who's going to watch Dave?'

They turn to look at the dog, who wags his tail enthusiastically, aware he's being talked about. Dave came from an animal shelter where Ffion had been taking a burglary report. As big as a Shetland pony and just as hairy, Dave is of indeterminate breed. He arrived with a host of behavioural issues, some of which have improved over the last few months, and powerful flatulence, which hasn't.

'Could you drop him off at Mam's for me?' Ffion says.

'Why can't you drop him off?'

'Because she likes you more than me.' She pulls on a pair of creased trousers, ignoring Leo's look of mild horror, then picks through the remaining laundry to find a top. 'She won't be able to say no.'

Leo contemplates Dave with a look of resigned acceptance. 'Come on, then, mate.'

'Oh . . .' Ffion takes a key from a dish on the windowsill. 'This is for you, by the way.'

'What's this?'

'What does it look like?' Ffion bends to put on her shoes, glad of the mass of curly hair that falls over her flushed face.

'Ffion Morgan, are you finally giving me my own key?'

'It's practical, is all.' She straightens. 'Don't get notions. Consider it a trial run for my new place – although I swear my solicitor's ghosting me. We're supposed to be exchanging this week and I've not heard a word for days.'

'Sure.' Leo grins at her. 'We're staying at mine tonight, though – I've got Harris for a few hours, remember.'

'I remember.'

'I won't be taking him back to Allie's till around six.' Leo's tone is light, but there's a tension to his expression that wasn't there a moment ago. 'If you want, we could wait till you—'

'Another time, yeah? Sounds like I'm in for a long day.' Ffion's phone rings and the dog launches into a cacophony of barks. 'For the love of—'

'Go.' Leo pushes her gently towards the door. 'I'll see you later.'

DI Malik is already talking. '. . . recovered from the lake. They'll meet you by the jetty.' Ffion leaves, glad of the diversion. It's not that she doesn't want to meet Leo's son, it's just that she doesn't exactly have a great track record as a parent. If she gives the whole thing a swerve, she can't mess it up.

She puts her breakfast on the roof of her car while she searches for the keys she had literally a second ago, then flings her bag on the back seat. She's halfway down the street before she remembers the bagel.

TWO

SUNDAY | DS LEO BRADY

This time last year, Leo's life was simple. Five days a week he would make the twenty-minute commute to Cheshire's Criminal Investigation Department, where he is a detective sergeant. He would go to the gym most evenings (and occasionally for a beer afterwards). Last, but by no means least, he would spend as much time with his seven-year-old son Harris as work (and his ex-wife) would allow.

Life is very different now.

Leo and Ffion divide their time between Leo's place and Ffion's rented cottage in her home town of Cwm Coed. A few months ago, Ffion's landlord gave her notice – the income potential of turning the place into a holiday let had become too good to ignore – and Leo had tentatively suggested Ffion might move in with him.

'It's too far from work,' she'd said. 'And Mam. And the lake. Anyway, I've saved enough for a deposit – I'm going to buy somewhere.'

'We could buy together. Somewhere closer.'

'It'll be a nightmare if we split up.'

In Ffion's world, Leo has come to understand, glasses are never just half-empty, they're bone-dry and being used as ashtrays. Her aversion to anything resembling commitment means there's no formal arrangement for where they end up each night, resulting in a nomadic lifestyle that Leo finds unsettling. He is forever discovering he has no clean socks, or that the suit he'd planned to wear for court is twenty miles in the wrong direction. He recently left a toothbrush in Ffion's bathroom, thinking it would make sense to at least keep toiletries in both houses, only to find it back in his overnight bag when he came out of the shower. His commute has tripled, and the gym has fallen by the wayside (along with the beers, which is probably no bad thing).

But Ffion . . .

Leo's face splits into a smile. He often catches himself smiling for no reason nowadays. Except it isn't for no reason, it's because, after making a mess of things for far too long, he and Ffion finally got it together. And by God, he loves her. Leo had thought he loved Allie when he'd married her, and maybe he had, but the way he feels now is off the scale. Ffion is infuriating, challenging, argumentative and unpredictable, but in spite of all that – or perhaps because of it – Leo adores her. She's also the hottest woman alive, which makes them both regularly late for work. All of this means Leo puts up with keeping a toothbrush in his car and chasing drifts of Dave hair around his previously immaculate house, with driving miles to get to work (and, really, the views around Cwm Coed almost make up for that), and with never being able to plan anything further than a few days ahead.

'We might not be together by then,' Ffion said once, after Leo had suggested they book a holiday.

Leo tries not to let it faze him. One day, when Ffion's ready, she'll commit. And then maybe they'll get a place together, and he'll introduce her to Harris, which is far more important than a

11

holiday or where Leo keeps his toothbrush. Even Ffion can't make excuses not to meet Leo's son for ever.

Ffion's mother, Elen Morgan, has the door open before Leo and Dave are halfway up the path. 'Ffi sent you to do her dirty work, has she? Thinks I won't say no to you, I suppose.'

'You're good, Mrs Morgan. I could use your powers of deduction in CID.'

'How you put up with that girl, I don't know.'

'I'm hoping she'll turn out like her mother.'

'*Fydd gweniaith yn mynd â ti i unman.*'

'Not a clue what that means, sorry.' Leo hands Elen Dave's lead. 'Thanks for looking after him.'

'I said flattery will get you nowhere,' Elen calls after him as he makes his way back to his car. 'And it's about time you learned Cymraeg!'

Leo pretends not to hear, waving goodbye without turning around. He'd tried to speak Welsh once, when he and Ffion had gone out for a drink with some of her friends. Leo had been practising for the occasion, almost losing his nerve, and then finally getting it together and asking in faltering Welsh whether anyone would like another drink.

The table had fallen silent. Everyone stared at him.

'What did you just say?' Mia's lips had twitched. Leo had wanted to die, but he mumbled it again, realising too late that he'd got two of the words in the wrong order and that the final bit wasn't Welsh at all, but GCSE Spanish. Mia burst into laughter and the others joined her, and Leo had burned with awkwardness.

Ffion had laughed too. She'd leapt to her feet and pulled Leo's arm aloft. 'My boyfriend the linguist!' Even hearing Ffion publicly acknowledge their relationship for the first time couldn't take the sting out of Leo's embarrassment. He hadn't tried again.

Weekends on CID run with skeletal staff led by a duty DS, which today is Leo. As always, he'll have a couple of detective constables with him, who will spend the day catching up on paperwork and praying nothing comes in to put the kibosh on their evening plans.

The second Leo walks into the office, he knows something's happened. There's an indefinable quality to the air, even though there are still only two detectives, even though both those detectives are sitting quietly at their desks.

'What's in?' Leo puts his bag on his desk.

'Burglary on The Hill.' DC Dawn Chambers doesn't look up. 'Three-million-pound detached property.'

The Hill, a wide tree-lined street on a steep slope in Tattenbrook, West Cheshire, is populated by bankers, minor league footballers and bored housewives. At the foot of The Hill, the houses look relatively normal (albeit far larger than anything Leo could ever dream of owning) but, as the incline increases, the builds become bigger and more extravagant. The properties at the top of The Hill, with views across the entire county, are listed for sale for sums that always make Leo think there's been a typo.

Dawn spins her chair around to face him. 'Tidy search. Small items taken, no large electronics, no art.' She pauses. 'Entry via the kitchen window, and the alarm didn't go off.'

Six months ago, a house on The Hill was broken into when the owners were away, and a number of small items were stolen. No large electronics, no art. Entry via the kitchen window, and the alarm didn't go off.

'Who called it in?' Leo says.

'The owners were away last night. Got back this morning to

find the back door open and the wife's jewellery missing. The dog unit was there within six minutes but couldn't find a trail.'

'CSI?'

'On scene now.'

Cheshire borders seven other counties, making it an easy target for travelling criminals who can be in and out of the force area in a heartbeat. Burglaries are a relatively frequent occurrence in Cheshire, and two break-ins in six months – even within the same street – could simply be unlucky.

But two break-ins in the same street with the same MO?

That's a series.

Facebook.com/groups/ WithoutConvictionSleuths

🔒 *Private group*

Simona Macleod

Hey, I've just downloaded ep 1 of Season 4 and I'm wondering if I need to go back and listen to Season 3 or whether I'll pick it up?

1h

All comments ▼

Kirsty Padden-Barr

You definitely need Season 3, it explains the murders and how Karl Munson was (wrongfully) convicted.

56m

James Goldsmith

There's a summary in the pinned posts, but, basically, Peter and Stephanie Carmichael were stabbed with a steak knife during a Valentine's dinner at their house (candles, flowers on the table, all that shit). The police nicked a homeless guy sleeping in a shed nearby, and the poor bloke got fifteen years. He died of liver failure about six years into his sentence.

54m

Kirsty Padden-Barr

Seven.

50m

James Goldsmith

I said about.

45m

Simona Macleod

Cool, thanks. How come Munson was pardoned?

44m

Kirsty Padden-Barr

This is literally all in Season 3.

42m

James Goldsmith

The witness who picked him out at the ID parade said she'd been put under pressure, and the DNA evidence should never have been allowed because the officer who arrested Munson had been at the house just before nicking him.

38m

Kirsty Padden-Barr

It's called cross-contamination.

37m

James Goldsmith

Ignore DI Padden-Barr @Simona Macleod. Season 4 picks up from the posthumous pardoning. The police overlooked loads of evidence at the scene. Like, there was that hexagonal locket that went missing, remember – they covered it at the end of Season 3 – Munson didn't have it anywhere and he hadn't had time to flog it.

33m

Simona Macleod

Cheers for the catch-up. I'm going in!

21m

THREE

SUNDAY | FFION

It's a peculiar contradiction to feel claustrophobic outdoors, but that is how Ffion always feels in Cwm Coed in August. Even on a Sunday morning, the high street is crammed with dawdling tourists who stop walking without warning, spill into the road and abandon litter within two metres of a bin.

Ffion drives down the narrow street with her windows down and the new season of the *Without Conviction* podcast playing through her earbuds. The presenters are called Joseph Flint and Gemma Lyrick, and they share the same rapid, almost breathless way of speaking.

. . . yet according to one of our listeners, Joseph is saying, *who we're calling 'A', Peter Carmichael didn't even like steak.*

Is 'A' a verified source, Joseph?

The Carmichaels were regulars at a restaurant A used to work at. Stephanie would always have the steak, and A claims Peter said on more than one occasion that he wasn't a fan.

So what are we saying, Joseph? Because when the police found Peter and Stephanie dead in their kitchen, there were two rump steaks waiting to be cooked.

I guess, Gemma, we're saying there's a question mark over whether Stephanie had planned that dinner for her husband, or for someone else . . .

A man wearing a wetsuit pulled down around his waist steps out in front of Ffion's car and she slams on the brakes, which shriek in protestation. Ffion throws up her hands in the universal sign for *What the fuck are you doing?* and the man mouths an apology and jogs to the other side. On the pavement, the newsagent, Haydn, is fixing a sheet of plywood across the broken window of his shop. He nods to Ffion, and she takes out her earbud. 'What happened here?'

'No idea,' Haydn says. 'It was like this when I came down this morning. Bloody pissheads.'

'Have you made a police report?'

'No point. No offence.'

'None taken.' From behind her, a car honks at Ffion to move, so she does. She takes out her other earbud. Anecdotal evidence of Peter Carmichael not liking steak is far from the 'tea' promised in *Without Conviction*'s explosive trailer, but the previous season had been gold, and Ffion has high hopes for Season 4.

There's nowhere left to park at the lake, so Ffion leaves her car on the road, next to the ice cream van, and walks towards the jetty. She takes out her phone and dials as she picks her way through the campervans and sunshades.

'Yes, it's me again.' Ffion steps over a lurid green inflatable watermelon. 'You'll miss me when we finally complete on this house, won't you? That's assuming we complete before one of us succumbs to old age and dies, which is looking increasingly unlikely. I'm sure you've got dozens of other clients leaving messages for you, and I'm sure those people are just as sick of living out of boxes as I am, but I have literally nowhere to go after the end of this month, so for the love of all that is holy can we *please* exchange this week?'

She ends the call. Her solicitor almost certainly won't pick up the message till tomorrow morning, but Ffion feels better for doing something constructive. She once read that moving house is as stressful as bereavement and divorce. Having experienced all three, Ffion entirely concurs.

Llyn Drych – so quiet and serene for much of the year – is a migraine of noise and colour. Ffion walks past a man banging in the final post of a series of orange windbreaks encircling himself and his wife. The windbreaks (presumably brought to protect them from other people, since the air is stiflingly still) successfully block the view of the lake and its overlooking mountain, Pen y Ddraig. Ffion wonders why the couple bothered to come at all.

She could use a few screens herself, she thinks, as she draws closer to the yellow kayak on the shore by the jetty. A line of police tape is woefully inadequate at keeping curious eyes away. Preserving crime scenes in busy locations is always a challenge, and crime scenes by open water especially so. In the shallows of Llyn Drych, a police community support officer with his trousers hitched above his boots shouts at swimmers to keep their distance. He's sweating, his peaked cap a poor substitute for shade.

'*Ti'n iawn*, Ffion?' he says, as she approaches.

'*Well na fo.*' She nods towards the kayak.

'Better than *her,*' the PCSO corrects. 'The victim's female.'

Ffion walks towards the other officers, her eyes fixed on the body slumped in the kayak – a body Ffion can indeed now see is a woman. She's wearing a swimming costume with a plunging neckline, and the exposed skin is mottled and purple. The woman's lower half is hidden beneath a waterproof skirt fastened around the opening of the kayak. The combination puts Ffion in mind of some macabre breed of mermaid.

'Alright?' Ffion recognises the female officer, Police Constable

Lucy Doherty, but doesn't know the guy she's with. His dark wavy hair is gelled into a quiff, and on his police-issue tie is a silver pin. She shows him her ID. 'DC Morgan. Bryndare CID.'

'Sam Taylor,' he says. He tilts his head forward in something that's less of a nod and more of a bow. 'A recent transferee from Cheshire. Hoping to apply for CID myself, actually, so I'll be looking for advice.' Sam smiles in a way that sets Ffion's teeth on edge. It's the smile of a man who doesn't think he needs advice and has only said so to ingratiate himself with someone who might be useful to him. Ffion glances at Lucy and catches the tail end of an eye-roll.

'Who found the kayak?' Ffion says.

Lucy opens her mouth to speak, but Sam gets there first.

'A man by the name of Steffan Edwards. He was opening up the boathouse when he saw what he thought was an abandoned kayak. Took a motorboat out to bring it in, and . . .' He gestures to the woman at their feet. 'Don't worry, we haven't touched it.'

'You checked to see if she was breathing,' Lucy says.

'Well, yes.' Sam flushes. 'But preservation of life outweighs preservation of scene. There wasn't a pulse,' he adds unnecessarily.

Ffion looks at Sam, who holds her gaze unwaveringly, almost challengingly. He's younger than her – maybe twenty-eight, at most. 'Over to you, then,' she says.

'I'm sorry?' Sam frowns.

'Consider it a dress rehearsal for CID. What are our next steps?'

'Oh. Right. Get CSI here.'

'What for?'

'To capture forensic evidence and photograph the body *in situ*.'

'But this could have been an accident,' Ffion says. 'You're going to use taxpayers' money to photograph something that might not be the result of criminal activity?'

'Absolutely.' Sam isn't thrown by Ffion's role play. 'By the time we know how the victim died, it'll be too late to go back and secure evidence. It has to be done now.'

'Okay, good. What other priorities do you have?'

'The kayak,' Sam says. 'Removing the body here could result in evidence being lost. I'd request that it goes to the mortuary as it is – in the kayak.'

'Not bad,' Ffion says grudgingly. 'Just one thing.'

'What?'

'This woman is someone's daughter, possibly someone's wife or sister. She's not an "it".' Ffion reaches for her radio and calls in the request for CSI and transport, her gaze fixed on the scene. The woman in the kayak isn't wearing a helmet or spray top. It's not uncommon for holidaymakers to take to the lake in the wrong kit, but it's less likely upriver, where the churning waters bring to their senses all but the most determined – or reckless. But reckless paddlers don't wear cutaway bathing costumes more suited to strolling along Caribbean beaches – at least not in Ffion's experience – and reckless paddlers who don't return are almost always reported missing within a few hours. Something doesn't add up, which usually means one thing.

Murder.

FOUR

SUNDAY | LEO

'It must be on the other side.' Leo spins the car around and drives slowly along the wide, tree-lined street. The houses are set back from the road, some behind imposing gates, others with wide gravel driveways. On the new-build development where Leo lives, all the houses look the same, but here on The Hill there's no common style. Sixties brick, then Cotswold stone, then faux Tudor beams. They pass (for the second time) a striking glass building that looks like an office block, and Leo wonders how the owners got planning permission for something so extraordinary. Money talks, he supposes.

'You just know these are the sort of people to put in a complaint about response times,' Dawn says, as she looks for the names of each house. 'If they had numbers like normal houses, it would be a million times easier to find them.'

'Tell that to my ex-wife,' Leo says. 'When she moved here, she took the number off the front door and gave her new address as "The Willows". She gets the right hump when the postman can't find it.'

'Your ex lives on The Hill?' Dawn points at a large boulder by the side of the road, where carved letters spell out 'Sunnyside'. 'Here it is.'

'She *tells* people she lives on The Hill.' Leo turns through the open gates at the end of the drive. 'Her new bloke inherited some money from his parents, and they bought a doer-upper at the bottom, around the corner.'

Stones crunch beneath the wheels of the car as Leo sweeps around the circular flower bed in the centre of the drive. The house is red brick, with floor-to-ceiling windows on the ground floor and stone pillars flanking the enormous front door.

Dawn pulls the bell, setting off a jangling inside which gradually fades away. There are several seconds of silence before they hear footsteps. The door opens.

'You took your time.'

For one brief, awkward moment Leo thinks Mrs Lennox has opened the door naked, before realising she's wearing a pair of flesh-coloured leggings with a matching crop top. Her dark hair is scraped into a severe ponytail which pulls the skin tight across her cheekbones.

'Sorry about that,' Dawn says. 'We couldn't find you.'

Mrs Lennox lets out a sharp sigh as she turns into the house. 'I'd ask you to take your shoes off, only there's no point: your colleagues have left fingerprint powder everywhere. Thank heavens they're almost finished; the house looks like a bomb's gone off in it.'

The hall at Sunnyside is bigger than Leo's entire ground floor, and there's no sign of the metaphorical bomb Mrs Lennox referred to. In fact, the place is immaculate. There's a wide staircase in the centre of the room which leads to a mezzanine landing from which a huge glass ceiling floods the hall with light. The rest of the room is empty, which seems rather a waste of space, although the Lennoxes clearly aren't short on that. There are several open doors off the hall and Leo catches a glimpse of a living room with four sofas arranged in a square.

Mrs Lennox leads them into the kitchen, where a man in straining shorts is leaning on the central island. There's a smashed window behind him, and Leo can see a white-suited CSI in the garden, working on the exterior frame. 'This is my husband, JP,' Mrs Lennox says.

'JP?' Leo extends a hand, which Mr Lennox ignores.

'John Paul Lennox. Everyone calls me JP. The wife's Camilla.' JP's hair has been artfully – but not hugely successfully – arranged over a large central bald patch. It would be presumptuous, Leo thinks, to conclude that Camilla Lennox is only with her considerably older husband for his money, but, from where Leo's standing, JP has little else going for him.

'Have you caught them yet?' JP says. He doesn't pause for breath, let alone an answer. 'Didn't think so. They'll be long gone by now. Do you know how long it took your lot to send a squad car?' He opens his mouth to answer his own question, but Dawn saves him the trouble.

'Six minutes,' she says brightly. 'Eight minutes under target.'

JP blinks. 'Yes, well. It felt a damn sight longer.'

'We'd like to ask a few questions, if that's okay?' Leo says.

'I'm not sure what I can add to what I told your uniformed colleagues,' JP says, but he gestures towards the table and pulls out an upholstered dining chair. 'Coffee?'

'If it's not too much trouble,' Dawn says.

'No trouble at all.' JP raises his voice. 'Jade!'

From the corner of the kitchen, a young woman in an apron appears from what looks like a utility room. Her skin is pale and her face heart-shaped with wide blue eyes. Her loose blonde hair looks as though it could do with a wash.

'Coffee,' JP says. 'Three cups. And a tea for Camilla. The detectives are here to ask some questions about the burglary.'

Jade stares at him, her mouth slightly open.

'Wakey wakey!' JP snaps his fingers in the air several times.

Jade blinks. 'Alright, keep your hair on,' she mutters, walking over to a cupboard.

'I'll pretend I didn't hear that.' JP sits back down and gives a short, forced laugh. 'You wonder how they get through the day, don't you?'

Leo and Dawn exchange glances. What a charmer.

'Getting decent staff around here is an absolute nightmare.' Camilla Lennox joins them. 'All the trades are the same – I had someone round to quote on a new kitchen and they literally ghosted me.'

'Well, the end result is lovely,' Dawn says. Leo has to admit, it's a beautiful kitchen. Marble counters sit on top of solid wood cupboards hand-painted in a light sage green. Three glass lamps hang above the island.

Camilla is momentarily confused, then she bursts out laughing. 'This? Christ, this is the *old* kitchen! The new one will be stunning.'

'Waste of money, if you ask me,' JP says.

'The estate agent didn't think so,' Camilla retorts. 'There's a house for sale on The Hill called Ormindale,' she explains to Leo and Dawn. 'Warren and Emmy Irvine are going through a rather unpleasant divorce.'

Leo, who still feels the aftershocks of his split with Allie, wonders if there's any other kind.

'Anyway, I saw what their place was on for, and I had the same agency over to value ours,' Camilla says. 'All the houses are different, you see. The Makepeaces did a loft conversion earlier this year, and the Jeffersons have extended theirs so much it's unrecognisable.' Camilla gives a little headshake, before allowing a smug smile to creep on to her face. 'Apparently ours will be worth a hundred grand more than Ormindale once we've had the new kitchen fitted.'

'The new kitchen that will no doubt *cost us* a hundred grand,' JP says under his breath. 'This break-in'd better not affect property prices.'

Leo notices a dustpan containing pieces of porcelain on the island. 'Was there much broken in the burglary?'

'Just that figurine,' Camilla says. 'It wasn't worth anything, fortunately.'

'Did you point it out to the crime scene investigator?' Leo pushes back his chair so he can take a look.

'Yes, yes, that's why it's there. No prints, apparently. He swept up the bits and left them there in case I wanted to try and mend it.'

Leo picks up the largest piece of the ornament and looks through the bits in the dustpan. The figurine is – or was – a shepherdess. She's holding a curved staff and has one lamb pressed against her porcelain skirt, and what looks like another under one arm. A bit twee for Leo's tastes, not that he'd ever say that to Mrs Lennox. 'It's a pretty clean break; you could probably glue it.'

'It was a silly present from a friend years ago – kitsch nonsense. I'll stick it in the bin later.'

'I understand you were in Abersoch when the break-in happened?' Leo says.

'We have a place there and some friends had invited us for supper. We couldn't really say no, even though it's a bit of a pain going just for one night. The traffic can be a nightmare, but we had to be back early this morning, because JP has a charity golf tournament.'

'*Had*,' JP says, looking at his watch. 'I should be teeing off now. I told you we should have said no to dinner.'

'Oh, right!' Camilla gives a sharp laugh. 'It's okay to offend my friends, but heaven forbid we miss your golf—'

'What time did you leave here yesterday?' Dawn stops the marital bickering before it takes hold.

'Around five,' JP says.

'And what time did you get home this morning?'

JP looks at his wife. 'Seven-thirty?'

'About that,' Camilla says.

Dawn makes a note. 'So the burglary could have happened at any point between five p.m. yesterday and this morning?'

'I guess so,' Camilla says.

Jade sets a tray on the table and begins laying out cups. Leo thanks her, trying to make up for her employers, who haven't even acknowledged her, but she doesn't look at him. She clatters his cup, spilling coffee into the saucer.

'When did you hear about the burglary, Jade?' Leo says.

'Mrs Lennox texted me.' She glances at him but continues to lay out the drinks. 'I – I wasn't here.'

'Jade doesn't work weekends,' Camilla says. 'I called her in today to sort out the mess.'

'You don't live in?' Dawn asks.

'I'm married. Got two little ones. We live on Stonebridge.'

Leo knows Stonebridge Gardens, a sprawling council estate a couple of miles east. 'And were you home last night?'

'I'm home every night – the baby still wakes a lot, and she won't take a bottle.'

'Would you be happy for us to confirm that with your partner?' Leo smiles to reassure her. 'It's just routine.'

'S'pose so.'

'Thank you.' Leo turns to JP and Camilla. 'We'll need details of anyone else who has access to the house, please. Do you have an alarm?'

'*Someone* forgot to set it.' JP glares at his wife.

'I *did* set it; it must be broken.'

'Well, either way, it didn't go off, and it wasn't set when we got home this morning.'

'Who has the code?' Dawn asks.

'Just the three of us,' Camilla says. 'JP, me and—', she looks accusingly at the cleaner, '—Jade.'

'I didn't – I never—' Jade looks as though she might cry.

Outside, the crime scene investigator is packing up. Leo stands. 'Excuse me while I have a quick chat with my colleague. Dawn, can you make a start on the statements?'

'No prints, sorry.' The CSI peels back his hood.

'Not even on that broken ornament?'

'Gloves.' The CSI shrugs. 'Looks like they knew what they were doing. Clean and tidy search, very little disturbed beyond what they took – and they didn't take a lot.'

'No vehicle, perhaps,' Leo says. 'Only took what they could carry.'

'Maybe, although there's a glass dish by the sink with several rings in it, and a few other bits which to my uneducated eye look like they might be worth a bob or two. Seems strange not to have taken them when they'd easily slip in a pocket.'

Leo nods to the grass around the broken window. 'Did you find any footprints?'

'None. It started raining in the early hours of this morning, which means the break-in probably happened before that.'

A six- or seven-hour window, then? Leo looks at the houses

either side, but they're so far apart – and the hedges separating each garden so high – that the chances of someone having seen an intruder are slim.

'You take this side of the street,' he tells Dawn, once the statements are done and they've left Mrs Lennox complaining she'll never get the fingerprint dust off the paintwork. 'I'll do the other side.' He loosens his tie and runs a finger between his neck and the collar of his pale blue shirt. 'God, it's hot.'

Dawn has her ear pressed to the phone, waiting for the results of the routine PNC check she'd requested on the occupants of Sunnyside. She's wearing a knee-length cotton dress which looks infinitely more comfortable than Leo's suit. She looks suddenly at Leo, her brows raised as she thanks the operator and ends the call.

'Well?' Leo says.

'Camilla and JP Lennox are clean.' Dawn pauses. 'But no wonder Jade looked so nervous – she did six months in HMP Styal. For theft.'

X.com

Duncan Murphy @duncanmurphy_16
Just finished episode 1 of @WithoutConviction and wondering
how those police officers can sleep at night! Stephanie
Carmichael had a SECOND PHONE hidden in her bedroom and
the police literally ignored it #carmichaelmurders
#defundthepolice

Sophie Barnett @eastlondonSoph
Do we know what's on it?

True Crime Fandom @truecrimefandom
@eastlondonSoph Call history shows multiple calls in and out
to a single number. No texts, which is weird

Sophie Barnett @eastlondonSoph
Boomers don't know how to text

Richard Sheldon @SheldonRichard1956
@eastlondonSoph that's a very sweeping generalisation. Some
of us are pretty tech savvy, actually, as evidenced by these
tweets. Regards, Richard.

Sophie Barnett @eastlondonSoph
@TrueCrimeFandom so who was she calling all the time?

True Crime Fandom @truecrimefandom
@eastlondonSoph the other number was a pay-as-you-go phone. Unlikely the police will be able to identify who it belonged to, given the time that's elapsed

Duncan Murphy @duncanmurphy_16
@TrueCrimeFandom @eastlondonSoph If they'd done their job properly ten years ago, Karl Munson wouldn't have died in prison #defundthepolice

True Crime Fandom @truecrimefandom
@duncanmurphy_16 @eastlondonSoph It makes you think, doesn't it? Obviously what happened to Stephanie Carmichael and her husband was awful, but she was clearly up to no good

DrCarlyMeyer @CLMeyer_PhD
@truecrimefandom are you seriously suggesting she brought this on herself? @duncanmurphy_16 @eastlondonSoph

True Crime Fandom @truecrimefandom
@CLMeyer_PhD @duncanmurphy_16 @eastlondonSoph No! I'm saying whoever she was keeping secret is obviously the killer . . .

FIVE

SUNDAY | FFION

Once Ffion has overseen the transfer of the kayak and its cargo into a private ambulance, she returns to her car, which is stifling hot after an hour and a half in the blazing sun. Ffion wrenches back the roof and drives the mile and a half from Cwm Coed to the rafting centre, the sound of the engine now far too loud to enable any more podcast-listening.

At the rafting centre, her colleague DC George Kent is sitting in a job car with the engine running. Ffion pulls up alongside her and feels an icy blast of air-con as George opens her door.

'Isn't this weather glorious?' George says. She's wearing black linen trousers and a matching short-sleeved top, both of which are miraculously uncreased.

'It's fucking awful.' The back of Ffion's neck is damp, and she snaps a hair bobble off her gearstick to tie back her hair.

'Makes a change from rain.'

'I like the rain.' Ffion gets out of her car. 'It keeps people away.'

'Bet Cwm Coed's mobbed today,' George says, as they walk towards the rafting centre.

'Yup, the lake was ninety per cent paddleboard.'

'And twenty per cent buoyancy aids, I'll bet.' George glances towards the riverbank, where a group of women are clipping each other into bright orange life jackets. 'It's all fun and games till somebody drowns.'

'That's a cheery slogan.' Ffion grins. '*Visit Wales* should have you doing their adverts.'

'They bloody well should – it might stop a few needless deaths. When will people learn that water kills?'

Ffion pushes open the door to the centre. 'I don't think a buoyancy aid would have stopped this one.'

'Let's see what the post-mortem says. Tenner says accidental drowning.'

'You're on,' Ffion says. 'I have to warn you, my reputation's at stake on this one – I told a transferee it was murder, and I can't be losing face in front of hot men.'

'Hot?' George stops walking.

'Objectively speaking. But a dick with it, so . . .' Ffion shrugs.

Fifteen-year-old Ed Clough doesn't look up as Ffion and George enter the café. He's sitting next to the centre manager, Donna, and has a pint of water clutched in both hands. Beneath the mop of blonde hair, the lad's complexion is tinged with green.

'How are you doing?' Ffion says. Ed doesn't answer.

'He hasn't been sick for a while,' Donna offers.

George sits opposite them. 'Well, it's not every day you come across a dead body.'

'Especially the morning after a big one, eh, Ed?' Ffion says cheerfully. 'I hear the Young Farmers were on form last night.'

Ed blanches. He takes a sip of water, closing his eyes as he forces it down. Ffion gets out her phone. She's about to present him with a photo she took of the lakeside crime scene, but George coughs and takes the phone from her.

'Hey, what are you—' Ffion stops as she realises George is

cropping the shot so the contents of the kayak can't be seen. 'Yeah, that's a fair shout.' She shows Ed the edited image. 'Is this the kayak you found this morning?'

Ed's eyes turn reluctantly to the phone, then quickly back to his glass of water. He nods.

'Great,' Ffion says. 'I mean, not *great* great, obviously. But good to know we don't have another one floating down the Awen.' She turns to Donna. 'Is it definitely one of yours?'

Donna nods. 'May I?' She reaches for Ffion's phone, then uses her finger and thumb to zoom in on the back of the kayak, where the number 87 has been handwritten in black marker pen. 'Seventy-five to ninety-five are kept in numbered racks at the back of the centre. When I opened up this morning, eighty-seven was missing, so I sent Ed to look for it.'

'What's this skirt around the opening of the kayak?' George points to the photo.

'That's a waterproof spray deck. It fastens around your waist and seals around the cockpit to keep out the water. One of the first things we teach people here is the wet exit – how to pull off the skirt and get out of the kayak if it tips over.'

'So a kayaker who couldn't do that,' George says, 'for example if they'd hit their head and were unconscious—'

'Would drown,' Donna finishes.

'Our Crime Scene Investigator will come by later to examine the racking,' George says. 'It would be helpful if you and your staff could give samples for elimination purposes.'

'Of course.'

'Is she dead?' Ed says suddenly. He looks at Ffion, who hesitates, then nods.

'Sorry.'

'I thought so.'

The break in his voice tugs at something inside Ffion. Teenagers are so noisy, so full of bravado, until something big happens. Ffion's seen it this summer in her own daughter. Seren had been born when Ffion was just sixteen, and the two girls were brought up as sisters. They're still more like sisters than mother and daughter, Ffion thinks, although that's changing, slowly. And now Seren is eighteen, and off to university. She'd been positively brimming over with excitement once her A-levels had finished, telling anyone who'd listen that she couldn't wait to leave Cwm Coed. She and Caleb had showed Ffion the house they planned to share with three others, and Ffion had bitten back the retort that it was so far from central London they might as well stay in Wales. As the summer stretched on, and the start date for uni had drawn near, Seren's bragging had become more subdued. She's still excited, Ffion knows – still wants the big adventure – but she's scared too.

'I'm really sorry I let go of it,' Ed says.

Ffion takes pity on him. 'I'd probably have done the same. Do you still live in the house by the bus stop?'

'Yeah. With the red door.'

'I know it. Go home. We'll take a statement once you're feeling a bit more human, alright?'

Ed looks at Donna, who nods.

'Get yourself some salt and vinegar Hula Hoops and a full-fat Coke,' Ffion says. 'That was always my go-to breakfast after a Young Farmers party. With a bacon sandwich, obviously.'

Ed lets out a moan and claps his hand to his mouth, then rushes from the room.

'Well, I think we can strike him off the suspect list,' Ffion says. 'He doesn't have the stomach for it.'

'Suspect?' Donna says. 'You don't think it was an accident?'

36

'We're keeping all options open at this stage,' George says, shooting Ffion a look.

'The woman who runs the campsite next door said she saw three tourists mucking about with a kayak yesterday evening.'

'Cefn Coed?' Ffion says. 'Do you know what time she saw them?'

'Around six.'

'Did she describe the tourists?' George opens her notebook.

'She said she only saw their legs. They were carrying the kayak over their heads, running across the field up towards Mervyn's holiday cottage. They were zigzagging all over the place and mooing.'

Ffion stares at her. 'Mooing?'

'That's what she said. If it's the people staying at Merv's, they're estate agents. They had a rafting session with us yesterday morning, and they were a bloody nightmare.'

'In what way?' George looks up.

'Messing about, not listening to the briefing . . .' Donna shrugs. 'They didn't like it when I told them off, they started calling me "Miss" and making out like it was school. I wish it bloody had been, I'd have given them detention.'

'How many in the group?' Ffion asks.

'Four. I had to pull the organiser to one side in the end and say I was *this close* to chucking them out. The older guy had just pushed one of his colleagues under the water, and you know when people act like they're messing about, but they're not?' Donna pulls a face. 'There was clearly no love lost between the pair of them.'

'What time did the group leave here?' George says.

'I signed them out at three-thirty.'

'Do you know where they went?'

'They said they were going back to their holiday let, then out for something to eat,' Donna says. 'They asked me to recommend – and I quote – "a restaurant with a good wine list, within walking distance".'

Ffion laughs. 'They haven't been to Cwm Coed before, clearly.' She pushes back her chair. 'Come on, George, let's find out what they went for: Caffi Coffi or the chip van.'

The holiday let at the top of the field is a converted barn with an exposed staircase at one end, leading to what would once have been a hay loft. The stonework has been recently repointed, and the slate roof looks new.

'What a gorgeous place to stay,' George says, turning to admire the view, which stretches down towards Cwm Coed.

'Mervyn owns half a dozen of them. All holiday lets.' Ffion knocks on the glossy black door. 'People bang on about Londoners pushing up property prices so locals can't afford to live in their own town, but half the farmers in Cwm Coed have got an Airbnb. Talk about shitting on their own doorstep.'

There's no sound from inside the house.

'You seem a little triggered,' George says.

'If you'd spent the last year trying to buy a house, you'd be triggered.'

'I take it you still don't have a moving day, then?'

'Don't ask.' Ffion knocks again. 'The chain's collapsed three times and my solicitor's ghosting me.' She moves to look through a window, but just as she's cupping her hand around her eyes, the door opens.

'Yes?' A woman in her fifties, with matted blonde hair stuck to one cheek, sways slightly in the open doorway. She puts out one hand to steady herself, the other pressed to her temple. Smears of mascara ring her half-shut eyes. She's wearing a deep red silk robe, carelessly pulled around her shoulders. She squints at them. 'What time is it?'

'Time for headache pills and a strong coffee, by the looks of things. I'm DC Ffion Morgan and this is DC George Kent. Could we come inside, please?'

'Police? Is there a problem?'

'Who else is staying at this property?' George says, as they follow the woman inside. A large basket in the hall is stuffed with lake paraphernalia: snorkels, wetsuits, buckets and spades. In the living room, there are brown leather sofas either side of a large fireplace, and a large footstool covered in a sky-blue Welsh woollen blanket. George gestures to the woman to sit down.

'I – look, what's this about? My head's killing me.'

Ffion stays standing. 'A kayak was stolen from the rafting centre at the bottom of the field. The culprits were seen heading towards this property.'

'It takes two detectives to investigate a stolen kayak?'

'It had a dead body in it.'

The woman's mouth works but no sound comes out. She stares at Ffion.

George opens her notebook. 'What's your name, please?'

'Carole Simmonds.'

'And you're staying here with . . . ?'

'My staff. I own an estate agency in Cheshire – Simmonds Sales and Lettings – and I take my team away for a couple of nights twice a year.'

Ffion grimaces. 'I can't imagine voluntarily spending the weekend with people I work with.'

'Cheers for that,' George says. 'Ms Simmonds, I'd like the names of your colleagues, please.'

'Employees. Mike Foster, Russell Steele and Natasha Brett.'

'Are they all here?'

'I assume so. As you can see, I've only just got up. We had rather a late one. You know what they say: all work and no play.' She attempts a smile, but the effort clearly triggers a headache, as she presses a hand against her temple.

'Down here, is it?' Ffion is walking down the narrow hallway leading from the sitting room.

'Yes, but—'

Ffion bangs on the first closed door she comes to, then continues down the hall without waiting for a response. The second door is open, and she notices the bed is neatly made, the curtains open. 'Whose room is this?'

'Mine,' Carole says. 'Natasha and I took the rooms with en-suites. The boys are sharing a bathroom.'

'What's going on?' A man around Carole's age has appeared in the corridor, clutching a towel around his waist.

'Who are you?' A second man opens his bedroom door. He's younger than the first, and wearing a pair of boxer shorts, his hair dishevelled and his eyes screwed up against the light.

Ffion bangs on Natasha's door, unwilling to delay things by answering the men's questions, or even by asking for their names, because she's quite certain now that Carole Simmonds's final colleague won't be here. That Natasha Brett is the young woman in the kayak.

Ffion opens the door to the fourth bedroom.

It's empty.

The three estate agents sit in silence on one of the brown leather sofas. George has made coffee, but no one is drinking it; the two sales reps have even worse hangovers than their boss. Mike Foster

40

is in his late forties, with slightly thinning fair hair and a hooked nose. The buttons on his hastily pulled-on shirt are crooked. Russell Steele is younger – perhaps mid-twenties – and dark-haired, with a beard so short and so meticulously shaped it looks as though it's been drawn on with a Sharpie. He's pulled on a towelling robe over his boxers.

'Are you sure it's Natasha?' Mike says.

'The description you've given us matches that of the woman recovered from the lake this morning,' Ffion says.

'But what on earth was she doing kayaking?' Carole says.

Ffion doesn't answer. 'Someone will need to formally identify her. Did Natasha have any next-of-kin?'

'She lives with her boyfriend,' Carole says. 'Luke. I can't remember his last name, but I'll have his details at the office. He's her emergency contact.'

'Parks,' Russell says. 'Luke Parks.'

'When did you last see Natasha?' George looks at each of them in turn.

Carole frowns. 'She came to the pub, didn't she?'

'I think so,' Mike says. 'We all went, didn't we?'

'Fucked if I know.' Russell winces. 'It's all a blur.'

'You went to Y Llew Coch, did you?' Ffion clarifies. 'In town?'

'That's the place.' Mike turns to Russell. 'See, I said you were pronouncing it wrong.'

'I don't even remember going there, mate,' Russell says, 'let alone pronouncing it.'

'What time did you leave?' George asks Carole.

The older woman shrugs helplessly. 'I know this sounds awful, but I honestly can't remember a thing about last night.'

'Try.' Ffion's tone is clipped.

'How about earlier?' George says. 'Do you remember taking a kayak from the rafting centre?'

'We were *at* the rafting centre,' Carole says. 'We had a group session there yesterday morning. No one took a kayak, though.'

'Are you sure about that?' Ffion says.

'Quite sure.'

There's a sound from one of the men – a throat being cleared – and when Ffion turns, she sees a glance pass between Mike and Russell.

Mike rubs his head, then looks up sheepishly. 'We did take a kayak. Russ, Natasha and me.'

'Why?' Carole says incredulously.

'We thought it would be funny, I suppose.'

'But what did you *do* with it?' Carole says.

Ffion answers for them. 'They put it on their heads and ran across the field back here.'

There's a long silence.

'Why on earth . . .' Carole gives a slow shake of her head.

'Were we . . .' Russell's brow furrows as he pieces something together. He looks at Mike. 'Were we *mooing*?'

Mike flushes. 'You said we were a six-legged cow.'

'Why would I say that?'

'You called it a cow-ak.'

Ffion digs her fingernails into the palms of her hand to stop the snort of laughter which threatens to erupt from her. 'The six legs being the pair of you plus Natasha?'

'Yes,' Mike says.

'What did you do with the kayak?'

There's a pause, as Mike and Russell stare blankly at each other. Russell shakes his head. 'I just remember falling over a lot, and then going to the pub.'

'We never went near the water,' Mike says. 'I'm sure of it. Our clothes would have been wet, wouldn't they? We'd have remembered that.'

There's a knock at the door and Ffion goes to answer it. She's just sending the cleaner packing when George comes out of the sitting room, pulling the door shut behind her.

'What do you reckon?' George says quietly. 'They swear blind they can't remember a thing about last night.'

'They're lying.'

'What makes you so sure?'

'They're estate agents,' Ffion says brusquely. 'And their lips are moving.'

SIX

SUNDAY | LEO

Leo has sent Dawn to check out Jade Upshall's alibi and is tackling the house-to-house inquiries alone, a task made easier by the fact that many of the houses on The Hill are empty. Several have shuttered windows and padlocked gates, and Leo wonders if they're 'lock-and-leaves', used as occasional boltholes or bought as investments and never lived in. He tries to imagine living on The Hill with Ffion – not that they could ever afford it – but all he can hear is her voice in his head, telling him it's too far from Cwm Coed.

Fairhaven, an imposing Victorian property with ornate gables, has had a makeover since it was burgled earlier this year. Notices above the front door, and on the separate garage block, warn of an alarm system linked to a private security firm.

'We had it installed the same time as the loft conversion,' Philip Makepeace says as they stand on the front doorstep, noticing Leo looking at the signs. 'Costs a fortune each month, but I'd like to see the buggers get past that.'

His wife has been gardening. There's soil stuck to her sun-creamed arms, and grass blade indents on her bare knees. She offers a hand, then thinks better of it and waves instead. 'Hi, I'm Suki.'

'Detective Sergeant Leo Brady,' Leo says. 'My team are handling the investigation into your burglary.'

'Investigation?' Philip snorts. 'Is that what you call it? It's been six months and you've still not caught them. We'd have been better off investigating it ourselves.'

'I can send you a link to our recruitment site, if you're interested in a career change?'

Philip narrows his eyes, unsure if Leo is joking. Like JP Lennox, Philip Makepeace is older than his wife. Unlike JP, Philip sports a full head of hair and the hint of a six-pack beneath his white Hugo Boss polo shirt. The collar is turned up at the back and Leo wonders if it's protection from the sun, or merely an affectation.

'Your neighbours were burgled last night,' Leo says.

'Oh, how awful!' Suki presses a hand to her chest. 'Who? Is everyone okay?'

'Sunnyside,' Leo says. 'The Lennoxes were out for the evening, so no one was hurt, but obviously they're very shaken.'

'The area's going to the dogs,' Philip says. 'Not sure what we pay our council tax for, but there you go – that's what happens when you let a Labour councillor in.'

'Darling, you can't blame Lia Cole – she was only elected a fortnight before we were broken into, and she's ever such a nice woman. She's in my book club.'

'I only hope this crime wave doesn't cancel out the value we've added to this place,' Philip says. 'We converted the loft into a hobby room for Suki,' he adds, for Leo's benefit. 'Simmonds say it's added twenty per cent.'

Suki turns to Leo. 'It's a studio.'

'She can spend hours up there, throwing paint around.' Philip ruffles his wife's hair. Leo wonders what would happen if he attempted to ruffle Ffion's hair. He suspects he'd end up in A&E.

'I'm an artist,' Suki says. 'I've had several exhib—'

'Happy wife, happy life – isn't that what they say?' Philip chortles indulgently.

'Were the two of you home yesterday evening?' Leo says. 'We think the burglary took place between five p.m. and midnight.'

'I was home all evening,' Philip says. 'Didn't see a thing, I'm afraid. Suki went to a committee meeting at the tennis club, though. Did you see anything, darling? Any men with striped jumpers and bags marked *Swag*?' He snorts at his own joke.

'Nothing. I took a look at Sunnyside as we drove home actually, in case Camilla had been telling porkies about being away in Abersoch.' Suki raises a cynical eyebrow. 'She says committee meetings bring her out in hives. Anyway, the place was in darkness.'

'We?' Leo says.

'I'm sorry?'

'You said "as *we* drove home". Who were you with?'

'Goodness, I can see why they promoted you.' Suki gives a girlish giggle. 'A friend gave me a lift, so I could have a few drinks. I find it keeps those pesky hives at bay.' She laughs again. A phone rings somewhere in the house, and Philip excuses himself to go inside.

'I did see Warren and Emmy Irvine's housekeeper leaving last night,' Suki says. 'I don't know if that's useful? They live at Ormindale.' She taps a manicured fingernail on her lips. 'It would have been about twenty past seven. Oh, and, just as I got back, Cara Jefferson ran past. I was literally putting my key in the lock, so I just gave her a wave. But maybe she saw something?'

'What time was that?'

46

'Um, some time after ten, half-past? Sorry, I didn't really notice the time.'

'You've been very helpful, thank you,' Leo says.

'My pleasure.' Suki pulls the front door closer, cutting them off from the inside of the house, from where Philip can be heard on the phone. 'If there's anything else, feel free to pop back. My husband works nine to five, but I'm generally at home.' She pauses. 'I rarely have anything on.' She holds Leo's gaze at this, a small smile leaving him in no doubt that the double entendre was intentional.

'I'll bear that in mind.' Leo says goodbye and makes a sharp exit, not checking his pace until he's safely off the driveway and striding towards the next house. Christ. He wishes he'd kept Dawn with him now.

The Irvines' housekeeper doesn't work Sundays, and neither Warren nor Emmy Irvine noticed any suspicious activity yesterday evening.

'We were supposed to have a viewing at some point.' Warren is in his mid-fifties, with a lithe, athletic build. He wears small glasses with a thick black frame, which give him an intellectual air. 'They never turned up – I don't know what that estate agent's playing at. She's sold several houses on The Hill – she told Emmy she's the boss's favourite, so gets her pick of houses, I don't know how true that is, but she's doing an appalling job for us.' Warren is standing in the doorway of their house, Ormindale. Emmy is a few metres away in the garage, with the double door raised. 'Mind you,' Warren continues, 'maybe the absence of acceptable offers has less to do with the incompetent agent and more to do with my *ex-wife* deliberately leaving filthy underwear strewn about the place.' He spits this last in Emmy's direction.

'DS Brady, would you be kind enough to inform my *husband* – yes, darling, we are still legally married, and will be until you agree a sensible settlement – that as long as he continues with his attempts to make me homeless, I shall continue to resist them. And if that involves staging a dirty protest, then so be it.'

'You're a grade A bitch.'

Emmy turns to Leo. 'Hear that? That's my thanks for twelve years of marriage.' Her voice is shaky and her eyes look red and swollen.

'Thanks for what, Emmy? For spending all my money, or for regularly getting drunk and embarrassing me in front of my friends?'

Leo takes a step back from the verbal whiplash. 'Well, if you remember anything—'

'I've done everything.' Emmy is still addressing Leo. 'I cook, I clean—'

'You order takeout and tell the housekeeper what to do!'

'Heaven forbid he should lift a finger and actually contribute!'

'A hundred and seventy grand a year – that's what I contribute!' Warren practically screams it. 'Plus bonuses!'

'JP's on two hundred,' Emmy says. 'Camilla told me.'

The front door slams.

'He's very sensitive about money,' Emmy says, but the fight has gone from her voice now her husband isn't there to hear it. She stares at the boxing gloves in her hand, as if she doesn't know how they got there, then drops them into a box.

'Are you going away?' Leo says.

'Away?' Emmy says sharply. 'Why would I go away?'

Leo motions to the boxes. 'Um . . . you're packing?'

'Oh,' Emmy says. 'No, I'm not going anywhere.' Her jaw tightens. 'This house is as much mine as it is his, whatever he thinks.'

In one half of the Irvines' double garage is a black BMW; the other half is full to bursting. Bespoke racking holds an array of tools, while brackets fix two bikes (mountain and road), a paddleboard and a surfboard to the wall.

'All the gear, no idea,' Emmy says, when she sees Leo looking. 'Most of it's heading for the yard sale. That's what the boxes are for.' She steers Leo back towards the drive. 'Actually, I do need to get on, so if you don't mind . . .'

Each box is marked with a price, Leo now realises. He spots a Paul Smith scarf thrown carelessly into the £10 box, and wonders if Emmy would take a fiver.

'It's a week on Saturday. Our garage is the biggest, so everyone's bringing their bric-a-brac here to be sorted.' Emmy tosses a wooden chopping board into a box marked '£1'. 'There was a yard sale years ago, organised by the woman who had Fairhaven before Philip and Suki, and we've been meaning to do another ever since.' She straightens. 'It's for charity, of course. I'm very committed to helping others.'

'Which charity?' Leo asks, relieved he didn't try to haggle over the scarf.

'Children in Ukraine?' Emmy wrinkles her nose. 'Or Gaza? I forget.'

Committed indeed.

'Everyone's coming here on Thursday evening to finalise the plans.' Emmy's brow creases. 'It was supposed to be a sort of committee meeting, and then Cara suggested bringing partners and Camilla said she'd make some salads, and now I seem to be hosting a party.' She lets out a long breath and presses the heels of her palms against her eyes.

'It looks as though you have a lot on your plate right now,' Leo says gently.

'You have no idea.'

'Getting divorced is really hard, whatever the circumstances.'

Emmy lets her hands drop. 'Right.' She looks up and gives a little smile, but Leo can see the exhaustion beneath her expertly applied make-up. 'It really is.'

There's a far more convivial atmosphere at Hollies, a large red-brick house with a rambling rose trained above the porch. Mikaela and Cara Jefferson take Leo into the garden, where they sit on large swinging chairs. They pour him a glass of water from a pitcher filled with ice and long curls of cucumber, and Leo tries to maintain some degree of professionalism despite his chair's insistence on bouncing him up and down. In front of them, a pool shimmers silver in the sunlight. Floating on the surface is an inflatable penis.

'Sorry about the cock,' Cara says. 'It was a joke present from a friend, but it turned out to be surprisingly comfortable, so we kept it. There's a cupholder in each testicle.'

'We expected our son to be mortified,' Mikaela says. 'Alec's nineteen – you know how they can be. But he thought it was hilarious. He's set up an Instagram account for it.'

'I understand you went for a run yesterday evening?' Leo addresses the question to Cara, who immediately holds out her wrists to be cuffed.

'It's a fair cop, guv. Do I need a lawyer?'

'You *are* a lawyer, you goof,' Mikaela says.

Leo is beginning to like the Jeffersons. 'Sunnyside was broken into last night – I was wondering if you saw anything out of the ordinary?'

Mikaela's smile vanishes. 'Oh, God – is everyone okay?'

'No one was home, fortunately.'

50

'I'm trying to think.' Cara has her fingers pressed to her temples. 'I ran down The Hill, did a loop, probably passed Sunnyside again about forty minutes later . . .' She shakes her head. 'I don't remember anything out of the ordinary, sorry.'

'Do you remember if the gates were open?' The Lennoxes had been adamant that they'd closed the gates before they left for Abersoch, only to find them ajar on their return.

'Closed.' Cara hesitates, then repeats her answer, more confidently. 'Closed. I'm sure of it.'

'And this would have been . . .'

Cara is looking at her wrist, scrolling through what Leo assumes is a fitness tracker. 'I pressed stop at ten thirty-five, so it would have been a minute or two before that.'

'That's really helpful, thank you.' That narrows their timings to between ten thirty-five and midnight.

The final house, in prime position at the top of The Hill, is the Coach House. *Location, location, location*, Leo thinks, as he waits for someone to answer the door. Parked on the driveway are two cars: a Toyota Yaris, and a hot pink Mercedes with pearlescent paintwork and personalised plates. *B14 NCA.* Away down the hill, Tattenbrook tails away into golden fields, Chester a model village in the distance. A shimmering haze has settled in the air, and Leo imagines having a job where Sundays mean barbecuing in the garden with a beer, instead of traipsing up and down The Hill in the blazing heat.

Leo hears a *woof woof!* from inside the Coach House. He's just thinking that he's never heard a dog sound quite so much like a human when the door is opened by a grey-haired man wearing a set of fluffy ears.

'Who is it?' comes a child's voice.

'I don't know yet, I've only just—'

'Dogs can't talk, Grandad!'

The grey-haired man sighs, then gives two short barks in the direction of the kitchen. He looks at Leo sheepishly. 'If you'd have told me twenty years ago that I'd be spending my retirement pretending to be a golden retriever, I'd never have believed you.'

'You're clearly very well trained, sir.' Leo grins. He fishes for his ID. 'I'm sure we've got vacancies in the dog section, if you're interested.'

'Grandad, who's at the—' A young blonde girl – perhaps six or seven – skids into the hall, then comes to an abrupt halt when she sees Leo. She's wearing a white lab coat with a plastic stethoscope around her neck.

The golden retriever takes off his ears. 'The name's Dennis. And this is my granddaughter, Scarlett.'

'Don't tell me,' Leo says. 'You're the vet.'

The girl nods shyly.

'I imagine you're a very good vet.'

'I am. I mended Grandad's broken leg, didn't I?'

'You did indeed.' Dennis looks at Leo. 'What can we do for you, officer?'

'There was a burglary in the street last night. I'm speaking with all the neighbours to see if anyone saw or heard anything.'

Dennis takes a phone from his pocket. 'I'll text my daughter – she's in her garden office. This is her house. I'm just the free childcare.' He rolls his eyes, but it's obvious he's having the time of his life. Scarlett's grandfather is clearly one of those active grandads. Leo, whose knees already click when he walks upstairs, tries to imagine looking after Harris's kids one day, but the idea seems impossible.

'Are you a *police officer*?' Scarlett asks Leo.

'That's right.' He shows her his ID badge and points to the word 'police'.

Scarlett's eyes light up. 'Let's play police officers, Grandad! You can be the baddie and I'll be the protective.'

'Detective, sweetheart. Ah, here she is.' Dennis steps aside as a woman in denim shorts walks into the hall. 'We'll leave you to it. Come on, Scarlett.'

'Thanks, Dad.' The woman watches them leave, then smiles at Leo and extends a hand. 'Bianca Dixon. So now you've met the whole family.'

'Your dad's great with your daughter.'

'They adore each other. Dad moved into a warden-assisted flat last year, but I worry about him being lonely, so he spends a lot of time here. Between you and me, I don't really need the childcare – Scarlett's such a good girl, she plays quite happily while I work – but he likes to feel useful, so . . .' Bianca smiles. 'And Scarlett loves it, of course.'

'Were you at home last night, Ms Dixon? There was a burglary at one of your neighbours' properties.'

'I was home all night, but I didn't see anything, sorry. Should I be worried? I've got a video doorbell and an alarm – although I confess I don't always set it. Dad's always nagging me about it. Says you can't be too careful nowadays.'

'He's right.' Leo takes out a card and writes on the back of it. 'That's the number for the crime prevention team. Give them a call if you'd like some advice.'

From the next room, Leo hears the unmistakable *nee-naw* of a police siren, followed by Scarlett's high-pitched voice. 'Hands up!'

'I surrender,' Dennis shouts. 'I said, I surrender!'

Leo laughs. 'Sounds like she might need back-up for that dangerous fugitive she's arrested.'

* * *

53

House-to-house inquiries complete, Leo makes his way back to the car. He checks the time, then drives to the bottom of The Hill and around the corner into Taplin Drive. The road here is still tree-lined, but it's narrower than The Hill, with fewer driveways, and cars parked on both sides. The wheelie bins, although tidy, are pulled up to the sides of the houses instead of hidden away in Farrow-and-Ball-painted bin stores. It's a nice street, but it isn't The Hill.

The Willows (formerly known as 24 Taplin Drive) is the second house along from the corner. Like its neighbours, it has a long garden with a gate leading to a scrubby footpath which runs along the back of the properties. It is this footpath that has given Leo's ex-wife delusions of grandeur, as it emerges directly on to The Hill. Leo has no doubt that if Allie ever takes a lift from a friend, she asks to be dropped off around the corner.

When Allie and Dominic bought the house, there had been a low garden wall surrounding the front garden. Now there are tall gates, with a golden lion on top of each post, and a buzzer above an engraved sign saying *The Willows*. Leo presses it. There's a pause, then the gates start to open with a loud juddering, before grinding to a halt. He presses the buzzer again and this time he hears Allie's telephone voice floating from the intercom.

'I've opened the gates. Just leave the parcel in the porch.'

'It's me. The gates don't work.'

'Yes, they do.' There's another loud juddering noise, but the gates don't move, so Leo squeezes through the gap. He's walking up the path when Allie opens the front door. 'Have you broken my new gates?'

'They were broken already. Why have you got them, anyway?'

'Do you like the lions?'

'They're very you.'

54

Allie narrows her eyes, unsure whether he's being rude. Not for the first time, Leo wonders how the two of them stayed married even for the few years they did. He knows *why* (the reason is seven years old) but the *how* eludes him.

'You're not due to have Harris till tonight.'

'I know, I'll pick him up after work. I just wanted to give you a heads-up about some burglaries in the area. It's unlikely you'd be targeted, but—'

'Why wouldn't we be targeted?' Allie is affronted. 'What's wrong with our house? Someone said the other day they thought the previous owner could have been a footballer, actually.'

'Who, a midfielder from Macclesfield under-nines?'

'Fuck you, Leo.'

'Right. Always a pleasure, Allie. I'll see you later.'

'You're not bringing that woman, are you?'

'Do you mean Ffion?'

'I've told you: I don't want her around Harris. It'll confuse him.'

'Dad!' Harris charges out of the house and throws himself at Leo. 'Do you want a coffee? Dominic's got a new machine, and he lets me press the button.'

'Maybe some other time.'

'No, it's okay,' Allie says. 'Come in.'

Leo is confused by her rapid capitulation – Allie usually leaves him standing on the doorstep – but it all becomes clear when he steps inside and Allie sweeps an arm around the dark and slightly poky hall.

'What do you think?' she says. 'We've had the whole place redecorated. The wallpaper's from Osborne & Little – it's the exact same one they've got in the master bedroom at the Coach House, at the top of The Hill.'

'When have you been in the master bedroom at the Coach House?'

'I haven't. I looked at old "for sale" photos on Rightmove.' Allie walks towards a console table at the back of the cramped hall. Her bare feet leave marks in the silvery grey carpet. 'You can find listings months, even years, after the houses have been sold, and the photos are brilliant for interior inspo.' She adjusts the position of a large vase filled with eucalyptus, then picks up a hideous china dog. 'This was twenty quid from Home Bargains. It's a dupe for the Staffordshire ones, which go for hundreds. There's a house for sale at the moment with one either side of their fireplace.' She brandishes it at Leo. 'A burglar would make a beeline for this sort of thing.'

'If you say so.'

'What's been stolen from The Hill? Is it mostly antiques? Or paintings?'

'Not much, to be honest. They might have been disturbed before they could get going, or maybe they didn't find what they were looking for.'

'Dad, shall I make your coffee?'

'You know what, mate, I think I'll skip the coffee.' Leo bends so he's eye-level with Harris. 'That way, I can get my work squared away and pick you up a bit earlier. How does that sound?'

'Yeah, that's cool.'

'This vase was from the middle aisle at Aldi, but it's exactly like one from Oliver Bonas.' Allie's still talking. 'I use Google image search to find the original, then look for a copy. Some of the stuff you see on Rightmove is insanely expensive, but I can always find a cheaper dupe.' She waves an arm around the hall again. 'And look! You'd never know.'

Leo thinks you probably would – there's something about Allie's house that's trying a little too hard; something that just misses the mark. Above the console table is what Leo had taken for a black-framed mirror, but now sees is nine mirrored tiles stuck on to a square of painted wall. Beside the table is a cardboard box filled with a mixture of clothing, toys and ornaments.

'More dupes?' Leo indicates the box.

'That's jumble. We're holding a yard sale the weekend after next.'

'Oh, right – I was at Ormindale just now, actually.'

Allie's eyes light up. 'Did Emmy mention me?'

'Why would Emmy Irvine mention you?'

'Because we're holding a yard sale,' Allie says, pausing between each word as though Leo is intellectually challenged. 'Emmy and me. A sort of committee. Of two.'

'Well, take a dessert or something to the party on Thursday – she's very stressed about it.'

'The party?'

'Or committee meeting. Whatever it is, she looked like she wanted to cry when she mentioned it.'

'She's getting divorced. It's a *very emotional* process,' Allie says pointedly.

'Quite.'

'Come and see the kitchen,' Allie says. 'It's IKEA, but Dom found a YouTube hack and it looks just like a Clive Christian—'

Leo is already at the front door. He finds Allie exhausting. He worries about Harris; worries about the influence of Allie's obsession with status and class. With *things*. Granted, Leo had perhaps gone too far in the opposite direction when he and Allie had first separated – Leo's spartan pad had been the very definition of bachelor pad – but he found a balance, and his house now feels like a home.

On his way back to the office, he sees several houses sporting 'For Sale' signs with the same logo he saw on the sign at Ormindale. Simmonds . . .

I had the same agency over to value ours, Camilla had said earlier, when they'd been talking about house valuations. And didn't Philip Makepeace say they'd done the same? *Simmonds say it's added twenty per cent.* Leo makes a mental note to find out whether the valuation happened before or after the burglary.

Experience has taught him there's rarely such a thing as coincidence.

SEVEN

SUNDAY | ALLIE

Allie feels annoyed. She often feels annoyed nowadays, and since thirty-eight is far too young to be perimenopausal, she can only attribute it (as usual) to her ex-husband. She should have known better than to expect Leo to show any interest in her newly decorated hall. Even if he'd secretly been impressed by the finish, pure spite would have prevented him from saying so. Leo's jealous, that's the problem. Allie's moved on. She's remarried, she has a gorgeous house on The Hill (well, it will be gorgeous, once they've finished the refurb), while Leo's still treading water. Sure, he's bought his own place now, but everyone knows new-builds are tacky, and right behind Leo's road is a housing association development, so who knows what sort of kids Harris hangs out with when he's there. Sometimes Allie's friends talk about what a great dad Leo is, but she soon puts them straight.

'Harris!'

There's no answer, so she goes into his room, where Harris is engrossed in a PlayStation game. Leo had said no to a PS5 last Christmas, that a Nintendo Switch was more than enough for a seven-year-old, but when Harris unwrapped it and threw his arms around Allie she knew she'd done the right thing. That said, it was proving increasingly hard to get Harris to leave the house.

'You're going to play with Scarlett.'

'I don't like Scarlett,' Harris says, without taking his eyes off the screen.

'Yes, you do.'

'I don't. She's a girl.'

'Well, I need to run some errands, so you're going. It'll only be for an hour.'

'Can I finish my game first?'

But Allie has already pressed the 'off' button.

'Mum!'

Allie is thrilled when Bianca herself opens the door of the Coach House. She has nothing against Dennis, who regularly dropped Harris at school last term – *I'm taking Scarlett anyway, it's no bother* – but Bianca is everything Allie aspires to be. The glossy nails, the plush silver carpet, the pink Mercedes . . . it's all so . . . *classy.*

'Oh, hi, Allie, how are you?'

'I'm good. Sorry to drop in unannounced, but I'm taking some jumble to Emmy' – she holds up the bag of items she's collected from home – 'and Harris has been begging to see Scarlett.' She lowers her voice conspiratorially. 'I think someone has a bit of a crush!'

'Mum, I never—'

Allie squeezes Harris's cheeks before he can finish. 'Aw, I'm teasing you.' She looks back at Bianca. 'Is Scarlett home, though?'

There's the briefest of pauses, then Bianca smiles. 'Sure. Come on in, Harris. Scarlett's in the playroom.'

Bianca accidentally lets the front door swing back after Harris steps inside, but fortunately Allie catches it before it closes. She follows them into the kitchen, where Grandad Dixon is watching football on an iPad. Harris heads through to the playroom.

'They get on so well, don't they?' Allie says. 'It's lovely to see.'

'Lovely.' There's another pause, then Bianca says, 'Coffee?'

Allie makes a show of checking her watch, even though this is exactly what she was secretly hoping for. 'Why not? Just a quick one.' She installs herself on one of the high stools at the breakfast bar. The marble counter is threaded with what looks like gold, and Allie wonders if she could get the same effect with a piece of Formica and a gilt Sharpie.

'I'll have to leave you with Dad, I'm afraid.' Bianca puts a flat white in front of Allie. 'I'm dealing with an HR crisis, and you know what it's like. I'll see you soon.'

Allie is barely able to enjoy the fact that Bianca thinks she looks like the sort of person who regularly deals with HR crises, so gutted is she to see the Queen of The Hill glide back to her inner sanctum. Allie has seen pictures of Bianca's office on her company website, which features Bianca in a velvet armchair next to a desk empty of everything except a laptop and a Neom candle.

'Actually I've just remembered I said I'd be at Emmy's by now.' Allie slides off the stool. 'Sorry to waste the coffee.'

'You're alright, love.' Dennis reaches for it. 'Bianca only lets me have decaf, so this'll be a treat.' He winks at her. 'Shall I give Harris tea later? Scarlett's having fish fingers.'

'Thanks, but his father's picking him up.'

'Part-time dads, eh?' Dennis raises an eyebrow, and Allie feels the tiniest prickle of guilt about the way she's slagged Leo off at the school gates.

At Ormindale, the garage door is open, and Emmy is sitting in a garden chair, scrolling through her phone. She jumps as Allie approaches.

'Sorry,' Allie says. 'Didn't mean to scare you.'

'It's fine. I was just . . .' Emmy gives a half-shrug, indicating her phone. She looks exhausted. Allie remembers the sleepless nights after she and Leo broke up; the arguments about money, the house, Harris. Emmy usually looks effortlessly stylish – the sort of woman who throws on a navy blazer over jeans and a white shirt and looks instantly catwalk-ready – but today she's wearing sweatpants and a stained vest top. Her caramel hair is in a messy scrunchie, instead of the slicked-back, perfectly sculpted bun she usually opts for.

'Divorce is so hard,' Allie says. 'Are things . . . progressing?'

Emmy gets up. 'Did you want something?'

'Oh.' Allie blinks. Emmy doesn't mean to be so curt, Allie knows, but even so . . . She holds up the bag of jumble. 'I found some more bits and bobs.' She has a whole heap of unwanted items on the bed in their spare room as well as in the box in the hall, but bringing it up in smaller bags has been the perfect excuse to spend more time on The Hill. She hopes Emmy doesn't lose the house in the divorce, otherwise Allie will have to start all over again with the new people.

'Great. The one-pound box is over there.'

Allie's never sure if Emmy is joking when she arbitrarily directs the treasures Allie has found towards the bargain buckets. Allie laughs anyway. Maybe she should go to TK Maxx this week and buy a few bits to bump up the quality of her donations. A nice cashmere jumper, maybe, or a cocktail shaker.

The thought reminds Allie of the party Leo mentioned. She clears her throat. 'Is everything ready for Thursday evening?' A subtle reminder that Emmy hasn't yet let Allie know the details.

Emmy's barely a metre from Allie, but she doesn't seem to hear her. 'My husband is such an arsehole,' she says instead. She sits back down and taps furiously on her phone. Allie is reluctant to leave the subject of the party (What should she bring? Is there a dress code?), but she dutifully pivots. She loves it when Emmy confides in her about Warren. It makes Allie feel like they're real friends, which she supposes they are now. After all, they've spent hours sorting jumble together, and, even if Allie hasn't actually set foot inside Ormindale, it's really no different from hanging out in the kitchen together.

'What's he done this time?' She sits in the chair next to Emmy.

'Actually, could you start folding those sets of curtains?'

'Oh.' Allie jumps up. 'Yes, of course.'

'He thinks I can live off five grand a month. I mean, does he even know there's a cost-of-living crisis?'

'How awful.' Allie's and Dominic's household income is a long way from five grand, but Allie imagines the running costs for Ormindale are exorbitant.

'Honestly, when I think what a charmer that man was when I met him.'

'Really?'

'Handsome, smooth-talking . . . and such a gentleman. He'd always open my car door for me.'

'The dream,' Allie says, battling with an unbelievably heavy set of drapes. *Who the hell has windows this big?*

'He's still a charmer with everyone else, of course. It's only me he treats like shit.'

Allie's phone pings with a message, and even before she drops the curtains to look, she knows it's someone posting on the WhatsApp group, because Emmy's pings at the exact same time.

Being accepted into the WhatsApp group for The Hill has been one of the greatest achievements of Allie's life. She had suggested to Emmy that now she was helping with the yard sale she could do with having everyone's numbers, and how would she go about joining the WhatsApp group? And Emmy had shrugged and said

Bianca had made her an admin, as it happened, and five seconds later Allie was in.

Allie had been so excited. She'd wanted to post on Facebook about it, but had settled for showing Dominic, who was a little bemused. 'But we don't live on The Hill,' he'd said, and Allie had sighed and muttered, 'You just don't get it.' If they leave their house by the back door and walk down the alley, they come out on to The Hill, and if that doesn't qualify them as living on The Hill, then she doesn't know what does.

'The Jeffersons are going away tomorrow night,' Allie says now, reading the message aloud, because Emmy seems to be in no hurry to open hers. 'Alec's going with them, so the house is going to be empty, and can we all please keep an eye out, given last night's break-in.'

Allie immediately replies. Yes of course @CaraJeffersonHollies. Are you going somewhere nice? She waits for a reply, but Cara doesn't even acknowledge her, which is a bit rude, but perhaps she's got a lot on her mind. Allie scrolls up the thread, in case she's missed anything interesting. Camilla Lennox has posted pictures from their burglary, including a smashed ornament and a broken window.

'My ex-husband is the detective investigating the burglary at Sunnyside,' Allie says, revelling in the chance to impart some gossip. 'He said the burglars didn't find what they wanted. I guess Camilla's and JP's stuff didn't appeal, which is a bit of an insult if you think about—'

'You're divorced?'

'Yes. I don't know what I ever saw in him.' Just then, Allie has an image of Leo on their wedding day, turning to watch her walk down the aisle. She gets a funny feeling in her stomach and pushes it to one side.

'Did he make you sign a pre-nup?'

Allie pretends to think about it, because clearly she is now moving in circles where pre-nuptial agreements are commonplace. 'Hmm, did he . . . ? No, we didn't have a pre-nup.' Nor did either of them have two pennies to rub together, but that was by-the-by.

Emmy sighs. 'Warren did. Insurance, he called it. It says if the marriage ends due to infidelity – mine, of course, not his – I'm not entitled to a pay-out.'

'You wouldn't get any money if you had an affair?' Allie is glad this is not something that occurred to Leo. She favours the term 'overlap' to describe the dual timelines of her marriage and her relationship with Dominic.

'Not a penny.' Emmy gives a little smirk. 'So it's just as well I've been entirely faithful to him, isn't it?' She frowns. 'You should pick those curtains up before they get creased.'

Allie goes back to folding fabric. She knows that Emmy wants to stay on The Hill and is trying to convince Warren to give her the house as part of the divorce settlement, and Allie wants that to happen too. She's put significant effort into becoming friends with Emmy (if she never sees another bag of jumble again, it'll be too soon) and she doesn't want it going to waste. Because of that, she won't read anything into the little smirk she saw just now.

The smirk that strongly suggested Emmy has been more than a little bit naughty.

EIGHT

SUNDAY | FFION

It's two p.m. by the time all three estate agents have given their statements and packed their bags into Carole Simmonds's car. With the holiday let now empty, Ffion and George are searching Natasha's room. They have found enough clothes and make-up for a fortnight's holiday, but nothing to suggest how the young woman wound up dead in the river.

'She doesn't come across as the outdoorsy type,' George says, surveying the glittery heels strewn across the floor. 'I wonder what she wore to go rafting.'

'The centre provides water shoes and wetsuits.' Ffion is digging through a make-up bag the size of a bread bin. 'Still no sign of her phone.'

'Carole said it never left her hand.'

'Maybe she took it in the kayak with her.'

'If she did, we've got no chance finding it.' Ffion straightens. 'We'll have to put in a request for cell site.'

A car pulls up outside, and George looks out of the window. 'Uniform are here. Oh . . . I'm going to hazard a guess this is your hot transferee.'

'He's not *my* hot transferee. Does he have a quiff and an air of smug superiority?'

'Yes.'

'Then that's him.'

'He's not a patch on Leo,' George says.

'I wasn't planning on trading.'

They walk outside, where PC Sam Taylor greets Ffion as though they're old friends, then turns his two-hundred-watt smile on George.

'I don't believe we've had the pleasure.'

'DC George Kent. Ffion was just talking about you.' The corners of George's mouth twitch, and Ffion shoots daggers at her.

'All good, I hope?' Sam grins.

He really does have an exceptionally slappable face, Ffion decides. 'You two our scene watch, then?' she says tersely.

'Yes.' PC Lucy Doherty shields her eyes from the sun and looks across the valley. 'Not a bad place for it.'

'That's just as well,' George says, 'because the DI won't authorise CSI until after the post-mortem, so you'll be here till the end of your shift, then handing over to nights. Have you got some water?'

'Yes, all set.'

Ffion and George drive in convoy to the housing development on the outskirts of Chester where Natasha Brett lived with her partner of three years, Luke Parks. Local officers did what is euphemistically referred to as 'the death knock' this morning, and Luke has agreed to accompany George to the mortuary to formally identify his partner.

'Natasha moved in with him about nine months ago,' George says, as they walk up the path towards the house. 'But get this: he's got a conviction for domestic assault.'

'Oh, now *that's* interesting.'

Luke Parks's house is a one-bed terraced starter home, and

Ffion wonders how the property prices compare with Cwm Coed, where the place she's buying is a similar size. *Supposed* to be buying, she corrects herself. It's been over a week since Ffion heard from her solicitor, and she has a horrible sense of foreboding. Is there a problem with her mortgage? Has the chain collapsed again? The thought of having to live with Mam and Seren, as she did for a year after her separation and divorce, makes Ffion's heart sink.

'The conviction pre-dates his relationship with Natasha,' George is saying, 'and there's nothing on the intel system to suggest Natasha is also a victim, but nevertheless it's a red flag.'

'Are you okay FLOing him?'

'Only one way to find out.' It's George's first assignment as a family liaison officer, there to support the victim's loved ones and keep them up to date with police activity. In principle, the FLO is a neutral party, separate from the investigation. In practice, many a murder case has changed focus thanks to intelligence provided by a FLO.

Especially when the loved one in question is a potential suspect.

The door is opened by a slightly built man. He's significantly older than Natasha, with thinning hair and frown lines etched between his brows. The tattoos on his forearms are a blur of dark ink, rendered indistinct either through age or by attempts to remove them.

'Mr Parks? I'm DC George Kent, your Family Liaison Officer. We spoke on the phone.'

Luke nods mutely.

'This is my colleague, DC Morgan. We're so sorry for your loss.'

When George had arrived in Ffion's department, Ffion had

thought her cold and unemotional. The new DC would never come for drinks after work, or even join the others in the canteen for a coffee. When the two of them had been tasked with finding a contestant missing from a reality TV show being filmed near Cwm Coed earlier this year, Ffion had found George infuriating, and it was clear the feeling was mutual. But as their missing person case became a murder investigation, George had unbent a little, and perhaps so had Ffion, and the two of them had found a way of working together. Now, Ffion sees what looks like genuine compassion on George's face.

'We'll have a quick chat here, if that's alright,' George says, 'then I'll take you to see Natasha.'

They decline Luke's offer of a cup of tea, and sit on the sofa. Luke takes the armchair, which has a handle on one side to make it recline. Ffion wonders whether Natasha would have been left with the sofa, which is hard and uncomfortable and positioned at an awkward angle for the television, a vast flat-screen directly opposite Luke's chair. Elsewhere, the room is an odd mix of styles. Brown utilitarian furniture is accessorised by what Ffion imagines arrived with Natasha: faux fur throws and hanging plants, an Oliver Bonas candlestick.

'When was the last time you saw Natasha?' George says.

Luke looks at her blankly for a second before answering. 'Yesterday morning, before she left for her team-building weekend.'

'The four of them travelled together, I understand.'

'Yes. Natasha took the bus to work, same way she normally would, then her boss drove them all to Wales.'

'And how did she seem?' Ffion says. To her left, just visible beneath the side table, there's something sticking out from under the sofa.

'What do you mean?'

'I mean, what sort of mood was she in before she left?'

Luke picks at something on his jeans. 'She was fine.'

'Fine?' Ffion leans over the arm of the sofa to get a better look at what she's sitting on. It's a duvet, screwed in a ball and shoved out of the way.

'We didn't really speak yesterday morning, to be honest.'

'No?' Behind the duvet is a pillow.

Luke looks up to find Ffion staring pointedly at the bedding. 'I . . . I actually slept down here on Friday night.'

Neither Ffion nor George says anything, and eventually Luke is compelled to fill the silence.

'It wasn't an argument, or anything. Just, like . . . a difference of opinion. Nothing serious.'

'What was it about?' Ffion asks. 'This *difference of opinion.*'

'I didn't want her to go away.' He lifts his chin, defensively. 'We don't see each other much in the week. I work lates, and by the time I get home she's asleep.'

'So the weekends were the only time you had together,' George says.

'Exactly.' When he speaks again, there's a break in his voice. 'If she'd only listened to me and stayed at home, she'd still be here.'

Ffion can't decide if Luke's declaration is one of regret or reproach. 'Where were you on Saturday night?'

'At home.'

It's quick. Defensive? 'All night?'

'Where else would I be?'

Definitely defensive. 'I don't know,' Ffion says. 'I suppose I'm wondering if you took a trip to Wales.'

'I was here all weekend.' He stares at Ffion. The hairs on the back of her neck prickle.

70

'Luke,' George cuts in. 'I'm sorry to ask this, but did Natasha ever express any thoughts of self-harm? Did she ever suffer from depression?'

'No.' Luke shakes his head. 'Never. I mean, she had low moods sometimes, same as anyone, especially when she was on her—' He flushes. 'You know. But she was happy. We were happy.' His voice cracks again, and he presses the heels of his palms into his eyes. He exhales, his breath uneven.

'How did she get on with her colleagues?' George checks her notes. 'Russell Steele, Mike Foster?'

'She didn't like Mike much – that's why she was so chuffed to get the bonus.'

'Bonus?' Ffion says.

'Every six months, the top seller gets a bonus. It's always Mike. Natasha always said it was a fix, and she'd never win, but this time she did. She said we should spend it on the house, but I told her to treat herself.'

'Did Natasha get on with her boss?'

'Carole sounded like a bitch, to be honest, always making backhanded comments about what Natasha was wearing, or how she'd done her hair. If you ask me, she was jealous. I kept telling Nat to get a new job, but she wouldn't. Said she was on to something at Simmonds.'

'You wanted her to go to another agency?' George says.

Luke shakes his head. 'Not another agency, another job. Something safer.' Ffion and George exchange glances. 'I was worried she'd be attacked, or kidnapped. You hear about it. Weirdos pretending they want to buy a house, just to get the estate agent there on her own.'

'Did Natasha say she felt vulnerable?' George says.

Luke shook his head.

'Did she mention any viewings that had made her feel uncomfortable?'

'No, but she had to deal with all sorts. One woman opened the door to her stark bollock naked.'

Ffion resists the temptation to tell Luke that isn't anatomically possible.

'Houses full of cat shit, vicious dogs,' he goes on. 'Last week, it was a woman shagging a bloke while her husband was at work. Nat takes it all in her stride.' His face pales. 'At least, she did.'

'It sounds as though Natasha was very special,' George says gently.

Luke swallows hard. He nods.

'Are you ready to see her?'

'Not really,' Luke says, but he stands up. He turns to Ffion, perhaps not having heard the same compassion in her questions as he had in George's. 'Natasha was my whole world. I'd do anything to have her back.'

Once again, Ffion feels a prickle on the nape of her neck. She doesn't doubt that Luke loved Natasha. The question is: how far might he have gone to try to keep her?

NINE

SUNDAY | LEO

As Leo leaves work, he passes the Portakabin in the back yard. The structure had presumably once been intended as temporary office accommodation but had instead become a permanent fixture which now houses the cold case review team.

Leo pauses in the open doorway. He recognises – although doesn't know well – the only officer currently in the room: John Evans, a DC in his fifties, with thinning hair and a lean, languid build. 'How's it going?' Leo says.

'Alright. What's happening on CID?'

'Burglary series on The Hill. And this is Operation Beech, right?' Leo looks at the walls of the Portakabin, on which are pinned photographs of Peter and Stephanie Carmichael, first living, then very, very dead, sprawled on the floor of the kitchen in their luxury home. 'My partner's obsessed.'

'Her and the rest of the world, mate. We've had to unplug the phones – someone got hold of the direct line and put the number on a true crime forum. You would not believe the number of "expert" crime investigators out there, ready to tell us exactly how to do our job.' John rolls his eyes.

'And the bosses have got you working weekends?'

'Something came in yesterday.' John puts his hands on either

73

side of a plastic box on his desk, in which are a number of items in clear plastic bags. 'The Carmichaels' house was sold as part of the estate, and the new owners just got around to changing the kitchen. When the old one was ripped out, they found a box hidden behind the kickboards.'

'Does it relate to the murders?' Despite himself, Leo's interested.

John nods. 'And to be fair to the true crime community – much as it pains me – the new owner only knew about the case because they listen to the *Without Conviction* podcast.' He spins his chair around. 'Come in, if you want. I'll put a brew on.'

Leo looks at his watch. 'I have to collect my lad. I might stop by in the week though, if that's okay?'

'I'll be here.' John turns back to his box of evidence, and Leo continues to his car. If Ffion knew he'd turned down the opportunity to hear about the Carmichael case first-hand, she'd never forgive him. But Harris comes first. Leo has learned to ignore the raised eyebrows that follow him out of the station on the days he leaves work early to collect Harris from school. *Part-timer*, Dawn often says, in an attempt to wind him up.

If only. Leo frequently spends his weekends off catching up on paperwork; regularly reads through files on a weekday evening when he could be watching the latest series of *Vera*. None of that bothers him, as long as he never has to let down his son.

Tonight, after tea, Leo listens to Harris read, then signs the accompanying sheet to say how many pages they've done. He sees Allie's name a couple of times, but mostly it seems to be Dominic who listens to Harris's reading, and Leo feels the weird mix of gratitude and envy that comes with knowing the man who now lives with your kid is fundamentally decent.

'Bath time,' Leo says. Allie has reluctantly conceded that as long as Harris is ready for bed, he can come back an hour later than normal.

At six-thirty, Leo is just starting to think about getting Harris in the car to go home when he hears the familiar sound of Ffion's Triumph Stag pulling up outside the house.

Shit . . . He completely forgot to let Ffion know about the change in timings.

Leo gets to his feet just as the doorbell goes. Ffion has a key, but for some reason Leo can't fathom, she never uses it if he's home. He opens the door and is immediately set upon by Dave, who puts two heavy paws on Leo's shoulders so he can lick Leo's face.

'I've had the sort of day,' Ffion says, as Leo pushes Dave off, 'that can only be salvaged by you taking me to bed and—' She stops abruptly as Harris appears behind Leo. 'Oh. I thought you said he'd be—' She cuts herself off again, pressing her lips together. 'I mean . . . hi!' She smiles at Harris. 'I'm Ffion.'

Harris turns his face away. Dave starts barking, excited by the presence of a potential playmate, and Harris shrinks closer to Leo.

'Change of plan, sorry,' Leo says. 'Allie said Harris could stay a bit later, so . . . I was just about to take him back, actually, but maybe we could . . .' Leo nudges Harris. 'Are you going to say hello?'

Harris shakes his head over and over, something which Dave seems to find disproportionately exciting. He jumps up again and Ffion grabs at his collar, prompting a volley of barks. Harris claps his hands over his ears, then tugs at Leo's jumper, pulling him down to his level. Leo makes an apologetic face at Ffion.

'Does she live in a cardboard box?' Harris says, in a whisper you could hear next door.

Leo laughs. 'Why would you think that? Ffion's a police officer, like me. She lives in a house.'

'Speaking of which,' Ffion says, 'Mia reckons she saw the estate agent showing someone around the house I'm buying. Why would they do that when it's sold, subject to contract? They're absolute ba—' She glances at Harris. 'Bathtubs,' she finishes carefully. She dumps her bag on the floor, muttering to herself, 'Absolute fucking bathtubs. Dave, for God's sake, calm down.'

'But Dad.' Harris tugs at Leo's sleeve. 'Mum says she's a dirty tramp. And tramps live in cardboard boxes, don't they?'

There is a long and agonising silence.

Leo wants to die. He thinks he *might* die, actually, under the furious heat of Ffion's glare.

She raises an eyebrow at Leo. 'A . . . tramp?'

'I'm sure she didn't mean—'

'Oh, I'm quite sure she did.' Ffion picks up her bag again. 'Well, I'd better be getting back to my cardboard—'

'Ffion, don't be like—'

'Is she, then, Dad?'

'Ffion, stay. Please. I'll let Allie know we're going to be late, and you and Harris can get to know each other proper—'

'No!' Harris turns away again, burying his head in Leo's trousers. 'I want to go home. I don't want to see her.'

Leo puts an arm around Harris. He looks at Ffion. 'I'd better . . .'

'Yeah. Whatever. Just go.'

'I'll be back in half an hour. We'll talk then.' He ushers Harris outside, talking nonsense about what they'll do next weekend, and how about if Leo picks up a couple of tickets for the football? Leo doesn't want Harris to feel he's done something wrong, but at the same time, who knows what he'll say if they hang around?

Bloody Allie. Leo feels a level of anger he's never once felt towards his ex-wife: not when he discovered she'd been having an affair; not even when she was stopping him from seeing Harris. Leo has never bad-mouthed Dominic, even though the guy has all the charisma of an overdressed salad; clearly Allie has no such scruples.

Leo looks back to see Ffion still standing in the open doorway, her bag in one hand. He winces. He's been asking Ffion to meet Harris for months, and it really couldn't have gone much worse.

TittleTattle.com

Forums > True Crime > Peter and Stephanie Carmichael

WhatKatyDid

I have goss! A friend's brother works at Chester police station, and
he just booked in some evidence found at the Carmichael house!
Member since 2022. 173 posts

RockyRose

Well dont leave us in suspence. Is it the missing locket?
Member since 2022. 54 posts

WhatKatyDid

Sorry, my dinner was ready. No, he said it was a shoebox full
of stuff like letters and theatre tickets. Apparently it was
hidden behind a kickboard.
Member since 2022. 173 posts

MartyJ

Did he photograph any of it?
Member since 2019. 298 posts

WhatKatyDid

My friend asked him, but he wouldn't. Says it's too much of a risk and he doesn't want to lose his job. He saw a theatre programme and two tickets for Cat on a Hot Tin Roof, a pressed flower, and . . . get this . . . a LOVE NOTE.
Member since 2022. 173 posts

MartyJ

Whoa . . . is he sure? What did it say?
Member since 2019. 298 posts

WhatKatyDid

He wrote it down. Here it is. 'Call me when you can. Can't wait for Paris! Love you always x'
Member since 2022. 173 posts

SuperSleuth

I knew it! I've literally been saying for YEARS that Stephanie was over the side!
Member since 2016. 455 posts

TEN

MONDAY | FFION

Ffion waits for the sound of the shower before she opens her eyes. She glances at Leo's bedside table. Taking his phone into the bathroom with him is a new habit, one which gives Ffion an uneasy feeling in the pit of her stomach, as though she's about to sit an exam for which she hasn't revised.

She rolls on to her back and stares at the bedroom ceiling. Leo's phone habits are the least of her problems. Arguing with Leo is nothing new (George maintains that arguments are Ffion's preferred communication method, and Ffion can't dispute this without proving George right, which is deeply irritating), but last night felt different.

She doesn't blame Harris – he's just a kid – but, just as it always hurts when Seren lashes out at Ffion, it hit hard to hear Harris call her a tramp. Perhaps because it was an echo of a time when Ffion, fifteen and pregnant, described herself the same way; perhaps because Ffion can only imagine what other slurs Leo's ex-wife has been bandying about. But mostly because Harris is the only person in the world Leo loves more than Ffion, and he will always, always put him first. Where does that leave Ffion?

'I told you it wasn't the right time,' Ffion had said last night, when Leo returned home. She'd still been in the hall, sitting on the stairs, not wanting to stay but unable to leave. 'You ambushed me.'

'It wasn't an ambush – I forgot to message you, that's all. It'll be fine next time, you'll see.'

Ffion had raised an eyebrow. 'Harris is okay about seeing me again, then?'

Leo's hesitation had answered for him.

Ffion gets out of bed and pulls on her clothes. Before Leo can emerge from the shower, she slips downstairs, retrieves Dave from the kitchen, and leaves for work.

At first glance, Simmonds Sales and Lettings looks like any other estate agent. There are property details trapped between Perspex and hung on twisted silver wire in the windows, and large desks at which vendors can be schmoozed and contracts signed. Simmonds, however, is nothing like the estate agents through which Ffion is buying her house. There are no pound signs in the window here, only a discreet 'price on application' beneath the flowery descriptions. There are no terraces or semi-detached; no houses that would *benefit from some modernisation* (Ffion has viewed several of those over the last nine months and come to realise this is estate agent speak for 'the house is a shithole and it will take every penny you possess – and then some – to renovate it').

Inside Simmonds, Ffion's loafers sink into plush carpet as Carole leads the way into her office. A striking pink orchid with large symmetrical petals sits in a moss-covered pot on one side of her desk. Ffion touches a petal between her thumb and forefinger and is surprised to discover it's real. She has never been able to keep a house plant alive.

'Stunning, isn't it?' Carole says. '*Phragmipedium kovachii.*

Expensive, but a real talking point.' She's fiddling with the air-conditioning display on the wall. 'Are you cool enough?'

'I'm fine.' The petal comes off in Ffion's hand, and she quickly shoves it in her pocket.

'I've put the *closed* sign on the door,' Carole says, 'so we won't have any walk-ins. I would have shut completely, out of respect for Natasha, but the boys have viewings, and I don't want to let people down.'

Ffion thinks darkly of her own estate agent, who, if Mia's story is true, is still doing viewings on *her* house. Bastards. She mentally rearranges the list of people she hates, putting estate agents in second place, above traffic wardens. She'd like to put them first, but politicians take some beating.

'Are you a homeowner, DC Morgan?' Carole sits at her desk and gestures for Ffion to do the same. 'No? Well, if there's ever anything we can do to help . . . We have some beautiful properties on our books at the moment.' She waves her hand at the wall, on which are displayed more house details. Ffion sees a stunning six-bedroom house faced with honeyed stone. *Ormindale, The Hill. A luxury residence in Cheshire's most desirable postcode.*

'Thanks, but I think my budget's a little lower than anything you'll have to offer.'

'Oh, you'd be surprised!' Carole flips open an iPad and taps at it efficiently before handing Ffion the screen. 'This one-bed is terribly reasonable; offers over four nine nine.' On the screen is a photo of a kitchen in which you couldn't even stroke a cat, let alone swing it.

'I'll give it some thought,' replies Ffion, whose absolute definite cannot-go-any-higher limit is half that.

'Excellent! I can set up a view—'

'I've thought about it.' Ffion hands back the iPad. 'It's a no. Was Natasha a good estate agent?'

'She was a born saleswoman. My top seller has always been Mike, but, more recently, Natasha had been outperforming him significantly.'

'How did Mike feel about that?'

'He was furious.' Carole gives a short laugh. 'I'd been hinting to each of them that they were in the lead, you see, so it rather came out of the blue for Mike.'

'You play them off against each other?' Ffion might demote politicians from first place after all.

'A hungry agent is a successful agent, and Natasha was hungry,' Carole says. 'She had so much persistence. The evening after a viewing, she'd email the prospective buyers with information on schools, or gyms, or whatever she'd discovered was their primary focus.'

'I'd like to see these emails. You said I could take her laptop?'

'Ah, about that.' Carole hesitates. 'It's not in the office, I'm afraid. Have you asked her partner if he's seen it?'

'Yes – he hasn't.'

'Well, it's not here, so she must have taken it home. I'm sorry you had a wasted trip.'

'Can you access her emails remotely?'

'I – I suppose so. Why?'

'Could you do so, please?'

'Now?'

'No, next year. Yes, of course now,' Ffion snaps.

Carole's eyebrows shoot upwards, but she turns to her computer and taps some keys.

'Did Natasha mention any creepy vendors? Pushy buyers? Anyone she was having hassle with?'

'We sell high-end homes, DC Morgan,' Carole says, as though that answers Ffion's question, when some of the biggest creeps Ffion's ever encountered have lived in stunning houses. 'Here you are. All our emails are stored on a central server in order to keep a digital trail of offers, negotiations and so on. This is Natasha's folder.' She turns the screen to face Ffion and pushes the mouse towards her.

There are thousands of sent and archived emails, but only a handful in Natasha's inbox. Ffion thinks of the red notification bubble on her own phone, which currently stands at 8,724 unread. 'Is it possible to download all this?' she asks Carole.

'I can try.'

While Carole looks for a USB stick, Ffion clicks back to Natasha's inbox and looks down the list of subject headers. She sees 'Ormindale', the 'price on application' house featured on Carole's wall, and she can't resist opening the email to see how much it is.

Yes, that's fine, the first email says. It's from a Warren Irvine. Natasha's opening email is further down, asking Warren and Emmy, who is presumably Warren's wife (Ffion notes that Natasha has emailed them on separate email addresses), about a viewing. *The buyers are particularly keen to see the romantic master bedroom, which is a priority for them*, Natasha's email reads. There's no mention of the house price, and Ffion closes the email. *Romantic master bedroom*. Fucksake. Ffion's priority is a garden capable of outwitting Dave-the-escapologist. No, strike that: her priority is simply finding a bloody house before she's forced to move back home to Mam's.

Ffion leaves Simmonds with the USB stick and precisely an hour to get to Natasha's post-mortem, which gives her time to indulge in another instalment of *Without Conviction*. Joseph Flint

84

is describing the house where the Carmichaels died: a two-bedroomed mews property in an exclusive gated community.

Literally no one is getting past those gates without a fob, he tells his co-host, with his usual breathless insistence. *Which begs the question: was the killer one of the other residents?*

Gemma Lyrick picks up the script. *The police spoke to the owners of the other five mews houses. And we know what you're thinking, and no, we didn't just take their word for it. Joseph and I donned our sleuthing hats and checked out everyone's alibis ourselves.*

Ffion is torn between admiring the young couple's tenacity and being outraged by their audacity. Bet they're bloody annoying at a crime scene, she thinks. They'll be the type to whip out a phone and start filming when a police officer tries to move them on, then post it online as an example of #policeoppression. She's just wondering whether Joseph and Gemma have checked out how many gate fobs had been issued, and whether any were missing, when she remembers she has a murder of her own to solve – the victim of which is currently waiting for her at Bryndare mortuary.

The pathologist, Izzy Weaver, takes her through to the mercifully cold morgue, where George is already waiting.

'I don't usually work Mondays,' Izzy says. 'I should be on the golf course.'

'Yeah, well, I should be a size eight.'

'How's that delicious man of yours?'

'Leo?'

'I wasn't aware you had more than one.'

Ffion ignores her and walks over to a steel gurney covered with a blue sheet. 'This ours?'

Izzy joins her. 'Yes, this is yours. Natasha Brett.' She pulls off the blue sheet and the three of them look at the naked woman on the gurney. Natasha is tiny, probably only five foot one or two at first glance. Her eyes are open, and her hair has been carefully tucked behind her ears. Izzy's flippancy only extends to the living, Ffion has learned; the dead are treated with the utmost respect.

'How was Parks during the identification?' Ffion asks George.

'He held it together pretty well.'

'In a murderous sort of way?'

George responds to Izzy's quizzical look. 'Ffion's got a tenner on it because she told some hot transferee it was murder, and she doesn't want to lose face.'

'Hotter than DS Brady?' Izzy says, one brow arched.

'No one's hotter than DS Brady,' George says.

'Will you two please stop objectifying my boyfriend?' Ffion feels the weird mix of pleasure and awkwardness she always feels when she calls Leo her 'boyfriend'. 'And for the record, the transferee might be hot, but he's also an arrogant arsehole.'

Izzy sighs. 'They so often are, aren't they? Right, let's push on. The canoe was a nice touch, by the way. My bodies don't usually come with packaging.'

'Kayak,' Ffion says.

'Pedant.' Izzy works her way from the woman's head to her toes, visually examining every centimetre of skin. 'Abrasions to the left hand and the left shoulder – likely sustained post-mortem.'

'She wasn't wearing a helmet,' George says. 'I wondered if she might have hit her head and been knocked out. If the kayak rolled and she was unconscious, she'd drown in seconds.'

'She has contusions to the right side of her head consistent with blunt force trauma, but see how the marks are yellow? At first glance they look old, but this laceration is fresh. I suspect she hit rocks on her way down the river towards the lake, after your young lad found her.'

'He said there were no marks on her face when he saw her,' Ffion says.

'There we go, then. Sustained post mortem.' Izzy's leaning over the woman's face, her fingers carefully prising open her mouth. 'This froth at the back of the throat – and in the nostrils, see here? – would support the theory that she drowned.' She looks again at the skin around the woman's face, head and neck. 'If she'd been forced underwater, I'd expect to see evidence of pressure, either on the top of her skull, or on her shoulders, but she's clean.'

'Accidental drowning, then?' George says.

'Don't go spending that tenner till it's in your hand.' Izzy runs her hands along the woman's torso. 'Now, the blood's settled in the upper portions of the body – the face, arms and torso – and this lividity is fixed. See how when I press her skin, it stays red? This suggests she was upside down either at the point of death or within two or three hours after it, and that she remained that way until the canoe – sorry, the kayak – was recovered.'

'Can you tell whether she died in the kayak?' Ffion says.

'Rigor mortis begins setting in around two hours after death, so if she didn't die in it, she was placed in it soon afterwards.' Izzy reaches for her scalpel and makes a single smooth cut from the woman's left shoulder to the centre of her chest. She repeats the process on the other side, before running her scalpel directly down the middle of the stomach.

Ffion crosses to the drying rack. She can deal with intact bodies, and she can deal with dissected ones, but the process of getting from one state to the other is never pleasant viewing. Natasha's swimsuit is hanging from the rack and Ffion pulls on a pair of latex gloves and looks for the label. *Pour Moi*, it reads. *Size 8.* The swimsuit is black, with cutaway sides and a plunging neckline partly filled in with a gauze panel.

'Lungs are enlarged – see how they're overlapping?' Izzy is saying. 'There's a significant amount of liquid in the stomach too, so either she was big on hydration, or she took on a load of water as she died.'

Ffion moves out of the way, as Izzy carries a lung – or possibly a stomach, Ffion doesn't look that closely – to the scales. The pathologist pauses, taking a closer look at Natasha's ankles.

'Maybe it's just a shadow, but it looks . . .' She trails off, moving Natasha's feet from side to side and comparing one foot to the other. 'Yes, it is.'

'Is what?'

'Remember I said I was looking for signs of pressure having been applied to her shoulders or head, from someone pushing her under the water?'

'Right,' Ffion says. 'But there weren't any.'

'No.' Izzy beckons them closer. 'But she might have been pulled.'

Ffion peers at the inside of Natasha Brett's left ankle, where Izzy is pointing to a small oval mark only a shade or two darker than the surrounding skin. 'A bruise?'

'I'll make sure it's been photographed.' Izzy weighs the organ – a lung, Ffion decides – then places it in a shallow plastic tray and makes a swift and decisive cut across the surface. Liquid pours into the tray. Izzy turns. 'Where did you say she was found?'

'In the Awen. Although she ended up in Llyn Drych.'

'Smell this.'

'I'd really rather not,' Ffion says.

Izzy takes a small pot from a shelf and unscrews it, removing a slip of paper and dipping it into the liquid. 'We'll need to wait for toxicology, but . . .' She looks at the paper. 'Yes, I thought so.'

'What?' George says.

'Chlorine.' Izzy snaps off her gloves. 'I think you've won your bet, Ffion. Wherever this young lady drowned, it wasn't in the river.'

ELEVEN

MONDAY | LEO

When Leo had emerged from the bathroom, rubbing his hair with a towel, he'd assumed Ffion had gone downstairs to make them both a cup of coffee. Even when he'd been standing in the empty kitchen, dressed and making his own coffee, it hadn't occurred to him that Ffion would actually have left without saying goodbye. In fact (Leo is embarrassed to admit it, even to himself) he had thought that Ffion had perhaps gone to buy breakfast and would come through the door bearing bags of fresh-baked pastries from the bakery down the road. He should have known such an act would be ludicrously off-brand for Ffion. A disappearing act was much more her style.

Unwittingly compensating for Ffion's silence is Leo's ex-wife, who has sent a barrage of angry texts since seven-thirty this morning, when Harris had presumably told Allie that he'd met 'Daddy's girlfriend'.

I told you I didn't want her anywhere near my son! Wtf are you playing at?

Swearing in front of a child! Not exactly the sort of behaviour the taxpayers expect from a detective, is it???

Harris is really upset and doesn't want to see you. I hope she's
worth it . . .

Leo usually finds it amusing to hear his hands-free software
read out Allie's text messages, which are generally peppered with
expletives and misspellings, but even the car's robotic AI voice
can't put a comedy spin on today's missives. Legally Allie might
not be able to stop Leo seeing his son, but that won't stop her
trying.

'You okay?' Dawn says, when he walks into the office. 'You
look rough.'

'Thanks.'

'Sorry. But if you're ill, go home. It's only a burglary, no one's
died.'

'I'm not ill.' Leo logs on. 'Seriously, I'm fine.' Work is a welcome
distraction, not to mention far more straightforward than his
personal life. In an investigation – even a complex one – there
are rules. Clear lines of inquiry to follow. Besides, it's never 'only'
a burglary. Philip and Suki Makepeace had been badly shaken by
the break-in at Fairhaven six months ago, and now the burglar
has struck again at Sunnyside it's highly likely another house on
The Hill will be hit. JP and Camilla Lennox seem to have brushed
off the incident, but what if the next victim is more vulnerable?
What if the occupants are at home when it happens? Not everyone
is as philosophical about a break-in as JP Lennox, who simply
said, 'Well, that's what insurance is for', as he listed the items
stolen from Sunnyside. Taking a burglar off the streets doesn't
only bring closure for the crimes already committed; it stops
countless other people becoming victims.

'Did Jade Upshall's husband confirm she was home all night?'
he asks Dawn.

She nods. 'The baby wakes constantly in the night and won't settle without her. I think he was telling the truth.'

'Take a look at her associates,' Leo says. 'Anyone she's been with in the past when she's been stop-searched or nicked. Find out who she was banged up with. She might not have turned over Sunnyside herself, but she could have passed information to someone who did.'

On his way back from the morning briefing, Leo heads out to the Portakabin in the back yard to see what he can learn about the Carmichael murders. His latest text to Ffion remains unanswered, but a juicy piece of intel about her latest obsession might do the trick.

Leo knocks on the open door, and it rattles on its hinges. 'Is that offer of a brew still on?'

'Tea or coffee?' John stands. 'We're out of milk.'

'Coffee, then. Cheers.'

Leo steps into the Portakabin and looks around. The crime scene photographs are brutal. He knows from Ffion that Peter and Stephanie Carmichael were both stabbed in the stomach with a steak knife believed to have been taken from the table, which had been laid for two. The knife had come from a set of six. One had still been on the table, four had been in a drawer, and the sixth – the murder weapon – had been found in the dishwasher.

'That was a bit of a fuck-up,' John says, following Leo's gaze. In one of the crime scene photographs, the dishwasher is open, the steak knife clearly visible in the cutlery basket. 'Officers were on scene ten minutes after the 999 call – a neighbour had heard Stephanie screaming – but no one thought to stop the dishwasher till CSI arrived, by which time it was too late.'

'What about DNA or prints elsewhere in the kitchen?'

'CSI did the usual, but there were no matches on the system, and by then Munson had been nicked and ID'd by a witness, so . . .'

It must be hard, Leo thinks, reinvestigating a case in which your own colleagues made mistakes, knowing evidence will have been lost in the ten years that have since elapsed.

John hands Leo a chipped mug with *Is it Friday yet?* on the side. 'Who do you like for your burglaries on The Hill?'

'The profile doesn't fit any of the usual suspects,' Leo says. 'Both break-ins happened when the occupants had planned to be away, but it's hard to say whether the burglar knew that in advance or just got lucky.'

'What did they nick?'

'Odds and ends. A few ornaments, a couple of expensive neck-laces, earrings and the like. I've circulated details to jewellery stores.'

'I've just drawn up a list of those "cash for gold" places, if you want it?'

'That would be great, thanks. Did whoever kill the Carmichaels turn the place over, then?'

John shakes his head. 'Stephanie Carmichael was missing a locket she often wore. The family insisted it had been stolen, but Stephanie had recently sold some jewellery, so there was a question mark over how relevant it was.' He reaches for his laptop and brings up a photograph. 'It's very distinctive, and it contained a photograph from their wedding, so it's very traceable, and it could have the offender's DNA on it, even after all this time, so we're still looking.'

'Assuming it's not been through the dishwasher.' Leo gives a wry smile. The image has been cropped from a photograph of Stephanie, the scalloped neckline of a peacock-blue dress just visible beneath

93

the necklace. The locket is gold – an uneven, bottom-heavy hexagon – and engraved with an intricate scroll design.

'Edwardian,' John says. 'I'll email you that list.'

'Did you find anything useful in that box you were going through yesterday?' Having started his questioning purely with the aim of getting Ffion back onside, Leo now finds himself wanting to know more about the Carmichael case.

'The true crime forums have theorised for years that Stephanie had a secret lover.' John rifles through a sheaf of paper to the side of his desk and pulls out a sheet. 'And now it looks like they were right.'

The photocopied image shows what looks like a sticky note from a Vauxhall showroom. There's a handwritten message below the logo.

Call me when you can. Can't wait for Paris! Love you always x

'Definitely not from her husband?'

'Hidden behind a kickboard?' John takes back the photocopy. 'Today's job is to attempt to convince the passport office to let me through their seventy billion layers of bureaucracy and tell me how many times, and when, Stephanie Carmichael travelled to Paris. Once I have dates, I can get data protection waivers in to the airlines to see who she travelled with.'

Leo looks pointedly around the empty office. 'How many on Operation Beech?'

'Two others. Both part-time.'

'Shout if you need more resources and I'll run it by the DI. We've got this burglary series, but otherwise we're pretty quiet right now.'

Just as Leo finishes speaking, his phone rings.

'Mate, never say the Q word,' John says. 'You've jinxed it now.'

Leo laughs. 'Thanks for the coffee.' He takes the call as he leaves the Portakabin, immediately recognising the voice of the station duty officer.

'DS Brady? Are you in the station? We've just had something handed in to the front desk . . .'

Leo stares at the sodden black bin bag dumped on the table. The top is open and water seeps out of holes in the plastic, covering the table with a thin film of stinking water.

'A member of the public pulled it out of the river,' the SDO says. 'I spotted a Wedgwood vase and had a quick look on the property register. It looks like the one from your burglary at Sunnyside on The Hill.'

Leo dons a pair of latex gloves and starts sifting through the contents of the black bag.

It's all there.

The Wedgwood vase, Camilla's necklaces, the silver photo frames . . . everything.

'Do you think he got spooked and dumped the bag?' the SDO says.

'Maybe,' Leo says. But he's thinking about JP Lennox saying *that's what insurance is for*. He's thinking about the randomness of what was stolen from Sunnyside. A few bits of jewellery, a few ornaments. The odd valuable piece, but not Camilla's prized rings, left in a dish by the kitchen sink. Aside from the broken shepherdess, there was no damage caused, no mess left for the family to clear up.

Almost, Leo thinks, as though the entire burglary was staged.

TWELVE

MONDAY | ALLIE

'We're going to be late.' Allie butters a piece of toast and drops the knife in the sink. 'Do you have your sports kit?'

Harris is standing in the hall. He lifts the hand carrying his bag, as Allie rushes past him and into her and Dominic's bedroom.

'God, why are mornings always such a rush?' she says, through a mouthful of toast. 'Have you seen my keys?' She drags a brush through her hair.

'They're on the table,' she hears Harris say, and, as she races back into the hall, he hands them to her.

'Come on, don't just stand there. We're late!'

The primary school Harris attends is a five-minute walk from home, and in the summer holidays they run a series of activity days, for which Allie is profoundly grateful. Allie sees Scarlett with her grandad up ahead (Scarlett is always on time) and she tugs Harris's hand. Another mum waves from across the street and she waves back. Allie can't remember her name. A few of the parents have invited Allie and Dominic for drinks, or to join their table at the PTA socials, but Allie likes to keep her evenings free in case there's something happening on The Hill.

'You're very quiet today.' Allie looks down at Harris. 'Are you thinking about what happened at Dad's?'

'Not really.'

'I'm not surprised – he should never have let that happen.' Allie has a knot of tension in her stomach. 'Although I suppose it was *her* doing.'

Harris says nothing.

'What's she like, then, this *Ffion* woman?'

'Dunno.'

'Is she pretty?'

'I don't know.'

Sometimes, when Allie has had a glass of wine, she searches for Ffion Morgan on social media. All she ever finds is a locked-down Instagram account with a profile picture of the ugliest dog Allie has ever seen. Which reminds her . . . She stops dead. 'Let me see your face.' She pulls Harris's chin up. The dog jumped up at him, he'd told Allie, and there hadn't been scratches then, but maybe it had left a bruise . . . She turns his face this way and that but can't see a mark.

They carry on walking. 'That awful dog. You must have been so frightened.'

'A bit.'

'Mummy was bitten by a dog like that once, you know. I had to be sewn up.'

Harris looks at her in horror.

'Don't worry, I won't let him come anywhere near you ever again, you hear me?'

Tears well at the corners of Harris's eyes, and as they get to the school gate, Allie stoops. 'Poor baby, I'm so sorry that happened to you.' She pulls him into a quick hug then sends him into the playground. 'I won't come in with you – Mummy's got to help a friend out today.'

The Hill's WhatsApp group has been very active since the

burglary at Sunnyside. Bianca has shared several articles with crime prevention advice, and even JP – who hardly ever posts – has reminded everyone to check their insurance cover is up to date. Camilla's messages have been more emotional. I feel so violated, she said, which prompted a flood of hearts and offers of support from the other women. Camilla had 'liked' all the messages except Allie's, which smarted a bit, because Allie had spent almost an hour looking through inspirational quotes to find something that hit the right note, before pasting it into Canva so she could add in a pretty background. Maybe Camilla hadn't seen it.

It had occurred to Allie that Camilla might prefer help of a more practical nature, and so Allie is spending this morning making a lasagne. She never makes lasagne – it's far too much faff just for her, Dom and Harris – but it feels like the right sort of meal to take to someone who's been burgled. It says *comfort*, Allie thinks. It says *here is a dish made by a good friend*.

She agonises over what cookware to use. Pyrex lacks class, and the disposable foil dishes she uses at Christmas to save washing up are hardly suitable for The Hill. She settles on a stoneware Le Creuset dupe she bought at Dunelm, which is impossible to distinguish from the real thing unless you tip it upside down, which no one is going to do when it's full of lasagne. She'll tell Camilla not to worry about washing it.

As soon as the lasagne is cool enough to carry, Allie takes it up the hill and rings the bell at Sunnyside. JP answers the door and looks at her quizzically.

'Allie,' she prompts. 'From The Willows?'

'Of course, the jumble lady!' JP looks ineffectually around him. 'Camilla did say there were some bags somewhere, but heaven knows what she's done with them. We're all sixes and sevens at the moment – we were broken into at the weekend.'

'I know.' Allie holds up the lasagne. 'That's why I'm—'

'Camilla!' he hollers up the stairs. 'The jumble lady's here!'

Allie's smile grows tight. He doesn't mean anything by it, she tells herself. It's no different from calling someone . . . Allie grapples for an equivalent . . . *the tall lady*, or *the woman from next door*. JP's older than Camilla, who is in turn older than Allie, which makes JP practically another generation. She shouldn't take offence.

'Ah, Alice!' Camilla runs lightly down the stairs.

'Um, it's actually Allie.'

'Would you mind coming back tomorrow? Jade's tidied the bags away and I can't look for them now, I'm going shopping.'

'Are you taking the car?' JP says.

'No, parking's such a hassle. I'll see if the Makepeaces' driver can drop me off. Ray won't mind, he's such a sweetheart.'

'I think he's away,' JP says. 'I'm sure Philip mentioned it the other day.'

'I brought you a lasagne,' Allie says, so suddenly that it sounds vaguely threatening.

There's an awkward pause.

Camilla stares at the lasagne, confused. 'Why?'

'Because of the burglary.'

'They didn't take the oven, dear.' JP laughs uproariously, then claps Allie on the shoulder, presumably to bring her in on the joke.

'It must have been such a terrible shock.' Allie persists. 'You must have felt *violated.*'

'Oh, we did! We do!' If Camilla notices Allie using the very word Camilla had used on the WhatsApp chat, she doesn't remark on it. She clasps her hands to her heart. 'And you're a sweetheart, Alice, you really are.'

'It's nothing, really.' Allie beams. The last three hours – and the encrusted pans waiting for her at home – have all been worth it.

'The thing is . . .' Camilla makes an apologetic face. 'I'm vegan.'

'Oh.' Allie looks down at the generous cheese topping, melted into the creamy white sauce. She looks at JP. 'Then I suppose—'

'Gluten intolerance.' He sighs. 'Bloody pain in the arse. Quite literally, actually.'

'I see.'

'I'm so sorry, Alice.' Camilla squeezes Allie's shoulder. 'And after you went to so much trouble.'

'Really, it's fine!' Allie can feel her cheeks reddening. 'I'm glad you're okay after the burglary.' She turns to leave, hearing the door close before she's halfway down the path. Then she takes her lasagne home.

THIRTEEN

MONDAY | FFION

It had taken mere seconds to check the Airbnb listing for Mervyn's holiday let and confirm the presence of a hot tub in the garden, overlooking the river and sheltered from the elements within a three-sided gazebo.

By the time Ffion pulls up at the house, the forensics van is parked outside. The uniformed PCs are on their second stint of scene watch, and as Ffion gets out of her car she sees Sam Taylor talking to the two crime scene investigators. They turn as Ffion walks towards them.

Debbie Stevens has dark brown hair with a white streak, tucked behind one ear. She smiles at Ffion. '*Iawn?*'

'Sorry to keep you.'

'*Dim problem.*' Debbie holds up a notebook. 'Your colleague's briefed us.'

Ffion glances at Sam, then turns back to Debbie. 'It's probably best if I—'

'Female victim – IC1, long blonde hair – found in an upturned kayak in the river yesterday morning, wearing a swimsuit.' Debbie squints. 'My writing's appalling . . . Chlorine in the lungs. Crime scene is believed to be a hot tub situated in a three-sided outhouse next to this house. You've conducted a visual sweep of the property, which has been under scene watch since shortly after the body was discovered, and there are no signs of a struggle.' She looks up. 'Okay so far?'

Ffion nods tightly.

'Now you'd like us to photograph and document the scene, with particular attention to the hot tub. Take a water sample for comparison with the sample taken from the victim. Locate and identify any blood, fluids, tissue and hair, and collect latent prints. Examine the path between the house and the hot tub for footwear evidence.' She looks up again. 'Anything else?'

Ffion can feel Sam's smugness radiating towards her. 'No, I think that's everything.'

'Great, we'll get started.'

'Not bad, huh?' Sam says, as Debbie walks away.

Ffion glares at him. 'Who asked you to brief CSI?'

'Nobody, but it took you a while to get here, so I thought—'

'You should have waited.' She starts walking around the perimeter of the barn conversion, careful to stay away from the well-trodden areas of grass. At the rear of the property, around twenty metres from the main house, is an outhouse with a slate roof and three sides made from timber. Inside, a hot tub makes a low humming sound.

In front of the outhouse, beyond the big stone slabs that surround it, there's a break in the long grass, as though someone has walked through it. Ffion moves closer and, as she does so, she notices scuff marks on the stone slabs. She lets her eyes travel across the field. The marks in the grass become obscured, but, assuming the line continues straight down, they'll end up . . .

Ffion's gaze lands on the river.

'Debbie!' she calls out as the CSI walks towards her, a heavy bag making her gait lopsided. 'If someone dragged a kayak over stone slabs, could you tell from the marks if someone was in it?'

'If I know the weight of it when it's empty.' Debbie puts her bag a few metres from the hot tub and gets to work. Over the next two hours, she retrieves tiny fragments of fibreglass from the rough surface of the stone slabs, and meticulously measures the drag marks in the grass to compare with the kayak in which Natasha Brett was found.

'See this?' Debbie points to a patchy section of grass.

'Footprints?' Ffion crouches to get a better look. It's not a full footprint, but the rounded imprint of the toe shows a distinctive zigzag pattern, and a section of the heel is just visible too.

'Big feet.' Debbie measures the imprint. 'Eleven, or thereabouts. I'll take a cast for tread comparison. Do you have a suspect?'

'Three,' Ffion says, thinking of Natasha's colleagues. Size eleven suggests the killer was male, or does Carole Simmonds have huge feet? Ffion tries to recall Russell Steele's and Mike Foster's, but all she can picture is shiny shoes beneath even shinier suits.

While Debbie swabs the rim of the hot tub for DNA and sweeps a fine net through the warm water, Ffion walks down the slope, following the marks to the bottom of the field, where they disappear down the steep banks of the river. Did one of Natasha's colleagues drown her in the hot tub then drag her down to the river? Had they planned it, or was there an argument? A struggle? Ffion will need to re-interview all three of them: pin them down on their movements after getting back from the pub. Now that Natasha's death has been confirmed as murder, an incident room has been established at Bryndare police station, and Ffion and George will be seconded to Major Crime for the duration of the investigation. It means more people to do the job, which is theoretically a good thing, except that Ffion so often finds that the more people on an investigation, the more they get in the way.

She rings George. 'Hey, can you press Natasha's partner on where her laptop is?' she says, without preamble.

'Luke's adamant she rarely brought it home.'

'Carole Simmonds says she took it home all the time.'

'Well, one of them's lying,' George says. 'Where are you?'

'Back at the holiday let.' She fills George in on Izzy Weaver's findings, and the marks that suggest Natasha was dragged down to the river. 'Even if forensics find prints from one of the estate agents on the kayak, they've got a plausible story for why they're there; the briefing area at the rafting centre is right by the racking.'

'Do any of them have a motive?' George says.

'Natasha won the bonus Mike usually gets.' Ffion starts walking back up the hill. 'I'm not sure about the other two. They all went to the pub on Saturday night, right before Natasha was murdered. I'm going to go for a pint tonight and see what I can find out.'

'The sacrifices you make for this job, right?'

'What can I say?' Ffion laughs. 'It's a tough job, but someone has to do it.'

When Ffion pushes open the door of Y Llew Coch, she's greeted with a burst of music and chatter. Carole Simmonds's statement said all four estate agents had spent the evening at the pub, but, like her colleagues, she was hazy about what they'd done, or when they had left. 'I just remember it was karaoke night,' she'd told Ffion. 'I don't like to boast, but my "Stand by Your Man" is a bit of a showstopper.'

'We don't have karaoke nights,' the landlord says now. 'Our machine broke, and we never replaced it.'

'They were just singing, then?' Ffion steps to one side as a barmaid raises a small section of the bar and ducks under it into the lounge.

'Loudly and badly. The older woman absolutely murdered a. Tammy Wynette song.'

Around them, the barmaid begins collecting empties. Ffion nods to her ex-husband, Huw, who is sitting at a table in the corner with some of the rugby lads. They get on well enough nowadays, although Ffion still feels a twinge of guilt at how brief their marriage had been. Huw had wanted children and Ffion hadn't (she'd hardly been Mother of the Year with Seren) and it was one of the few things in life on which there was no compromise.

'Can I have a pint of the Hafod, please?' Ffion says.

The landlord takes a glass from the rack. 'I had to throw two of them out in the end. The older couple had already left – I told them they'd had enough – but the young lad was still here, and so was the girl.' He nods towards a shock of pink hair on the far side of the pub. 'You know she had a fight with Mia?'

'Mia?' Ffion says. The pink-haired woman turns at her name and comes over.

'When did you do this?' Ffion flicks Mia's hair, which is dramatically different from her usual blonde.

'Saturday. What do you think?'

'It's subtle.'

Mia grins. 'I haven't seen you for ages.'

'Been busy at work. I hear you had a fight on Saturday.' Ffion waits, but Mia's face is blank. 'Small, quite pretty. English.'

'Oh, her! I wouldn't call her pretty. She tried to snog Bobby.' Mia takes a swig of her pint. 'He says he was so shocked it took him a second to stop her. Well, you can imagine how that went down with me. She must have been half his age, for God's sake.'

Ffion thinks of Luke Parks. Natasha certainly had a type. 'What did you do?'

'What do you think I did? I had a word with her.'

'A word?' Ffion raises an eyebrow and Mia laughs.

'Okay, so I might have given her a bit of encouragement to sit down.' Mia grins. 'But seriously, Ffi, the girl was bang out of order.'

'She was murdered a few hours after she left here.'

Mia's mouth drops open. 'Holy crap, that was her? Do you know who killed her?'

'Not yet. Did she cause trouble with any other locals?'

'She had a right barney with one of the blokes she came in with. And you know they let John Williams's sheep out on their way home?'

'A barney? With which bloke? The one in his twenties or the one in his forties?'

'This lad was the same age as her. So much product in his hair he looked like he had one of those Lego wigs on.'

Russell, Ffion thinks. 'What were they arguing about?'

'I couldn't hear what they were saying, but the bloke kept looking over at me and Bobby, so I reckoned he was pissed off with her about that, same as I was. She was tossing her hair, all defensive like, and he was fuming. Proper angry. I figured they were together. *Slebog.*'

'Hey, it's bad enough when the men call women slags – let's not shit on our own, yeah?'

'She wasn't all over your boyfriend though, was she?' Mia says.

'Leo wouldn't have known what to do with himself.'

'You know your mam still thinks you might find yourself a nice Welsh man?'

'In Cwm Coed?' Ffion raises an eyebrow. 'Nah, Mam quite

106

likes Leo, I think.' She'd just like him more if he spoke Welsh, Ffion knows. Elen Morgan is fierce about what she calls the 'dilution' of the language.

'The problem,' she told Ffion, the last time the subject came up, 'is that, with Leo not speaking Welsh, you won't speak it at home. So then your children don't speak it at home, and before you know it we've lost a whole generation.'

'Well, we're not having children, so you don't have to worry about it,' Ffion said firmly.

'You're not even thirty-five, Ffi, you—'

'Mam.' Ffion had given her *the look*. End of conversation.

In the corner of Y Llew Coch, a man in a checked shirt has been enjoying a solitary pint in the corner of the pub. Ffion noticed him when she came in, but, as he turns to look towards the bar, she realises who he is. Her eyes narrow. 'Laters,' she tells Mia. 'I need to have a word with Idris.' She strides over to him, and he gets to his feet.

'Ffion! I've been trying to get hold of y—'

'Bollocks you have. I've had my phone on me all day. What's going on? Are we ready to exchange, or what?'

Idris's mouth opens, but for a few seconds, nothing comes out. He glances past Ffion, as though looking for an exit. 'There's been a . . . development,' he says finally.

'My landlord needs me out by the end of the month – this can't drag on much longer.'

'Ffion—'

'If we exchange next week, could we complete on the same day?'

'You've been gazumped.'

There's a long pause.

'You what?'

'Turns out the estate agents carried on doing viewings and the vendor's taken a higher offer from a London couple who want a weekend bolthole up here. You've lost the house, Ffion. I'm so sorry.'

'That can't be legal.'

'I'm afraid it is.'

Ffion lifts her pint and downs her drink in three gulps.

Estate agents . . .

Fuck the lot of them.

[alt text: the image is a letter written on blue paper. The text reads: *My darling Stephanie, you looked so beautiful sleeping, I didn't want to wake you. Thank you so much for getting the cash out for my aunt's casket. I called the bank, and they said loads of people's accounts are down. Such a pain! You're a sweetheart for helping me out. I wish Auntie Paula could have met you, she would have loved you like I do. If only we had met years ago, but now that I have you, I don't ever want to loose you. Love you always x*]

WithoutConviction Here it is, Instagrammers! The letter found in Peter and Stephanie Carmichael's house, read out in episode 3 of Season 4 (which incidentally now has more than one million downloads! Thank you guys so much!).
When we heard on the true crime grapevine that the new owners of the Carmichaels' house had found crucial evidence hidden in the kitchen, we wasted no time in tracking them down. They'd already handed the box to the police (good luck with that one – lol!) but fortunately for us (and you!) they took pictures of the contents first. Swipe to see the rest.
#CarmichaelMurders #TrueCrimestagram #InstagramTrueCrime #WithoutConvictionPodcast

View all 47 comments
18 minutes ago

Suzylovescrime
You guys are doing amazing work! Has anyone checked funeral records for women called Paula, so we can identify the nephew (Stephanie's lover)?

RachaelAppleby

Which banks have had outages? I'm with HSBC and I don't remember anything happening like this. @Lloyds @Natwest @Halifax?

SaimaHadi79

The police will be able to date the paper

Myslimmingjourney

Guess we're looking for a man with bad spelling then lol

FOURTEEN

TUESDAY | LEO

They need to check Eurostar too, reads Ffion's message.

Leo is eating breakfast. He taps a response. And the ferries? He adds a winking emoji, which Ffion either doesn't notice or ignores.

Who the fuck takes a ferry to Paris?!

As Leo had predicted, Ffion hadn't been able to resist Leo's teasers on the Carmichael case, and they had exchanged several messages late last night.

He risks a return to more personal territory. Missed you last night. Stay at mine tonight?

Just you and me? comes Ffion's message. No ambush . . .

It wasn't— Leo stops. He hits delete and starts again. Yes, just you and me x

Okay. Just don't mention estate agents. I'm raging.

Standard Ffion, then?

Ha ha. Go away, I'm very busy and important xx

Leo's phone rings before he can tap another response. He presses *accept* only when he's certain it isn't Allie.

'Sarge? It's Dawn. There's been another break-in on The Hill, and this time someone's been hurt. Badly.'

*   *   *

Leo gives his name to the uniformed officer standing in front of the Jeffersons' driveway, and ducks under the police tape. The front door is closed and as he walks around the side of the house, Dawn emerges from the back garden.

'Alec Jefferson's been moved to ICU.'

'Is he conscious? Talking?'

Dawn shakes her head. 'He's in a medically induced coma in the hope the swelling on his brain will go down. The FME is taking samples now.'

'His parents must be frantic.' Leo will catch up with the force medical examiner as soon as he finishes here. If there was a confrontation, Alec's body may hold crucial evidence. Fingernail scrapings could provide DNA that could take them straight to their man. Or woman, Leo reminds himself, although, statistically, burglars are rarely female.

'The Jeffersons went straight to the hospital when they got the call.' Dawn leads the way into the garden, where more tape blocks off the back door. 'All three of them were supposed to be visiting family last night, but Cara and Mikaela ended up going on their own. Alec stayed home.'

Leo looks through the kitchen window. He can't tell where Alec was assaulted – there's no blood on the floor, no sign of a struggle – but it doesn't take a genius to establish the method of entry. 'Another smashed window.'

Dawn nods. 'And the back door propped open, presumably to make a quick getaway. Just like the others. Cara Jefferson's coming back briefly, to tell us what's been taken, then she'll go back to the hospital.'

'Who found Alec?'

She turns, and Leo follows her gaze to a pretty wooden summer-house on the far side of the swimming pool. Inside, a man sits on a rattan chair, his head in his hands. 'He did.'

Duncan Cragg is a white man in his sixties, with a lined face and a full head of thick grey hair. Despite the heat, he's wearing a long-sleeved sweatshirt, a cotton bandana tied around his neck.

'I come once a week to maintain the pool,' he tells Leo. 'I check the chlorine levels, clean out the leaves, change the filter.'

'What time did you get here today?'

'A couple of minutes after seven. I was a bit late.' He hasn't yet met Leo's gaze, instead directing his answers to somewhere above Leo's right ear. 'The kitchen door was open, which surprised me, because I thought they'd gone away. I went to make sure everything was alright, and that's when I saw Alec.' He rubs his face vigorously. 'After that, it was all a blur. I called his name, but he didn't react and even when I ran in, he didn't move and—' Duncan stops and lets out a breath. 'I thought he was dead. I didn't know what to do. I know how to do mouth-to-mouth, but he was still breathing, so . . . He was just lying there, totally still, and so white.'

'Would you say you were here by five past seven?' Leo says.

'Yes. It was two minutes past when I got out of the car – I remember looking at the clock, because I'd been stuck in traffic. I guess by the time I'd walked around to the back, it would have been a minute or so after that.'

'Our records show that Control Room received a call from you at 07.17.' Leo pauses. 'Ten minutes seems like a long time to wait to call 999 when someone's unconscious.'

'I called upstairs first, to see if Cara or Mikaela were home. Came back and checked for a pulse, then . . .' Duncan shakes his head. 'It didn't feel like ten minutes. Everything happened really quickly until I was waiting for the ambulance, then it felt like for ever.'

'Was the alarm going off?' Leo has already seen the telltale box at the front of Hollies and the wires neatly fed through the frame of the door.

'If it had been, I'd have known something was wrong, wouldn't I?'

Leo doesn't bite, but he's even more certain now that there's something Cragg isn't telling him. 'Do you have the code for the alarm system?'

'Yes, but I told you, it wasn't going off.'

'I'd appreciate some personal details please – date of birth, address and contact number – then my colleague will take a written account of what happened.'

While Dawn makes a start on Duncan Cragg's statement, Leo walks further into the garden to run a PNC check. He keeps his gaze on Cragg, who shifts in his seat as Dawn questions him.

'Cragg, Duncan Peter,' comes the voice in Leo's earpiece. 'January 18th, 1963, born Glasgow. Previous convictions for affray, breach of the peace and Section 18 wounding with intent.'

Leo, his eyes still on Duncan Cragg, puts his radio back into his pocket. He wonders if the Jeffersons know about Cragg's past; wonders whether it's a coincidence that both of the break-ins in the last few days have taken place in households where the staff have criminal records.

Cara Jefferson arrives just as the crime scene investigators are setting up. At first glance she looks angry – her lips pulled so tight that the edges are white – but Leo can see the redness around her eyes; hear the quiver in her voice. She clutches her phone, continually looking at it, as if she doesn't trust she'll hear it ring.

'They say we just have to wait and see. They won't know the extent of the damage done to his brain until he wakes up.' Cara starts crying, and Leo can imagine the postscript playing silently in her head.

If he wakes up.

'We won't keep you long,' Dawn says. 'I know you'll want to get back to Alec as soon as possible. I don't expect you to be able to list everything that's been stolen, but if we can take details of a few key items, we can circulate them to antique dealers and pawn shops. It's possible the burglars will try to move them on quickly.'

Cara nods. The CSI gives them paper suits, masks and shoe coverings, and instructs them to walk on the transparent stepping plates that mark a path through the kitchen and into the hall. There, Cara turns slowly in a circle, looking at each room through the open doors.

'There should be a paperweight.' She points. 'On that coffee table. Blue glass – it's not expensive. And I don't see the walnut snuff box on the mantelpiece. Unless Mikaela moved it.' She lists a handful of other things – a silver-plated photo frame, an antique clock – then points to an ornament lying on its side on a sofa. 'That figurine shouldn't be there, obviously. It lives on that table.'

'This might sound like a strange question,' Leo says, 'but is there anything here you're surprised *hasn't* been stolen?'

'The paintings,' Cara says, right away. 'We collect art, and there are several pieces worth tens of thousands of pounds.'

'Anything else?' Leo says, looking at the paintings, all of which are large and would be cumbersome for a burglar to take.

'Oh . . .' Cara indicates a glass-fronted cabinet. 'My grand-mother's tea set. I can't be a hundred per cent certain, but it looks like it's all there. I've never had it valued, but it's solid silver.'

The milk jug and sugar bowl are dainty and easily slipped in a bag; they seem obvious items to steal. Leo can't get a handle on their burglar's profile. Savvy enough to disable alarms so they can work undisturbed, yet with no apparent system once inside. Most burglars who target high-value properties know exactly what they're looking for. They pick out the expensive jewellery and the valuable paintings. They drill into the safe and take wads of cash. Whoever broke into Hollies, Fairhaven and Sunnyside doesn't seem to have a clue what will fetch a good price. Yesterday, when Leo had picked through the contents of the bag dumped in the river, he had wondered if Sunnyside had been an insurance job – copycatting the original burglary at Fairhaven to make it seem more convincing – but how does Hollies fit into that theory? Even if Cara and Mikaela Jefferson had been collaborating with JP and Camilla – and the thought seems unlikely – they wouldn't put their own son in danger.

'Who knew you were going away last night?' Leo asks Cara.

'Duncan knew – I told him we wouldn't be here when he arrived to check the pool – and my mum, obviously, because we were going to stay with her. Alec might have mentioned it to a mate, I suppose, but his friends are all lovely. There's no way they'd break into our house, and they certainly wouldn't hurt Alec. Oh, and I put it on the group chat.'

'What group chat?'

'We have a residents' group on WhatsApp. After Sunnyside was burgled, I felt nervous about leaving the house empty. Ironically, I was relieved when Alec decided to stay home. It never occurred to me something like this would happen.' She dissolves into tears.

'May I see the messages?' Leo says.

Cara takes a deep breath, composing herself. She opens her phone, pulls up a message thread and scrolls back. 'Here, I posted a couple of days before we headed off.'

It's an active group, with a flurry of messages in the aftermath of the Lennoxes' burglary, and even more after Alec was attacked. Leo finds Cara's message and swipes to the side to see which group members read it. He recognises most of the names. Warren Irvine, Camilla Lennox . . . He looks up. 'Who's Klingon?'

'I can't remember her actual name,' Cara says. 'She lives at the bottom of the street and her son goes to school with Bianca's daughter, Scarlett.'

Leo's stomach fills with misgiving. Surely not?

'We call her "Klingon" because she's impossible to get rid of,' Cara says. 'One of those social climber types, if you know what I mean?'

Leo does. All too well.

They walk back through the kitchen, keeping to the stepping plates. Leo notices a flyer on the table for an estate agency. 'Are you moving?'

For exceptional homes in Cheshire, the leaflet reads, *speak to Simmonds.*

'No, they must have put it through the door this morning – it was on the mat when we got home. I know Carole Simmonds through a networking group we both attend. They've got buyers queuing up for The Hill, apparently. We've got no plans to sell.' Cara's face darkens. 'At least, we didn't. But knowing someone's been here . . .' She shivers.

'Do you have somewhere you could stay tonight?' Dawn says.

117

'The forensics team will be here for some time, and in the meantime, perhaps you could speak to our crime prevention team about a few things that would make you feel more secure?'

'Yes.' Cara nods. 'That would be good. We can go back to my mum's.'

Outside, Cara peels off her paper suit and checks her phone. 'Do you have everything you need? I'd like to get back to the hospital.'

'Just a couple of things,' Leo says. 'How long has Duncan Cragg worked for you?'

'A year or so. I'd have to check.'

'Did he disclose any convictions to you when he applied for the job?'

'No.' Cara frowns. 'I went through an agency and to be honest, I just assumed—' She breaks off. 'Are you saying he has a criminal record?'

'That's not something I can share,' Leo says. 'Perhaps if you check with the agency . . .'

'Oh, I will.'

'I understand you've given him the alarm code.'

'Yes. The plant room, where the filter and so on is, is accessed via the garden, but it's part of the house, so if we're away he needs to be able to disable the alarm.'

'Does he have a key to the house?'

'No, only to the plant room. There's no internal door.' Cara opens the contacts app on her phone. 'Would you like the number for the alarm company? They'll be able to confirm it was set, and whether it went off.'

'That would be very helpful, thank you.'

Cara turns to look at Duncan, still sitting in the summer house. 'Do you think he hurt Alec? Because if he did, I swear—'

'Focus on your son, Mrs Jefferson,' Leo says gently, putting a hand on her arm. 'That's the most important thing. Leave the investigation to us.' He walks with her around the side of the house, stopping briefly by the garden gate. 'No lock?' he says, touching the latch.

'There didn't seem much point,' Cara says. 'All you'd have to do is stand on the wall and you could easily climb over the gate.'

'Our crime prevention team will be able to suggest something.' Leo steps up on to the low wall and looks at the top of the gate. 'Maybe anti-climb paint, or some kind of—' He breaks off. Pulling his phone from his pocket, he takes a photo of the top of the gate, then jumps down. 'Does this mean anything to you?'

On Leo's screen is the wooden surround that edges the gate, on which are written four digits in black marker pen.

2905

Cara's mouth falls open. 'I don't understand. I didn't write that, and Mikaela wouldn't have—' She stares at Leo. 'That's the code for the alarm.'

FIFTEEN

TUESDAY | FFION

There is only one incident room at Bryndare police station, and it's currently being used for a drive-by shooting. Major Crime's senior investigating officer, DCI Christine Boccacci, has instead assembled the team in the ground-floor briefing room, much to the disgruntlement of a uniformed PC who had been about to tackle his paperwork tray there.

With several Major Crime officers already committed to the shooting, the team allocated to Operation Garnet – the name assigned at random to the investigation into Natasha Brett's murder – is small. George will remain as Luke Park's FLO, and DI Malik has reluctantly allowed DCI Boccacci to keep Ffion.

'But only for this week,' he'd told Ffion. 'I've told the DCI I need you back in the office after that.' Malik's office had – as usual – been chaotic. There'd been a pile of files on his desk, slipping in several different directions, and at least four mugs of half-drunk coffee dotted about the room.

'Actually, I'm going to need next Friday off,' Ffion had said. 'I'm supposed to be moving house.'

'I'll make a note, but put a leave request in. I gather you and George attended Natasha Brett's post-mortem.' Malik had paused. 'How was she?'

'Pretty dead.'

Malik had given an unamused sigh. 'I meant George.'

'Alright, I guess.' Ffion had frowned. 'Why?'

'Keep an eye on her. Family liaison work is intense, and working closely with someone who's lost a partner could be—' Malik had stopped. 'Well, she might want to talk, that's all.' His phone had rung and he'd glanced at the screen. 'I have to take this.'

Ffion had been bemused by the DI's sudden concern for George, an experienced detective who was surely more than capable of dealing with the emotional fallout of a FLO case.

As Boccacci introduces herself, Ffion looks around the briefing room at her temporary colleagues. The hastily assembled team includes four Major Crime detectives – two of whom are simultaneously working on the shooting – two civilian investigators, an indexer, and . . .

Ffion stares at the final member of the team, who is wearing a navy-blue suit with a silver pin on his pale pink tie. His hair is gelled into a quiff. She turns to the DCI. 'What's he doing here?'

'This is PC Sam Taylor,' the DCI says. 'Borrowed from uniform. Sam's looking to apply for CID, so he volunteered to bolster our numbers.'

'A pleasure to help out, ma'am.'

Ffion resists the urge to stick her fingers down her throat.

'It seems our estate agents had a fine old time on Saturday,' Boccacci is saying, 'but we have gaps in the timeline, and I'd like them filled. They spent the morning at the rafting centre, where the manager reported some tension between Mike Foster and Natasha, and DC Morgan has heard a similar story from locals in the pub.' Boccacci looks at Ffion, who nods. Mia has agreed to give a statement about the exchange she saw between Natasha and Russell Steele. 'Do we know where they went between the rafting centre and the pub?'

'Back to the holiday let, then to Caffi Coffi,' Ffion says. 'They ordered food, and what Steele describes as "a fair amount" of alcohol.'

'Speak to staff at the café and see what the atmosphere was like among the group,' Boccacci says.

'No problem.'

'Take PC Taylor with you.'

'What?' Ffion sits up straight. 'I'll be fine on my—'

'Moving on,' Boccacci says firmly. 'I'd like someone to look into Natasha's background. We know she has no convictions or warning markers, but who were her friends? What did she do on her days off? Look at her emails and messages. Was she getting hassle from anyone? What viewings had she recently done at work? Which valuations did she do? Did she flag any concerns to her boss about sleazy clients?'

'I'll take that one, ma'am,' a civilian investigator says.

From across the room, Sam gives Ffion a double thumbs-up. Ffion ignores him. She feels irrationally annoyed with George for taking the FLO job and leaving her to babysit this overly groomed man-child.

Boccacci closes her notebook decisively. 'Well, get to it, then.'

The bell above the door of Caffi Coffi jangles as Ffion pushes it open. The owner, Julie Potter, comes out from the kitchen, wiping her hands on a tea towel.

'Alright, Ffion? Your mam was in here earlier – she said you're investigating a body in a boat? Sounds exciting.'

Ffion despairs of her mam, who claims to disapprove of gossip yet will be first in line to pass on a juicy titbit. 'It wasn't exciting for the woman who died,' she says drily.

The retort goes over Julie's head. '*Paned?*' she offers.

'God, yes, I'm gasping. Coffee, please.'

'Instant alright? The machine's on the blink.'

'Tea, then. *Diolch.*'

Julie turns to Sam. 'How about you, handsome?'

'Oh, puh-lease . . .' Ffion yanks a chair out from under a table and sits down.

'Tea sounds wonderful,' Sam says. 'You're too kind.'

Ffion flips open her notebook. 'The woman who died was in here on Saturday afternoon.'

'You what?' Julie's eyes widen. 'Not the estate agents?'

'The very same. What can you tell me about them?'

'That they're obnoxious arseholes who racked up a huge bill then ran off without paying.' Julie pours boiling water into a metal teapot with such ferocity it splashes over her hand. She presses the scalded skin against her apron. 'And I'd never wish ill on anyone, but if one of them's ended up dead, maybe that's karma at work.'

Ffion, whose own misspent youth included far worse than a café bilking, considers this a little harsh.

'The things they said about this place . . .' Julie puts the teapot on the table and goes back for two cups. 'Slagging it off as though I couldn't hear them. *Stuck in a time warp*, apparently – the cheek! I had the whole place redecorated last winter.'

'It looks lovely,' Sam says.

Ffion shoots him an incredulous look. Caffi Coffi does an excellent bacon sandwich, but the peach-coloured walls and mint-green chairs are giving eighties vibes – and not in a good way. 'What time did they come in?'

'Around five. Well on their way, if you know what I mean.' Julie waggles an imaginary glass near her mouth. 'They had two bags-for-life full of beers, and the two women were drinking those gins in cans. When I told them they couldn't bring their own booze in here, they asked what wines I had, and when I said, "red or white", they ordered both.'

'Did they eat?' Sam asks. Ffion realises he doesn't have a notebook out, and she closes hers pointedly. She's no one's secretary.

'Did they?' Julie barks a laugh. 'Burgers and large chips all round, and onion rings on the side, followed by apple pie and ice cream. Then they ask for another two bottles of wine. By this time, they're really pissed. The two women went to the loo, and I heard them having a right ding-dong. The kitchen's right next to it, you see.'

'What were they arguing about?' Ffion says.

'No idea – my extractor fan makes a hell of a racket – but the older woman, the boss, told the young girl to keep her mouth shut. That's what she said: *If you want to keep your job, you'd better keep your mouth shut.* They went back to the table after that. That's when my chair got broken.'

'What happened?' Ffion says.

'The older woman stood on it to make a speech. Something about sales figures and bonuses – I wasn't really listening, I was more concerned about my chair, the way she was wobbling about. Anyway, next thing I know, she's on the floor and my chair's in pieces.'

'What happened then?' Sam says.

'I took the broken chair out back. I was in the yard when I heard the bell above the door go, and by the time I got back here they'd scarpered.'

'What time was that?' Ffion asks.

'Just after six, I reckon. A hundred and twenty-four quid, they owe me. And a new chair.' Julie looks at Ffion and Sam in turn. 'You can record that as a crime, right?'

'Our focus is on the murder inquiry,' Sam says. 'We can request a uniformed officer to come and take a full report from you in relation to the theft.'

'Oh, come on, Sam,' Ffion says. 'I'm sure we can do better than that.' She turns to Julie. 'As luck would have it, PC Taylor usually works in uniform, *and* he's just come over from Cheshire Constabulary, so he'll have all the contacts to deal with those estate agents. He'd be delighted to take a report from you right now.' Ffion pushes back her chair. 'I'll leave you to it, Sam.'

'But—'

Ffion gives him a double thumbs-up as she leaves the café.

So all three of Natasha's colleagues had taken issue with Natasha in the hours leading to her death. Ffion isn't ready to let Luke Parks off the hook, but the evidence against Carole Simmonds, Mike Foster and Russell Steele is mounting. Ffion walks to her car, calculating what time she can get to Simmonds. If one of those estate agents has size eleven feet, they're coming in.

SIXTEEN

TUESDAY | LEO

Duncan Cragg had refused a lift home. He's getting one anyway, because Leo doesn't want him phoning his wife before Leo's had a chance to hear her account of where Duncan was last night. Not that the man seems anxious to contact anyone. He leaves his phone in his pocket and stares out of the front passenger window.

A few streets away from The Hill, Leo sees Allie. She's standing by the front door of a large townhouse, talking to a man in a shiny suit. Above their heads is a 'for sale' sign. Leo shakes his head. Allie's deluded if she thinks she can afford a house that size. He almost feels sorry for Dominic.

'It's just here, on the right,' Duncan says, as Leo pulls into a narrow street with cars parked either side.

'Will someone be home?' Leo reverses into a space a few metres down from the Cragg's house. 'You've had quite a shock.'

'Annie'll be there. She looks after her granddaughter on Mondays.'

Leo glances at the gold band on Duncan's ring finger. 'Second marriage?'

'Third.' He gets out of the car, and they walk towards the house, a neat terrace with a small front garden and a bench by the door. 'Doing it right this time.'

'Do you have any kids of your own?' Leo says.

126

Duncan looks at him sharply. 'Nosy, aren't you?' He puts a hand on the door handle and waits pointedly. 'Thanks for the lift.'

'Mind if I come in for a few minutes?'

'I do, actually.'

Leo holds Duncan's gaze. 'Important we rule out potential suspects early on. Saves dragging them down to the station when—'

'Alright!' Duncan glares at Leo but he opens the door and calls out. 'Annie? The police are here. I'm not in any bother, but something's happened at work.'

Annie Cragg's forehead creases into well-worn furrows when she comes out of the kitchen. A toddler sits on her hip, bottom lip wobbling in preface to a wail. Annie listens in silence as Leo explains about the burglary at Hollies.

'Thank God you found him.' She's looking at Duncan, and Leo realises she's searching her husband's expression, looking for something. 'Are you okay?'

'I'm fine. Alec's the one in ICU.'

'Mrs Cragg,' Leo says, 'I understand Duncan was at home last night.' He watches her face carefully, but she doesn't miss a beat.

'We both were.'

'He didn't . . .' Leo shrugs '. . . pop out for anything, for example?'

'He thinks I did it.' Duncan's voice is half-hard, half-mocking.

'Because of what happened before?' Annie shifts the toddler higher on to her waist. She lifts her chin. 'You lot really don't believe a leopard can change his spots, do you?'

'This is a very serious investigation, Mrs Cragg. I wouldn't be doing my job properly if I didn't—'

'The first time I met Duncan, he told me he'd been inside, and he told me what for. But it's all in the past. Years ago, back when he was drinking.'

Leo turns to her husband. 'You don't drink now?'

'I can't,' Duncan says. 'I stay away from alcohol and I stay away from trouble. Simple as that.'

'Do you need me to give a statement?' Annie says. 'Because I'll give one, willingly. We were home all night. We watched that new crime drama at nine o'clock, then I rang my sister and Duncan was on the Xbox playing *Call of Duty* with a couple of mates. They'll tell you. We went to bed about eleven, I suppose. Duncan was out like a light, like always. I'm a terrible sleeper, so I'd know if he'd got out of bed.'

'That's really helpful. I'll take a quick statement now, if that's alright, and—' Leo turns to Duncan '—I'm afraid I'll need to take your outer clothes.'

'You what?' Duncan stares at Leo, who meets his gaze, unblinking. After several seconds, Duncan lets out a grunt and heads up the stairs.

'He's a good man,' Annie says, when he's gone. The statement is defensive, as though she expects Leo to argue with her.

'I'm sure he is.'

'He'll be finding this hard.'

'A police investigation?'

'That, yes, but . . .' Annie glances upstairs, checking the bedroom door is still closed. 'Duncan's got a son a couple of years older than Alec Jefferson. They're not in contact. Things were difficult at home when James was young, and Duncan was drinking and—' She holds up a hand. 'Look, I wasn't there. But I know Duncan misses his lad and it's been good for him to be around the Jeffersons. He's been helping Alec fix his car, talking to him about his uni course, that sort of thing. Finding him unconscious . . . well, it's a lot, that's all.'

'I'm sure it is.'

The bedroom door opens, and Duncan comes down the stairs, his shorts and long-sleeved top exchanged for joggers and a T-shirt. He pushes the clothes at Leo. 'Knock yourself out, but you're looking in the wrong place.'

'Where should I be looking?'

'How am I supposed to know? That's your job. All I'm saying is, I'd have to be pretty stupid to do over my own employer.'

Stupid? Leo thinks. Or cocky enough to front it out? He opens his notebook at a blank page and hands Duncan a pen. 'I'd like you to write something down for me.'

'What?'

'Write these numbers,' Leo says. 'Two, nine, zero, five.'

The pen quivers slightly in Duncan's hand, but he doesn't start writing. 'That's – that's the code for the Jefferson's alarm.'

'I know.'

Still the pen doesn't move.

'Just write it down, Duncan. Two, nine, zero, five.'

There's a long silence, then he moves the pen slowly over the paper.

2905

Leo takes back the notebook and pen. He's no handwriting expert, but it's not the sample he's interested in; it's the sweat that's broken out on Duncan's forehead, and the twitching hand that won't be stilled, not even when Duncan pushes it into a pocket.

'You wrote the alarm code on the top of the gate,' he says. It's a statement, not a question. A punt, perhaps, but Leo doesn't want to wait for forensics; he doesn't want to wait for someone else to get hurt.

'I didn't turn the house over.' Duncan's voice is quiet, but forceful.

'That's not what I asked.'

'Oh, Duncan . . .' Annie moves to stand next to her husband, her hand pressed against the small of his back, as though he's another toddler. 'What have you done?'

He turns to her. 'They said they'd hurt you.'

'Who did?' Leo says.

'I don't know. I got a note – through the post, here, to this house. It said I was to put the code for the alarm on the top of the gate, or Annie would cop for it.' He pulls away from his wife. 'What was I supposed to do?'

'Do you still have the letter?' Leo says.

Duncan shakes his head.

'Who knows you work for the Jeffersons, and also knows where you live?'

'I don't go about telling people, but it's not like it's hard to find out. People inside – they talk, right? I know stuff about people I wasn't even banged up with. Knowledge is power, so people trade facts. Who goes around with who, who's coughed to what job.' He looks at Leo. 'But all I did was write the number down. That's it.'

Leo is inclined to believe Duncan, who is now looking at Leo directly, unlike earlier, when the man wouldn't make eye contact. He still looks nervous, but he also looks relieved. Leo aims a pointed finger at Duncan's chest. 'We'll leave it there for now, but you're not out of the woods yet, Mr Cragg. If I find out that you know more than you're letting on—'

'I don't, I swear!'

'—you'll be back behind bars so fast you won't have time to say your goodbyes.'

130

SEVENTEEN

TUESDAY | ALLIE

There's a uniformed police officer at the front of Hollies, but just as Allie approaches, he's summoned to speak to a neighbour on the far side of the drive, so Allie walks around the back of the house and into the garden.

She's empty-handed this time.

Last night, Dominic had served himself an enthusiastic portion of the ill-fated lasagne intended for the Lennoxes. 'This is delicious.' He'd looked up. 'Aren't you having any?'

'I'm not hungry.' Allie had still been smarting from her foolishness. Of course Camilla was vegan. And gluten intolerance was everywhere nowadays, wasn't it? Allie should have made something less risky, like . . . She couldn't think of anything. She'd look online. Maybe buy a cookbook.

Today, Allie intends simply to offer moral support. The news about the break-in and the attack on Alec has sent shockwaves through the residents' WhatsApp group, and Allie will make sure Cara and Mikaela know they're not alone. She's made several attempts to get to know them since she moved to The Hill, but they're incredibly busy people. Cara has such a hectic schedule, and every time Allie's popped over, she's been about to take an important call.

A line of police tape blocks off the back door, but the French doors into the living room are open, and Allie calls out as she crosses the garden towards them. 'Hello? Mikaela? Cara?'

'If you're after the owners, they're at the hospital.' A woman in a white paper suit is brushing dark powder over an ornament lying on the sofa. She straightens. Above her mask, her eyes narrow. 'Are you from Major Crime?'

'No, I'm a neigh—' Allie corrects herself. 'A friend. From down the road. I popped by to see if I could help out.' The Jeffersons' sofa is seriously cool. It's a biscuity-coloured leather, low and modular, with three distinct yet connected sections. Allie wonders if she could take a quick picture, so she can reverse image search it.

'Hang on a sec.' The woman walks towards the hall and calls out. 'Leo!'

Damn. Allie takes a step back, but it's too late, Leo's in the living room. His expression turns from polite curiosity to abject annoyance when he realises who it is. 'What the hell are you doing here?'

'I'm friends with Cara and Mikaela.'

'Since when?'

'Don't interrogate me; I'm not one of your suspects.'

'Allie, this is a crime scene, not a social climbing frame.' Leo stares at her, then rubs a hand vigorously across his face. 'Have you any idea what I'm dealing with at the moment? Someone has broken into three houses within a hundred metres of each other. They've put a nineteen-year-old lad in hospital. He could have died – he might still die, for God's sake!'

'Don't shout at me!' Allie thinks she might cry. Why does Leo always have to be so *mean*?

'Out. This is a crime scene.' Leo's fingers dig into Allie's elbow as he marches her out of the garden.

She shakes him off. 'Oh, I see: it's not enough that you let Harris get hurt – you have to manhandle me too!'

'What are you talking about?'

'That dog needs putting down.'

'He's a bit exuberant, that's all.'

'Exuberant?' Allie gives a humourless laugh. 'He lunged at Harris!'

'He didn't lun—'

'Harris hardly slept a wink. He's absolutely terrified.'

'I'll speak to him.' Leo starts back towards the house.

'I've a good mind to report it.'

He turns. 'Allie, please don't do that. Dave's not dangerous, and Ffion adores him – she'd be devastated.'

Allie feels a stab of jealousy. It's not that she wants to be with Leo – that ship has well and truly sailed – but hearing him say another woman's name makes her feel . . . Well, she isn't sure how it makes her feel, but she doesn't like it.

She sniffs. 'It's the responsible thing to do. Imagine if it bit another child; I'd never forgive myself.'

Harris didn't exactly *say* he'd been bitten, but he definitely said the dog had jumped up, and that it had had enormous teeth. *Like a wolf*, he'd said. Or maybe Allie mentioned the wolf – she can't really remember. Either way, Harris had been terrified.

'What are you talking about? Dave didn't bite Harris.'

'By all accounts you were more concerned with your *girlfriend*, so excuse me for believing Harris over you.'

'This is all about Ffion, isn't it?' Leo says.

'I don't care about—' Allie can't bring herself to say the woman's name. 'My only concern is Harris.'

'Right. So concerned, you're moving house again, when he's only just got settled.'

Allie frowns. 'What are you talking about?'

'I saw you looking around a townhouse this morning,' Leo says.

'What?' Allie feels panic rising in her chest. 'That wasn't me.'

Leo looks quizzical. 'What wasn't you?'

'I mean . . . you can't have seen me because I haven't been looking at a townhouse. Or any house. We're very happy where we are.' Allie walks away before Leo can press her further.

At home, she makes herself a coffee from Dominic's posh machine, and settles down with her tablet to look for the Jeffersons' sofa. She finds it at Gamma & Dandy for just over seven thousand pounds. The thought of having seven grand to spend on a sofa! Allie can just imagine Dominic's face should she suggest it. Fortunately Allie loves a challenge, and two hours later she's found the perfect dupe at Wayfair for under two thousand. Granted, they don't actually have two thousand at the moment, and their existing sofa is only a year old, but it's something to work towards. Allie saves it to her vision board.

She's just contemplating a nap – Leo has no idea how exhausting full-time parenting is – when her phone pings with a text. When Allie sees the name on the screen, she pulls the phone close to her, even though there's no one there to see it but her.

Are you free tomorrow morning? the text reads. I've got another job for you.

EIGHTEEN

TUESDAY | FFION

'You look like shit,' George says. 'Are you okay?'

They're standing in Starbucks, waiting for their drinks. George's cropped hair is slicked back behind one ear, a tortoiseshell clip keeping it in place. Ffion puts a hand to her own nest of curls before deciding it's a lost cause.

'I think I'm coming down with something,' Ffion says. Behind her, a barista shouts a name for the second time; a woman orders a Frappuccino with extra ice. It's even hotter today than yesterday, the headlines a curious mix of environmental doom-mongering and *Cor, what a scorcher!*

'It's called stress.'

'It's called over-exposure to estate agents.' Ffion stretches her neck to one side and then the other, feeling a *click* as something releases. 'Maybe I'll buy a van and live in that instead.'

'Can you imagine Dave confined to a van?'

'He'll love it.'

'He'll eat it,' George says. 'You need a bit of self-care.'

'Are you FLOing me, DC Kent?' Ffion nicks a handful of sugar sachets for the tea cupboard at work and puts them in her pocket.

George laughs. 'Only a bit. And it's for your own good.'

The exchange reminds Ffion of her bizarre conversation with DI Malik. 'Um, how are you feeling?'

George raises an eyebrow. 'Are you okay?'

'That's literally what I just asked you.'

'In all the time we've worked together, Ffion Morgan, you have never once asked me how I'm feeling.'

'Yeah, well. Family liaison work can be intense, and—'

'Did the DI put you up to this?' George eyes Ffion suspiciously.

There's no point trying to deny it. 'Yeah. But seriously, what's it like? I can't think of anything worse than being someone's shoulder to cry on.'

'I don't think there's much danger of that happening.'

'Hey, I can be very supportive, I'll have you know.'

'Ffi, you're about as supportive as a training bra.' George grins. 'Anyway, there hasn't been any crying on shoulders. It's all been the practical stuff so far. When Natasha's body will be released, what deathmin needs doing—'

'Deathmin?'

'Death admin. Notifying people, registering her death, that sort of thing. It's a lot to deal with when you're grieving.'

'Or when you're racked with guilt for brutally murdering your partner?'

'I thought you'd decided it was one of her colleagues?'

'I'm keeping an open mind.' Ffion grins. 'Fancy coming with me to Simmonds?'

George shakes her head. 'I'm a FLO, I'm supposed to stay out of the investigation.'

'There are three of them. If they're in it together and they get tasty, I don't fancy my chances.'

'I thought Boccacci had paired you with the hot transferee? Why can't you take him?'

136

'I binned him off.' Ffion leans on the table. 'Oh, go on, it'll be fun.'

'Fine. But if Boccacci finds out, I'm screwed.'

'Cheers. I don't trust estate agents. I'm convinced Carole Simmonds knows where Natasha's laptop is, although I don't know whether it's something specific to Natasha she's trying to hide, or simply their gazumping shittery.'

'Who ordered a flat white and a breakfast tea?' the barista calls out.

Ffion waves. 'I did.'

'I've been calling for five minutes. Do you not know your own name?' He points to the takeaway cups, on which is scrawled 'Ian'.

'Seriously?'

'Come on, Ian.' George steers Ffion away before she can hit her stride. 'Gazumping shittery?'

'I'll tell you on the way.'

As Ffion and George walk towards Simmonds, the door opens and a couple emerges, talking animatedly as they cross the road. They're both in tailored shorts and short-sleeved shirts, with tasselled boating shoes and expensive sunglasses. One of the men wears a straw hat tipped towards the back of his head. Ffion wonders if they're buying or selling.

She puts a hand on the door just as Mike Foster is closing it.

'So sorry.' He pulls it wide and gestures for Ffion and George to enter, his wide smile sobering when he recognises them. 'Is there any news?'

'Yes.' Ffion studies him. He still looks like shit, which could either be guilt or the lingering consequences of Saturday night. The further Ffion gets into her thirties, the longer her own hangovers last.

'That's good,' Mike says.

'Natasha was murdered.'

'Murdered?' Carole says it at the precise moment that Russell's mouth drops open, giving him the air of a ventriloquist's doll.

In his shiny suit and fat-knotted tie, Russell looks older than he did yesterday morning, hungover and sleep-deprived; but, unlike Mike, Russell's face still carries the rounded glow of youth. He blinks rapidly and Ffion realises he's choking back sobs.

Carole doesn't try to stop hers. She sinks on to a desk, tears trickling down her powdered cheeks. 'That sweet, beautiful girl . . . who would want to do something so evil?'

'Have you . . . have you caught the person who did it?' Russell manages.

'Was it someone from the village?' Mike looks at Carole. 'I said we should have gone to the Lake District.'

It occurs to Ffion that Mike and Russell are standing by their respective desks, which means the third desk – on which Carole is currently sitting – must be Natasha's. Ffion looks at the laptop cable trailing uselessly across the desk. 'Why would Natasha take her laptop home but leave the charger?' she says.

'They've got really good batteries,' Mike says. 'Mine lasts for days.'

Ffion crosses the office and sits at Natasha's chair. She opens the drawers one by one, but there's no laptop inside; nothing of interest at all, in fact, just neatly organised pens and stationery.

George joins her. She stoops to pull something from between the desk and the wall. It's a padded laptop case. Empty. 'And why would she take it home without the case?'

No one speaks for a moment.

'Maybe it wouldn't fit in her bag,' Russell says.

Ffion has had enough of this. 'What size shoe do you take?'

she asks Russell. She has already clocked Carole's tiny feet and felt disappointed not to have the pleasure of arresting the boss.

'Um . . .' Russell looks panicked. 'Eight.' He thrusts his right leg forward, showing Ffion a narrow foot encased in a brown loafer.

'And you?' Ffion turns to Mike.

'Eleven. Why?'

'I need you to come with me.'

'What? Why?'

'I want to take a look at your shoe collection.'

There are no walking boots at Mike's house, nor trainers or shoes with the distinctive zigzag pattern Ffion saw in the footprints left around the hot tub. The trio continue to Chester police station, and wait to be allocated an interview room.

George nudges Ffion, then nods towards the glass wall adjacent to the front desk, behind which staff cross from one side of the station to another. Standing with his back to the glass, chatting to a uniformed officer, is Leo.

Ffion sends him a message.

Do we know who Stephanie Carmichael went to Paris with yet?

She watches him take out his phone, apologise to the woman he's talking to, then tap out a response. Sorry, busy x

You don't look very busy to me . . . Ffion adds the 'eyes' emoji and presses send. A second later, Leo spins around, and then his face lights up in a way that fills Ffion with a warmth she's never before experienced in a relationship. Leo gestures to the side door, and she walks towards it.

'What are you doing here?' he says.

'Voluntary interview.' Ffion indicates Mike. 'Although "voluntary" is doing a lot of heavy lifting in that sentence.'

139

'I've seen that guy somewhere.' Leo's brow crinkles as he looks at Mike Foster.

'Listen . . .' Ffion pauses. She owes him an apology, but she wishes she could be somewhere else to do it.

'Allie!' Leo says suddenly.

'Please tell me you didn't just call me by your ex-wife's name.'

'No! God, I promise you there is zero chance of my mixing you two up.' Leo looks at Mike. 'That man was with Allie, this morning. Showing her a house, although she swears blind it wasn't her. I couldn't give a rat's arse where she lives, but it wouldn't be fair on Harris to have to move again so soon.'

'About Harris,' Ffion says, because if she doesn't do it now, she might not do it at all. 'I'm sorry for my French exit yesterday.'

'I assumed you'd been called into work early.'

'Did you?'

'No, of course not. I assumed you were angry with me because of what happened with Harris, and in true Ffion style, decided avoidance was easier than having a grown-up conversation about it.'

'Ouch.'

'He's only seven,' Leo says softly. 'He didn't mean anything by it.'

'I know.'

'And I didn't engineer the timing, it just—'

'I know.'

'We'll talk properly tonight, okay?'

'Okay,' Ffion says. 'I need to disembowel an estate agent first, though.' Leo glances at Mike Foster, but Ffion shakes her head. 'Not him. At least, not only him. I've been gazumped on my house.'

'You're joking.' He takes in her expression. 'You're not joking. That's awful. What are you going to do?'

'Start house-hunting again, I suppose.'

'Maybe this is a sign.' Leo gives a small smile. 'I could make room in the wardrobe.'

'It'll just get messy when . . .' Ffion trails off.

Leo raises an eyebrow. 'When we split up?'

'I wasn't going to say that,' says Ffion, who had absolutely been about to say that.

'I love you, Ffi. I'm not going anywhere.'

'Me neither.'

'Well, then.' Leo touches her briefly on the arm, letting her off the hook. 'Now: go and disembowel an estate agent.'

Mike makes a half-hearted attempt to convince Ffion and George that he couldn't have cared less about Natasha beating him to the six-monthly bonus.

'I don't really think about my sales figures, to be honest,' he says.

Ffion gives an incredulous laugh. 'But your boss said she played you all off against each other. Isn't that right?'

Mike flushes. 'Yeah. Maybe.'

'So, there you were, thinking you were about to get your usual juicy bonus,' George says, 'only for Natasha to get it. That must have been annoying.'

'A bit.'

'Annoying enough to give her a scare at the rafting centre by holding her under the water.'

Ffion watches Mike's face as he realises he might actually be in the frame for Natasha's murder.

'I wouldn't have actually hurt her.'

141

'But you did hold her under?' George asks.

A beat. 'Yes.'

'And just a few hours later, someone held her underwater in the hot tub.' Ffion leaves the statement hanging.

'It wasn't me.'

'Who else did Natasha piss off?' Ffion says.

'I don't know.'

'I mean . . .' Ffion holds out both hands. 'You're the one who missed out on a bonus, so if no one else had beef with Natasha, that kind of looks like you're the only one with a motive for killing her, right?'

'She had an argument with Russell.' It comes out quickly, as though Mike hadn't entirely expected to say it.

'When?' George says.

'At the pub. Russell was drunk and flirting with Natasha. He was pissed off because he'd expected to get it on with her, and she wasn't up for it. She turned him down flat.'

'Did Russell know Natasha was in a relationship?' George asks.

'Yeah.'

'Then why would he *expect* her to sleep with him?'

Mike looks at her as though the answer was obvious. 'Because it had happened before.'

Facebook.com/groups/ WithoutConvictionSleuths

🔒 *Private group*

Helen Lancaster

If you haven't listened to episode 3 yet, look away now! Spoilers to follow . . .

So . . . what are your theories about the cash withdrawals Stephanie was making before she died? Almost twenty in total, over a period of eighteen months.

5h

All comments ▼

Debbie Mackie

Some people still use cash. I hate that the pandemic made us a cashless society. I run a small business and the card costs are crippling.

5h

Ffion Morgan

She was taking out between £500 and £1,000 each time though

5h

Linda Sperrin

I think she was planning to leave Peter. She was building an escape fund. Do we know if he was violent?

3h

Humasah Çakıroğlu

Maybe she was being blackmailed?

2h

NINETEEN

WEDNESDAY | LEO

'Did the Carmichaels have a history of domestic abuse?' Ffion is looking at Facebook and simultaneously slotting two slices of bread into the toaster.

'I have no idea.'

'Stephanie might have been building an escape fund.' Ffion puts both hands flat on the worktop and jumps up, planting herself next to the toaster. Ffion rarely sits like a normal person, Leo has discovered. She perches on tables; turns chairs around and rests her chin on the back; sprawls on the lounge carpet with her back against the sofa.

'Ffion, this is bordering on obsession.' Leo adjusts the knot on his citrus-yellow tie, using the glass door of the microwave as a mirror.

'I wonder if the cold case team has checked to see if she'd made inquiries with divorce lawyers.' She looks at Leo. 'Could you—'

'Don't even think about it,' Leo says. 'I felt a right idiot calling John up to see what the passport office said – he must think I'm one of those crazed "true crime" groupies.'

'But at least now we know when she was in Paris.' Too impatient to wait for the toast to finish toasting, Ffion fishes it out with a knife. 'And even if she and her lover booked their flights separately, it still narrows it down to one of the men on the same plane.'

'One of these days you're going to electrocute yourself.'

'Ooh . . .' Ffion stops, an open jar of peanut butter in one hand. 'Unless her lover was a woman.'

'I have to go. I want to see if someone wrote the alarm code for Sunnyside on the gate, the way they did at Hollies.'

'Can you ask John if Stephanie was bisexual?'

'No,' Leo says firmly. He puts his hands on Ffion's shoulders. 'I have a nineteen-year-old lad in a critical condition in ICU. I have three burglaries with no witnesses, no forensics, and absolutely no idea of which house might be next. So unless Stephanie's extra-marital activities can produce a viable line of inquiry for me, I am one hundred per cent not interested.'

'But—'

'And nor should you be. Focus on your own investigation.'

Leo's voice is stern, and he thinks for a second that Ffion's pissed off, that he's about to get a lecture about not telling her what to do. But then she wraps her legs around him and pulls him closer. 'You're *very* sexy when you're trying to be assertive, you know.'

'Thanks.' Leo kisses her, then breaks away. 'Hang on: what do you mean, "trying"? I *am* assertive.'

Ffion laughs and wriggles free, hopping off the counter. 'Wish me luck – I have to work with that wanker from uniform today.'

'He'd better not try to be assertive. Not now I know the effect it has on you.'

Ffion smiles and kisses him. 'It doesn't work when it's someone else,' she says softly.

Leo watches her leave, thinking that there is no one quite like

Ffion Morgan, and no feeling quite like being in love with her. He straightens his jacket collar in readiness for leaving the house himself, only for his fingers to come away sticky. There is a large smear of peanut butter all down his left lapel.

The garden gate at Sunnyside has no convenient wall nearby, so Leo holds up his phone to film the top of the gate. He reviews the footage, shading the screen with his hand as four numbers come into view, then takes a screenshot.

6490

He shows the numbers to Camilla Lennox. 'Is this your alarm code?'

Her eyes widen. 'Yes.'

'Change it right away.' Leo looks around. 'Is your cleaner working today? I'd like a word.'

Camilla installs Leo in the study and fetches Jade Upshall, who hovers nervously until Leo invites her to sit down. He politely but firmly ejects Camilla and closes the door, then he hands Jade his phone. On the screen is the photograph of the top of the fence.

'Who told you to write the alarm code on top of the gate?' Leo says.

'I don't know what you're talking about.' Jade puts the phone on the coffee table, setting it screen-side down, as though that will make the whole situation go away.

'We know about the letter, Jade.'

Jade remains mute.

'You received an anonymous note through the post, didn't you?' Leo tries to make her look at him, but her eyes are fixed on the floor. 'I imagine it gave you a scare. They threatened you, right?'

A single tear runs down Jade's cheek.

'Said they'd hurt your family?'

'The baby.' She whispers it. Another tear races the first, then traces her jaw and drops on to her leggings. 'The note said they'd come for my baby if I didn't put the code on the gate.'

'Why didn't you call the police?'

Now she looks at him, her lips curled in disdain. 'And what would you lot have done about it? You'd have taken one look at my record and binned the whole thing off.'

'No,' Leo says. 'We'd have—'

'Do you know what my probation officer said once? I said I was meeting up with a girl I'd been in HMP Styal with – a nice girl, not a skank – and he said, "People who lie down with rats get fleas." That's how he thought of us. Like rats. Infecting each other. Dragging each other down, instead of what we actually do, which is help each other.'

'Was writing the alarm code on the gate a way of *helping* someone? Someone else you met inside, perhaps?'

'You're as bad as that probation officer. I told you, the note was anonymous.'

'What did it say?'

'I'll show you.' Jade reaches into her back pocket.

'You've still got it?' Leo feels a spark of excitement.

'Yeah, well, it shit me up, didn't it? I wasn't going to report it, but I thought, what if they do something anyway? What if they hurt my baby? I'd need it as evidence.' In Jade's hand is a Galaxy phone with a cracked screen. She peels off the plastic case and takes out a folded piece of paper.

The note has been written on white A4 paper, the message itself a few brief lines at the top of the page.

148

Jade. You've made a nice life for yourself since you got out. If you want to keep it, and if you don't want to loose that pretty baby of yours, I need you to do something for me. Write Sunnyside's alarm code on top of the garden gate when you're next at work. There's a good girl.

Leo reads the note twice. There's no signature and nothing distinctive about the paper. 'Do you have the envelope?'

'I threw it away.'

'Did it come through the post?'

'I thought it had, at first – it was on the mat with some bills – but there wasn't a stamp. I think someone put it through the door.' Jade picks at a piece of loose skin around her fingernail. 'That made it worse. Knowing they knew where I lived, that they'd seen me with the baby . . .' She starts crying again.

'Jade, how well do you know Duncan Cragg?'

'Who?'

'He manages the pool at Hollies, where the Jeffersons live.'

'Never met him.'

'I find that hard to believe,' Leo says. 'You're both working in big houses on The Hill, both doing similar jobs . . . you've never got together over a coffee and bitched about the bosses?'

'No.'

'What about the other staff on The Hill? Do you meet up with anyone else?'

'This isn't Downton fucking Abbey,' Jade snaps. 'I just want a quiet life. I come to work, I do my job, I go home to my family. That's it. That's all I want.'

Isn't that what we all want? Leo thinks, suddenly feeling sorry for Jade. Aiding and abetting a burglary is a serious offence, but she clearly felt she had no choice. She hadn't known it then, but whoever burgled Fairhaven and Sunnyside would later break into Hollies and leave Alec Jefferson for dead. Who knows what they would have done to Jade or her baby, if she hadn't complied?

The burglar is looking for something specific. But what? And did he find it at Hollies? Because if it wasn't there, he'll strike again, Leo is quite sure. He mentally walks up The Hill, picturing each of the houses he now knows as well as the ones in his own street.

Which one will be next?

TWENTY

WEDNESDAY | FFION

PC Sam Taylor is wearing a cornflower-blue shirt under his jacket, with red braces that put Ffion in mind of braying stockbrokers. There had been nowhere to park on the high street, and as they walk from the car park to Simmonds, Sam makes a show of changing sides to position himself between Ffion and the road.

'DCI Boccacci says if I'm serious about getting on to CID I should get myself a mentor,' he says.

'Is that right?' Ffion walks faster. Sam has relatively short legs, she realises, and it's funny watching him try to keep up.

'I wondered if you . . .' Sam pauses. 'Fancied a bit.' The final three words come with a very deliberate change in tone.

Ffion stops walking. 'If I *fancied a bit*? A bit of what, exactly?'

'A bit of mentoring.' Sam's eyes are wide and innocent. 'Why, what did you think I meant?' Ffion is just wondering if she misread the innuendo when he raises an eyebrow. He takes a step forward, until he's uncomfortably close to her. 'If you think you could handle me, of course . . .'

Nope, definitely wasn't imagining it, then. She starts to move, but Sam puts a hand on her arm. 'What do you reckon?' He gives a lopsided smile. 'Would you like to tell me what to do?'

Ffion thinks of a different time, a different Ffion, a different

151

man. She remembers the way her body had felt as though it belonged to someone else; the way she'd laughed off her fear and pretended she wanted what he wanted. 'Yes,' she says. 'I would very much like to tell you what to do.'

'I knew it.' Sam smiles. 'I could see it the first time we met.'

'I would like you to back the fuck up.' Ffion extends a finger and pushes it hard into his chest. 'There will be no other warnings, understand? If I see even the tiniest hint of your disgusting, creepy behaviour – to me or to any other officer – I will haul your arse into a disciplinary so fast your feet won't touch the ground.'

Sam blinks at her. 'I wasn't—'

'Yes, you were.'

'It was just a bit of banter.'

'It's not acceptable. Not at work, not anywhere. Got it?'

A long pause, then Sam slowly nods.

'Go back to the nick.'

'But I'm supposed to interview Russell Steele with you. What'll I tell the DCI?'

'That,' Ffion says, walking off, 'is not my problem.' She takes out her phone, because she knows he'll be watching her, and she's suddenly hyper-aware of her limbs, her hands. She texts Leo.

How much wardrobe space would I get? Hypothetically.

He texts back right away.

As much as you want.

Ffion is about to put her phone away when he texts again.

I should warn you, there's considerable interest in this prime real estate.

She smiles. Leo is the antidote to all the shit men out there. Even if he has been a bit possessive over his phone lately. It doesn't mean he's up to no good.

152

What's the asking price? Ffion types, and she sees the dots that mean he's already replying.

I'm open to offers . . .

Five minutes later, Ffion is in Carole Simmonds's comfortable leather chair, with Russell perched on the wooden chair on the other side of the desk. Ffion resists the urge to ask Russell what qualities he can bring to the company, and where he sees himself in five years' time. Somehow, she doesn't think he'd find it funny. The office is air-conditioned, but nevertheless, thick dark circles have appeared around the armpits of Russell's pale blue shirt. He loosens his tie.

'We only slept together once.'

'When was that?' Ffion says.

'December. After the work Christmas do. We stayed at a hotel in Manchester and she . . . we . . .' He coughs.

'Why didn't it happen again?'

'We both agreed it was a mistake.'

'You *both* agreed?'

A muscle twitches near Russell's jaw. 'Yeah.'

'So if Natasha had wanted a rematch, you'd have said, *nah, you're alright, I'm good.*'

He chews at the inside of his top lip. 'We're just mates. We *were* just mates.'

'Sure. Did anything happen between you and Natasha at the weekend?'

'No. Swear down. Nothing happened.'

'You were drunk, though, weren't you?' Ffion says. 'I mean, you can hardly remember what you guys got up to, isn't that what you told me?'

'Well, yeah, but—'

'Then how can you be so sure nothing happened?'

Russell is silent.

'Tell me about Natasha,' Ffion says. 'What was she like?'

'She was clever. Like, a lot of girls don't have a lot up top, you know? But Nat was smart. And ambitious. She was going to set up her own agency, said it would be the start of a massive chain. She even found premises a few doors down from Simmonds.'

'She was going to set up in direct competition?'

'Natasha reckoned Carole was out of touch. She wanted to get Simmonds on TikTok – do really cool house tours, top tips on styling your home to sell, that sort of thing – but Carole wouldn't go for it. Nat just went ahead and did it on her own accounts.' Russell takes out his phone and opens Instagram, turning the screen to face her.

Ffion always finds it hard to see a murder victim's social media feed. To be so full of life, sharing nights out and meals made, and then . . . nothing. An unexpected full stop.

Natasha's Instagram account is called @NatashaSellsHouses. Her grid is glossy and oversaturated, and reminds Ffion of adverts by American realtors, who seem to be as much of a product as the properties they're selling. Interspersed with the shots of luxury living, Natasha gives glimpses into her own life, including nights out with the girls and nights in with Luke. Ffion scrutinises a picture of the couple together, trying to get the measure of their relationship. There's a photo of their house too, which has been cleverly cropped to make it appear detached, with no hint of the sprawling development in which it sits.

Natasha's last post is hashtagged #weekendvibes. It was taken in the garden at Luke Parks's house, the background blurred to disguise the overlooking houses. In the foreground, in sharp focus, several objects are artfully arranged on a turquoise metal table.

A glass of something colourful and cold, beads of condensation running down the outside. A plate of melon slices. Headphones, with the wires shaped into a heart.

If you need me, I'll be here! reads the caption. Anyone else binge-listening #WithoutConvictionPodcast? Late to the party but catching up fast! No spoilers please!

Ffion makes a mental note of Natasha's handle, so she can look at the comments later, even though most of the theories she's come across online about the Carmichael murders have been batshit crazy. So many people fancy themselves as armchair detectives, just because they once got out of an escape room.

'When you were getting ready for the trip' – Ffion makes herself focus on the matter in hand – 'were you thinking something might happen between you and Natasha?'

'No. Absolutely not.' Russell's answer comes quickly.

Too quickly.

'A witness in the pub saw you behaving in a threatening manner towards Natasha.'

'No, that was—' Russell stops himself. 'Yeah.' He can't meet Ffion's eyes. 'She said she wasn't interested and I . . . I was upset about it.'

Ffion studies his face. What had he been about to say? *That was something different*? Something worse? 'Upset enough to continue the argument when the two of you were back at the holiday let?'

'I didn't see Natasha after I left the pub.' Russell rubs the back of his neck. 'Look, have you spoken to her boyfriend? You know he used to follow her when she went out?'

'Is that right?'

'He'd call the office and ask to be put through to Natasha because she wasn't answering her mobile – he checked up on her all the time. Wanted to know which houses she was doing view-ings at, who lived there, what they did for a living . . .' Russell shakes his head. 'Natasha said he went full-on psycho when he found out about me.'

'Luke *knew* you'd slept with Natasha?'

'Yeah. That's why Natasha said it could never happen again.' Russell holds Ffion's gaze. 'She said if she cheated on Luke again, he'd kill her.'

TWENTY-ONE

WEDNESDAY | ALLIE

It's almost pick-up time from the holiday club and Allie has finished what she privately refers to as her 'side hustle'. She hasn't told Dominic she's earning a bit of pin money; she suspects he wouldn't approve. He can be very old-fashioned in his views. But it really doesn't affect him, she reasons. The house is always tidy and dinner is always cooked (well, *heated*; Allie is not a born chef) and if it means she can have a guilt-free spree in Homesense, then where's the harm?

Allie's about to leave when her phone rings. 'Grandad Dixon' flashes on the screen and Allie scrambles to answer it. Scarlett must have asked for another play date with Harris! Allie's so overexcited, she almost drops the phone.

'Hi, Dennis! How are you?'

'Sorry for the late notice, but would you mind picking Scarlett up? I'm at the doctor's and they want to send me to the hospital for surgery.'

Allie gives an excited little jig. How brilliant! Only friends ask for favours, and even though it's Dennis asking, Allie will really be helping Bianca. Bianca Dixon, needing a favour from Allie Green! With the exception of Emmy, none of the other residents of The Hill has ever called Allie, even though she's gone to great lengths to make sure they have her number.

'Of course!' Allie's voice has gone a bit squeaky. She coughs to clear her throat, and says it again, more nonchalantly. 'Of course. Shall I bring her back to The Willows?' Allie feels the warm glow she always feels when she gives her address as *The Willows*. Dominic thought it was silly to name their new house, but it was all part of Allie's big plan, and look how it's paying off! Would Scarlett Dixon be coming over to 24 Taplin Drive? Allie thinks not.

'No, love, don't worry. Bianca's on a call, that's why she can't pick her up, but assuming you're walking, she'll be done by the time you drop Scarlett home.'

'Can you let the school know I'll be collecting Scarlett?'

'Will do, love. Ta very much for this.'

'My pleasure. What are friends for?' Allie ends the call and spins in a delighted circle, giddy with excitement. It occurs to her that Dennis might have to stay in hospital, and that Allie could be called upon to take Scarlett to the holiday club tomorrow too. Obviously Allie hopes Dennis is okay – she did say that to him, didn't she? – but maybe she'll let Bianca know she can be on standby just in case. Allie pictures the relief flooding Bianca's face as she realises Allie is a friend she can lean on.

'Day or night,' Allie says. Dennis had been right: Bianca had finished her call by the time Allie and the two children reached the top of The Hill, and had been effusive with her thanks.

'That's very kind of you,' Bianca says. 'But Dad'll be home in an hour or so.' They're sitting in Bianca's perfect kitchen, and Allie is trying to make her drink last. It's iced lemonade from some cool brand Allie will have to find for when she invites Bianca over to The Willows.

'But if he . . .' Allie drops her voice respectfully. 'If he takes a turn for the worse, you must call me. Harris adores Scarlett and—'

'A turn for the worse?' Bianca frowns. 'He's gone in to have an ingrown toenail cut out.'

Allie blinks.

'His GP spoke to minor injuries, and they said it was quiet and if he popped over now they'd sort it for him.'

'Oh.' Allie reddens.

'He's such a drama queen.' Bianca laughs. 'I expect he told you he was at death's door, did he?'

Allie seizes on the explanation. 'Men, eh?'

'Oh, tell me about it! Why do you think I'm divorced?' Bianca rolls her eyes.

'Best way to be, right?' Allie's heart soars. It's happening! She's best friends with Bianca Dixon: two women helping each other out with childcare and gossiping about men. Maybe they'll go shopping together, and Bianca will ask Allie's advice on—

'But you're married, aren't you?' Bianca says.

Allie swallows. 'Um. Yes. But I meant, when you first get divorced, it's the best way to be.'

'Right.' There's an uncomfortable pause. 'What was your first husband like?'

'God, where do I start? Leo was a nightmare.'

'Was he abusive? Mine would lay into me when his football team lost.'

'More emotionally abusive, I'd say.' Allie feels a bit guilty maligning Leo like this, but it's not as though Bianca's ever going to meet him. 'He's a police officer. Talk about "married to the job": I used to think he cared more about his victims than he did about me.'

'I bet you did all the cooking and cleaning, right? All the childcare?'

Allie pauses. Leo pushing the vacuum cleaner around on his day off wasn't exactly *cleaning*, was it? And did sticking pork chops under the grill count as *cooking*? 'Exactly.' She glances at Harris, but he doesn't seem to be listening.

'They're all the same.' Bianca shakes her head. 'I was talking to Emmy about this only the other day. Warren doesn't lift a finger around the house. And now she's organising the yard sale too, poor thing. She must be run ragged.'

'It's a huge job.' It's actually Allie who has sorted all the donations, but Emmy's probably been hard at work behind the scenes. 'Emmy was so relieved when I said I'd step in.'

'Oh, are you helping?' Bianca tilts her head. 'That's nice of you, given you don't live on The Hill.'

Allie gives the same tinkly laugh she's heard from Camilla Lennox. 'We're at the bottom, in The Willows.'

Bianca's expression is part-sceptical, part-pitying, and before Allie knows it, her mouth is open again.

'We're thinking of buying Ormindale, as it happens.'

'Really? Emmy didn't mention that.'

'It's a sensitive subject for her.' Allie swallows. 'With the divorce and everything . . . . Probably best not to bring it up.'

'Of course. She's so on edge at the moment.'

'It's a stressful time.'

'I suggested I host tomorrow's get-together here,' Bianca said, 'but Warren caught our conversation and said he wouldn't hear of it.'

Tomorrow's get-together. The committee party that Leo mentioned, that Allie still hasn't been invited to. But perhaps the invitation is implied? An open invitation for anyone helping with the yard sale . . .

'He said as a single mother I do enough running around, and I should enjoy being looked after for a change.' Bianca laughs. 'You know what he's like: that man could sell sand at the beach. Suki insisted on taking over the food, at least. In fact, I must call her – I can't remember what she had me down for.'

'And it's at seven, right?' Allie opens the calendar app on her phone, as though the party is already in there. 'Or . . .'

'Seven-thirty.'

'Ah, yes, there it is. Seven-thirty.' Allie slides off her bar stool. 'Well, I guess I'll see you tomorrow night.' She wishes she could stay and talk more to Bianca, but she needs to get home: she has a party to get ready for.

By eight p.m. that night, Allie has been through her entire wardrobe and picked out three potential outfits for tomorrow. Harris is in bed, and Allie is scrolling on her tablet while Dominic watches a documentary about cheesemaking. She usually finds Pinterest relaxing, but tonight the mosaic of aspirational images on her boards is failing to soothe her. She's worrying about what food to take to tomorrow's party, given the unfortunate lasagne incident. Should she go for vegan? Gluten-free? What if people have allergies? Imagine if Allie were to send someone into anaphylactic shock with a plate of Marks & Spencer chicken satay – she would *die* of shame.

'What's a safe dish to take to a party?' she asks Dominic.

'Sausage rolls,' he says, without hesitation. 'Everyone likes sausage rolls. When's the party?'

Allie hesitates. She hasn't decided whether to take Dom with her tomorrow night. She loves him, but he can sometimes be a bit . . . boring.

Dominic turns back to his documentary. 'Did you know, there are more than seven hundred types of cheese in the UK alone?'

No. She won't take him.

Allie gets up. 'I'm going out.'

'Where?'

'I need to pick something up for the yard sale. I won't be long.'

'Tell them to sort their own jumble. They're taking advantage of you.'

'They're friends. Friends help each other.'

'Oh, Allie . . .' Dominic starts, but Allie doesn't hang around to listen. She leaves the house by the back door, so she can squeeze down the overgrown footpath and emerge directly on to The Hill, and the second she does, she feels calmer. This is where she belongs.

When Suki opens the door and sees Allie, she frowns. 'Are you a Jehovah's Witness?'

'Ha ha!' Rich people often have an odd sense of humour, Allie finds. 'I'm helping Emmy with the yard sale. I picked some bric-a-brac up from you a couple of weeks ago? Allie. I live at the bottom of The Hill.'

'Oh, yes, I remember now. I put a rather nice Ralph Lauren jacket in the bag by accident. Apparently Philip had left it out to be dry-cleaned, not thrown away.' Suki is wearing a long silk dress in burnt orange, and Allie wonders where it's from.

'I'll have a look for it next time I'm at Emmy's.'

Suki waves a hand dismissively. 'I've replaced it now.'

'You said you'd probably have some more bits and bobs for the sale.' Allie mentally crosses her fingers. Suki had said nothing of the kind, but Allie was right to assume she wouldn't remember.

'Almost certainly. It's for charity, isn't it? I'll have a look for you.'

'Great.' Allie waits.

'Oh. You mean now?'

'If it's not too much trouble?' Allie steps inside. 'What a lovely home you have. Actually, would you recommend the company who did your loft conversion?'

'Hmm?'

'I'm thinking of doing something similar. I'd like a studio,' Allie adds, remembering what Emmy told her about the work carried out at Fairhaven.

'You paint?' Suki's eyes light up.

'Well . . .' Allie flushes.

'You must come up and see it! It's the most wonderful space. What medium do you use?'

'Um . . . a bit of everything,' Allie says, deciding it would be a mistake to commit.

'You clever stick. I'm strictly oils, although I did dabble in watercolour for a time, but gosh, isn't it hard to get the depth?'

'So hard.' Allie can hardly believe she's walking up the stairs to Suki Makepeace's studio, chatting away as though they're old friends. And it's not really a lie, is it? I mean, Allie did GCSE art (she got a D, but still) and she could easily take it up again. She and Suki could go on a painting retreat together, to Tuscany or the South of France.

' . . . had to fight to get the dormer windows, but honestly, Velux ones would have ruined the light.'

'Absolutely.'

The studio is stunning. The art, on the other hand . . . Allie arranges her face into what she hopes is suitably awestruck. It's probably just that Allie's used to a different *sort* of art. Landscapes, or portraits, or bowls of fruit next to flagons of wine. Suki's art is more . . . experimental.

'This is a vagina,' Suki says, pointing towards a four-foot-tall canvas daubed in red paint. 'Except that of course it's actually a commentary on the destruction of femininity.'

'Of course. And you'd recommend the company you used for the conversion?' Allie feels on safer ground with interior design chat.

'They were great. I forget the name, but I'll dig it out for you. They even cleared out the junk the previous owner had left in here. Our solicitor asked her several times to take everything away, but she totally ignored us.'

'Did she stay on The Hill?'

'No, couldn't wait to leave, apparently. Her husband had done the dirty on her and she was so desperate to sell up, she accepted our first offer.'

'It's a lovely house,' Allie says, although she prefers the Coach House to Fairhaven.

'People are always putting notes through the door, asking if we'd consider selling.' Suki leads Allie back downstairs. 'You know the estate agents, Simmonds?'

'Very well,' Allie says. She flushes again.

'They had a call from someone wanting to buy our house last year. Hadn't even seen it! Just wanted the postcode, I suppose. He bought at some other house on the top of The Hill, in the end.'

'Your house is much nicer than Ormindale,' Allie says.

'You think? You're the sweetest!'

'It's good of Emmy and Warren to host the party there tomorrow night, given what they're going through right now.'

'Isn't it?'

'I just wanted to check if there were any allergies to be aware of,' Allie says.

'Gosh, do you know, I don't think I have you on my list . . .' Suki opens the Notes app on her phone.

'Emmy said she didn't want me worrying about cooking when I wasn't feeling a hundred per cent. She's such a sweetheart. But I absolutely must bring—'

'You're ill?' Suki takes a step back. 'I don't mean this to be rude, but I don't think anyone would want you at the party if you're sick.'

'I'm better now!' Allie says quickly.

'It's not Covid, is it? Because you can still be contagious for days after—'

'It's not Covid. It's . . .' Allie tries to think of an illness that sounds serious enough to be excused cooking, yet mild enough not to present a threat to The Hill. She has a brainwave. 'It's stress.'

Instantly, Suki's face floods with compassion. 'You poor thing. Have they given you metoprolol? Don't even bother. Tell them you want forty milligrams of citalopram and some sleeping pills. I've got some you can have in the meantime.' She holds Allie's gaze earnestly. 'Don't suffer in silence.'

Allie feels such a wave of happiness she has to fight not to let it show on her face. 'Thank you,' she says. The phone in Suki's hand pings, and at the exact same moment Allie's own phone vibrates. Both women look at their phones.

'It's Cara,' Suki says. 'She wants to know if anyone's passing the hospital tonight and could take them some toiletries.'

Allie's pulse picks up. She can do that! She's now managed to make friends with all the people who matter on The Hill except for Cara and Mikaela Jefferson, so this is perfect . . . But even as Allie is thinking it, another message pings on to the screen.

Be with you in twenty mins. Lots of love, Suki xxx

Allie looks up, dismayed, to see Suki putting her phone back in her pocket. 'Philip!' she shouts towards the kitchen. 'We need to go to the hospital. Such a terrible thing to happen,' she says to Allie, as she shows her out.

'It certainly is,' Allie says. And she means it. Because now, instead of coming to the Jeffersons' rescue, she's going to have to go home and hear more about cheese.

TWENTY-TWO

WEDNESDAY | LEO

Back at the station, Leo goes directly to the CSI office and submits Jade Upshall's anonymous note for forensic testing, then he walks up a flight of stairs to the carpeted floor occupied by the members of staff colloquially referred to as 'the grown-ups'.

Leo knocks on the door of the LPA commander. 'Ma'am, do you have a minute?'

'Literally two; I'm meeting with the Safety Advisory Group at half-past.' Superintendent Femi Reid gestures for Leo to take a seat. 'What's on your mind?' She rests her forearms on her desk and gives him her full attention.

'I'm dealing with the burglary series on The Hill, and I'm concerned there'll be another attack. I'd like a uniformed presence in the area overnight.'

'I can flag it as a tasking area,' Supt Reid says, 'but a dedicated unit just isn't possible. We're under-resourced as it is. Do you have a suspect?'

'No, ma'am. But we're making progress,' Leo adds quickly, seeing the superintendent's face. 'Staff at two of the targeted properties were coerced into giving over the alarm codes, and a member of my team is looking into the criminal associations of all the domestic staff on The Hill. We're running light on CID at

167

the moment, with DC Hardman on honeymoon and DC Swindley off sick. If I could borrow a couple of—'

'Did you miss the bit where I said we were under-resourced?' The superintendent stands up and picks up her notebook. 'I've just put another three officers on the cold case review team – you're up to speed on the Carmichael murders, I presume?'

'Yes, ma'am,' Leo says tightly. How could he fail to be, when everyone around him is more interested in a ten-year-old murder investigation than what's happening right before their eyes?

'Facebook is a hell pit,' Dawn says, as Leo walks into the CID office. He has tasked her with trawling social media for insights on the residents and domestic staff on The Hill.

'This is not new information.' Leo deleted his own Facebook account several years ago and has never regretted it. He looks over Dawn's shoulder at a post peppered with exclamation marks.

> Yard sale on The Hill today but everything outside my house is FREE to take, so please help yourself! Eighteen years' worth of crap from a dickhead who could never keep it in his trousers!! From now on I'm putting ME first. NO MORE SNAKES. If you know, you know! xxx

Beneath it are dozens of comments from concerned friends.

> You okay hun?

> @Sheryl Kingsbridge DM me!

> Is the treadmill still available and can you deliver?

The accompanying photograph shows a plethora of clothes, household objects and personal effects dumped in front of a house.

'Talk about a woman scorned.' Leo looks closer at the house. 'Is that Fairhaven?'

'Yes, she must have lived there before the Makepeaces.' Dawn scans the post. 'It was posted in 2016.'

'There must be something in the water on The Hill,' Leo says. 'Bianca Dixon's divorced, Warren and Emmy Irvine are separating, and Camilla Lennox is wife number three for JP.'

'Money can't buy you happiness.' Dawn clicks on to another tab, bringing up an Instagram page full of filtered selfies of Emmy Irvine. Leo scrolls through the captions.

When a woman realises her worth, she's unstoppable.

Tough times don't last. Tough women do.

'Emmy spends a lot of time on Instagram,' Dawn says. 'Mostly on lifestyle accounts; entering competitions, commenting on other people's posts. Warren is on X.' She brings up a third tab. 'He doesn't post, but he responds a lot, particularly to women.' She scrolls down a page of replies, all in a similar vein.

Stunning!

Have a great day, beautiful!

Thanks for brightening my timeline x

Dawn grimaces. 'Definitely the type to *slide into your DMs*.'

'Anything on the Jeffersons?'

'Mikaela doesn't do social media at all, as far as I can tell. Cara's mostly on LinkedIn – all very professional – and Insta, but her account there is private. Oh – I did find this . . .'

Dawn's screen fills with pictures of a pool float in the shape of a penis.

Leo remembers Cara's comment about the cup-holders. 'Alec Jefferson's behind that one.'

'He's funny,' Dawn says. 'Nice too: the posts are all to raise awareness of testicular cancer. There's a fundraising link in the bio.'

'What about the domestic staff? Any links between Duncan Cragg and Jade Upshall?'

'The crime analysts are looking at their associates but haven't thrown up anything so far. Cragg and Upshall don't follow each other on social media and I haven't found any mutuals, although it's possible there's a bigger degree of separation than that.' Dawn looks at a page of notes on her desk. 'Philip and Suki Makepeace have a driver called Ray Tinnion—'

'—who spent eight months in HMP Hatfield for theft back in the late nineties,' Leo says, remembering the details from the Makepeaces' burglary. 'He had a cast-iron alibi for the night Fairhaven was broken into, though. Have we run a PNC check on him recently? I'd like to know if anything's changed in the last six months.'

'I'll do it now. The Makepeaces say he's straight as they come, but who knows? Maybe he's lapsed . . .' She logs on to the Police National Computer, and Leo instinctively looks away as she enters her password.

'Oh . . .' Dawn says. 'Interesting.'

Leo turns back. 'What have you found?'

'An intel report from Manchester police a couple of months ago. A silver Audi was pulled over for kerb-crawling and the driver was given a warning. The car's registered to Fairhaven.' Dawn looks at Leo. 'And the driver was Ray Tinnion.'

TWENTY-THREE

WEDNESDAY | FFION

There's a welcome breeze coming from Llyn Drych, cutting through the stifling heat. Ffion and Leo are walking close to the water's edge so that Dave can cool off, and every few steps the dog stops to bark furiously at his own reflection. All around them, day trippers are reluctantly packing sunshades and folding chairs into cars, deflating paddleboards and calling to children to *come out of the water – I've told you three times now!*

'Do you think he killed Natasha?' Leo says. Ffion has been filling him in on her interview with Russell Steele.

'I don't know.' Ffion calls to Dave, who has his nose in the air, sniffing at something delicious (or possibly revolting – it's all the same to Dave). 'There's something off about Simmonds. The three of them are keeping something back, but Russell wouldn't crack, no matter how hard I pushed.' She identifies the object of Dave's attention at the same time he does: a couple laying out an evening picnic on a red and white checked blanket. 'Don't even think about it,' she tells him.

'Will you bring Natasha's partner in?' Leo says.

'On what grounds? We know he was angry about Natasha having been with Russell, but there's no evidence he came to Cwm Coed on Saturday night, and— oh, fuck!' Ffion breaks into a run as Dave bounds towards the picnicking couple, who are opening a bottle of champagne. '*Ty'd yma! Ty'd yma!* Come here!'

Dave pays no heed whatsoever to Ffion's increasingly frantic commands. There are looks of horror on the young couple's faces as they see an enormous, hairy hound lolloping towards them, his tongue hanging out of his mouth in anticipation of the delicious feast he is certain must be for him.

'*Gad o!*' Ffion shouts. 'Leave it!' She's almost within touching distance of him now, but Dave is hell-bent on a Scotch egg. As he puts on a burst of speed, Ffion dives for his collar, and the two of them slide on to the red and white checked rug, sending the picnic flying.

'Oh, my God.' Ffion scrambles to her feet, dragging Dave with her. 'I am so, so sorry.' The couple stare at her. They're Japanese, Ffion now sees; their wicker picnic basket bearing the name of a Michelin-starred hotel a half-hour drive away.

'It is no problem,' the man says.

'It really is. Look, can I pay for the picnic?' Ffion realises as she says it that she doesn't have her wallet. She looks around for Leo, who is doing his best to pretend he's not with her. 'Do you have any cash on you?'

'Please,' the man says. 'It is no problem. Just if you could . . .' He looks at Dave, who is breathing heavily over the man's feet.

Ffion pulls at Dave's collar, then clips on his lead. 'I really am sorry. And . . . um . . . *croeso i Gymru*. Welcome to Wales.'

'You've probably made their holiday,' Leo says, as he and Ffion walk away. 'They'll be talking about it for years. *Remember that time a hairy maniac landed in our picnic?*'

'He's not a maniac.' Ffion keeps a firm grip on Dave's lead.

'I wasn't talking about Dave.'

'Funny. When do you think you'll get a result from forensics on the anonymous letter?'

'Tomorrow,' Leo says.

'Tomorrow? I'm in the wrong force – our turnaround time's about six weeks at the moment.'

'I had to promise Jaffa Cakes.'

'That'll do it.'

They turn to take the footpath that runs along the length of the river Awen, and spot a familiar figure walking towards them. Elen Morgan has headphones on and is striding as though she's taking part in a speed-walking competition. 'Mam likes to get her steps in as quickly as possible,' Ffion explains. 'She'll be listening to an audiobook on double-speed too.'

'How efficient,' Leo says. He waves to Elen, who pulls off her headphones as they approach, but doesn't check her pace.

'*Sut wyt ti, Ffi?*' she calls. She looks at Leo. '*A ti, Leo?*'

'*Iawn,*' Ffion says. 'And he's fine too. Don't speak Welsh to him, Mam, you know he doesn't understand it.'

'Which is why he needs to hear it. Isn't that right, Leo?'

'Yes, Elen,' Leo says, obediently.

'*Ydy,*' Elen translates. She draws level with them but doesn't stop. 'Is everything going okay with the house?'

'You haven't heard?' Leo says. 'She's been gaz—'

'Gazebo-hunting.' Ffion gives Leo a look. 'For my new garden. Anyway, we won't keep you from your audiobook.'

'It's not an audiobook, it's that podcast you put me on to.' Elen raises her voice as she continues down the footpath. 'Did you get to episode four yet? Turns out they paid cash for the tickets to *Cat on a Hot Tin Roof*, and of course there's no CCTV, not after all this time, so that's a dead end.' She strides off, putting her headphones back on.

Leo shakes his head. 'Am I the only person in the world not listening to *Without Conviction*?'

'Yes.' Ffion loops her arm through his.

'How come you haven't told your mum about being gazumped?'

'She'll hear soon enough – this is Cwm Coed – but she'll only suggest I move back home, and I can't deal right now.'

Leo stops walking and gently pulls her to face him. 'Move in with me.'

'I'm thinking about it.'

'Think faster.' He smiles. 'It would be so good.'

They carry on walking. It *would* be good, Ffion thinks. Until it isn't, and then it will be horrendous, just like it was with Huw, just like it's been with every relationship she's ever had. Leo will tire of her, or find her 'too much' (as one particularly frustrated boyfriend concluded), and then it'll be sniping and point-scoring until Ffion moves out. Rinse and repeat.

As Ffion, Leo and Dave round the bend to where the river climbs towards the rafting centre, she sees a man on a quad bike in the neighbouring field. Beside him, a black and white collie runs freely.

'Two secs,' Ffion tells Leo. 'There's someone I need to speak to.' She walks towards the fence and waves an arm, and the quad bike heads towards them. There's a sharp whistle, and the collie turns, sprints towards the bike and jumps on to the back in one fluid movement. Ffion looks at Dave sternly. 'Are you watching this?'

The quad bike comes to a stop, and the farmer cuts the engine.

'*Sut dach chi,* Mr Williams?' Ffion says. He peers at her, and she helps him out. 'Ffion. *Merch* Elen Morgan.' Elen's daughter.

'*Ffion Wyllt, ydy?*' John Williams chuckles.

Ffion gives a polite smile, although the nickname 'Wild Ffion' makes her wince. It belongs to someone she outgrew a long time ago. 'I didn't realise your land extended this far.'

'Not far off sixty acres, all told.'

'That's a lot of work.'

The old man shrugs off the suggestion. John Williams had already been ancient when he'd been Ffion's maths teacher, almost twenty years ago. He had run his farm alongside teaching, once bringing an orphaned lamb to class because there had been no one home to keep it fed.

'Did you see much of the people who were staying up at Mervyn's place at the weekend?' Ffion asks him.

'People?' Mr Williams harrumphs. 'I'd call them animals, only it's an insult to the good ones.' He bends to stroke the collie.

'I hear they let your sheep out.'

'Traipsed through my field, leaving all the bloody gates open. Mixed up two flocks and let a load of them escape on to the road – I only found out because Dai *Parsel* was doing Amazon deliveries and he knocked to let me know. I'm still missing two ewes.' As he talks, he gets gradually louder, colour rising from his neck to his face. 'I marched up there to give them a piece of my mind.'

'What did they say?'

'They weren't there. Lights all blazing – Mervyn'll be paying for that, mind, come the end of the month. I banged on the door a few times – bear in mind I'd spent the best part of the afternoon rounding up my stock, so I wasn't in the most patient of moods – but no one came.'

'What time was this?'

'Eight-thirty, or thereabouts. I figured they must have walked into town – that Range Rover they turned up in was still parked outside, and there was another car there too.'

The Range Rover would have been Carole's. Ffion had clocked the details on Sunday morning when she and George had first gone to the holiday home. 'What make was the second car?'

'Some electric kind – I saw the green bit on the number plate.'

'I don't suppose you remember any of the index number, do you?'

'I can do better than that.' Mr Williams leans down and puts a hand in the deep pocket on the side of his trouser leg. 'I took a photo.' He retrieves the latest model of iPhone – the screen crazed with cracks – and makes several attempts to unlock it before passing it to Ffion with a *tsk* of frustration. 'Damn thing never recognises my face, and I need my glasses to do the code.'

'What is it?' Ffion says, poised to enter the number.

Mr Williams gives a sly grin. 'Pi.'

'Pie?'

'Did I teach you nothing, Ffion *Wyllt*? The value of Pi to three decimal places – rounded – is three point one four two.'

'I got a D in GCSE maths, Mr Williams. I never even got to grips with long division.' Ffion taps in 3 1 4 2 and the iPhone unlocks. She opens the photo app.

'If any of my ewes died, I was going to report the buggers for leaving the gate open, see? So I took photos of their cars, just in case.'

Mr Williams's photo album is mostly full of sheep. Ear tags, inflamed limbs, a revoltingly maggoty fleece, and the largest pair of testicles Ffion has ever seen.

'Scrotal oedema,' Mr Williams explains. 'Nasty case. It's right at the end.'

Ffion is – somewhat unwillingly – peering at the poor ram's swollen appendage, when she realises her former teacher is referring to the photograph of the electric car, which is the last picture in the camera roll. Relieved, she opens it and feels a rush of cortisol.

The electric car is a red Nissan Leaf.

And it belongs to Natasha's partner, Luke Parks.

To: Joseph Flint and Gemma Lyrick
<withoutconviction@gmail.com>
From: Louise Preston <louiseprestonhair@gmail.com>
Subject: Stephanie Carmichael

Hi,

I've just discovered your podcast and I don't know how relevant this is, but I met Stephanie Carmichael about a month before she was murdered. I heard it on the news at the time, but I didn't make the connection till I saw her photo on your Facebook page.

In 2014, I was in my first hair stylist job, working in a salon in Manchester. Stephanie was a walk-in, looking for a blow-dry before she went out for dinner. I remember her because she said a few things that troubled me. She was in a relationship with a younger man who liked fancy things but never seemed to pay for them. She said how she'd treated them both to a weekend in Paris, and how she'd bought him an expensive watch for his birthday. She said he was having problems with his bank account – something about it being frozen – so she'd lent him some cash. He was waiting for some investment to come good, apparently. It all sounded really sus, to be honest. I didn't get how she couldn't see the red flags, but she seemed totally loved-up. I remember thinking, if that was my mum, I'd be really worried about this bloke she's met.

Like I said, I don't know if it's relevant. My boyfriend said I should tell the police, but I don't know if they'll think it's silly

– it was literally just a half-hour conversation, with the hairdryer going the whole time. Anyway, I thought I'd email you just in case it's helpful.

Kind regards,

Louise

TWENTY-FOUR

THURSDAY | LEO

Leo arrives at the station twenty minutes late, thanks to getting stuck behind a caravan on the road out of Cwm Coed. Last night had been good, though. He and Ffion had cooked dinner together and agreed not to talk about work. They both needed a break from thinking about their respective investigations.

'That doesn't mean I want to hear about the Carmichael murders, though,' Leo had said.

'Okay. Although I think they're setting too much store on the sticky note with the Vauxhall showroom logo.'

'Did you even hear me?'

'Everyone's saying Stephanie's lover worked there, but I'm thinking it could just as easily have been someone who bought their car from them. What do you think?'

'I think this rice is done.'

'About the sticky note, though?'

'I think I have enough cases of my own without trying to solve someone else's.'

After morning briefing, he goes to the CSI offices with the packet of Jaffa Cakes he stopped off for earlier. He holds them up as Jo approaches.

180

'You did say you might be able to turn it around quickly. But if it's too soon . . .'

'As it happens, I came in early.' Jo takes the Jaffa Cakes. 'A pleasure doing business with you.' She takes him over to the bench that runs along one side of the room, on which is a long row of labelled boxes filled with sealed exhibits waiting for processing. Leo sees a lighter, a wine glass, and what looks like the severed hand of a shop mannequin. He tilts his head to read the label, curious to see what job it's from. Next to the table is the fuming cabinet, its racks already filled with the next batch of exhibits. When the cabinet is switched on, droplets of Superglue are heated into a gas and circulated through the space, sticking on the ridges of invisible sweat left behind. Leo got to try it out once when he was training and remembers the thrill of then sweeping the exhibit with fingerprint dust and seeing it cling to the previously hidden prints.

Leo's own exhibit, the anonymous note received by Jade Upshall, is in a tray marked 'for collection'. The sealed bags here are all paper-based – letters, sweet wrappers, a flyer for a cleaning company. These porous items won't have been processed in the cabinet but by hand, a CSI carefully brushing them with powder to reveal a print, before lifting it with tape and transferring it to a piece of acetate.

'Sorry to be the bearer of bad news,' Jo says. She lays the bag in front of them, the letter inside grubby with powder. 'Whoever wrote this wore gloves.'

Leo should have known it wouldn't have been that easy. It rarely is. Even so, he feels a barb of disappointment. Ffion left for work this morning with a clear plan for her investigation, while Leo feels as though he's going around in circles. He looks at the letter.

Write Sunnyside's alarm code on top of the garden gate when you're next at work. There's a good girl.

Who wrote it? Who is systematically breaking into houses on The Hill – and Leo feels certain there will be another – and who left young Alec Jefferson for dead?

. . . if you don't want to loose that pretty baby of yours, I need you to do something for me.

'Thanks for processing it so quickly.' Leo picks up the exhibit. 'I'll take this back to Property. Do you want me to book anything else in? Save you a job?'

'Great! This lot's all done – no prints on any of it.' Jo puts a hand on the full-to-bursting tray, and Leo regrets his impetuous offer, which means he will need to enter each exhibit reference into the property log, ensuring an unbroken chain of evidence, should it ever be needed in court. He lifts the first exhibit – a screwed-up cigarette packet – and sees a magazine behind it; a flattened takeaway cup behind that. The next bag contains a sticky note with edges curled from age.

Leo stops, the bag in his hand. 'What's this from?' The note is large – bigger than a standard yellow Post-it note – and bears an image of a car, outlined in blue. *Salisbury Motors*, reads the text. *Authorised Vauxhall dealers since 1979.*

'The cold case review team,' Jo says. 'They've sent up all sorts, I'm still working my way through it all. It's badly damaged by damp, unfortunately.'

Leo goes to put it down, but the blue sheet beneath it catches his eye.

My darling Stephanie, you looked so beautiful sleeping, I didn't want to wake you.

Leo reads the final line.

If only we had met years ago, but now that I have you, I don't ever want to loose you.

He looks at his own exhibit: the letter to Jade Upshall.

If you don't want to loose that pretty baby of yours . . .

Lots of people mix up *loose* and *lose*, Leo knows, but it isn't only that. It's the slope of the 'W' in *wake* and *work*; the sharp downward stroke of the 'y' in *you*.

The letters were written by the same person, Leo's sure of it. He can't make sense of it, but the facts are staring Leo in the face. The person behind the burglaries on The Hill killed Peter and Stephanie Carmichael.

TWENTY-FIVE

THURSDAY | FFION

George meets Ffion outside Luke Parks's house. 'For the record, I don't agree with what we're doing,' she says. 'And I don't believe DCI Boccacci will, either.'

But Ffion's already halfway up the path. 'We have photographic evidence of his car at the scene of Natasha's murder, despite his repeated claims that he was home all evening.' Ffion knocks at the door. 'He's coming in.'

'He didn't do it.'

'The evidence says otherwise.'

'At least let me speak to him first,' George says. 'He's emotionally unstable and he won't be expecting this.'

'Only because he thought he'd got away with—'

'For fuck's sake, Ffion!'

It's so rare for George to raise her voice that Ffion falls silent. George's jaw is rigid, her eyes glistening, and Ffion wonders if DI Malik was right to worry about her; maybe George isn't cut out to be a FLO. She's getting personally involved, getting emotional about someone who could be a murderer. Who *is* a murderer, Ffion thinks, but something about George's expression makes her pause.

As the front door opens, Ffion steps to one side and gives George the floor.

'Hi.' Luke Parks looks and sounds like a man who hasn't slept in days. His clothes are rumpled and there are patches of dry skin beneath his eyes.

'Can we come in?' George asks, and Luke shrugs and walks away from the door, leaving Ffion and George to follow him inside. He falls into his chair, which is so moulded to him, it seems almost a part of him. Ffion wonders if this is where he's spent his nights, racked with grief . . . or guilt.

'Luke, there's been a development in the case,' George says. Luke's mouth opens, but she speaks over him, knowing there's no time to waste. If Luke says anything incriminating, it needs to be under caution. 'In order to speak to you about it, my colleague needs to arrest and caution you. I know this will come as a shock, and you'll have the opportunity to speak to a lawyer once you're at the station.'

'What? This is—'

'I'm arresting you on suspicion of murder,' Ffion says. Luke's standing now and she takes hold of his arm, although he's rooted to the spot, his mouth agape. 'You do not have to say anything, but it may harm your defence if you do not mention when questioned something which you later rely on in court. Hands in front of you, please.' Ffion cuffs him in the front stack position, both forearms parallel to the ground, and, all the time, Luke looks at George as though she's betrayed him.

'Section 32 of the Police and Criminal Evidence Act 1984 gives me the power to search your property for anything which might be evidence relating to an offence,' Ffion says. 'Specifically, I'm looking for walking boots or shoes, and for Natasha's laptop, so perhaps you could save us all some time and tell me where I'll find those things.'

'I didn't kill Natasha.' Luke speaks quietly.

'Walking boots?'

'I don't have any.'

Sometimes Ffion forgets that not everyone lives surrounded by fields, that not everyone has dogs who need dragging out of swamps. She looks anyway – on the rack by the back door, and in the tangled heap of shoes in the bottom of the wardrobe – but finds only a few pairs of trainers with pristine soles. Natasha's side of the wardrobe is arranged by colour. Beneath the hangers, her shoes are in clear plastic boxes, and the care with which they are stored makes Ffion feel at once desperately sad for Natasha, and determined to bring her killer to justice.

Natasha's laptop is nowhere to be seen.

'She never brought it home,' Luke says, when Ffion returns to the living room. 'It was heavy – one of those old, clunky types – and Nat didn't like carting it home on the bus. She used my computer if there was something urgent, but she knew I—' He clams up.

'What?' Ffion demands.

He pauses, his cheeks slowly mottling red. 'I didn't like it when she worked at home. Like I said before, we didn't get much time together.'

'In the car.' Ffion grips his arm above his left elbow. She glances at George as they walk Luke out of the house, and raises an eyebrow. *Told you*, she wants to say. Luke killed Natasha. Ffion's never been surer of anything in her life.

TWENTY-SIX

THURSDAY | LEO

So much for the superintendent's claims of insufficient resources, Leo thinks. He looks around the packed briefing room, where Leo's team and the cold case review team have formed the nucleus of a new taskforce. There are officers here Leo has never seen before, pulled from other stations and seconded from lower-priority units. Leo's boss has lost the battle of jurisdiction, and at the front of the room stands Detective Superintendent Jake Sturrock, who is taking on the role of senior investigating officer.

'Settle down,' he says. 'We've got a lot to get through. You will all have received the background information about the Carmichael murders and the recent burglary series on The Hill, so I won't waste time going over it now. We have a handwriting expert looking at the two letters now, but we're in no doubt they were written by the same person.' Sturrock looks to the back of the room. 'DC Evans has been leading on the cold case. John, what can you add to the picture?'

'We believe Stephanie Carmichael was the victim of a romance fraud,' John says. 'It's likely the large amounts of cash she withdrew from the account she shared with her husband Peter were given to her lover, who will have concocted a variety of stories for why he needed it. Notes found hidden behind a kickboard in the kitchen reference an aunt's funeral, a problem with a frozen bank account and an overseas investment opportunity.'

'Are there forensics on the notes?' a female detective asks.

'Not on everything – a washing machine flood has degraded a lot of it – but we have two clear sets of prints on the theatre playbill for *Cat on a Hot Tin Roof*: Stephanie Carmichael's and an unknown set. There's no match on PNC, so all we can definitively say at this stage is that they're not Peter Carmichael's.'

'Did any of Stephanie's relatives or friends mention an affair?' Sturrock asks.

'No. But that's not unusual in romance scams. The perpetrator seeks to isolate their victim from friends and family who might see the red flags and try to intervene. We've taken a statement from a hairdresser who came forward as a result of *Without Conviction*.'

A DS with a bald head and small, round glasses lets out a sharp exhalation. 'That bloody podcast. They'll have to pull the whole season if we charge someone, or they'll find themselves in contempt of court.'

'Don't be too quick to condemn them,' John says. 'If we do get to court, it's highly likely it'll be down to what they uncovered. The hairdresser said Stephanie was coy about her lover's identity, but did say he was younger than her. Stephanie was sixty-eight when she died.'

'DS Brady.' Sturrock turns to Leo. 'How does this link to your burglary series?'

'Domestic staff at two of the targeted properties received notes – which we now know to be written by Stephanie Carmichael's lover – intimidating them into facilitating the break-ins.' Leo pauses. 'We thought from the outset that the burglar had been looking for something particular, and now I'm wondering if that "something" came from the Carmichaels.'

'A piece of Stephanie's jewellery went missing around the time of the murders,' Sturrock says, 'right?'

'Right,' John says. 'An Edwardian locket. Karl Munson didn't have it when he was arrested, and there was a question mark over whether Stephanie might have sold it before the attack; a few of her pieces turned up on the second-hand market.'

'But not the locket,' Leo says.

'No.' John taps a few keys on his laptop then turns it around to face the room, showing them a photograph of the six-sided gold locket. 'Stephanie wore it regularly, according to her sister. It's eighteen-carat gold and it contained a photograph of Peter and Stephanie on their wedding day.'

'You think this is what our burglar has been looking for?' Sturrock asks Leo.

'That wouldn't make sense,' John interjects. 'Stephanie's sister said the locket had enormous sentimental value for Stephanie but it was worth a few hundred if that. It seems disproportionate to break into multiple houses for it. We did think the killer might have been worried about DNA, but we've had a confirmed sighting of the locket on Monday by a dealer at We Buy Gold in Warrington – several hours *before* the break-in at Hollies that night. A white woman in her forties attempted to sell it, but left abruptly. The dealer thinks she was spooked by the dummy CCTV cameras above the counter.'

'*Is* there CCTV?' Sturrock asks.

'Not in the shop or covering the front, but we've looked at the footage from the street cameras and we have the registration number of the car that picked her up: a silver Audi registered to Philip Makepeace, Fairhaven, The Hill.'

'How old is Makepeace?' Sturrock directs the question at Leo, but it's Dawn who answers, the details of all The Hill's residents at her fingertips.

'Fifty-seven,' she says.

'It's not Philip Makepeace who drives the Audi, though,' Leo says, remembering the intelligence report from Manchester police. 'It's their live-in driver, Ray Tinnion. And, as it happens, I'm due to pay Tinnion a visit today.'

Suki Makepeace opens the door of Fairhaven with a sultry smile. 'I saw you coming up the drive. So very lovely to see you.' She's wearing a strapless dress, and she pulls at the elastic holding it up. 'It's so hot, isn't it? Shall we sit by the pool?'

'It's actually your driver we need to speak to,' Leo says.

'Lucky him.' Suki glances at Dawn. 'Actually, I was hoping you could give me some advice on security marking. Perhaps your colleague could speak with Ray, and you and I could—'

'I'll ask the crime prevention team to get in touch,' Leo says firmly.

Suki sighs. 'Ray's not in any trouble, is he? We'd never manage without him.'

'Just routine inquiries. Do you happen to know where he was on Monday?'

'I wouldn't have a clue – Philip deals with everything to do with Ray and the cars.'

'And where were *you* on Monday afternoon at three p.m., Mrs Makepeace?' Leo has a frustratingly basic description of the woman who tried to sell Stephanie Carmichael's locket. *White, in her forties, wearing a long dress and a sunhat* could be any number of women in Cheshire.

'Me?' Suki thinks. 'Oh! I had an online yoga session. I probably

190

took a selfie . . .' She opens the photo app on her phone and scrolls through dozens of selfies – it was only a few days ago, Leo thinks, how many has she taken since then? – before showing him a picture of her cleavage encased in Lycra. 'My yogi will vouch for me too, if you need a statement.'

'I don't think that will be necessary. Thank you.'

'Will you need to . . .' Suki drops her voice '. . . take down my particulars?'

'Absolutely not,' Leo says firmly. 'But I would like to speak to your husband.'

'He's at work. I'll ask him to phone you when he gets home.'

'Mr Makepeace works for Livingstone Asset Management, right?' Dawn says, checking her notes.

'Yes, but don't call him at work – they've introduced some boring policy about domestic calls. He even turns his mobile off; it's such a pain when there's an emergency. A couple of weeks ago I couldn't find any part-baked baguettes in Waitrose, and—'

'Could I possibly have a look at your garden gate, please?' Leo says quickly. He walks towards it.

Suki jogs to catch up. 'I often thought I'd make an excellent police officer, although the hats are terribly unflattering, aren't they?'

Leo carries a chair over from the patio to stand on. Suki insists on holding the chair – 'I'd never forgive myself if you fell' – which puts her head inappropriately close to Leo's groin. Dawn makes a noise that is definitely more snort than cough. There's nothing on the top of the gate, and Leo jumps down from the chair as quickly as he can.

'Was this gate here when the burglary occurred?' Dawn asks.

Suki nods. 'It's years old.' She points to the garage block to the side of the drive, above which two tiny windows have been pushed wide open. 'Ray has the studio above the garage.'

'Thanks,' Leo says. 'We'll be fine from here.'

'I'll be in the garden,' Suki purrs. 'If there's anything you want from me.'

'Studio' is a generous term for the dark, poky room above the double garage, in which Ray Tinnion has a single bed, a sagging sofa, and a kitchenette with a plug-in hob.

'They're not bad,' he says, when Leo asks how he gets on with his bosses. 'Suki's a sweetheart – always gives me a bit extra if she keeps me up past midnight.' He sits on the bed and gestures for Leo and Dawn to take the sofa. It's low, and Leo can see storage boxes under the bed; a pair of shoes kicked out of sight. Next to the shoes, uncoiled in the dust, is a thin leopard-print belt with a neon pink trim. Leo wonders exactly what form Suki's 'extra' takes.

'And Philip?'

'No comment.' Ray gives a lopsided grin. 'I know what side my bread's buttered.'

'Why do they need a driver?' Dawn asks.

'I've never asked. They both like a drink, so maybe it's that. Philip used to work in the back of the car, but nowadays he's mostly on his phone, or sleeping. To be honest, it's all about status for this lot. If the Joneses get a housekeeper, the Smiths want a butler.' He shakes his head. 'I'm just grateful to have a job and a roof over my head.'

'You're aware of the recent burglaries, I imagine?'

'Yes. How's the Jefferson lad?'

'In a bad way.' Leo examines Tinnion's face but finds nothing except seemingly genuine compassion. 'Have you seen anything suspicious? Anyone hanging around the neighbourhood?'

'Nothing that stands out. I wasn't here at the weekend. The

Makepeaces aren't good at respecting my time off, so I take myself away. I went to my sister's in Brighton on Saturday morning, and came back on Monday. I can show you the train tickets if you need an alibi.' He laughs, then he sees Leo's face and sobers. 'Christ, you really do, don't you?'

'Just covering all bases. Could you give me contact details for your sister?'

'Sure.' There's a note of resentment in Ray's voice, but nothing more. If Leo had to bet, he'd say the guy was telling the truth.

'We're looking into some anonymous letters that were sent to some other members of staff working on The Hill.' Leo pauses, but there's no recognition on Ray's face. 'Have you received anything?'

'What sort of letter? I don't get much post.'

'A request to do something.' Leo doesn't want to give too much away, although his instincts are telling him Ray's not hiding anything.

Ray frowns and shakes his head. 'Sorry, mate, you've lost me.'

'You drive Mr Makepeace around in a silver Audi, is that correct?' Dawn reads out the licence plate number, and Ray nods. 'Are you allowed it for personal use too?'

'Within reason. I'll nip to Sainsbury's, that sort of thing.'

'That Audi was stopped by police in Derby Street, Manchester, on June the tenth this year.' Dawn pauses. 'The driver was issued with a warning in relation to kerb-crawling.'

'Not me, mate.'

'The driver showed the officer ID in the name of Ray Tinnion.'

'He could have showed off his arse with my name tattooed across both cheeks – it wasn't me.' Ray gets out his phone. 'When did you say? June tenth?'

'Yes. It's not the first time you've been in trouble with the police, is it?'

'When I was a kid, yeah.'

'You went to prison.'

'I was in my twenties.'

'It didn't bother the Makepeaces that you had a criminal record?'

'I don't know what the agency told them.' Ray walks closer to Leo and Dawn, a photo showing on his phone. 'I got the job through Bianca Dixon. She lives in the Coach House at the top of The Hill. Runs an agency called Prestige Home Help.' Ray thrusts the phone at them. 'See? The only place I was crawling in June was back to my bed after a few too many piña coladas.' In the photo, Ray is standing on a sandy beach in front of a sparkling blue sea and sipping from a cocktail laden with fruit and decorated straws. 'Swipe up, and you can see the date. June tenth. Antigua, ten days, all inclusive, fifteen hundred quid. Not bad, right?'

The metadata checks out. Leo looks at Ray. 'Can I see some ID?'

'My driving licence is in the Audi – I'll get the keys.'

'You keep it in the car?'

Ray shrugs. 'Seems like the most likely place I'll need it.'

'How many sets of keys are there?'

'Two. I have one, and Mr Makepeace has the . . .' He trails off, his mouth dropping as the truth dawns on him. 'Bastard!'

'I can add a note to the intelligence report,' Leo says, 'to say you weren't driving the car at the time of the offence.'

'Makes you wonder what else he gets up to on my days off, doesn't it?' Ray grimaces. 'How many other times he's given my name.'

'There's nothing else on the system.' Dawn looks at Leo as she speaks, and he knows she's thinking about the second-hand gold dealer in Warrington. Had it been Phillip Makepeace behind the wheel?

'Nothing he's been caught for, maybe,' Ray says grimly. 'Rich people hold all the cards, that's the problem, and they know it. I get a flat, my bills paid . . . how else could I afford to rent around here?'

'Where were you on Monday?' Leo asks.

'I told you, I was coming back from my sister's. I got back around lunchtime.'

Leo keeps his gaze locked on Ray's. 'Did you drive the Audi later that day?'

'No, I wasn't working.'

'Any personal trips?'

'No.' Ray's voice has darkened, the volume a touch too loud for such a small space.

'You didn't drive to Warrington?' Dawn says.

'What is this, the Spanish Inquisition?'

'A woman was seen getting into the Audi,' Leo says, 'outside a second-hand gold merchant in Warrington on Monday aftern—'

'Oh, he's taking the piss now!' Ray stands and paces to the kitchenette. 'He gets away with it once, and he thinks he's invincible.' He pours himself a glass of water from the tap and drains it in one, then he turns to face Leo. 'We're the easy targets for you lot, aren't we? The cleaners, the housekeepers, the drivers . . . Especially when we've got a bit of a past. But I'm telling you, that lot in the fancy houses are no better than us. In fact, they're worse.'

Leo takes in Ray's flushed face and evident anger towards his employer.

You're looking in the wrong place, Duncan Cragg had said. Leo pictures Philip Makepeace, cruising slowly down Derby Street, looking for kicks; then putting the blame on his driver when he got caught. Who knows what else is going on behind the glossy gates and ornate porticos of the other houses on The Hill?

Leo's been focusing on the staff, but maybe the rot isn't below stairs. It's above them.

TWENTY-SEVEN

THURSDAY | FFION

Luke Parks slumps in the chair opposite Ffion and George.

'My client would like DC Kent present at interview,' Luke's solicitor had said, when she had emerged after consulting with Luke. Ffion had explained that it wasn't appropriate; that George was Luke's family liaison officer and, as such, separate from the investigation.

'It's your call,' the solicitor had said, 'but – off the record – I think it'll be a more useful interview if he has someone he trusts there.'

Consequently, a decidedly reluctant George is sitting next to Ffion in the small, rather shabby interview room, which smells of cigarette smoke despite no one having lit up in here since 2007.

'You've been arrested on suspicion of murder,' Ffion begins. 'You do not have to say anything, but it may harm your defence if you do not mention when questioned something which you later rely on in court.'

'I didn't do it.'

'When we asked you where you were over the weekend,' George says, 'you told us you were at home.' She reads from Luke's statement. 'You said you *didn't leave the house*, and that you spent Saturday evening *watching TV and having a few beers*.' She looks up. 'Can you confirm this is the statement you gave me?'

'It is.'

'The statement you declared was true, *to the best of my knowledge and belief*?' George reads the printed declaration at the top of the statement. '*I make it, knowing that if it is tendered in evidence, I shall be liable to prosecution if I have wilfully stated in it anything which I know to be false, or do not believe to be true.*' She puts the statement on the table and waits.

Luke looks down at his hands. 'I lied.'

'Let's try again, then, shall we?' Ffion says. 'Where were you on Saturday evening?'

There's a long silence, during which Luke looks at his solicitor, who gives the briefest of nods. Whatever the agreed script is, Luke is going to stick to it.

'I followed Natasha to Wales.'

'Why?' Ffion says.

'I got a DM on Instagram. It said Natasha was away on a dirty weekend with Russell, and they thought I should know about it. Said if I went now, I'd catch them together.'

'Who was the direct message from?' Ffion glances at George. Luke's story is easily verifiable; his phone had been taken from him when he arrived in custody.

'I don't know. A load of numbers and random letters. No bio, no photo, no posts.'

'But you believed them?' George says.

'It wasn't the first time.' Luke picks at his fingernails. The clock on the wall fills the silence with a rhythmic *tick tock*, *tick tock*. 'We'd had an argument the night before – I told you about that.'

'That was the truth, then?' Ffion says.

'Yes, but . . .' Luke rubs his face. 'I didn't tell you what it was about. Not all of it. I said it was because Nat was going away, and that was part of it . . .' He puts his fingernail between his teeth and pulls at the loose bit he's been fiddling with. 'It was because the last time she went on a work trip, she slept with Russell.'

'How did you find out?' George asks.

'She told me. Said she was eaten up with guilt and couldn't bear lying to me any more. Said it was a mistake, she didn't even like him, blah, blah, blah.' Luke's voice is bitter. 'She said it would never happen again.'

Ffion watches his body language: the nervous fingernail picking, the shift of his torso towards the door. 'But you didn't believe her.'

'No.' He hesitates. 'She'd bought a sexy new swimsuit, just for the weekend. It was bugging me, and then that message came in about Russell and . . .' He exhales heavily. 'Natasha was stunning. Younger than me, cleverer, more ambitious . . . I was punching, I knew that. Why wouldn't she go off with him?'

Ffion isn't about to soothe his ego. 'What time did you leave home on Saturday evening?'

'Seven. I got there around eight.'

'What was your plan?' George says.

'I took a bottle of champagne to give Nat, to celebrate her bonus. If it really was a work thing – if Carole and Mike were there too – I'd give them the champagne and go home. But if she was just there with Russell . . .'

'Yes?' Ffion prompts, when the sentence ends there.

'Well . . . then I'd go home. But at least I'd know for certain.'

'And that's it?' Ffion laughs. 'You drive across the border in a blinding rage because you suspect your girlfriend of cheating on you, yet if Nat opened the door in a bathrobe, draped over Russell, you'd just . . . go home.'

Luke flushes.

199

'So what did happen?' George says.

'I knocked, but no one was in, so I waited in the car, and eventually Nat's boss came back with the older guy – Mike.'

'Did they see you?'

'They were a bit too wrapped up in each other, if you know what I mean?'

'What about Natasha?'

'She came back about twenty minutes afterwards.'

'Was she with Russell?'

'No. She was on her own.'

'Did you speak to her?' George says.

'No. I started to feel a bit . . .' he struggles to find the word. 'Like, would Nat maybe think I was being a bit—'

'Stalkery?' Ffion says.

'—protective,' Luke finishes. 'There was no sign of Russell, and Nat just looked . . . normal. Pissed, but normal. So I drove home.'

'I don't think you did.' Ffion leans on the table. 'I think you waited. I think Natasha got changed and went out to the hot tub, and maybe you thought she was meeting Russell there, or maybe you just saw an opportunity to confront her away from the others, so—'

'That's not what happened!' Luke slams a fist hard on the table.

'—you followed her and you lost it, just like you're losing it now.'

'I'm not losing my temper!' Luke stands up, pushing against his chair so hard that if it hadn't been bolted to the floor it would have smashed into the wall behind.

'Sit down, Luke.' George speaks calmly, and Luke looks down at his chair as though he doesn't remember getting to his feet. Slowly, he sits back down.

There's a long silence.

'There was another car there,' Luke says suddenly. 'I just remembered.'

'You. Just. Remembered.' Ffion leaves a deliberate pause between each word.

'Honest to God. When I drove away from the house, there was a car parked at the bottom of the track. I didn't see who was in it, but maybe that's who killed Natasha.'

'What colour was this car?' George says.

'Black.'

'Make?'

'I don't know. Something big though, like a Range Rover, or a BMW X5.' George blinks. 'I don't remember the number plate, except that the last three letters were ROB. I remember it because, well, it's a name, isn't it?'

'And you think the driver of this car murdered your girlfriend?' Ffion says.

'Maybe.'

'The girlfriend you're devastated to have lost.'

The solicitor coughs. 'Where are you going with this, DC Morgan?'

'So devastated that you'd do anything to find the person responsible, except for passing this possibly crucial piece of information to the police.' Ffion laughs. 'I'm sorry, but you can't expect us to believe—'

'If I'd told you about the car, you'd have known I was there too, and you'd think I killed Natasha.'

'That's exactly what I think.' Ffion keeps her eyes on Luke's. 'I think you drowned Natasha in that hot tub, and then you panicked, so you put her in the kayak and dragged her down to the river to make it look like an accident.'

'No.'

'Natasha's body has been examined,' Ffion says. Luke flinches at the word 'body'. 'Numerous samples have been taken. If your DNA is found on her swimsuit, or—'

'I did the laundry; I touched her clothes all the time. My DNA is bound to be—'

'On a brand new, just-picked-up-from-the-shop swimsuit?' Ffion says.

Luke clutches his head. 'You're just trying to catch me out now.'

'The thing is, Luke.' Ffion leans towards him. 'I don't need to try.'

Luke is released on police bail, pending further evidence.

'A single fingerprint on the hot tub,' Ffion says. 'That's all we need.'

'I don't think he did it,' George says. They're on their way back to the incident room. The corridor is only wide enough for two people, and whenever someone comes the other way, one of them has to drop back to let them pass.

Ffion stares at George. 'Were we in different interview rooms? Did you not see how quickly he flared up?'

'He's lost his girlfriend.'

'And have you seen a single tear leave his eye?'

'Not seen, no.' George slows her pace and tucks in behind Ffion as a uniformed officer comes towards them.

'Well, then.'

'That doesn't mean he hasn't cried.'

'You have to admit,' Ffion says, 'he doesn't present as a normal grief-stricken partner.'

'What does that look like?'

'Well, he looks guilty as hell, for a start.'

George falls back into step with Ffion. She looks as if she's about to say something.

'What?' Ffion pushes open the double doors at the end of the corridor, and they head up the stairs towards Major Crime.

'Nothing.'

'You're as bad as Seren. Spit it out.'

'All I was going to say is that there's no such thing as "normal" when it comes to grief.' George hesitates. 'I didn't cry for weeks after my husband died.'

A sudden pounding sound comes from above, as several sets of boots race down the stairs on their way to an immediate. Ffion and George flatten themselves against the wall.

'*Diolch!*' says one of the officers, as he jumps the last three steps.

Ffion feels as if the wind's been knocked out of her. 'I didn't know,' she says, when the stairwell is quiet again.

'I didn't want you to. I didn't want anyone at work to know.' George is silent for a moment. 'The thing is, I felt guilty as hell. Still do, if I let myself think too much about it, which I don't. The last conversation Luke Parks had with Natasha was an argument; of course he feels guilty. That's going to haunt him for the rest of his life.'

'Is this why the boss wanted to know if you were okay?'

'He didn't want me to do the FLO course. He thought it was too soon, that it might stir up some emotions.'

'Has it?'

'Maybe a bit.' George pushes open the door to the incident room.

'If you ever want to talk . . .' Ffion says.

'Thanks.'

' . . . can you find someone else?' Ffion throws a sidelong grin at George.

George laughs. 'You're more sensitive than you admit, Morgan.'

'Yeah well, maybe I am, but I'm still not letting Parks off the hook. Until I'm shown evidence to the contrary, he's our number one suspect.'

'What about the car he saw?'

'Oh, come on! You don't seriously think he saw a car?'

The briefing room is quiet, and there's no sign of Sam; Ffion wonders what he told the DCI when he skulked back to the station. She turns to a detective in Boccacci's team.

'Have you seen the lad who was on secondment? Sam Taylor?'

'The boss sent him back to uniform.' The detective shrugs. 'He gave her some cock-and-bull excuse for coming back to the nick, and she wasn't having it. He's done himself no favours if he's planning to apply for CID, that's for sure.'

Ffion feels a flash of guilt, then she reminds herself of the way Sam spoke to her. It will do him good to be taken down a peg or two. 'Is this desk free?'

'Knock yourself out.'

Ffion logs on to the Police National Computer. Time to disprove Luke Parks's desperate attempt to throw the suspicion on anyone but himself.

TWENTY-EIGHT

THURSDAY | ALLIE

During the week, Allie's days follow a similar pattern. A quick tidy-up after dropping Harris off, then a couple of hours of daytime TV while she looks through Pinterest and orders a few bits for the house. She used to go to the gym in the afternoon, but ever since she heard Camilla and Emmy discussing the relative merits of reformer Pilates versus David Lloyd spin classes, Allie's off-peak leisure centre membership has lost its appeal. Now she wears her Sweaty Betty to clean the kitchen.

Today, though, she has dressed up. She's wearing wide taupe trousers with a sleeveless shift top in the same colour, paired with a tan belt she found at sixty per cent off in TK Maxx. Around her shoulders Allie has looped one of Dominic's navy sweaters, even though it's twenty-eight degrees today and she's already sweating. The finished look is almost identical to a picture in the 'This is What Old Money Really Looks Like' article she saw online a few weeks ago.

In the hospital car park, Allie adjusts the sweater, which keeps falling off her shoulder (people's shoulders must slope less when they have Old Money), and picks up from the back seat the food parcel she's brought. The plastic bag rather spoils the aesthetic, but she doesn't have a basket. And it is Waitrose, at least.

'Surely the Jeffersons are coming home to eat and to sleep?' Dominic said this morning, when Allie was lightly toasting sourdough bread for the sandwiches. Harris had basic white sliced in his lunchbox, but Allie felt she should level up for Cara and Mikaela.

'You know what hospital canteen food is like, though.' Allie layered buffalo mozzarella and thinly sliced beef tomato on to the sourdough, which she'd already spread with pesto. 'And they need to keep their strength up.' Also, although she didn't say this, everyone else had been to visit Alec in the hospital, and Allie didn't see why she should miss out.

'You don't think it's a bit . . .' Dominic put a gentle hand on the small of her back, '. . . much? Taking lunch to people we hardly know.'

'You might not know them, Dominic, but I do. The whole of The Hill is rallying around them. And before you say we don't live on The Hill, even Grandad Dixon has been to visit, and his flat is in Fairbourne, which is a darn sight further than Taplin Drive. So I think it would be odder if I *didn't* offer to help, don't you?'

Dominic didn't answer.

Alec Jefferson is still in a critical but stable condition. Allie knows this from the WhatsApp group, which Cara and Mikaela have used to keep everyone updated, and to stagger visiting times so Alec isn't overwhelmed.

When would be the best time for me to drop in? Allie had posted on the group yesterday, but she hasn't had a reply, and now her message has been pushed out of sight by a dozen more. It's understandable, Allie thinks: Cara and Mikaela must be beside themselves with worry, and the reception at hospitals is always patchy. She should just turn up, she had decided, scrolling back through the thread to check the visiting times.

She looks at the clock as she reaches the reception desk, her Waitrose bag clutched in both hands. Perfect timing.

'I'm sorry, I can't let you through to the ward.' The woman behind the desk looks at Allie above blue-framed glasses.

'I'm a friend of the family.'

'Name?'

'Allison Green.'

The woman runs a finger down a handwritten list and Allie cranes her neck to read it. She sees *Dixon, Lennox, Makepeace.*

'Wait – I'm probably down as Allie.'

'Sorry, no Allie.'

'But I brought sandwiches for Alec's parents.' Allie puts the Waitrose bag on the counter. 'They're sourdough!'

'I'll make sure they get them.'

Allie feels tears pricking at her eyes. She turns to leave, and through the glass panels in the double doors that lead to the ward she sees Emmy hugging Cara. Behind them, Warren is talking to Mikaela. Allie feels a burst of resentment towards the gatekeeping nurse. There must be some mistake. Allie will try again, maybe when there's someone else on the desk, or maybe the officious receptionist will go to the loo and Allie will be able to slip past and on to the ward. Cara and Mikaela will be pleased to see her, she knows they will. Allie will wrap her arms around Cara and say, *You poor thing, what a nightmare this is. What can I do to help?* and she'll feel Cara's relief as she realises Allie is the perfect friend to have when times are tough; that Allie positively thrives in a crisis.

Back in her car, Allie's stomach grumbles. She had planned to eat lunch with Cara and Mikaela (Allie would have insisted they all eat – *we have to keep our strength up, for Alec's sake*) and now her own sandwiches are behind the counter with the officious receptionist. Had Cara and Mikaela missed Allie's name off the visitor list by accident, or has Allie been deliberately shut out? She imagines them eating the sourdough sandwiches without bothering to ask who made them; or, worse, laughing about Allie's attempts at friendship.

Allie's lips tighten. She gets out of the car again and walks back towards the hospital.

TWENTY-NINE

THURSDAY | LEO

Bianca is on the phone when she opens the door to the Coach House. She frowns slightly when she sees Leo.

'I'll have to call you back, Dad, there's someone at the—' She stops. Leo can hear the low timbre of a male voice at the other end of the phone as Bianca tries in vain to speak over it. 'Yes, but can I call— Okay, well, try turning it off and— Dad, I really have to go.' She hangs up.

'Sorry to interrupt,' Leo says.

'He can't get his laptop to work. It'll be something else tomorrow, bless him. Technology is not Dad's strong point – he fetches Scarlett when he wants to turn the TV on.'

'My dad's the same.' Dawn smiles. 'Do you have a few minutes to talk?'

'About the burglaries?'

'About the number of domestic staff in the street who have criminal records,' Leo says.

Bianca hesitates, then she steps back. 'You'd better come in.'

'I've placed six so far,' she says, when they're installed in the kitchen. The bifold doors are open and the tiled floor continues seamlessly into the garden, where a bright pink hot tub is surrounded by sun loungers. 'My signature colour,' she says, when she sees Dawn checking it out.

'So far?' Leo prompts.

'A woman at the bottom of the street wants a cleaner, but only for an hour a week. Most of my guys want more substantial roles, but I'll find someone.' Bianca takes a jug of water from the fridge and goes to the cupboard for glasses.

'You have Ray Tinnion at Fairhaven, Jade Upshall at Sunnyside and Duncan Cragg at Hollies.' Leo looks up. 'That's only three.'

'I placed a full-time housekeeper at Rushmead, a couple of doors down, and a nanny at Oak View. My gardener is number six.' Bianca looks through the open bifolds on to the beautifully kept lawns. 'He's one of the reasons Prestige Home Help exists.'

'How do you mean?' Leo says.

'Geoff did some ad hoc gardening for me at my old house. We got chatting and he told me how hard it was to find full-time employment when you have a criminal record, particularly if you've been in prison, as he had.' She puts down the glasses and pours the water.

'Thank you,' Dawn says. 'Did it concern you, finding out Geoff had been inside?'

'Not in the slightest. I'm a good judge of character. Geoff made some mistakes when he was younger, but all he wanted was a fresh start. I couldn't afford to hire him full-time back then, but it made me think. I was working in HR, but I'd just had Scarlett and I was looking for a way to work from home. So I started PHH.'

Leo takes a sip of water. 'Do your clients know they're employing criminals?'

'*Reformed* criminals.' Bianca pushes back her hair, and her bracelets jangle. 'Most don't even ask. They trust me to match them with someone reliable, honest and hard-working. Which I do.'

'Would you normally place so many workers in one street?' Dawn says.

'Word-of-mouth is a powerful advert. Dad hands out my business cards on the school run, bless him.'

'Somewhat unfortunate, isn't it,' Leo says, 'that there's been a spate of burglaries on The Hill since these *reformed* criminals started working here?'

Leo's echoed emphasis isn't lost on Bianca, who raises an eyebrow. 'I'm disappointed to see such cynicism from a police officer. Incarceration isn't just about punishment, DS Brady, it's an opportunity for reflection and restorative justice. Most people who leave prison have no intention of ever going back.'

'Just a coincidence, then,' Leo says.

'Everyone who comes through my agency is someone I'd be happy to have in my own home. Do you seriously think I'd fill my own neighbourhood with ex-criminals if I had any doubt about their good character? Hardly a good advert for my agency, is it?'

It's a fair point, Leo knows, except that both Duncan and Jade have admitted handing over the alarm codes to their respective employers' homes, which is stretching the definition of 'good character' somewhat.

'I'm sure if you looked into all the other domestic staff in the area – the ones who haven't been personally vetted by my agency – you'd uncover all manner of unsavoury secrets,' Bianca says. 'A clean record doesn't mean someone's honest, DS Brady. It just means they haven't been caught yet.'

'I need some background information on all the individuals you've placed on The Hill,' Leo says. 'The person responsible for the break-ins has been putting pressure on some of the staff to facilitate the burglaries. If we can establish how he knows them, we may be able to identify him. I'd like to see the files you have on each of them.'

'Absolutely not.' Bianca shakes her head. 'That's confidential information. It would be a breach of—'

'Intelligence suggests the burglar is also responsible for a double murder.' Leo holds her gaze. 'I need those files, and if I have to come back here with a warrant, I will.'

There's a long silence.

Bianca stands. 'Wait here.'

There's limited information in the files, but Leo requests copies regardless. Next-of-kin details will provide another layer of associates to check out, and Leo can request intelligence checks on Duncan's and Jade's previous places of employment.

'Maybe Stephanie Carmichael's lover worked with them both in the past,' Leo says, as Dawn drives them back to the station. 'Or he met Duncan in prison.'

'And Jade?'

'Was visiting?' Leo shakes his head. 'I don't know.' He's googling the company where Philip Makepeace works. Suki said Livingstone Asset Management had strict rules about personal calls, but a police inquiry is not personal.

'There's no one here of that name, I'm afraid.' The switchboard operator has a sing-song voice that manages to sound at once welcoming and bored stiff. 'Is there anything else I can assist you with?'

'He's a trader, if that helps?' Leo says.

'I'll put you through to that floor.'

A man answers the phone with a barked 'Yes?' and Leo repeats his query.

'Makepeace?' the man says. 'Fired.'

'I beg your pardon?' Leo puts a steadying hand on the car door as Dawn takes a roundabout a little too quickly.

'Months ago. Insider trading. Lucky not to end up behind bars, the fucking idiot.'

As Leo ends the call, he hears Bianca's words in his head. *A clean record doesn't mean someone's honest, DS Brady. It just means they haven't been caught yet.*

Philip Makepeace has been lying about going to work.

Which makes Leo wonder what else he might have been hiding.

At precisely five-thirty, Philip Makepeace arrives home. He's wearing a suit, the tie loosened and the collar unbuttoned, and he carries a briefcase. Leo gets out of his car and walks towards Fairhaven, reaching the front door at the same time as Philip.

'Can I help you, detective?' Philip puts his key in the lock.

'I hope so,' Leo says.

Suki is in the kitchen, adding water to a vase of flowers. 'How was your day, darling?'

'Long,' Philip says. 'Dull. Detective Sergeant Brady wants a word.'

'Again?' Suki turns around. 'Twice in one day, detective – people will talk.'

'I'm trying to establish who was driving the silver Audi on Monday afternoon,' Leo says.

'Ray, I imagine,' Suki says. 'Did you ask him?'

'Yes, he said it wasn't him.'

'Then no one would have driven it.' Suki says. 'We have our own cars.'

213

'You don't drive the Audi at all?'

'I literally never have.' She picks at a paint spatter on her left arm.

'How about you, Mr Makepeace?'

Philip shakes his head. 'Hardly ever. I can't remember the last time I drove it.'

'Could it have been Monday?'

'No, I was at work.'

Leo holds his gaze. 'Are you sure about that?'

'Totally,' Philip says, but his eyes slide away from Leo's.

Suki looks between the two men. 'What's going on?'

'It's Livingstone Asset Management you work for, is it?' Leo says.

The faintest flicker of concern passes across Philip's face. 'That's right.'

'Only, when I called, they told me you'd left.'

'Well, I—'

'What's all this about?' Suki turns to her husband. 'Why would they think—'

'They said you'd been fired for insider trading,' Leo says.

Philip closes his eyes for a second.

'Darling?'

There's a long silence. 'I had an opportunity to make a bit of extra money,' Philip says eventually. 'You wanted to go to Mauritius again, and it seemed like an easy way to . . .' He sighs. 'But I lost my job over it, and the boss threatened to bring in the police.' He glances at Leo.

'Oh, God!' Suki's hands fly to her throat. 'This is awful!'

'It's okay, I managed to talk him out of it.'

'No, but Mauritius! How are we going to pay for Mauritius?'

Leo clears his throat. 'So where *were* you on Monday afternoon, Mr Makepeace?'

'I was in a café, updating my LinkedIn profile. Fat lot of good that's done me so far,' he adds bitterly.

'Can anyone verify that?'

'I don't know . . . look, what's all this about?'

'As I said, I need to establish who was driving the silver Audi on Monday afternoon.'

'And as *I* said, I hardly ever drive it.' Philip's face reddens, his voice rising in volume.

'You drove it in Derby Street, Manchester, on June the tenth this year.'

Leo speaks deliberately slowly, his eyebrows slightly raised as he waits for the penny to drop. When it does, Philip reddens further. He glances at his wife.

'If you say so,' he mutters to Leo.

'What were you doing in Manchester?' Suki says sharply.

There's a long silence. Eventually, Philip speaks. 'Detective, my wife and I need to talk. Could you give us some privacy?'

Leo stands. 'If either of you remember who was driving the Audi on Monday, please let me know.' As he leaves the house, he hears Suki's voice rising in anger.

Could Philip have taken Suki to the gold dealer? Ray Tinnion denies driving the Audi, and so does Philip, but which man should Leo trust? A former prison inmate, or a stockbroker who lied about losing his job and gave false ID when stopped by police?

Leo's glad to leave The Hill for the day. It might be luxurious and exclusive, but it's crawling with lies and deception, and being here makes Leo itch.

THIRTY

THURSDAY | ALLIE

Allie has been ready for hours. She has changed three times, redone her make-up twice, and changed her silver sandals for a pair of heels with red soles, which could almost be Christian Louboutin if you don't look too closely. She hovers in the kitchen, too wired to sit.

Dominic looks hopefully at the foil-covered platter on the table. 'Is any of that for supper?'

'Sorry, I didn't get that far. I think there's some breaded cod in the freezer? This is for the par—' Allie breaks off. 'Committee meeting.'

It's not exactly a lie. The get-together at Emmy's is to finalise details for the yard sale, which is pretty much the same thing as a meeting. If Allie tells Dominic it's a party, he'll wonder why she hasn't invited him, and the truth of the matter (although Allie would never dream of telling him this) is that Dominic simply doesn't fit in on The Hill. He and Allie once bumped into Bianca on the school run, and, when Bianca asked where they were holidaying that year, Dominic actually said, *We're staying in a caravan in Dorset.* A caravan! When Bianca was taking Scarlett and Grandad Dixon to Tuscany! Allie had almost died of embarrassment. *A cabin,* she'd said quickly, and Dominic had looked at her, confused.

216

It's so hard to know what time to turn up. Too late and she could appear rude; too early, and her new friends might think her gauche. Allie looks at the clock. If she walks slowly, she should time it right.

'Don't wait up,' she tells Dominic. It's a beautiful evening and Allie imagines Emmy's garden strewn with fairy lights; Allie sitting on a rattan sofa between Camilla and Suki. Someone will produce blankets from the White Company (Warren, probably, in his ongoing attempt to secure custody of his and Emmy's mutual friends) and the girls will gossip and drink rosé long after the sun goes down.

Allie's red-soled shoes are hard to walk in, and the plastic digs into the backs of her heels as she makes her way up The Hill. As she draws closer to Ormindale, she can hear the strains of conversation and laughter, and her heart beats faster. It's finally happening: she's finally going to a party on The Hill! She takes a deep breath and smooths her dress. It's long – almost to her ankles – with a full broderie anglaise skirt and a nipped-in waist. The high neckline and long sleeves make it a little warm for the current temperatures, but the finished look is perfect for a garden party. Add a hat, and she could be off to watch the polo, she thinks.

'It's very . . .' Dominic had hesitated when she'd asked him what he thought.

She gave him a twirl. 'Stylish?'

'Amish.'

Men. They don't know the first thing about fashion.

Allie pauses at the garden gate to take the foil off her platter. It had been so hard to know what to bring, but then she'd seen an advert on Facebook from a woman who did fruit carving. Allie can't wait to see everyone's reactions.

She opens the gate.

Warren's and Emmy's garden is long and beautifully landscaped, with mature trees and thoughtful planting. Close to the house is a large semi-circular patio, furnished with L-shaped sofas with squashy cushions. Two enormous parasols shade a long trestle table on which the food and drinks have been laid out. Allie sees a multi-pack of burger buns, still in their packet, and a packet of Lidl cheese slices. A sharing packet of salt and vinegar crisps has been torn open, their contents spilling on to the table.

Warren is standing by a barbecue, waving a pair of tongs. 'Anyone for any more?' Allie lingers on the sidelines, waiting to be welcomed. 'Camilla? Can I interest you in some of my sausage?'

Camilla giggles. 'Warren Irvine, you are incorrigible!'

'Encourageable, more like,' JP says. 'Steady on, old chap, that's my wife you're flirting with.'

'It's never stopped him before.' Emmy's voice cuts across the banter. There's an uncomfortable pause, into which Allie steps with her fruit platter.

Everyone stares at her.

'Allie!' Emmy says. There's another excruciating pause. A glance bounces between the women like a grown-up game of pass the parcel. Emmy, Camilla, Suki, Bianca. Back to Emmy.

'Those kebabs need turning,' Warren returns his attention to the barbecue.

Philip joins him. 'They'll dry out if you keep them on any longer.'

'You should think about upgrading to the Weber Genesis,' JP says. 'Best barbecue I've ever had.'

'Allie,' Emmy says again. 'I didn't expect to . . .' She tails off, staring at the platter in Allie's hands. 'Is that . . . is that *my house*?'

'Isn't it incredible?' The fruit-carving woman has done a

sensational job with the photograph Allie provided. She's used pineapple for the honeyed stone building, with a melon porch and windowpanes carved from slivers of grapes. A kiwi lawn surrounds the house.

'It's extraordinary.' Emmy can't take her eyes off the platter. She's wearing cut-off jeans and a vest top, her feet in flip-flops that have seen better days.

'I'm so glad you like it.' Allie moves towards the trestle table. 'I'll just put it here, shall I?'

'The thing is, we're actually having a party.'

Allie adjusts a strawberry flower that was already perfectly placed, her face flushing.

'Hello, love. Well, don't you look a picture?' Dennis Dixon appears by Allie's side, one hand holding Scarlett's. 'We were just exploring the garden.'

'Is Harris here?' Scarlett says. 'There's a tree we can make a den in.'

'Sorry, he's at home.' Allie glances at Emmy, who is whispering to Suki. 'I should probably get back, actually.' She'll tell Dominic it was a quick meeting.

'You haven't even had a drink yet.' Dennis puts an arm around her. 'Come on, love, what do you fancy? Pimm's?'

'That would be lovely.' Allie hopes he'll stay and chat with her – the other women are standing in a circle that seems impenetrable – but no sooner has he found her a glass than Scarlett drags him off to find more trees to climb. Allie stands self-consciously next to the trestle table. Her dress is too hot, and she looks wistfully at Bianca's loose cotton dungarees, which are almost identical to ones Allie owns but had dismissed as being too casual.

Allie has finished her drink without noticing. Just as she lifts the jug to pour another, Camilla comes over to the trestle table.

Thank goodness! Allie hadn't been sure how much longer she could stick it out on her own. She smiles warmly at the other woman.

'A dry white wine, please,' Camilla says.

'Oh.' Allie stares at her. 'Um. Sure.' She finds a bottle of wine in an ice cooler.

'Anyone else for a top-up?' Camilla calls to the others. There is a chorus of yeses, and Camilla snaps her fingers at Allie. 'You might as well bring the bottle.'

There's no break in the women's conversation as Allie tops up their glasses.

'*Cheshire Life* said they'll send a photographer after we know how much we've raised from the yard sale,' Suki is saying. 'They're asking if we can do one of those photos with the giant cheques.'

The wine runs out halfway through Emmy's top-up. 'There's another bottle in the drinks fridge in the garage,' Emmy says, without looking at Allie.

Allie hesitates, then turns. It's fine, she tells herself. How many parties has she been to where the guests all muck in? Serving drinks, washing up . . . it's just what friends do.

'Don't touch the Chablis!' Emmy shouts after her.

There's a lump in Allie's throat and she feels as though she might cry. This isn't how she'd imagined tonight would be.

Warren is in the garage, pulling a four-pack of beer from the bottom of the fridge. 'Everything alright?'

'I was just getting some more wine.' Allie holds up the empty bottle in explanation.

'Help yourself. Stick that one in the recycling.'

Allie walks across to the blue plastic boxes lined up by the wall – she knows the Irvines' garage as well as her own now – and adds the bottle to the pile of empty glassware. She bends and picks up a porcelain figurine in two pieces. 'Oh, what a shame!'

Warren looks over. 'The estate agent broke it when she was staging the house. Didn't fit her "aesthetic", apparently.'

The ornament is a shepherdess, and Allie feels as though she's seen it somewhere before.

'Emmy was furious,' Warren says. 'But then, Emmy's furious about everything nowadays. It was from a set, apparently – something Cara Jefferson gave her and Camilla from the last yard sale they had on The Hill.'

Allie remembers now. Camilla had posted a photo of her broken ornament on the group chat; and Allie had seen the CSI dusting a similar one for prints after the break-in at Hollies. Allie feels the delicate edge of the figurine in her hand and can see how easily it might break. 'This could be glued together,' she tells Warren. 'It's a clean break.'

'Sweetheart, the days of doing favours for my soon-to-be-ex-wife are long gone.' He takes the beers back to the party, leaving Allie standing alone in the garage. She contemplates the shepherdess. What if she were to mend it? Emmy would be so grateful . . .

Allie hides the broken pieces in the folds of her dress. She opens the big garage door and slips on to The Hill and away from the party.

Cheshirecabbies.com/chatroom/ generaltaxichat/backofmycab

@big_baz
I had Jamie Oliver in the back of my cab today. Top bloke. Big tipper

@C4BB1E
Nice. I had his wife once

@big_baz
LOL you wish

@Alfonso
Tell you who I had – going back a few years now though. That one who was stabbed with her husband. Stephanie Carmichael

@big_baz
Seriously??

@Alfonso
It wasn't her old man she was with though. You can always tell can't you. I picked them up from the theatre. The Lion King I think or Cats. Something with a cat in it anyway

@Susies_Cabs_Chester
What was she like?

@Alfonso
No idea. I dropped her off and her bloke made me wait till she was inside, then I took him home. He lived in one of them massive houses on The Hill

@big_baz
Fuck me I took a bird from there shopping once and you should of seen the stuff she came back with. She must of been loaded

@C4BB1E
I'm not being funny but have you told the police about this @Alfonso? They banged up the wrong guy for it and now they think her lover killed them both

@Alfonso
Are you saying I had a murderer in the back of my cab???

@C4BB1E
Did he pay by card? You could give the cops his name

@Alfonso
Nah, I didn't have a card machine then. She used his name but I'm blowed if I can remember now

@Susies_Cabs_Chester
Do you think you'd recognise it if you saw it? I'm a bit of a genealogist, I can pull the electoral register from 2014. Hang on, I'll post a screenshot . . .

ELECTORAL REGISTER   DECEMBER 2014

THE HILL, TATTENBROOK, CHESHIRE, CH4 9NS

The Coach House	Peter Grey, Verity Grey
Rose Cottage	Ross Clough, Simona Macleod
The Barn	Scott Smart
Fairhaven	Sheryl Kingsbridge
Orchard House	Maxwell Cartwright, Elizabeth Cartwright
Sunnyside	Jean Paul Lennox, Camilla Lennox
The Gables	Ioan Bled, Aisha Bled
Hillcrest	Markham Dyer, Clare Dyer, Graham Lang
Hollies	Mikaela Jefferson, Cara Jefferson
Yew Tree Cottage	Keith Charlesworth, Rebecca Charlesworth
Four Winds	Anthony Spencer, Sara Spencer
The Poplars	Mathew Woodward, Dawn Woodward
Ivy Cottage	James Goldsmith
Ormindale	Warren Irvine, Emmeline Irvine
Conifers	Lynda Checkley
Braeside	Robert Padden, Kirsty Padden-Barr

@Alfonso
Nothing rings a bell, sorry

224

THIRTY-ONE

FRIDAY | LEO

Next to Alec Jefferson's hospital ward is a relatives' room containing two sofas, a small table with four chairs, and a galley kitchen with labelled tins. *Tea, Coffee, Sugar, Biscuits.* Someone has left a plate of cupcakes on the side, with a note saying *Dropped off by the Khans – help yourself!* Despite the floor-standing fan, which emits a faint whine as it whirs from left to right to left, the room is hot and airless. Leo loosens his tie. A week ago, the caseload on CID had been so light, Leo had been contemplating taking some time off. Now, his head was throbbing with the complexity of an investigation which had started as a straightforward burglary series and become a cold case double murder investigation.

'I just don't understand how this could have happened.' Cara Jefferson is sitting on one of the sofas next to Mikaela. Dark circles ring her eyes.

'A thorough investigation is under way,' the ward sister says. 'I'm so sorry.'

'He could have died,' Mikaela says. She leans her head against Cara's, their hands interlaced and their legs pressed together, as though they were one person, not two.

Leo had come to the hospital at the request of Detective

Superintendent Sturrock, to reassure the Jeffersons that progress is being made, without giving away exactly what that progress is.

'Thanks to information just received from a taxi driver,' Sturrock had told Leo, 'we now know that Stephanie Carmichael's lover lived on The Hill around the time of the murders. I've asked one of the case investigators to pull the electoral register for 2014. We're getting close now, so keep the Jeffersons on-side and let's keep speculation to a minimum.'

But when Leo had arrived on the ward, he discovered it had been an eventful night for Alec Jefferson.

'A nurse found him choking,' Mikaela told Leo. 'They gave him oxygen, but his vital signs were dropping and they thought he was having some kind of seizure.'

'We should have been here.' Cara's voice was hoarse with emotion and lack of sleep. She looked at Leo. 'We went back to The Hill. The hospital staff had been insistent Alec was doing well, and we desperately needed a good night's sleep. We wanted to show our faces at the Irvines too.'

'Not that we were in the mood to party,' Mikaela said, 'but everyone's been so kind, we felt we owed them half an hour, at least. Just to say thank you.'

'But when we got back here—' Cara broke off into a sob.

'They'd found something lodged in his throat,' Mikaela said. 'We're only thankful they got it out in time.'

The obstruction is on the table in front of Leo. A small piece of cotton wool, slightly bloodied, secured in a plastic specimen pot labelled *Alec Jefferson*. The pot is in turn sealed in a police evidence bag, marked with an exhibit reference and Leo's shoulder number.

'The cotton wool must have been in his mouth,' the ward sister says. 'Unconscious patients can still make involuntary movements, and we think Alec's tongue moved the cotton wool around his mouth until it ended up in his throat, where it caused a blockage.'

'But how did it get there?' Cara says.

'As I said, we're conducting a full investigation. We use cotton wool to wipe around patients' eyes and mouths, but of course nothing should ever be left behind. But – and I don't want this to sound defensive – this may not be down to negligence.' The ward sister looks at Leo, who nods.

'We're not ruling out the possibility that this was done deliberately,' he says. 'Alec had begun breathing independently, which significantly increased the likelihood that he might wake . . . and be able to name his attacker.'

Cara's eyes widen. 'You think whoever broke into our house tried to kill him?'

'I think it's a distinct possibility. I'd like a list of everyone who's had access to Alec in the last twenty-four hours. Staff and visitors.'

'I have that here.' The ward sister hands Leo a list, split into two columns. Leo will need to speak to all the members of staff, but it's the visitors he's most interested in. There are a few names he doesn't recognise – grandparents, perhaps, or friends of Alec's – but a long list of those he does: *JP Lennox, Camilla Lennox, Bianca Dixon, Dennis Dixon, Warren Irvine, Emmy Irvine, Philip Makepeace, Suki Makepeace, Duncan Cragg.*

'All your immediate neighbours,' Leo says.

'As I said, everyone's been so kind. Visiting, bringing food—' Mikaela stops. 'You surely don't think . . .'

'We have to consider all possibilities,' Leo says. He looks at the list again. He thinks about Duncan Cragg, and the teenage son he no longer sees. *Things were difficult at home*, Duncan's wife had told Leo. *Duncan was drinking. He's been helping Alec fix his car, talking to him about his uni course.* Could Duncan Cragg be drinking again? Might he have become fixated with Alec because the boy reminded him of his own son? But then why assault him? Why break into the other houses? Leo dismisses the idea. Stephanie Carmichael had been an affluent middle-class woman with expensive tastes. Leo can't imagine her planning a new life with Duncan Cragg.

Philip Makepeace. Philip, who for months has been pretending to go to work. Who picks up Manchester sex workers and gives someone else's ID when stopped by police. Had Philip been living on The Hill in 2014? Could he have been Stephanie's lover?

'Could anyone else have visited Alec?' Leo asks the ward sister.

She shakes her head. 'If their name's not on the list, they're not coming in.'

'Have you had to turn anyone away?'

'A few people. We had a reporter say he was Alec's cousin, and a woman tried to blag her way in with a picnic.'

'A picnic?'

'In a Waitrose carrier bag,' the ward sister says. 'The receptionist put it in the office behind the desk and came to tell me. We have to be careful with packages, as you can imagine. She was only gone a few minutes, and when she got back, the bag had disappeared.'

'You think the woman came back for it?'

'Who else would have taken it? Makes you wonder what was in it, doesn't it?'

It does indeed, Leo thinks. 'Is it possible she could have got on to the ward?'

'You need a pass, but if someone else was going through . . .' The ward sister sighs. 'The consultants are the worst for it, you know. Too busy and important to challenge someone following behind them.'

228

Leo adds his own handwritten name to the bottom of the ward sister's list. *Woman with Waitrose bag.*

Leo walks back to his car, hugging the shade of the oak trees that line the grounds of the hospital. Detective Superintendent Sturrock has sent through the 2014 electoral register and Leo scans the names, looking for ones he recognises. He's reading it for the second time when Ffion calls.

'Hey, stranger,' he says. 'Miss you.'

'Miss you, too, but this is a work call.'

Leo sits on a bench beneath a tree. 'It had better be something simple. This job is doing my head in.' He fills Ffion in on the call from the taxi driver. 'The person who broke into Sunnyside, Fairhaven and Hollies is close enough to The Hill to know the occupants' movements,' he says. 'Close enough to know where Duncan Cragg and Jade Upshall live, and how to put pressure on them.'

'And now you think the person who killed Stephanie and Peter Carmichael was living on The Hill in 2014?'

'Right.'

'So if any of the current residents of The Hill were also living there in 2014 . . .'

'They're our suspects,' Leo finishes.

'Fuck me, you're almost there!' Ffion's excitement is palpable and Leo grins. He wishes she were working this job with him. 'Have you already cross-referenced the two sets of names?'

'I was literally doing it when you called,' Leo says. 'It has to be either be Warren Irvine or JP Lennox.'

'Warren Irvine?'

'Or JP Lennox. Except for Cara and Mikaela Jefferson, who are both female, everyone else on the 2014 register has moved away, so wouldn't be privy to the comings and goings of the street now.'

'I am about to complicate your life,' Ffion says.

'Does this mean you're finally going to say yes to moving in together?'

'No. I mean, maybe. We'll see. Like I said, this is a work call.' Ffion takes a breath. 'We arrested Natasha's partner yesterday,' she says.

'Do you have enough to charge?' Leo glances at his watch.

'Not yet, and he's thrown something up that's rather muddied the waters,' Ffion says. 'He claimed to have seen a car at the holiday let where Natasha was killed, and he gave us a partial index. To be honest I thought it was bollocks, but we've run a DVLA check against the details.'

Leo really needs to get back to the office, but Ffion's been so interested in his investigation, he can't cut her off just as she starts telling him about hers. He begins walking towards his car.

'There are a fair number of possibles,' Ffion says, 'but once we narrowed it down to cars within an hour's drive of Cwm Coed, there are only a handful. And one of them . . .' Ffion pauses. 'One of them is registered to an address on The Hill.'

Leo stops dead. 'Is it a silver Audi, registered to Fairhaven?' He's thinking about the mysterious woman trying to sell Stephanie Carmichael's locket; about Philip Makepeace using the driver's car for his nefarious acts. The Makepeaces had their house valued after Suki's studio conversion. Might Natasha have been their estate agent?

'No.' Ffion sounds surprised. 'It's a black BMW X5, and it's registered to Warren Irvine, at Ormindale.'

230

THIRTY-TWO

FRIDAY | ALLIE

Allie wakes up to find a message from Emmy. She opens it eagerly. No doubt Emmy's wondering why Allie left the party without saying goodbye. Emmy will want to thank Allie properly for the fruit platter; perhaps even ask for the creator's details. She might (although even Allie doubts this) want to apologise for her rudeness. *I've not been myself lately*, she might say, which Allie will (gently and compassionately) agree with.

More jumble to sort, Emmy's message reads. 10am okay?

Allie's thumb hovers over the keypad. A tiny voice in her head tells her to say that she's busy. That she doesn't want to help with the yard sale any more. She ignores it. She's making progress, she really is.

Sure! Looking forward to catching up. We hardly got to chat last
   night! Xxx

Two blue ticks appear immediately, but Emmy doesn't reply.

Just before ten, Allie arrives at the Irvines' house. She's carrying a shoebox, in which is nestled Emmy's broken shepherdess. Allie has painstakingly glued the two pieces together, and if you didn't look closely, you wouldn't know anything was amiss.

There's a note on the garage door.

Had to go for an emergency hair appointment, Emmy has written. *Start without me.*

Emmy has left the garage unlocked, and when Allie lifts the heavy double door she finds an enormous heap of jumble to be sorted. Allie exhales. When she volunteered to help Emmy with the yard sale, she had imagined the two of them gossiping as they sorted bric-a-brac, perhaps giggling a little over some of the less desirable items. She had thought there would be Aperol spritzes in the garden, and long lunches in Emmy's kitchen with the other women on the street, until Allie was as much a part of The Hill as the rest of them.

The reality has been somewhat different. Allie has sorted the donated items single-handedly, while Emmy has sat watching, or – more recently – excused herself on the grounds of a forgotten appointment or last-minute committee meeting at the tennis club. Far from being accepted into the fold, Allie feels increasingly unwelcome. She was ignored at the party despite her show stopping gift; she was turned away from the hospital, when all she wanted to do was offer support. Allie thinks guiltily of her behaviour on the ward, then pushes the thought away. She was upset; people behave irrationally when they're upset.

She gets to her knees on the cold concrete and starts to sift through the new donations. Given the tax brackets of The Hill's residents, there's a surprising amount of cheap rubbish among the clothes and trinkets dumped in Emmy's garage, and Allie suspects some people are seeing the yard sale as an easier option than driving to the dump. She picks up a pair of laddered tights between finger and thumb and drops them into the bin.

The pile slowly grows smaller as Allie sorts the donations into her carefully organised boxes. On the day of the sale, they will set out a table in front of each house to display the contents of each respective box. £1 items by one house, £5 by another, and so on.

'This way it involves the whole street,' Allie had explained, when Camilla Lennox had demanded to know why they couldn't just hold the entire thing at one house.

'At least ensure our driveway has the table with the fifty-pound box,' she said. 'I don't want the hoi polloi kicking gravel all over the begonias.'

Allie remembers a taxidermy owl she'd asked Emmy to move, and checks to see it's in the right box. It isn't, of course, and, as she reaches for its base so as not to damage its feathers (and because touching its body freaks Allie out), her hand closes around something shiny and cold. She pulls it out. It's an iPhone – newer than Allie's own – and when she turns it on, the screen springs to life. There's no wallpaper photo, only the date and time of a standard home page. Some of the residents of The Hill think nothing of casting aside brand-new belongings, but a phone? It must have been thrown out by accident.

Allie takes out her own mobile and snaps a photo of the iPhone. She'll post on the WhatsApp group to see if anyone's lost it, and then – Allie feels a zip of excitement as the thought occurs to her – she'll say that the owner can pick it up from her house. Despite Allie's frequent invitations, none of her friends from The Hill has dropped into The Willows for coffee, or taken up her offers to show them the refurbishments she and Dominic have done. But the owner of the phone will have no choice but to visit!

Allie hopes it's one of the girls. Imagine if it's Bianca's phone! Allie will put some nibbles out in little bowls, and maybe get some proper olives from the deli counter at Morrisons, instead of the ones in a jar that Dominic claims are nicer. Allie will open a bottle of prosecco, and once they've had a glass or two she could say something like *Shame the others are missing out – why don't you text them and see if they want to join us?* and, since no one ignores messages from Bianca, it will be a party in no time. A party at Allie's house! She wonders if she should say they're having work done at the front of the house, and to use the back gate. *Yes, the little path right off The Hill, that's the one . . .*

'You know only drug dealers have two phones?'

The voice jolts Allie out of her daydream. She looks up to see Leo standing in the entrance to the garage.

'What are you shifting?' Leo says. 'Fentanyl or crack cocaine?'

'Don't be ridiculous. It's lost property, if you must know. I was about to message to see if anyone's missing one.' Allie scrambles to her feet. Leo's looking at Warren's BMW X5, no doubt wishing he could afford one. 'What are you doing here?'

'Looking for Warren Irvine. Is he home?'

'Neither of them are. I'm . . .' *Sorting jumble*, Allie was about to say, but she doesn't want Leo thinking she's some kind of hired help. 'I'm looking after the place.'

Leo is unclipping something from his keys. 'I've got a UV pen here; I'll check the phone to see if it's been security marked.'

Allie's so relieved that Leo has moved on, she hands over the phone and watches as he shines the blue light over the front of the phone and then the back. A lurid green dot flashes into view.

'See that?' Leo passes the light over it again. 'That's SmartWater security marking. It holds the owner's contact details – kind of like DNA for personal possessions. I'll book it in with Property when I get back to the nick, and they'll get in touch with whoever's lost it. Or had it nicked; mobile phone thefts are through the roof at the moment.'

'But it was in with the donations.' Allie gestures to the boxes of jumble. 'It will have come from one of the houses on The Hill. It'll be easy to find—'

'I should follow the correct procedures,' Leo says. He puts the phone in his pocket. 'If you do hear from the owner, feel free to give them my number.' He glances again at Warren's BMW, then back at Allie. 'No need to tell the Irvines I came over. I'll catch up with them another time.'

Allie feels like crying as she watches Leo walk away with her last-ditch attempt at cementing the friendships she's tried so hard to make happen. She looks at the final bits of jumble left to sort and feels a sudden, uncharacteristic burst of defiance. 'Emergency hair appointment, my arse,' she says out loud.

In Allie's bag is the shepherdess in its shoe box coffin. Emmy doesn't deserve it. Allie's proud of the dupes she finds, but lately she's been wondering if they don't look just a little bit . . . (Allie's loath to admit it, even to herself) . . . cheap. Having a genuine *objet d'art* in her house – one that was part of a set shared by Emmy, Camilla and Cara, no less – will add a spot of . . . what's that other French thing people say? A spot of *je ne sais quoi*. Allie leaves the garage and slams the door down hard.

As she walks home, she gets a text from Mike Foster. Her heart thumps, the way it always does when she hears from Mike.

The money should be in your account now, reads the message. Thanks again.

Allie deletes it, glancing around, even though there's no one in sight; even though Mike says they're doing nothing wrong, that it's all perfectly above board. Allie tries not to think too much about it, but deep down she knows that's not true. She knows that, if anyone were to find out what she's been up to, she'd be in a whole heap of trouble.

THIRTY-THREE

FRIDAY | FFION

No sooner is Ffion off the phone with Leo than she's hauled into DCI Boccacci's office. Luke Parks has lodged a formal complaint about his arrest.

'You seem to be under the impression you are the senior investigating officer on this case,' Boccacci says.

'He lied about his whereabouts on Saturday night. He needed to be questioned.'

'By the right people, at the right time, in line with the investigation strategy!' Boccacci raises her voice. 'I need everyone to work as a team. The young lad from shift came crawling back to the office because he was "feeling a bit under the weather", and now you're running around arresting people without my authority.'

Ffion opens her mouth to protest, but Boccacci doesn't give her the chance.

'You're an experienced detective, Ffion, you know how a murder investigation works.' She picks up her bag. 'I have to get to a briefing. For the avoidance of doubt, there are to be no arrests made without my express authorisation. Do I make myself clear?'

'Perfectly,' Ffion says through gritted teeth.

Boccacci narrows her eyes. 'There's no "i" in "team", DC Morgan. Remember that.'

No, but there's one in *piss off*, Ffion thinks, as she marches out of the station. She hates being told off, especially when it's justified. She knew she shouldn't have brought Luke Parks in without Boccacci's say-so, but she'd hoped he'd cough to the job and Ffion's bending of protocol would be overlooked. As it is, Boccacci's so incandescent, she didn't even want to know what Luke said, which means Ffion is still sitting on the information that a suspect in Leo's burglary series – and consequently in the murders of Peter and Stephanie Carmichael – was seen at the holiday let in Cwm Coed on the night Natasha was murdered. Ffion will feed this new information into the system in due course; she first wants a few hours to scope it out herself.

On her way to The Hill, Ffion stops in at Simmonds. She's wondering whether Natasha's relationship with Warren Irvine might have been more than just professional, particularly given the somewhat loose morals already demonstrated by members of the team. Luke Parks said Mike and Carole were *wrapped up in each other*, and now Ffion remembers Carole's bedroom in the holiday let: the bed perfectly made, despite Carole's dishevelled state.

'I just have a few more questions for you.' Ffion doesn't sit down. Instead, she walks slowly around the room, looking at the house particulars on the walls, the paraphernalia on the estate agents' desks.

Carole watches her warily. 'I've already told you everything I remember about the night Natasha died. Which is very little: as you know, we'd all had far too much to drink.'

'That, I don't doubt. But even though you did look as rough as a badger's arse when we saw you the next morning—'

'I beg your—'

'—I don't believe you got black-out drunk.' Ffion presses the keys on a calculator on Russell's desk. 'Let me tell you what I think. I think you spent the night with Mike and then woke up with shagger's regret, so you pretended you had no memory of the night before.'

'How ridiculous.' Carole laughs, but her face is flushed.

'Your bed hadn't been slept in.'

'I always make my bed as soon as I get out of it.'

It's Ffion's turn to laugh. 'With a hangover so bad you could only open one eye?'

There's a long pause.

'Fine. I spent the night with Mike. But I didn't have *shagger's regret*, as you so charmingly put it; we've been seeing each other for some time.'

'You're having an affair,' Ffion clarifies.

'I prefer to call it a relationship.'

'Is your husband aware of this *relationship*?'

'Well, no, obviously not.' Carole coughs. 'Which makes it a little . . . delicate. Hence not wanting to go into detail about my movements that night. I'm sorry if I've seemed rather evasive.'

Ffion puts the calculator to one side. All three estate agents have been cagey from the outset. Is it simply their extracurricular bed-hopping they've been trying to hide, or is there more to it? 'How did you and Mike get back to the holiday let?'

'We walked. Mike was a bit unsteady as we left the pub. He put his hand out to get his balance and . . . er, he broke a window.'

Ffion recalls seeing Haydn boarding up the front of the newsagents when she was on her way to the lake on Sunday morning. *Bloody pissheads.*

'I'll contact the shop and pay for the damage.' Carole shakes her head. 'I know we've behaved appallingly, DC Morgan, but it really was just high jinks. We're devastated by what happened, but none of us had anything to do with Natasha's death.'

'I understand Natasha was the agent looking after Ormindale, on The Hill,' Ffion says. 'Do you know if she saw the vendors socially?' She's thinking about the email Natasha sent to Warren Irvine, cc'ing his wife. *The buyers are particularly keen to see the romantic master bedroom*, she'd written. It had felt pointed, as though Natasha had been sending some kind of message. Toying with Warren, perhaps? A subtle threat to tell Emmy what was going on?

'Socially? Goodness, I doubt it.' Carole laughs. 'Sorry, this is very unprofessional of me, but the Irvines are . . . challenging to work with. Divorcing couples often are, especially when they're still living in the same house. I can't imagine Natasha wanting to spend more time with either of them.'

Ffion sits at Natasha's desk. There's a pen pot containing several biros and a yellow highlighter, and an A4 hardback desk diary.

'We use an online calendar for appointments,' Carole says, as Ffion picks up the diary. 'But Natasha loved her stationery.'

The cover is pink leopard-print with embossed gold lettering spelling SLAY GIRL across the front. There's a matching pencil tucked into an elastic loop on one side. Inside, there's evidence both of Natasha's ambition – monthly goals are meticulously documented and tracked – and her organisational skills, with a to-do list written to the right of each weekly schedule. Ffion scans the entries leading up to Natasha's death, looking for anything that seems out of place. Most of the entries relate to property viewings or meetings with clients, but there are personal appointments too: a GP appointment, a call with the bank.

Ffion flicks forward to the current week. There's always something sad, she thinks, about calendar entries written by someone who can't now see them through. Under today's date, something has been rubbed out; there are still tiny flecks of grey from what Ffion assumes is the eraser on the end of the leopard-print pencil. She moves her head, changing the light on the page to try to read what Natasha had written. Elsewhere in the diary, Natasha's pencil entries are crossed through, often with small notes beside them. *Moved to 28th. Cancelled.* Was there some reason Natasha wanted to erase this entry completely, or has someone else interfered with this diary?

Ffion takes a piece of scrap paper from Natasha's desk and places it over the diary page. She gently rubs the pencil over her paper until a series of letters emerge from the imprint of the entry.

Call with Richard Wright.

Ffion closes the diary. 'I'll be taking this with me,' she says, and the look on Carole's face tells her she's on to something.

It turns out there are hundreds, possibly thousands, of Richard Wrights. Ffion calls George.

She picks up on the second ring. 'Before you ask, the answer's no.'

'You don't know what I'm going to say.'

'Boccacci's given me a right bollocking, thanks to you. I told you I shouldn't have done that interview with you.'

'How's Luke?'

'What, now he's had his trust in his family liaison officer completely undermined, you mean?'

Ffion winces. 'Sorry.'

There's a pause, then George says, 'Did she tell you there was no "i" in "team"?'

'She did.'

'Did you tell her there was one in *piss off*?'

'Am I that predictable? Listen, I need a favour.' Ffion speaks over George's protestations. 'Can you ask Luke whether the name Richard Wright means anything to him? Natasha was due to have a phone call with a Richard Wright today, but someone's rubbed out the diary entry.'

'I'll ask him,' George says, 'but I can't guarantee he'll be helpful.'

'Tell him thanks for the information about the car,' Ffion says. 'It's looking like a significant development.'

'The car you said wouldn't exist?'

'Yeah, that one.' Ffion grins. 'Turns out it's registered to a bloke who lives on The Hill. A suspect in Leo's burglary series.'

'Wow.' George pauses. 'So . . . you've passed this up the chain of command and are waiting for Boccacci's instructions, right?'

Ffion doesn't answer.

'Right?' George says again.

'Boccacci said I wasn't to make arrests,' Ffion says. 'She didn't say anything about asking a few questions.'

'Ffion—' George starts, but Ffion has already ended the call.

'Last Saturday? I was at home all evening.' Warren holds Ffion's gaze. His eyes are large and brown with gold flecks, his lashes enviably long. He's tanned and lean, and if it weren't for the greying hair and lined forehead he would pass for a man twenty years younger. 'Life is a little stressful at the moment, and I haven't been socialising much.'

'Can anyone vouch for the fact that you stayed home?' Ffion says. They're in Warren's study on the ground floor, which has a large corner desk and floor-to-ceiling bookshelves. Ffion wants to jump right in and tell the man they have a witness who saw his car near the holiday let where Natasha was killed, but she can't

241

do that without cautioning him, and Boccacci has been very clear on that front.

'I'm afraid not,' he says. He turns his gaze towards the window, which looks out on to the garden. 'My wife and I are separating, and we're not on good terms. The house is large enough that we don't need to see or hear each other if we don't want to and, well—' He exhales. 'That's the point we've reached, unfortunately.' He shakes his head, as though dislodging the thought. 'Do you have a suspect for the burglaries? I just ran a test on our alarm, actually, in case we're targeted.'

'I'm not here about the burglaries,' Ffion says.

'No?'

'I'm investigating the murder of Natasha Brett, your estate agent.' She glances at his feet. They look large. Would he wear size eleven boots? She thinks of the distinctive zigzag prints left at the crime scene.

Warren looks surprised, but not shocked. He sighs again. 'That was a terrible thing to happen.'

'What was she like?'

'Natasha? Young. Attractive. Competent, although she hadn't managed to get the asking price for this place.'

Ffion finds it interesting that Warren's primary observations are physical ones. 'Did you see her socially?'

'Good grief, no. She was an estate agent.' Warren leans forward, clapping his hands on his knees. 'Is that everything, officer? I have a Zoom appointment with my divorce solicitor.'

He shows her out, and as the front door closes, Ffion sees that the garage door is open. Inside, a woman is filling a box with junk. Ffion walks towards her.

'You must be Emmy.'

'Who's asking?'

'Detective Constable Morgan, North Wales CID.'

'I'm really busy, actually, I—'

'This won't take long.'

Ffion sees Emmy glance towards the house, and wonders if Warren is violent towards her. She certainly seems anxious.

'Are you here to arrest my husband?' Emmy says.

'Should I?'

'I don't know: is being a bastard an arrestable offence?' The woman gives a weak smile.

Ffion laughs. 'If it were, I'd have a few exes locked up.'

'They're all hearts and flowers at the beginning, of course, but then . . .' Emmy dumps the box on the floor and dust puffs up around the sides. 'We're having a yard sale,' she explains. She points to a row of neatly labelled boxes. 'I had someone doing the grunt work, but she's buggered off and left me to do everything on my own.'

'Were you at home on Saturday night?' Ffion asks.

'When the Lennoxes were burgled? Yes, I told the other detective I was. I woke up briefly some time after midnight – I thought I heard a noise down here – but I take sleeping pills and they make me really groggy. Almost as soon as I had the thought, I was flat out again.'

'What kind of noise?'

'The garage door squeaks when it opens. When I heard about the burglary, I wondered if they'd had a go at this place too, but nothing was disturbed. I think I must have imagined it.'

Warren? The timing would fit. Ffion makes a show of examining the yard sale boxes, moving towards the black BMW parked on the far side of the garage. 'Wow, there's a lot of good stuff here.'

'You're welcome to come. It's next weekend.'

'Cheers.' The wheels of the BMW are dirty, and the rear bumper is covered in mud spatters. Emmy has turned back to her box of junk, and Ffion takes the opportunity to peek through the rear window. She only has a second – Emmy and Warren might not be on speaking terms, but Ffion doesn't want to run the risk of her alerting him – but a second turns out to be all she needs.

Carelessly thrown in the boot of the car is a pair of men's walking boots, one upright and one fallen to one side. The boots are muddy, but, even through the dirt, Ffion can see the distinctive zigzag pattern on the sole.

THIRTY-FOUR

FRIDAY | LEO

Cheshire Constabulary covers almost a hundred square miles, so Leo is used to seeing other parts of the force represented on video screens at various meetings. But when he arrives back at Chester nick for the end-of-day briefing, he doesn't recognise the empty room currently shown on the screen.

'What's going on?' he asks Dawn.

'No idea. Sturrock said there's another job coming in.'

'You're joking.' Leo already feels as though his head might explode with the strain of trying to straighten out all the strands involved in the burglary series, and now the Carmichael murders. On the screen, the room is starting to fill up. A woman Leo recognises sits at the head of the table. 'That's DCI Christine Boccacci,' he tells Dawn. 'North Wales.' Boccacci had overseen the last job he and Ffion had worked on together; a murder on a reality TV show being filmed in the mountains above Llyn Drych. She'd offered Leo a job, but he hadn't wanted to be so far away from Harris.

Leo messages Ffion – Are you in this briefing with Boccacci? – but even as it sends, he sees her on the screen. She sends him a waving emoji. He's about to ask for the inside story when Detective Superintendent Sturrock walks in and everyone falls silent.

'Evening, everyone. DCI Boccacci and team, thanks for dialling in. Christine and I have already agreed on a strategy, so this is a brief meeting to ensure everyone's on the right page. Warren Irvine will be arrested at six o'clock tomorrow morning.' Sturrock looks directly at the camera. 'Christine, I'm conscious your team won't be up to speed on the Carmichael murders.'

Leo hides a smile. Between the *Without Conviction* podcast and Ffion's obsession, he doubts anyone within a twenty-mile radius of Bryndare police station has escaped without a thorough briefing.

'In short, Peter and Stephanie Carmichael were murdered ten years ago by someone we believe to have been Stephanie's lover, who lived at the time on The Hill, in Tattenbrook, West Cheshire. A series of burglaries has recently occurred on The Hill, and we now believe these were committed by Stephanie's former lover, in an attempt to retrieve something connected with the murders.' Sturrock pauses. 'We suspect this is a gold locket, worn by Stephanie, but we're not clear why he wants it so badly.'

'We're struggling to make sense of some conflicting information with regard to the locket.' John Evans, the cold case review team DS, picks up the thread. 'A woman attempted to sell it in Warrington, and was accompanied by someone in a silver Audi usually driven by Ray Tinnion, a live-in driver employed by Philip and Suki Makepeace of Fairhaven, The Hill. However, this was on Monday afternoon, the day before the most recent burglary on Monday night when nineteen-year-old Alec Jefferson was attacked.'

'Because of this,' Sturrock says, 'we can surmise that if the locket was the reason for the break-ins, then the driver of the Audi is not our burglar, and the actual burglar didn't know on Monday night that someone else had it. And we also can't be a hundred per cent certain that Warren Irvine is our man, even though he was living on The Hill at the time the Carmichaels were killed and he fits the profile of her lover. We simply don't have enough to arrest him. However . . .' The detective superintendent extends an arm towards the screen, where DCI Boccacci is waiting for her turn.

'*We* do,' she says. 'Natasha Brett was an estate agent engaged by Warren Irvine to sell his house, Ormindale, on The Hill. On Saturday night she was drowned in a hot tub at a holiday let in Cwm Coed, then dumped in a kayak in the river. Warren Irvine's car was seen in the vicinity around the time of the murder, and we have identified evidence in his car which could potentially link him to the offence.' The DCI looks pointedly in Ffion's direction but Leo can't tell if it's in admiration or admonishment; Ffion has a tendency to go rogue. Leo would never tell her this, but if she worked for him, one of them would be submitting their resignation within the first week.

'A mobile phone was found in Warren Irvine's garage and handed in to one of your officers,' Boccacci is saying, and Leo realises she's talking about him, about the phone Allie found. 'The phone belonged to Natasha Brett.'

There's an audible hum around both briefing rooms. Leo often thinks of his cases as jigsaw puzzles to solve: a slow but methodical process of finding the edges, then letting the middle take shape. Discovering that his burglary offender is also the suspect in a ten-year-old murder investigation had been the equivalent of piecing two separate puzzles together; now someone has dumped the contents of a third box on Leo's desk.

He messages Ffion – Did you know? – and sees her on-screen, tapping a response.

Nope, brand new information. Heard Boccacci and Sturrock on the phone earlier, having a pissing contest about who'd be lead officer, but didn't know why . . .

Do you want to stay at mine tonight, since it's such an early start?

Can't. The dog-walker's picking Dave up from mine first thing.

Detective Superintendent Sturrock is speaking again. 'Arresting Irvine for the murder of Natasha Brett gives us an opportunity to search his house for evidence of that crime, while also being . . . *proactive* in relation to anything else of interest.'

There's a slight twitch at the corner of his mouth. The law is clear about house searches. In theory, you're only authorised to search for what relates to the offence under active investigation, which means if you're looking for a stolen TV, you can't open drawers. In practice, there are always ways around it. After all, who's to say that drawer doesn't contain a remote control?

'DS Brady,' Sturrock says.

Leo focuses. 'Sir?'

'DCI Boccacci's team will interview Irvine in relation to Natasha's murder. I'd like you and DS Evans to be ready to question him over the burglaries and the Carmichael murders, the moment we feel there's sufficient to arrest him on them.'

'Yes, sir.'

'The cleaner at Sunnyside, Jade Upshall, has been very co-operative. She's informed us that Warren Irvine is attending a charity dinner and auction this evening with her employers, JP and Camilla Lennox – the Irvines are trustees, I understand – hence the decision to arrest first thing in the morning.' Sturrock looks

248

around the room. 'Any questions? No? Then I'll see you all bright and early tomorrow.'

The video screen freezes momentarily, then fades to black.

Leo calls Ffion. 'Can I stay at yours tonight, then?' If he were to stay in his own house he could fall into bed in twenty minutes from now and only be twenty minutes from work in the morning . . . but he'd still rather be with Ffion.

'Sure. I might be in bed, though.'

'You gave me a key, remember?'

As Leo opens Ffion's front door, Dave bounds down the stairs. He gives Leo a sniff, then, finding no biscuits, lollops back upstairs to Ffion.

'Fine guard dog that one makes.' Ffion is sitting up in bed, her laptop screen casting a glow across her face. 'Imagine if you were a burglar.'

'Don't. I've had my fill of burglaries.' Leo eyes Dave, who has climbed on to the bed. The dog makes a grunt like an old man, turns in a circle then lies on Ffion's legs. Leo thinks about Allie's threat to report Dave to the authorities. 'Um, he's okay, is he?'

'Yeah, he always does that.'

'No, I mean . . . no one's complained about him, or . . .'

'People are always complaining about Dave,' Ffion says. 'I tune it out.'

Leo starts to undress. If Allie had followed through on her threat to report a dog bite, Ffion was unlikely to keep it to herself.

'How's Alec Jefferson?'

'They think he'll be okay.' Leo continues undressing, folding his clothes and putting them on the chair by the bed, on which is a heap of (possibly) clean laundry. Only when he's naked does he remember his wash bag is still in the boot of his car. He groans.

'What?'

'I forgot my toothbrush.'

'Top drawer.' Ffion nods to the dresser at the end of the bed.

Leo opens it. 'You bought me a toothbrush?'

She answers tersely, not looking up from her screen. 'It's a spare, that's all.'

Beside the toothbrush is a can of men's deodorant and a bottle of Leo's favourite shower gel. Leo takes the toothbrush and silently closes the drawer, grinning to himself like a kid who's stumbled on a stash of Christmas presents.

'Why have you started taking your phone to the bathroom?' Ffion says suddenly, as Leo is about to leave the bedroom.

'I've got a couple of emails to read, that's all.'

Ffion doesn't say anything.

'But they can wait.' Leo drops his phone on the bed. 'I'm too tired to concentrate, anyway.' He tries to sound casual, but it's clear from the way Ffion's looking at him that she's suspicious, and as he washes his face he wonders if she's picked up his phone. He itches to go back for it.

'John's still waiting for the airlines to get back to him.' Leo calls from the bathroom, half-hoping it will distract her. 'If Stephanie travelled to Paris with Warren Irvine, it'll give us the link we need.' The phone's locked, anyway, so all Ffion will be able to see is notifications, and at this time of night there shouldn't be—

'Has Warren ever bought a Vauxhall from Salisbury Motors?' Ffion says.

It takes Leo a moment to remember the sticky note with the car showroom logo. 'I'm not sure.' He speaks through a mouthful of toothpaste, standing on the landing between the bathroom and the bedroom. 'I'll check with John tomorrow.' He returns to the bathroom to rinse his mouth.

'We'll have to get a handwriting sample from him when he's in custody tomorrow,' Ffion says, 'to compare with the love letters, and with the threatening notes to Jade Upshall and Duncan Cragg.'

'Good thinking.' Leo moves closer to Ffion and nuzzles her neck, sliding a hand beneath the covers.

She bats him off. 'I've just offered you my expert advice on your investigation, Brady. Are you not even going to ask about mine?'

'You're right, it's very rude of me. Is Boccacci letting you interview Warren?'

'She took some persuading, but yes.'

'What's your strategy?'

'It's very difficult to concentrate when you're doing that with your hand.'

'Sorry.' Leo stops. 'Tell me.'

'It'll be a doddle. His car was pinged on an ANPR camera on Saturday night, so now we have that as well as Luke's witness statement. I'll just keep letting out the rope till he has enough to hang himself.'

'Have you completely ruled out the estate agents?' Leo says.

'Regrettably, yes; it would have been a pleasure to slap cuffs on all three of them. They're up to something, and it bugs me that I can't work out what it is.'

'I'd cross-examine Allie over it, but she's adamant it wasn't her I saw with Mike on Tuesday.'

'She wouldn't tell you even if she knew. Not if it was to help me. She loathes me.'

'You, me, Dave . . .' Leo sighs. 'I've come to the conclusion she doesn't really like—'

'Dave?' Ffion stares at Leo. 'When you asked if anyone had complained about Dave, you meant Allie, didn't you?'

There's a long pause. Leo had been hoping to avoid this. 'She thinks Dave bit Harris.'

'Bollocks!'

'That's – sort of – what I said.'

'Did he tell her that?'

'No,' Leo says firmly. He doesn't know what Harris has said, but he's certain this has all come from Allie.

'That woman is poisonous.'

'I'm sure she won't *actually* make a complaint.' Leo isn't sure at all, but he hopes that saying it might make it true.

'I've a good mind to speak to her myself.'

'Please don't.'

'She's got no right to—' Ffion stops, as Leo's hand returns to the place it was a few minutes ago. 'That's a cheap trick, Brady.'

'Will it work?'

Ffion's breath catches.

'I'll take that as a yes.'

The first time Leo's phone rings, he ignores it. The second time, he rests his forehead briefly on Ffion's, whispers a *sorry*, then rolls off her and answers the call.

'Sorry to bother you, DS Brady.' The caller's voice is accompanied by the familiar soundscape of Control Room. 'There's a note on the system to call you if a job comes in on The Hill.'

Leo swings his legs out of bed. 'What have you got?'

'The call came in on the nines from a Mrs Emmy Irvine, address Ormindale, The Hill,' the operator says. 'She returned home from a dinner this evening to find the house had been broken into. Her husband Warren's been attacked.'

'Is he badly hurt?' Leo is already getting dressed, the phone wedged awkwardly beneath his chin.

'He's dead.'

THIRTY-FIVE

FRIDAY | ALLIE

Allie can hear a police siren wailing – not right outside, but close enough to have woken her. She turns over to go back to sleep, but then a second car passes right by the house, blue lights casting eerie shadows around the edges of the bedroom curtains.

Something's happened.

Allie slips out of bed. The windows are wide open, but the air is still, and Allie is sticky from sleep. She pauses to check that Harris is sleeping soundly, then pads into the kitchen and opens the back door. The sirens have stopped, but above The Hill the sky pulses with blue. Someone has moved Allie's flip-flops, so she shoves her feet into Dominic's gardening clogs and races down the path and out of the gate. The too-big clogs make a bid for freedom with every step, and she runs awkwardly, her toes pointing skywards.

As she emerges from the overgrown path on to The Hill, the blue pulse in the sky grows brighter, and Allie's heart rate quickens to match it. Which house is it? Has the burglar struck again? Or maybe Grandad's staying the night with Bianca and has had a funny turn. Allie runs up the street, clogs flapping, heart pounding.

It's Emmy's house.

There are three police cars, haphazardly parked, and an ambulance with its rear doors open. A few metres away is a small cluster of people, their faces ashen.

Allie joins them. 'What's happened?'

JP stares at her. 'Who are you?' He's wearing black tie, his stiff white collar unnaturally bright in the blue-tinged light.

'It's the woman from round the corner.' Camilla's fully dressed too, in a long evening gown with diamante straps. She gives Allie a smile so fleeting it's gone before it's fully formed. 'Sally, isn't it?'

'Allie. Is it another burglary?'

'Worse,' Bianca says. 'Warren was home. No one's telling us anything, but we think he's been hurt.'

'I can't believe this is happening again.' Cara lets out a sob, and Mikaela puts her arms around her.

'Three burglaries in a week,' Philip says. 'Two serious assaults. I mean, what are the police doing?'

'It's terrible,' Allie says, but no one even glances in her direction.

'That's a Labour council for you,' JP says. 'Painting rainbows and telling everyone their pronouns, when they should be tackling crime and disorder.'

'Oh, don't be ridiculous, JP,' Camilla snaps at him.

'Where's Emmy?' Allie says. 'Is she okay?'

'All I'm saying is that all these break-ins have happened since Rupert Weston-Barr lost his seat.'

'Do shut *up*, JP.'

'Does anyone know how Emmy is?' Suki says.

'She's been with the paramedics since we got back.' Camilla indicates the ambulance, and now Allie sees that Emmy is inside, a paramedic sitting beside her. Allie can't see Emmy's face, only the incongruous sparkle of an evening gown puddling on the floor of the vehicle. Emmy must have been out with Camilla and JP,

Allie realises. The three of them are the only ones who are dressed. Everyone else is in nightclothes, although even in nightclothes they ooze money and style. Suki wears navy silk pyjamas with a pale gold trim; her husband is in loose joggers with a T-shirt tucked into the waist.

'I think Emmy sensed something was wrong at home, you know,' Camilla is saying. 'Ray drove us to the auction, and I sat next to Emmy in the back; she didn't seem quite herself. She left the table after the main course and by the time she came back, she'd missed dessert. She said she wasn't feeling well.'

'That's so extraordinary,' Mikaela says. 'A similar thing happened to me the night Alec was hurt, didn't it?' She and Cara are wearing matching kaftans, their feet in neat black slides. Allie looks down at her Winnie-the-Pooh T-shirt dress and the ugly, oversized gardening clogs.

Cara nods. 'Alec's been home alone overnight loads of times, but that night, Mikaela just couldn't settle. You kept saying something felt *off*, didn't you?'

Mikaela nods. 'Some people have a sixth sense, I really believe that.'

'Poor Emmy,' Camilla says.

Everyone turns to look at the ambulance in which Emmy is sobbing. Allie snatches off the stupid clogs and walks home barefoot. She doesn't fit in on The Hill. She will never fit in.

Facebook.com/groups/ WithoutConvictionSleuths

🔒 *Private group*

Shaun Chance

Episode 6 has finally dropped!!! It was worth the wait. Hats off to the Without Conviction team, your investigative powers know no bounds!

25m

All comments ▼

Joseph Flint

We couldn't do it without you guys, to be fair. Our Patreon's gone interstellar lately. We appreciate every subscriber and every single donation. Your support helps us do what we do!

23m

Karen Louise Bradfield

The interview with the jeweller was amazing! How did you track him down?

22m

Joseph Flint

That one's down to my genius co-host! 🏆 😈 The police had circulated a picture of the locket to jewellers and gold dealers, but we figured they wouldn't have done the leg work. Right @Gemma Lyrick?

20m

Gemma Lyrick

takes a bow Yeah, we didn't know if the killer tried to sell the locket locally, but I made a list of all the jewellery shops in a fifty-mile radius and visited them all. It's been a l o n g process lol! This one jewellery guy recognised the locket straight away as one he did a repair on for the Carmichaels. I was gutted, because how was that going to help our murder investigation? But something made me switch on my voicenotes and get an interview anyway . . .

15m

Karen Louise Bradfield

So glad you did. When he said there was a second photo behind their wedding photo, I was like WHAT???

13m

Peta Miller

Imagine being stoked that your wife carries you close to her heart, but it's actually because there's a picture of her lover behind it. Gutting!

11m

Jennifer Barrett

It's quite a romantic story when you think about it

8m

Karen Louise Bradfield

Maybe look up the definition of romantic? Her lover brutally stabbed her and her husband!

6m

Margaret Young

The picture of the locket has been circulated so widely now I can't imagine there's anyone in the country who wouldn't recognise it as Stephanie Carmichael's. If it's found, and the photo of her lover's still inside, there's no way he can claim there's no connection between them. He's 'bang to rights', as they say.

5m

Shaun Chance

He might not have known she hid a photo of him inside. He covered his tracks really well in every other respect.

3m

Peta Miller

I agree. If he knew the locket would identify him, he'd do everything he could to get rid of it.

2m

THIRTY-SIX

FRIDAY NIGHT | LEO

Warren Irvine is lying on his stomach in a pool of blood, the back of his T-shirt stained deep crimson. Leo has asked for the on-call forensic pathologist to attend to examine the body in situ, and while they wait, two white-suited CSIs take photographs. Emmy Irvine is outside, being treated for shock.

Leo had expected to see a broken window at the rear of Ormindale, as there have been in the other three burgled properties, but all the glass is intact and the windows locked. Warren is fully dressed, and the burglar alarm has not been set.

'No sign of forced entry,' says a uniformed officer.

The front door has been cordoned off, and a steady stream of officers and CSIs move between the street and the crime scene via the back garden.

'What time did his wife leave?' Dawn says. Like Leo, she's wearing a white paper suit over her clothes.

'Ten to seven. She went out with JP and Camilla Lennox.'

'It was a fundraiser,' Camilla said, when Leo asked where they'd been. 'Dinner, drinks, a silent auction.'

'I won Silverstone tickets,' JP added. 'Looking forward to it, actually, it should be a good—' He caught Leo's expression and fell silent.

Leo hasn't yet spoken to Emmy. He saw her being led away from the house by the ambulance crew, and her eyes were wide and haunted. However acrimonious her separation from Warren, discovering his body in such a brutal state must have been horrific.

A silver Volvo XC90 pulls up next to Ormindale and a woman in her late fifties gets out. She makes a beeline for Leo and shakes his hand firmly. 'Izzy Weaver. We've met before.'

'Have we?' Leo tries to place her. 'I'm sorry, I can't quite—'

'You're Ffion's bit.' She winks, then nods towards the crime tape across the front of Ormindale. 'Round the back, is it?'

Ffion's *bit*?

Dawn stifles a laugh.

Leo remembers where he met Izzy Weaver now. She did the post-mortem on Rhys Lloyd, a singer murdered at his lakeside holiday home during a New Year's Eve party. It was at the mortuary that Leo had met Ffion, although, technically, their first encounter had been in the rather less professional setting of Leo's bedroom. It still makes Leo smile to remember Ffion's expression when they'd come face to face in the morgue just hours later.

'You're a long way from Bryndare mortuary,' he says, showing Izzy around the side of the house.

'Tell me about it. *On call* used to mean popping out for half an hour to check over a scene, then sending a fat invoice. Now we're driving halfway across the country.' She looks up at Leo. 'Ffion keeping you on your toes, is she?'

'You could say that.'

'She's besotted with you, of course.' They reach the back door and Izzy takes the paper suit proffered by a CSI. 'Has the scene been interfered with in any way?'

261

'No, death was confirmed by the attending officer, then the scene was secured,' Leo says. 'Um . . . besotted?' He feels himself blushing.

'God, yes, totally.' Izzy walks into the kitchen and surveys the scene. 'Although I imagine she doesn't tell you so.'

'Er, no, not really.' Leo is suddenly aware of Dawn and the CSIs, all of whom are within earshot. He focuses on the body in its pool of blood. 'So, what are your thoughts?'

'Christ, how should I know?' Izzy says. 'Marry her?'

Leo coughs. 'I meant the crime scene.'

'Oh, that!' Izzy laughs. 'Stabbed, by the looks of it. See the hole in his T-shirt?' She walks slowly around the body. 'You have to get up close and personal to stab someone. Is it possible he knew his attacker?'

Leo opens his mouth, then closes it again. Where to start? 'This is the latest in a series of break-ins on The Hill,' he says. 'We believe the person responsible is also behind a double stabbing back in 2014.'

'Not Peter and Stephanie Carmichael? Such a fascinating case – the podcast has me absolutely hooked.' Izzy kneels to get a closer look at Warren.

'We're working on the possibility that the murderer lived on The Hill at the time of the attack, still lives here, and is responsible for the recent burglaries.'

'Then you must have a suspect?'

'We did,' Leo says. 'You're looking at him.'

Izzy sits back on her heels. 'Well, he didn't do this to himself, so you'll have to find another one.'

Leo finds Emmy Irvine in the back of an ambulance. Someone has given her a huge blue fleece to wear over her evening dress, which makes her look tiny and fragile. She hugs herself, tears streaking her make-up.

When she speaks, her voice is weak. 'I can't stop thinking about it.' Emmy shakes her head, as though trying to dissolve the image. 'All that blood . . . and Warren just, just *lying* there. I know we were getting divorced, but . . .' She glances at Leo. 'It's complicated.'

Leo briefly allows himself to imagine Allie being brutally mown down. 'I'm sure it is.'

'I'm surprised you don't think I did it.' Emmy gives a broken laugh. She looks up at Leo, then stops laughing. 'Oh! You do.'

'I was under the impression your husband was attending the fundraiser last night, Mrs Irvine?'

'He was supposed to. Well, we both were, to be honest – we're both trustees – but since he can't stand to be in the same room as me, he said I couldn't go.' Emmy shakes her head. 'He did this all on the residents' WhatsApp, incidentally, despite Camilla's best efforts to take it into a separate chat. Anyway, at the last minute he changed his mind and said he wasn't going himself, so I had to scramble to get ready.'

'Where was the fundraiser?'

'Nolan Hall. Bit of a schlep, so we borrowed the Makepeaces' driver.'

'And the three of you were there all evening?'

'We couldn't exactly nip home – it was a three-course meal with auction lots in between.'

'What happened when you got home?'

'I told the officer who—'

'And now you're telling me.' Leo smiles.

There's a flash of irritation in Emmy's eyes, but she doesn't argue. 'I said goodnight to Camilla and JP, then I walked home.'

'Alone?'

'No.' Emmy picks at a fingernail. 'The Makepeaces' driver, Ray Tinnion, walked me home. He said because of the burglaries, he wanted to make sure I was safely inside.' Emmy's voice starts to wobble. 'I used my key, and when I opened the front door . . . You can see right through into the kitchen, you see. I didn't even notice Warren at first, I just saw all that blood and—' She swallows hard. 'I screamed. After that, it's all a blur. We called 999 and by then I'd gone into the house, and I found – I found . . .' Emmy buries her face in her hands.

'I'm sorry, I know this is hard.' Leo watches her closely. It wouldn't have been possible for Emmy to stab Warren – not if she was with the Lennoxes all evening, as she says she was – but that doesn't mean she isn't involved. Could someone have killed Warren at Emmy's behest? Leo wonders where Ray Tinnion spent the evening, while Emmy, JP and Camilla were at dinner.

'I'd like you to come back to the house with me,' Leo says.

'No, please don't make me!' Emmy bursts into anguished tears.

'I need to know if anything is missing.' The unbroken windows aren't the only thing different about this burglary. The other three had been what they called 'tidy searches', with little disturbed beyond a few accidental breakages. Ormindale, in contrast, has been trashed. Every drawer has been pulled out, and every cupboard opened; their contents tipped on to the floor. The bathroom cabinets, underbed drawers, bedside cabinets . . . all ransacked.

'Will Warren—' Emmy swallows. 'Will he still be there?'

'He's been taken to the mortuary. The crime scene investigators will still be at work – it'll be a few days before you can move back, I'm afraid.'

'I'm not living there any more.' She shakes her head furiously. 'Never. I can't.'

'We can organise for someone to clean everything up,' Leo says gently.

'But what if the burglar comes back?'

'None of the other houses on The Hill has been targeted twice,' Leo says.

'Can I have some kind of police protection?'

'That won't be possible, I'm afraid.'

'But what if . . .' Emmy's voice is a whisper. 'What if it was me they wanted?'

Leo looks at her levelly. 'Is there something you're not telling me?'

'No, of course not, I—' She covers her face with her hands. 'This doesn't seem real. It's like being in a film. A horror film.'

'If we could just walk through the house,' Leo says, 'then maybe you can try to get some rest.'

Emmy looks at him, her bottom lip trembling. Then she nods. 'Okay.' She lets out a short, audible breath. 'Let's see what's been stolen.'

As Leo steers Emmy gently towards Ormindale, Ffion joins them. They had travelled separately, not knowing if they would need two vehicles later on. Leo had felt rather guilty as he'd pulled away from her ancient car, leaving her far behind.

'You okay?' Leo says.

Ffion nods. 'Boccacci's spitting chips. I said I'd update her once I'd seen you.'

The three of them enter the Irvines' house through the French doors in the dining room, avoiding the bloodstained kitchen. Ffion sucks in air as she takes in the mess.

'I can't bear this.' Tears stream down Emmy's face. 'Please, please can we leave?'

'I know it's difficult to tell,' Leo says, 'but is there anything obvious missing?'

Emmy looks helplessly around the trashed dining room. 'I don't think so.'

Ffion indicates a rectangular patch on the wall which is a shade brighter than the surrounding paintwork. 'Was there a picture there?'

'Yes, but it hasn't been stolen. I sent it to auction.' Emmy flushes. 'Divorce is expensive.'

Leo doesn't pass comment. He still resents having to sign over half his pension to Allie, when she was the one who had an affair.

They do the same in the hall, in Warren's study, and in the drawing room, which contains several easy to steal items. A silver candelabra lies on the floor in front of a glass-fronted mahogany cabinet. The contents – a collection of jade figurines – are scattered on the carpet.

Leo looks at the fireplace. 'Is there something missing from the mantel?'

'I don't think so?'

'Next to the candlestick, where that space is.'

'No, it's always been like that,' Emmy says, and she should know, of course, but something passes across her face, so fast Leo can't pinpoint it. Why does he get the feeling she's hiding something?

Outside, Leo takes Emmy across the street to where the neighbours are gathered in a tight huddle. Apart from JP and Camilla Lennox, everyone's in nightwear, some with jackets pulled hastily on over pyjamas. Standing a little further away, as though he knows his place, is Ray Tinnion.

'You can stay with us as long as you need to,' Camilla says.

'Or come to me,' Bianca offers. 'Dad sleeps over sometimes if he's babysitting, but mostly he goes home in the evenings, so it's just me. It would be no trouble, Emmy.'

'No, I—' Emmy pulls the fleece tightly around her. 'Absolutely not. I wouldn't feel safe. I'll go to a hotel.'

'Oh, Emmy,' Suki says. 'You can't be all on your own in a hotel, not when Warren's just—' She stops. 'Not after this,' she finishes.

'I'm going to a hotel. I'll get a cab.' She looks around, as though there might be a taxi rank she hadn't previously noticed.

'Nonsense,' Philip says. 'Ray will take you.'

'I don't want to be any trouble.' Emmy dissolves into tears, and the other women cluster around her.

'Warren must have had the locket,' Ffion says, as she and Leo watch the residents of The Hill from a strategic distance. 'That's what the intruder was searching the house for.'

'But the locket is hardly worth anything,' Leo says.

'It had a photo of Stephanie's lover inside. Behind her wedding picture. I listened to yesterday's *Without Conviction* podcast on my way here. The photo connects the lover to the double murders. That's why it's valuable.'

'Right.' Leo tries to keep up. 'But if Warren had the locket and someone else wanted it back . . .'

' . . . then Warren can't have been Stephanie's lover,' Ffion finishes. 'But who was?'

Leo doesn't know. But then he watches Ray Tinnion leading Emmy towards his car, a strong arm around her shoulders. He remembers the leopard-print belt coiled under Ray's bed, and the indignation when Leo accused him of having driven to the gold merchants.

Ray wasn't on the electoral register for The Hill in 2014.

But that doesn't mean he wasn't living here.

THIRTY-SEVEN

SATURDAY | FFION

'This case involves far too much time on the wrong side of the border for my liking,' Ffion says. She and George are sitting on a bench by the side of the River Dee, which is a poor substitute for Llyn Drych in Ffion's opinion, but nevertheless a preferable option to Chester nick.

'I think Cheshire's got a lot going for it,' George says.

'You're not thinking of jumping ship, are you?'

'I was thinking you might, actually. Once you move in with Leo, I mean.'

'I haven't said I'm definitely moving in with him,' Ffion says. 'It's too far from the lake, for a start. And from Mam,' she adds as an afterthought.

'You could swim in the Dee.'

Ffion looks at the river, where brown foam has formed around pieces of flotsam. 'I think I'll pass.' She yawns loudly. 'Did you ask Luke about the entry in Natasha's diary?'

'Yes – he'd never heard Natasha mention a Richard Wright, and he's not a Facebook friend or an Instagram follower of hers. But . . .' George looks smug. 'I've found him on LinkedIn.'

Ffion screws up her eyes for a second. 'I have so many questions right now, but the overriding one is, what the fuck are you doing on LinkedIn?'

'It's a good networking platform.'

'It's Facebook for narcissists.' Ffion picks up a stick from by her feet and picks at the bark.

'Richard Wright's posts aren't narcissistic.'

'Are they about how he got up at five o'clock this morning, drank a green shake then jogged seventeen miles to work, only stopping to hand dollar bills to a beggar who later turned out to be the CEO of Apple?'

'You're very cynical, you know,' George says. 'As a matter of fact, he mostly posts links to the investigative work he carries out into corrupt estate agents. He's a property ombudsman.'

'Oh. That *is* interesting.' Had Natasha been under investigation? Ffion throws George a sidelong look. 'Sorry.'

'Although he does also advocate getting up at five.' George grins and stands up. 'I'll keep you posted.'

On the way to Bryndare police station, Ffion tries to listen to *Without Conviction*, but the latest episode won't download. She chucks her phone on the passenger seat and spends the drive with only her thoughts for company.

Things between her and Leo seem . . . Ffion feels for the word . . . *disconnected* right now. It's inevitable when work's busy, and it's not as though she wants them to live in each other's pockets – Ffion guards her independence fiercely – but nevertheless she feels as though they're orbiting around each other, never quite aligning. Last night, when Leo had been getting ready for bed at Ffion's, he'd made a point of leaving his phone behind when he went to the bathroom, but she'd seen him looking to make sure she wasn't touching it. What is he hiding from her?

* * *

270

Warren Irvine's BMW has been recovered to a secure unit where forensics officers will analyse the mud spattered on the tyres and bumper and compare it to samples taken from the ground around the hot tub where Natasha was killed.

'The boots are a match,' DCI Boccacci tells Ffion. 'Both for size and for tread pattern.'

'Right.'

'You could at least pretend to be pleased.'

Ffion shrugs. 'It seems a bit pointless now, doesn't it?' She isn't the only one to feel that way; Warren Irvine's murder has caused a shift in the team's collective energy. Yesterday, the office was buzzing with tension. Today, they're going through the motions. Ffion imagines it will be a very different atmosphere in Leo's team, as they try to identify which of the men on The Hill had been Stephanie Carmichael's lover.

'It's never pointless.' Boccacci gives her a stern look. 'We owe it to victims of crime – not to mention their loved ones – to bring closure to a case, regardless of circumstance.' She picks up her daybook. 'We also owe it to the perpetrators to be one hundred per cent certain of their culpability, which is why—' she raises her voice to reach the rest of the team '—I don't want to lose momentum. Check with petrol stations between The Hill and Cwm Coed to see if we can get CCTV of Irvine behind the wheel. Cheshire's Major Investigation Team has seized his tech, so liaise with them and ask for a heads-up on anything that could relate to our case.'

'Yes, ma'am.' The chorus of agreement comes from everyone but Ffion.

'Natasha's mobile phone is with digital forensics,' Boccacci says. 'The SIM has been removed, and the handset's been restored to factory settings; they're working to see what data can be retrieved. Ffion, may I have a word?'

271

As Boccacci leaves the room, Ffion trails behind, feeling as though she's at school again.

'You spoke to Warren Irvine within twenty-four hours of his death,' Boccacci says, when they're standing in the corridor.

'Oh, bollocks.' Ffion knows exactly what that means.

'Indeed. That makes it a death following police contact, which means we've had to refer ourselves to the IOPC.'

'Brilliant.' The Independent Office of Police Conduct investigates the police for suspected wrongdoing; Ffion has definitely had better days. She wonders if Leo will find himself in the same boat.

'It's a technicality, Ffion, no one's suggesting you did anything wrong, but Professional Standards will need to interview you.'

Ffion feels suddenly, bone-crushingly tired. Boccacci stops talking and looks at her, and, when she speaks again, she doesn't sound like a DCI.

'Are you okay?'

'I'm fine,' Ffion says, but, to her horror, her voice cracks and her eyes are stinging with tears.

'Is everything alright at home?'

Ffion scrubs angrily at her face. She clears her throat. 'I'm fine,' she says again, with a fraction more control. 'I've got a lot going on, that's all. The house I was buying fell through, and my daughter Seren leaves for uni the week after next, which is a big change for both of us, and there's been the murder investigation, obviously, and . . . and . . .' Ffion tails off.

And I think my boyfriend might be keeping something from me.

'That sounds like a lot,' Boccacci says. 'Do you have someone you can talk to?'

Ffion isn't much of a talker. She takes herself off up a mountain instead, or plunges into Llyn Drych, where, no matter what the season, the water's always cold enough to freeze out whatever's on her mind. And if Ffion did want to talk, who would she talk to? Mam's the biggest gossip in Cwm Coed, and Seren's head is too full of the big move to London.

'Yes,' Ffion says finally. 'George.'

Boccacci nods approvingly. 'Good choice.'

Downstairs, Ffion is making a coffee when her phone rings and she's summoned to the front desk. 'Can someone else deal?' she says. 'I'm on my knees.'

'Sorry, Ffi, uniform need to speak to you. It's urgent, apparently. Room two.'

She makes her way to the corridor behind the station duty office. The four small rooms there are used to debrief witnesses, carry out voluntary interviews and – in the case of at least two officers Ffion knows – have a cheeky nap on a long night shift.

She opens the second door without bothering to knock, and finds Sam Taylor sitting at the small table there, reading through a witness statement.

'Sorry, I thought . . .' Ffion looks at the number on the interview room door. Number two. 'Did you . . . did you want to see me?'

'Take a seat.' Sam half rises and gestures to the chair on the other side of the table.

'What's all this about?' Ffion stays where she is. 'There's been a development in the Natasha Brett murder investigation and—'

'This is important,' Sam says.

'More important than murder?'

'I just think you'll want to get it sorted out as . . .' Sam clears his throat, '. . . discreetly as possible.'

'Seriously, mate, what the fuck are you talking about?'

'I'll have to notify Professional Standards, of course.'

273

Twice in one day? That's a record, even for Ffion. She hesitates, then closes the door and sits down.

'This is a voluntary interview,' Sam says. 'You do not have to say anything, but it may harm your defence if you do not mention something when questioned that you later rely on in court. Anything you do say may be given in evidence.'

'What exactly am I supposed to have done?'

Sam's pen hovers above his notebook. 'I believe you're the owner of a large grey dog?'

'You have got to be kidding me.'

'We've received a report from a member of the public who alleges your dog is not being kept under proper control, and that it attacked a six-year-old child.'

'He didn't attack—'

'What breed is the dog?'

'I don't know.'

Sam looks up from his notebook. 'You don't know?'

'Even Dave doesn't know what breed he is.'

'So he could be a banned breed?' Sam flicks back to a page in his book on which he has made a list. 'A pit bull terrier? Japanese Tosa? If it's an XL bully, the law requires an exemption certificate and—'

'Dave's not an XL bully!' Ffion would laugh if she wasn't so angry. 'He's at least fifty per cent giant Schnauzer and he's soft as butter.'

'I'm afraid the complainant sees it rather differently.'

'I bet she does,' Ffion says grimly. 'How come it's not Cheshire Constabulary speaking to me? The *alleged*—' she draws out the word '—offence took place in their area.'

'The complainant knew the dog's owner was a detective with North Wales Police, so she rang here. I saw the job come in, and, rather than bat it back to Cheshire, I thought I'd deal with it.' He gives a smile that doesn't reach his eyes. 'Take the initiative, you know?'

Right. So that's how it goes. Ffion's being punished twice: once by Allie for daring to go out with Leo, and a second time for calling out Sam Taylor's 'banter'.

She folds her arms across her chest. 'Get on with it, then.' Ffion will answer Sam's questions. Then maybe she'll go and pay 'the complainant' a visit.

THIRTY-EIGHT

SATURDAY | LEO

At Allie's house, the broken gates are still jammed, and a note on the intercom says, 'Ring before entering!'

Leo ignores it, pushes through the gap, and rings the doorbell.

'Your gates are still broken,' he says, when Allie opens the door.

'The engineer's supposed to call me with an appointment time.' Allie must have been in the garden. She's wearing a sundress with the straps pulled down over her shoulders, her skin a mottled mix of sunburn and fake tan. 'Have you found out who stabbed Warren? It's so awful. I've been trying to get hold of Emmy all day. She must be distraught.'

There's an easy familiarity to Allie's words, as though she's talking about her best friends, and Leo thinks about his conversation with Cara Jefferson after the burglary, when they were looking through the residents' WhatsApp group. *We call her 'Klingon' because she's impossible to get rid of.*

'Why are you in a residents' chat group for The Hill?'

'It's not a crime.'

'Answer the question.'

'I'm not one of your suspects – you can't interrogate me.'

'You don't live on The Hill, Allie.'

'As near as dammit, we do. Harris plays with Scarlett Dixon

all the time – he adores it when Grandad Dixon picks them both up from school – and I've become very friendly with Cara and Mikaela Jefferson. They're lesbians, but ever so nice.'

'I'm sure your endorsement means a lot to them,' Leo says drily. 'What happened to your old friends?'

'Which old friends?'

'Hayley, was it?' Leo racks his brains for the names of the mums Allie used to talk about. 'Oh, and Becky – you really liked her. You were always taking the kids out together.'

'I don't really see them nowadays.' Allie shrugs. 'Most of the couples on The Hill are older, so their socialising isn't based around the sprogs. Such a relief!' She rolls her eyes in what Leo hopes is a joke, because, in her desire to make 'better' friends, has Allie really forgotten their own 'sprog'?

'Bianca's dad is always happy to have Harris – Dennis says it means Scarlett has someone other than him to boss about, bless him.'

'Two kids is a lot to handle. He's getting on a bit, Allie.'

'He says it keeps him young. And it's great for me, it gives me time to catch up with my friends.' Allie frowns. 'Although of course, everyone leads such busy lives. Every time I see Cara, she's on her way to an important meeting.'

'I bet she is,' Leo says.

'Did you just come round here to insult me?' Allie looks at her watch. 'Only I have to make a call.'

'I need your fingerprints.'

'What for?' She narrows her eyes at him.

'That phone you found is connected to an ongoing investigation. I need your prints so we can eliminate them from the inquiry.'

'Is it to do with Warren?'

'I can't give you any more information. Can I come in?'

With obvious reluctance, Allie lets him into the hall. She looks at her watch again. 'Thing is, I have to make a call. Like, right now.'

'It'll take me a few minutes to get everything ready,' Leo says. 'Make your call, I'll wait here.' He puts the fingerprint kit on the console table, moving the vase and the hideous china dog to make room. Allie's collection of ornaments seems to be breeding; there are at least two more since he was last here.

'You always did have to get your own way,' Allie snaps. She goes into the kitchen, slamming the door behind her.

'Oh, how I miss being married to you,' Leo says under his breath. He can hear her speaking on the phone and can't resist moving closer to the door to hear what was so urgent about her call.

'One point two million,' Allie is saying. 'But that's our final offer.' She pauses, then says, 'Yes, we're proceedable, with no chain.' Another pause. 'Okay, well, let me know.'

What is Allie playing at? Leo hears her footsteps coming towards him, and quickly moves away from the door. He's standing by the console table when she returns. 'Everything alright?' he says.

'Why wouldn't it be?'

Leo takes each of her fingers in turn, pressing them into the ink pad, before rolling them into the relevant box on the form.

'Ow, that hurts.'

'Well, relax, then.'

'It's hard to relax when you're hurting me!'

'Since when could you and Dominic afford a house worth one point two million?' Leo says.

Allie snatches back her hand. 'How dare you listen to my private conversations!'

'I think if you're planning on moving house, I have a right to know where our son will be living.'

'We're not moving.'

278

'Then—'

'It's none of your business, Leo. I'm giving Harris a stable family environment in a nice area, which is more than I can say for you and that woman you've dragged into his life.'

'Don't.' Leo is so angry he can barely speak. 'Just don't, Allie.' He looks around at Allie's bungalow. 'I was amazed you could even afford this place, to be honest. I mean, I know it needs a lot of work, but it still cost a bomb.'

'It was a very reasonable price, actually.'

Leo laughs. 'You made me look at the house details at the time, remember?'

'Ah, but that's not what we ended up paying . . .' Allie gives a secretive smile. She bites the inside of her cheek, looking up at Leo through her eyelashes. It's a look Leo knows well; a look that means Allie has done something underhand and won't be able to keep it to herself. 'We had a little something going on with the estate agent.'

'If it involves a threesome, I don't want to know.' Leo hands Allie a wipe to remove the excess fingerprint ink.

'God, no.' Allie grimaces. 'No, this was much better. And so simple! We made an audaciously low offer on the house, then we slipped the estate agent a little something not to pass on any higher offers. The vendors held out for a while, but with a little persuasion from the agent they took the only offer on the table.' She beams. 'Ours.'

'Isn't that illegal?'

'The agent suggested it.' Allie shrugs. 'It wasn't hurting anyone. You should be glad Harris is growing up in such a desirable area. People are literally queuing up to buy on The Hill, you know. My friend Suki had an offer out of the blue from Simmonds last year – some bloke in Spain who hadn't even *seen* the house. Everyone wants this postcode.'

Simmonds again. Talk about fingers in pies. 'You bought through the same estate agency, didn't you?'

'Yes, Mike Foster. Clever, isn't it? The vendor sold their house, we got a bargain, and he got a cheeky backhander.'

Not Natasha, then. Leo's relieved not to find himself with another jigsaw puzzle dumped on his desk, although he's beginning to agree with Ffion's opinion of estate agents. His mobile rings, interrupting his thoughts, and he sees Dawn's name on his screen.

'Get to the hospital now,' she says, without preamble. 'Alec Jefferson's waking up.'

WithoutConviction

To all our loyal followers, here on Instagram and on our other channels. We have been advised by our lawyers to temporarily take down the podcast and stop commenting on the Carmichael murders as this is now an active criminal investigation. We are proud of everything we have achieved so far and have handed everything to the police. We'll be back in Season 5 with another incredible case for you! Till then, keep sleuthing, truth-tellers!

With grateful thanks for all your cheerleading. Gemma & Joseph xxx

#CarmichaelMurders #TrueCrimestagram #InstagramTrueCrime #WithoutConvictionPodcast

The user has turned off comments

25 minutes ago

THIRTY-NINE

SATURDAY | LEO

Alec Jefferson is deathly pale. Sweat glistens at his temples and in the hollow at the base of his neck. Tucked beside him is a threadbare rabbit, the legacy of a childhood not long left behind. His mothers sit either side of him, relief and worry etched on their faces.

'I can't believe he's awake.' Cara's final word morphs into a sob.

'My head's banging.' Alec winces. 'It's like the worst hangover ever.'

Mikaela gently strokes his hair. 'There are still lots of tests they have to do,' she tells Leo, 'but they think he's going to be fine.'

'Alec.' Leo is standing at the end of the young man's bed. 'I apologise for asking questions when I'm sure you just want to be with your family, but we really want to find the person who did this to you. What can you tell me about that night?'

'I went to bed around midnight and—'

'Did you lock up?' Mikaela looks at Leo. 'He's always leaving the door open.'

'I locked up.' Alec aims a weak slap at her. 'Are you going to let me talk?'

'Sorry.' She draws an invisible zip across her mouth.

'I woke up a couple of hours later. I wasn't sure why at first, but then I heard a noise downstairs. I thought my parents had

282

come home for some reason, so I got out of bed to see if something was wrong, and that's when I saw torchlight moving around in the hall, and realised we were being burgled.'

A nurse bustles into the room and takes the clipboard from the end of Alec's bed. 'Obs,' she says briskly, whipping out a blood pressure cuff. 'You need to let him rest soon, please, Detective Sergeant.'

'What happened then?' Leo is making notes. He'll take a formal statement when Alec has regained some strength.

'I went downstairs.'

'You could have been killed,' Cara cries. 'Why on earth didn't you call the police?'

He turns his head slightly on the pillow. 'Because you insist we all leave our phones downstairs at night.'

'I've always thought that was a stupid rule,' Mikaela says under her breath.

'When I got to the bottom of the stairs, I couldn't see the torchlight at first. I was still a bit groggy – I'd been in a really deep sleep – and I thought maybe I'd imagined it. I turned on the hall light, then I walked into the kitchen and . . .' He winces again, reliving the moment. Cara chokes back a moan.

'I was hit with the torch, I think.' Alec closes his eyes. 'It all happened so fast.'

'Did you see the person who attacked you?'

'Only his arm. I know that's not much help to you. It was definitely a man's arm, with a tattoo, here.' He touches the underside of his right forearm.

'Tattoo?'

'It's weird, it's the only bit I remember clearly. An arm going up – I guess holding the torch – and a tattoo. Round, like a full moon.' He closes his eyes again, exhausted.

283

'Can you remember any other details about it?' Leo says. 'Any colours?'

'No, it was dark in the kitchen; I just got a glimpse of it in the light coming from the hall.'

'I'm afraid you'll have to continue this tomorrow.' The nurse moves to stand in front of Leo, her physical presence adding weight to her proclamation. 'Relatives only, for another hour, and then this young lad needs to sleep.'

He isn't the only one, thinks Leo. Last night he had managed a broken hour's sleep in his office chair with his feet up on his desk, and is now functioning solely on coffee and adrenaline.

Back at the incident room, Leo takes the details of the tattoo Alec Jefferson described to the indexer, who feeds it into HOLMES. By the time Leo reaches his desk, the computer system will have allocated an action to the intelligence team to search the systems for core nominals with tattoos on their inside forearm.

Although, as it turns out, Leo doesn't get as far as his desk.

'DS Brady!' Detective Superintendent Sturrock calls out as Leo passes his doorway. Leo does an abrupt 180 and walks into the office, where DS John Evans from the cold case review team is looking extremely pleased with himself.

'Stephanie Carmichael flew to Paris with British Airways,' John says, the second Leo appears. 'She booked via a travel agent in Wrexham and paid for two business-class seats.'

'Do we have a name?' Leo says.

'Ronald Kingsbridge.'

'Date of birth 7th September 1959,' Sturrock says, 'making him nearly sixty-five.'

Kingsbridge. Leo frowns. 'I've come across that name recently.'

'It's on the electoral register from 2014,' Sturrock says, 'although not Ronald specifically. A Sheryl Kingsbridge was the only adult living at Fairhaven who was registered to vote in December 2014, but if we look back to 2010, there's another adult registered at that address. Ronald.'

'I'm thinking he left Stephanie Carmichael's locket at Fairhaven,' John says. 'Maybe he'd hidden it; maybe his wife threw him out and he couldn't go back for it.'

Sheryl Kingsbridge. Leo remembers where he'd seen the name: it was in the post Dawn had found on Facebook.

'No big deal, he thinks,' John says, 'because some other mug goes down for the murders. Kingsbridge is in the clear. Only then Munson's pardoned, and the case is live again, and Kingsbridge knows that locket's bad news for him.'

'But why break into the other houses?' Sturrock says.

Leo thinks of the Facebook post.

Yard sale on The Hill today but everything outside my house is FREE to take, so please help yourself!

'Because the locket wasn't at Fairhaven any more,' he says. 'His wife had put it in a yard sale.'

Eighteen years' worth of crap from a dickhead who could never keep it in his trousers!!

'But the locket could have ended up anywhere,' John says. 'What makes Kingsbridge think it's still on The Hill?'

'I don't know,' Leo says. 'But maybe his wife does.'

Sheryl Kingsbridge lives in a modest semi-detached house on Maple Avenue, about five miles from The Hill. She opens the door wearing navy blue Crocs and a cotton dress patterned with cherry blossom.

'Ronnie's dead, is he?' she says, when she sees Leo's ID.

Leo's a little taken aback. 'What makes you say that?'

'Wishful thinking, I s'pose.' She gives a hoarse laugh that turns into a coughing fit.

'When was the last time you saw your husband?'

'Ex-husband. About five months ago.' Sheryl tugs at the bra strap on her left shoulder, then releases it with an audible *twang*. 'It's too bloody hot, innit?'

Five months would have been soon after Fairhaven was burgled. 'Where did you see him?'

'He came here. Bloody cheek. Gawd knows how he found me, but that's Ronnie for you. Friends in all the wrong places. The years haven't been kind to him, that's for sure. I hardly recognised him.'

'And before then? When had you last seen him?'

'The day I found some tart's knickers in my bed, that's when. Spring of 2014, it was.' Sheryl hoiks up her bra strap again. 'Oh, I knew Ronnie was having affairs, but he was always discreet about it, and to be frank he was bringing in the money and I wasn't working, and well, that's just how we had it. Ask no questions and I'll tell you no lies. But those knickers were the final straw. I threw him out.'

'Where did he go?'

'To hers, I suppose, till she chucked him out as well, then he'd have gone on to the next one, and then the next one.' Sheryl shakes her head. 'I'm well out of it. Course, when he came over, he said he'd straightened himself out, but I'll believe that when I see it.'

'Why did he come to see you?'

'He wanted his stuff.'

'After ten years?' Leo says.

286

'That's what I said. You're having a giraffe, I said. I'd packed his stuff up the day I kicked him out. He'd tried to convince me to let him back in so he could check I hadn't forgotten anything, but I knew his game: he'd have pocketed all sorts. So I held my ground and changed the locks, and that was that. A couple of years later I had to sell the house – I was behind on the mortgage, and the bailiffs were on my back. As it turns out, Ronnie had been right; I'd forgotten all the crap in the loft. But by then I had no idea where he was living, so I chucked it all in the yard sale.' Sheryl fishes a pack of Marlboro Lights from her bra and takes out a cigarette. 'Do you want one?' She offers the pack to Leo.

'No, thanks. Mrs Kingsbridge—'

'I go by Adams now.'

'Ms Adams, was there anything in that yard sale that Ronnie might want back? Perhaps something very valuable, or—'

Sheryl gives a throaty laugh. 'I'd have sold it if there had been. Ronnie had a tidy sum put away, but he didn't give me a penny of it when we split.'

'Jewellery, perhaps?' In Leo's pocket is a copy of the police poster featuring Stephanie Carmichael's stolen locket. He unfolds it. 'How about this?'

'That's lovely, that is.'

'Did you see it among the possessions Ronnie left at Fairhaven?'

'Honestly?' There's a gleam in her eye, and Leo's pulse picks up. His hopes are quickly dashed. 'I'd have kept that one myself, even if it was nicked off some slapper.' She laughs uproariously, and the force sets off a coughing fit that doubles her over for several seconds. 'No, love,' she says, once she's regained her breath. 'It was just a pile of crap he'd picked up from gawd knows where. I remember an exercise bike – or was it a treadmill?'

287

'Treadmill,' Leo says, remembering the Facebook post.

'No one wanted it, anyway. I took it to the tip the next day. Most of the knick-knacks went, as I recall. I emptied the loft, and you wouldn't believe the shit I cleared out from the shed.'

'Who came to this yard sale?'

'Only locals. One of the neighbours took the Worcester; another one had the exercise gear. I think JP – he and Camilla lived in Sunnyside – had the golf clubs.'

'The Lennoxes still live on The Hill,' Leo says. 'Tell me: did you know Cara and Mikaela Jefferson?'

'The lesbians? Caused quite a stir back then. Ronnie was gone by the time they arrived, though.'

'What about Warren and Emmy Irvine?'

'I don't recognise the name, but there were a few people who moved in around the time I threw Ronnie out, and I pretty much kept myself to myself after that. Too much bloody gossip for my liking.' Sheryl drops her cigarette and grinds it on to the step with her Croc. 'Look, you're asking all the same questions Ronnie did, and I've given you all the answers I gave him. I don't know where his stuff is now and I don't care. I'm just the idiot who married him.'

'Do you have any photos of Ronnie you could show me?'

'Now *you're* having a giraffe!' Sheryl laughs again. 'Why would I want that ugly mug staring at me? I deleted him off my phone and burned our wedding photos, and it felt bloody good, I can tell you.'

As Leo leaves Sheryl Kingsbridge's house, he calls Ffion to let her know it's going to be another long day. Sheryl doesn't recall the locket, but everything else fits their theory that Ronnie's been breaking into houses looking for it. It had to have been taken

288

from the yard sale by someone who was living on The Hill at the time.

'Alright?' The tone of Ffion's voice tells Leo she's in the middle of something. 'Can I call you back?'

'Sure.' There's a grinding noise in the background which is oddly familiar. 'You okay, though?' He wonders if she's in the middle of an arrest; if she's about to deal with a violent suspect. He shouldn't worry about her – Ffion is more than capable of looking after herself – but of course, he does.

'I'm fine.'

The phone goes dead. Leo stares at the blank screen, trying to place the noise he heard. It was something mechanical, like an old-fashioned lift or a—

His heart sinks.

A gate.

Ffion isn't tackling a suspect.

She's tackling Allie.

FORTY

SATURDAY | FFION

Allie's house isn't at all what Ffion had anticipated. She had expected something grand, something more like the properties shown off in the windows at Simmonds. The details for this rather ugly bungalow would be kept in a drawer, brought out in desperation when all the beautiful show homes had been exhausted.

It's more of a house than you'll ever have, says a voice in Ffion's head. Allie's house might be shabby, but the plot is enormous. There's a yellow 'notification of planning permission' fixed to the telegraph pole next to the gate, and Ffion supposes Allie and Dominic will build upwards, turning this dated bungalow into something more covetable.

And what does Ffion have? Ten days left on a rental lease, several boxes of books, and a flatulent dog with behavioural issues.

The thought of the last snaps her out of her wallowing. Dave may have issues, but he's never bitten anyone. Ffion had been right *there*, for God's sake, and okay, Harris had been scared (and, frankly, the less Ffion thinks about that particular encounter, the better), but Dave didn't touch the kid.

Ffion rings the bell. She doesn't know what Allie looks like, she realises; and, as the front door opens and a dark-haired woman smiles politely at her, Ffion realises the same is true in reverse.

'Hi,' Allie says. 'Can I help you?'

Ffion is momentarily destabilised. Over the past few months, Leo's ex-wife has assumed ogre-like proportions in Ffion's head. Ffion had pictured Allie's features etched in a permanent scowl; imagined a voice like fingernails down a blackboard. But the woman in front of her looks warm and friendly. She looks, Ffion realises, like someone Ffion might be friends with.

'Are you alright?' Allie says. And then, very slowly, her brows knit together. Ffion can almost see the connections being made inside the other woman's head. She wonders what Harris has told Allie about her, or – and this is more likely, she thinks – what snippets Allie has wheedled out of her son. *What colour is her hair? Is she pretty? Slim? Funny? What does she talk to Dad about?*

'You,' Allie says.

It is astonishing, Ffion thinks, how much venom can fit into one small word. Allie's expression is no longer warm; she no longer looks like the sort of person with whom Ffion might be friends.

'Can we talk?' Ffion says.

'Isn't that what we're doing?'

'Inside?' Ffion looks at the houses around them. 'Unless you particularly like airing dirty laundry.'

Allie glares at her for a second, then pulls open the front door and steps to one side.

Ffion stands in the hall – clearly as far as she's going to be allowed in – and tries to stay calm. 'My dog didn't bite your son.'

'Are you allowed to be here?'

'You should get your facts straight before you make accusations.'

'Isn't there some law that says you can't harass witnesses?'

'Did Harris actually tell you he'd been bitten?'

'He was terrified!'

'That's not what I said. I said, did Harris—'

'Get my son's name out of your mouth.'

Ffion laughs. 'Can you hear yourself? You're like a middle-aged *Love Island* contestant.'

'I beg your—'

'This isn't about Harris at all, is it? You just can't bear seeing Leo happy.'

'Happy?' Allie snorts. 'He couldn't be happy with someone like you.'

'Is that right?'

'Do you know what he said to me once? Just after we got together?'

Ffion sighs. 'I have a feeling you're going to tell me.'

'He was crewed with a female officer one time, and . . .' Allie sniffs. 'Well, I didn't like it, to be honest. And Leo said, "You've got nothing to worry about, Allie, I'd never go out with a copper. Not even if I was desperate." *Desperate*, he'd have to be.'

'Is that right?'

'He'll cheat on you.' Allie's voice is shrill.

'Leo would never cheat,' Ffion says, but she thinks about Leo snatching up his phone and taking it into the bathroom; turning away the screen so Ffion can't see what's behind the *ping* of another notification.

'Sure about that, are you? You can get pre-nups for cheating, you know; my friends Warren and Emmy got one. It'll protect your assets for when Leo runs off with another woman. Which he will.' Allie spits this last.

Ffion laughs. The only asset Ffion has is Dave, and she doubts

Leo would want him. 'Look, can't we be grown-ups about this? You've moved on, and Leo says that Harr—' Ffion stops herself, and concedes a point to Allie. 'He says *your son* gets on well with your husband, right?'

'Dominic's a wonderful stepfather.'

'Great, so can't we just—'

'Harris doesn't need another mother.' There's a shift in Allie's voice on the last word; a tiny crack as anger gives way to something else.

Despite herself, Ffion unbends a little. 'I'm not trying to be his mother,' she says, more calmly than the situation merits. If Allie knew but a tenth of Ffion's complicated relationship with motherhood, she'd know she had nothing to fear. Ffion thinks of Seren, growing up believing Elen was her mam; that Ffion was just her annoying big sister, who told her what to do and occasionally wrapped her up in fierce hugs that came from nowhere.

'You know,' Ffion says, and suddenly there's a lump in her throat, and she swallows it down because she will not cry in front of Allie, 'it can be good for kids to have two women in their lives. Two strong, independent women,' she adds.

There's a long silence. Ffion holds Allie's gaze and silently congratulates herself for being the bigger person. There had been a time when she would have lost her temper, when this would have ended up in full-on fisticuffs; the pair of them scrapping on the floor. But as they stand there, Ffion sees a softening in Allie's face, and she thinks that she might just have got through to—

Allie's open palm lands on Ffion's cheek with a sting that makes her eyes water.

Just as Ffion's fingers are curling into fists, she feels a hand on her shoulder.

'Hey,' Leo says.

FORTY-ONE

SATURDAY | ALLIE

Nobody moves. Leo keeps his hand on Ffion's shoulder and his eyes locked on Allie. Ffion's shocked expression has morphed into fury, her face a violent shade of red, except for the stark white imprint of Allie's hand on her left cheek.

Allie is shaking. She's never hit anyone before. Never thought she was capable of it. She squeezes her right hand in her left, trying to stop the tingling in her fingers. She wants to cry, but she won't. Not while Ffion's still here. She thinks of the way Leo rushed to Ffion's side. Was he ever that protective of Allie, when they were together? Did his eyes ever light up the way they do when he talks about *her*?

Allie doesn't care about Leo, not any more, but she does care about Harris. If Leo loves Ffion, then Harris might come to love her too, and the thought of that makes Allie's heart hurt.

The kitchen door opens and the cleaner steps tentatively into the hall. 'That's everything done, Mrs Green. I didn't have time for the en-suite, but I've done the family bathroom and given the kitchen a good going over.'

'Thank you, Tanya.' Allie has to force the words past the lump in her throat.

Tanya looks nervously at Leo and Ffion. She glances again at

Allie, then opens and closes her mouth, as though she'd been about to say something but had thought better of it. 'I'll see you next week, then,' she says.

'What's going on?' Leo says, when Tanya's gone.

'She just showed up out of the blue,' Allie says, 'and forced her way inside.'

'I didn't *force* my way in.' Ffion shakes off Leo's hand. 'Throwing her weight around, trying to intimidate me into dropping my complaint.'

'Sorry – who slapped who?' Ffion rubs her cheek. 'Although seriously, mate, if you're going to hit someone, learn to throw a proper punch. Bitch-slaps belong in high school.'

Allie feels the rage rising inside her again. 'You think you're better than me, don't you?'

'Yes.' Ffion gives a deliberate yawn. 'Next question?'

Leo steps between them. 'Dropping *what* complaint?' He looks at Allie, but she doesn't answer.

'She reported Dave,' Ffion says.

'Seriously?' Leo rubs his face. 'Christ, Allie.'

Allie adjusts the placement of the porcelain shepherdess on the console table. It's nothing personal, she tells herself; she's protecting Harris, that's all. Making sure he's not around unsuitable people. And let's face it, a woman who lets a dog attack a child is far from suitable. Dominic said Harris had forgotten all about it, but the poor boy had simply pushed it to the back of his mind. When Allie had reminded him about it, Harris had got upset all over again.

Ffion clears her throat. 'I need to go.' She looks at Allie. 'It would be easier if we could all just get on, you know.'

'Just leave,' Allie says.

Leo lightly touches Ffion's arm. 'See you later?'

A shadow passes across her face – 'Yeah. Maybe.' – and then she's gone.

Leo doesn't speak for a second or two after the front door slams. Allie's never seen him like this before, as though something's simmering under the surface.

'Why do you want to ruin the one good thing that's happened to me in years?' he says eventually.

Allie can't look at him.

'I love her, Allie. She's going to be in my life whether you like it or not, and it would be so much better for Harris if you could at least pretend to be okay with that.'

'I don't want her around him.' Allie fiddles with the detailing on the edge of the console table; adjusts the position of a photo frame featuring Harris standing between Allie and Dominic. The shepherdess still doesn't look right, and Allie moves it to the opposite side, next to a stack of fabric-bound books.

'When did you get a cleaner?' Leo says.

'She started today. Not that it's any of your business.'

'You're home all day and you can't clean your own house?'

'Everyone has a cleaner, Leo.' Allie tuts. 'I was literally the only person on The Hill who didn't have one.'

'For the hundredth time, Allie, you don't live on The—' Leo breaks off. 'Did you get her through Bianca Dixon's agency? She said a woman at the bottom of The Hill had asked her for one.'

'So what if I did?'

'I think that's a bad idea.'

'First your girlfriend, now you,' Allie says. 'How come everyone's having a go at me today?'

'Were you given an employment history?'

296

'Bianca thoroughly vets everyone before taking them on,' Allie says. 'I trust her.'

'You should at least ask for details of any criminal convictions.'

'Don't be such a snob.'

'*I'm* a snob?' Leo laughs. 'That's rich, coming from a social climber like you. Do your new friends know you're copying everything they do?'

'I'm sure they'd be flattered to know they inspire me,' Allie bites back, but Leo has stopped listening. He's staring at Allie's console table.

'That shepherdess.' Leo points. 'Where's it from?'

'A friend gave it to me.' Allie colours slightly.

'What friend?'

'Emmy Irvine, if you must know. It used to be on her mantelpiece.'

'I've seen it before, but not in the Irvines' house.' Leo frowns.

'It's one of three,' Allie says. 'They're very sought-after, actually. Royal Worcester.'

'Worcester?' Leo picks up the shepherdess.

'*Royal* Worcester.'

'Where are the other two?'

'Camilla and Cara had one each. Please be careful, Leo – I've already mended it once.'

Leo is holding the figurine upside down, putting his fingers through the firing hole at the bottom. 'Was there anything inside it?'

'Inside . . .' Allie isn't following this; Leo's behaving quite bizarrely. 'No, of course not. The estate agent selling Ormindale broke it, and the Irvines were throwing it out, so I . . .' Allie hesitates. 'I said I'd mend it.' There, that wasn't a lie. Allie had mended it, she just hadn't told the Irvines.

'I have to go,' Leo says.

'Hey – that's mine!' Allie shouts, as Leo makes his way down the drive with her shepherdess.

'I'm seizing it as evidence of a crime.'

'But—'

It's too late, Leo has squeezed through the gates and is at his car.

Allie shuts the front door and leans heavily against it. Evidence of a crime. He must know she stole it. Has he gone to ask Emmy if she wants to press charges?

Allie takes out her phone. She'll come clean with Emmy. The restored shepherdess was always meant to be a surprise for Emmy; no one need know that Allie decided to keep it. She's scrolling down her WhatsApp chats to find her latest one with Emmy when something strikes her as odd. The chat thread for The Hill is almost always at the top, bumped up by frequent messages. Now that Allie thinks about it, she hasn't had a notification all day.

She wonders if she's accidentally muted it. After what happened to Warren last night, Allie imagines the group has been bustling with concern for Emmy. She opens the chat.

You can't send messages to this group because you're no longer a participant.

Allie stares at her screen.

Bianca Dixon (The Coach House) removed you.

It must be a mistake. It was only a few hours ago that Allie had been with them all, having run up The Hill to see what was

298

happening, to see if she could help. Allie's a supportive neighbour, a friend, a—

She chokes out a sob. She's got everything wrong. The lasagne, the fruit platter, her clothes, the hospital visit, the yard sale, the shepherdess, Leo, Ffion, that bloody dog . . .

Allie sinks to the floor, her back against the door, and lets weeks of pent-up tears spill over her cheeks.

FORTY-TWO

SUNDAY | LEO

The video screen once again shows Bryndare's briefing room, but Leo doesn't need to look for Ffion this time: she and George are right next to him. The rest of the North Wales team are in Bryndare, with the exception of Detective Chief Inspector Boccacci, who stands at the front of the room next to Detective Superintendent Sturrock.

'They're having their pissing contest in person this time.' Ffion keeps her voice low; Boccacci is renowned for her bat-like hearing. 'Cold case murders go head-to-head against estate agents.'

'Corrupt estate agents,' Leo says. 'Allie said Mike Foster took a bribe not to pass on higher offers, so Allie and Dominic could undercut.'

Ffion's mouth drops open. 'Dammit, why didn't I think of that?'

'Don't be too hard on yourself, I imagine Foster covered his tracks well. I looked it up, and agents are legally bound to pass on—'

'No, I mean if I'd done that, I wouldn't have been gazumped.'

'Right, let's make a start.' Sturrock raises his voice above the chatter. 'DS Brady?'

'Thanks.' Leo clears his throat. 'Sheryl Kingsbridge has confirmed that the three Royal Worcester shepherdess figurines were hers. They were an anniversary present from Ronnie, although she says she never liked them and at some point – she reckons around 2012 – she put them in the loft.'

'Before the Carmichaels were murdered,' says a detective sitting by the window.

'Yes. When Ronnie wanted to hide the locket, I guess the shepherdesses seemed like a good place,' Leo says. 'They're hollow, with firing holes in the base. If he wrapped the necklace in a piece of cloth and pushed it inside, you'd never know from looking at it.'

'We now believe Ronnie Kingsbridge to be a serial romance scammer who has operated under both his own and a number of different names,' DS John Evans says. 'Our intelligence system has thrown up three potential reports of romance fraud in Cheshire and the surrounding area, committed by a white male matching Kingsbridge's profile. There are likely to be many more women out there who haven't reported him, because they feel ashamed at having been taken in. We suspect Stephanie Carmichael was just one in a long line of female victims.'

'Let me get this straight.' A male detective with his shirt-sleeves rolled up leans on the table in front of him. 'Kingsbridge found a shepherdess at the Lennoxes' house, but it wasn't the right one, so he broke into the Jeffersons' house, but that wasn't the right one either.'

'Sounds like *Goldilocks and the Three Bears*,' someone calls out from the back of the room. There's a ripple of laughter.

'Correct.' Detective Superintendent Sturrock brings the room to order. 'So he went to the final house on his list of suspects. Warren and Emmy Irvine's. Only he was too late – someone had already found the locket.'

'Warren,' says the detective with the rolled-up sleeves.

'No.' Detective Chief Inspector Boccacci has been silent until now. She steps forward. 'Natasha Brett.'

FORTY-THREE

SUNDAY | FFION

'Natasha broke the shepherdess when she was staging Ormindale for a viewing,' DCI Boccacci says. 'We don't know whether she took the locket away with her, but we do know she later sent a text message to Warren Irvine, saying she had some information he would be interested in.'

'Data from Natasha's phone shows they had arranged to talk on Monday,' says a slightly built man with glasses.

'Natasha's Instagram post said she was following the podcast *Without Conviction*,' Ffion says. 'She would have known the locket was Stephanie Carmichael's – it was discussed at the end of Season 3 – although she wouldn't have known about the hidden photo.'

'It's possible Natasha came to the same conclusion we did,' Boccacci says. 'That Warren Irvine had been Stephanie's lover.'

'Could she have been planning to blackmail him?' Leo asks.

'Funny you should mention that,' the slightly built man says. 'We also found messages from Natasha to her boss, Carole Simmonds, demanding money or Natasha would "release the file".' He looks up from his notes. 'No mention of what the file contains.'

'I can help there.' George waves a hand. 'Natasha had been compiling evidence against her colleagues.' She brings the screen of her laptop to life and Ffion sees the title page of a Word document. *Simmonds Sales and Lettings.*

'The dossier was started more than nine months before Natasha died,' George says. 'The final change was made ten days ago, right before she made an appointment to speak with Richard Wright. Richard is a property ombudsman, the first port of call for sales agents who are concerned about unethical or illegal practices within their own organisation.' George looks up. 'Natasha was a whistleblower. Or would have been, had she not been murdered.'

Ffion leans towards George's laptop so she can see the document. It's twenty-two pages long and meticulously researched, with an executive summary that makes Ffion's jaw drop.

Practices include inflating valuations to secure business, erecting 'for sale' signs outside empty properties, offering cash inducements to householders to display 'for sale' signs, setting up fake viewings, taking fake offers on speakerphone in the presence of other prospective buyers, failing to pass on offers in order to sell to another buyer offering a kickback, and undervaluing properties in order to sell to personal contacts.

'This is appalling.' Ffion scrolls through pages of evidence, including screen captures from WhatsApp and email, and a transcript from a conversation Natasha recorded between Carole Simmonds and Russell Steele.

CS: Mr and Mrs Patterson have booked a second viewing on Albert Terrace. They've said their upper limit is six fifty, but I took their mortgage broker out for lunch, and he said they can borrow more than that. If they offer less than the asking price, don't trouble the vendors with it. They'll go higher.

Ffion thinks about the dozens of houses she's viewed; all the offers she's made that have been turned down. She thinks about the phone calls from agents, telling her she'll *have to move fast – there are already offers on the table*. She looks at George. 'What a bunch of crooks.'

At the end of Natasha's document, among the appendices, is a list of people who, the heading explains, could be approached as witnesses. Some of the names are victims – Ffion sees the unwitting Mr and Mrs Patterson among them – but there's a second list, entitled *Collaborators*. As Ffion's gaze moves down the list, her jaw drops again.

'There are stiff penalties for corruption, according to Richard,' George is saying. 'Heavy fines, even prison sentences. Natasha was taking a huge risk compiling all this evidence.'

'It's a fair assumption,' Boccacci says, 'that one of Natasha's colleagues erased the entry in her schedule for her call with the property ombudsman, and that one or all of them got rid of her laptop, which we still haven't found. But . . .' She holds up a finger. 'Mud on Warren Irvine's car matches samples taken from the scene, and the tread on his walking boots fits with the pattern found on footprints around the hot tub. Traces of chlorine have been found on his boots, and on waterproof trousers and a jacket seized from the garage at Ormindale.'

'Could Luke Parks have found out that Warren Irvine killed Natasha?' says one of Sturrock's team. 'Judging from his previous, he's a bit of a vigilante.'

'You think he killed Warren in an act of revenge?' Boccacci says.

'That's not possible.' George lifts a hand. 'I was with him the night Warren died.'

'It wasn't Warren,' Ffion says suddenly. How is it that she's only just realised? She looks around the room. 'Emmy's the murderer.'

'Emmy Irvine was only absent from the charity event for forty-five minutes,' Detective Superintendent Sturrock says. 'There wouldn't have been time for her to get home, kill her husband, then return to the dinner. The timings have been confirmed by Camilla and JP Lennox, and we have her on CCTV during that time, talking to the Makepeaces' driver outside the hotel.'

'Of course.' Ffion grins. 'That fits too. And I don't mean Warren.'

'Any chance you could share your thoughts with the rest of the class?' Boccacci says archly.

Ffion turns to George. 'Luke Parks worried about Natasha's job because she "had to deal with all sorts", remember?'

'Right. Naked vendors, houses full of animal waste. I remember.'

'And a woman cheating on her husband.' Ffion waits, but she's surrounded by blank faces. 'Emmy was cheating on Warren, quite possibly with the Makepeaces' driver, Ray Tinnion, which would explain why she spent half the charity dinner outside with him.'

'I thought she and Warren were splitting up anyway?' says a woman on the opposite side of the table.

'They are.' Ffion remembers what Allie told her. 'But they had a pre-nuptial agreement. Infidelity means no divorce settlement.' *It'll protect your assets for when Leo runs off with another woman.* 'Natasha caught them together,' Ffion continues. 'That's what her email was about, referencing the buyers who wanted a *romantic master bedroom*. I thought it was because something was going on between Natasha and Warren, but it was a dig at Emmy. Laying the groundwork for yet more blackmail, perhaps.'

'So Natasha thought she had dirt on both the Irvines?' Boccacci says. 'Warren, because she thought the locket meant he killed the Carmichaels. And Emmy, because she caught her having an affair.'

'Right,' Ffion says. 'But Emmy got to her first.'

Boccacci and Sturrock exchange glances.

Sturrock nods. 'Bring her in.'

FORTY-FOUR

SUNDAY | ALLIE

Over the past twelve months, Allie has seen more Shaker-style kitchens than she can count. Today's is painted in Farrow and Ball Cornforth White, with an island in Hague Blue. It's a popular choice – Allie must have seen at least a dozen in the same combination – but perhaps a little safe. She preferred yesterday's Calamine cabinetry against the Breakfast Room Green walls. Still, it's a beautiful kitchen, with huge glass doors that disappear into pockets in the walls, and tiles that flow seamlessly on to the garden terrace.

'They're here!' Mike has been standing in the hall, watching from the window. Allie picks up her bag, casts one final, longing look at the kitchen, then steps out to join him.

They have their double act off to a fine art now, and Mike opens the front door at the precise moment the prospective buyers are getting out of their car. He greets them warmly. 'I'm so sorry, I'm running a few minutes behind today. I'll be with you in just a second.'

Allie doesn't make eye contact with the couple, whose children are now spilling out of the back seat of an old Škoda. She tells herself that anyone viewing this sort of house must have money to burn; so what if they end up spending a few thousand more than it's worth? She follows Mike towards the road, leaving the family to admire the house.

'Oh, look at those porch tiles!' the woman is saying, and Allie swallows the needling, uncomfortable feeling it gives her.

'Would I have my own bedroom if we moved here?' says the youngest kid.

Allie forces herself back into the part she's playing. She shakes Mike's hand. 'Thanks so much, I think it's everything we're looking for.'

'We do have considerable interest, as you can imagine.'

'I'll speak to my husband this evening, but we're happy to go to the asking price.'

'Great,' Mike says. 'Speak later.' He walks back towards the house, and as Allie walks away she catches the exchange of glances between the husband and wife. By the time the viewing's over, Mike will have his offer. He always does.

Allie and Dominic wouldn't be living on The Hill without Mike Foster's help. Not only had he persuaded the owner to accept an offer far below the asking price, he had also produced a payslip for Allie after their first mortgage application had been refused.

'This says I'm a dental nurse,' she'd said, looking at the document.

'It's only the figures they're interested in,' Mike had said.

Allie hadn't mentioned it to Dominic. She told him there had been an 'administrative hiccup', but that she'd managed to sort it.

So when Mike had asked Allie to help him out in return, she hadn't hesitated. He liked to do practice viewings on a new house, he said, and it was useful when those viewings happened to overlap with genuine ones. Allie had jumped at the chance to look around properties she would never otherwise have set foot in, collecting interior ideas and taking photos of furnishings she would later attempt to replicate on a budget.

The first time Mike had given Allie a speaking role, she'd fluffed her lines and blushed so intensely, she'd been certain the woman who had just arrived to view the house would know she was a stooge. But Mike had texted her later to say it had all gone swimmingly, and could Allie send him her bank details for 'a little thank you'.

Today's 'little thank you' is in Allie's account by the time she gets home, which means the Škoda family have offered on the spot. Allie feels momentarily sad that she won't be able to entertain friends in that lovely kitchen with its huge glass doors, before remembering that she and Dominic could never afford to even consider a house like that. The thought makes her even sadder. Maybe Camilla would have accepted Allie's numerous invitations to lunch had she and Dom lived in a bigger house. Maybe Cara wouldn't always have been 'just heading into a meeting' had Allie lived further up The Hill, instead of at the bottom. If Allie's house had been nicer, maybe Bianca wouldn't have thrown Allie out of the WhatsApp group.

The sudden eviction from the group has cut deep, and thinking of it makes Allie tearful all over again. At home, she forces her way through the broken gates (those bloody gates! Allie wishes she'd never had them fitted) then pulls up short when she sees who is standing outside her front door.

'What's happened to you?' Ffion says, with zero concern.

'This is harassment, and I won't stand for it.' Allie pushes past her and puts her key in the door. 'Get off my property, or I'll call the police.'

'Good idea.'

Allie stares at her. There's a smug expression on Ffion's face that makes Allie want to slap her again. She doesn't know what Leo sees in the woman. She's not even pretty.

'I'm sure they'll be interested to hear about your activities with Simmonds Sales and Lettings.'

Allie freezes. It isn't illegal, Mike says. Every estate agent has a few tricks up their sleeve, and at the end of the day you can't force someone to buy a house if they don't want to. 'I don't know what you're talking about.' She steps inside and pushes the door hard, but Ffion's foot gets there first.

'Mortgage fraud is a serious offence. You could go to prison.'

'Leave me alone!' Allie starts crying again. She puts all her weight against the door, but Ffion doesn't budge, and eventually Allie gives up. The door swings open. 'What do you want?' she says dully.

'I want you to call PC Taylor and tell him you got it wrong. Dave didn't attack Harris.'

'I'm not doing that; he'll think I'm mad.'

'I've seen the forged payslip, Allie. I know about the calls to Mike Foster, the fake viewings. We can add conspiracy to commit fraud, if you—'

'Fine,' Allie snaps. 'I'll do it.'

'And I want you to stop badmouthing me to your son.'

'I say what I see, that's all.'

'Bollocks. You don't even know me. I don't give a flying fuck what you think about me, but if you care about the relationship Harris has with his dad, stop with the shit-stirring.'

'Do you seriously think I'm going to let my son be exposed to that sort of language?'

Ffion lets out a long, noisy breath. 'For the love of all that is holy, Allie, take the poker out of your arse and look around you.'

Allie frowns.

'You've got an amazing son and a husband who loves you. A nice house in a nice part of town. An ex who adores his son, contributes financially, and plays an active role in his life. How is my existence taking anything away from that?'

Because if Harris learns to love you, he might love me less.

Allie can't say it, but the thought of it brings more tears to her eyes.

'You're his mother,' Ffion says, and her tone is less harsh now. She takes a step back, away from the door. 'That's never going to change.'

FORTY-FIVE

SUNDAY | LEO

Emmy Irvine has been staying at the Cheshire Hyatt since the early hours of yesterday morning. Leo waits patiently at reception while a group of tourists ask about theatre tickets and tour options. There are two uniformed officers waiting outside, should they be needed, although Leo doubts they will. Emmy doesn't strike him as the type to put up a fight.

'I need to speak to the woman staying in room 362.' Leo shows his warrant card to the receptionist. 'Could you call up and say there's a visitor for her? No need to mention it's the police.'

The receptionist's eyes widen a fraction, but she nods and picks up the phone. Leo hears the faint sound of the ringing tone.

'Sorry, there's no answer.' The receptionist replaces the receiver and clicks the computer mouse, her eyes darting across the screen between her and Leo. 'Oh . . . it looks like Mrs Irvine checked out about half an hour ago.'

Leo wastes no time in getting back to the police car. Emmy Irvine had told her family liaison officer she'd be staying at the Hyatt for at least a week.

'Where to?' says the uniformed officer behind the wheel.

'The Hill,' Leo says. 'Sharpish.'

*　　*　　*

When Leo had first visited The Hill, he'd felt envious of its occupants. The wide avenue with its set-back houses. The private driveways and electric gates. The views over Cheshire, stretching as far as the eye could see. He'd pictured the rarefied lives of the residents, and imagined they had few concerns beyond whether to open the Whispering Angel or the Mirabeau with dinner.

Now, as they drive up The Hill towards Ormindale, the street has a very different feel. Leo notices the slipped roof tiles on a house halfway up; a pair of gates in need of paint. He hears the strains of barking dogs and children arguing. Even the tree-lined street seems a little narrower, a little shabbier. Funny what a few days can do to your perspective. Money doesn't inoculate you from crime, or sadness, or trauma. People are people the world over.

'Just here,' he says, and the driver pulls over.

As Leo walks up the drive to the Irvines' house, he sees movement in an upstairs room. The front door is locked, and he signals to the uniformed officers to watch the front of the house, while he jogs around to the garden. As he'd hoped, the back door is unlocked. Leo slips inside. Quietly, he checks each of the downstairs rooms, before going upstairs one slow step at a time. He hears a cupboard door open; the jangle of coat hangers. A muttered curse as something falls to the floor.

Emmy is in the master bedroom. Two large suitcases are open on the floor, a tangle of shoes, clothes and toiletries thrown haphazardly into them.

'Hello, Emmy,' Leo says.

Emmy cries out. She backs up, one hand pressed flat to her chest. 'You scared me. I thought . . .'

'Packing?'

'It's jumble.' She blinks rapidly. 'For the yard sale.'

313

Leo looks deliberately to the bed, where a passport protrudes from Emmy's open handbag. 'You won't be needing that where you're going.' He walks towards her. 'Emmy Irvine, I'm arresting you on suspicion of murder. You do not have to say anything, but it may harm your defence if you do not mention when questioned something which you later rely on in court.'

Emmy bursts into tears.

She doesn't say a word as they drive to the police station, where she gives her full name – Emmeline Sophia Irvine – in a whisper to the custody officer.

'Empty your pockets, take off your belt and any jewellery,' Leo says, and Emmy begins dropping items on the counter. A lip salve and tissue from her pocket. A pair of hoop earrings. A hair clip. Leo watches as she undoes the clasp of a narrow leopard-print belt with neon-pink edging and pulls it from the loops of her white linen skirt.

'Is that the lot?' the custody officer says.

Emmy hesitates. She's wearing a high-necked sleeveless T-shirt in a soft sage green, and as she reaches behind her neck Leo catches a movement beneath the collar. Emmy brings her hands forward again, and a hexagonal gold locket spins on its chain, sending prisms of light dancing across the filthy custody walls.

FORTY-SIX

NINE DAYS EARLIER | FRIDAY | NATASHA

Natasha stashes her bicycle in a bush. She's got another driving test booked next month and she simply *has* to pass this time. Rocking up to value a two-million-pound property on what her mum used to call a sit-up-and-beg bike is not at all the image Natasha wants to project.

She stops her audiobook as she nears the Irvines' house and takes out her earbuds. She alternates between podcasts and self-help books, and even though she's got another episode left of Season 3 of her favourite podcast, *Without Conviction*, before Season 4 starts on Sunday, she can't stop listening to *Manifest a Million: Your Path to Wealth*.

Natasha is going to be rich. Really rich. Like: can't spend the interest fast enough rich. Everyone knows property is the key to serious wealth, and Natasha isn't wasting any time. Right now, she's focusing on building her little black book. When she leaves Simmonds and opens a rival agency, she'll take all Carole's property developer clients with her. In the meantime, she's saving every penny she can. Next year she'll have enough for her first investment property: the start of her portfolio. Luke doesn't ask for much towards his mortgage and bills, which makes it worth putting up with his jealousy and bad moods.

'Natasha!' Emmy Irvine throws her arms around her as though they're best mates. 'Coffee? Or a martini? It's almost four, after all.'

'How about an espresso martini?' Natasha says.

'Clever!'

While Emmy flits about the kitchen, grinding beans and filling a shaker with ice, Natasha casts a practised eye around the drawing room. She's had mixed feedback from the viewings so far, and she wants to pep things up a little.

'Okay if I move some things around?'

'Don't make it look too good!' Emmy laughs. It's a running joke between them: Emmy not wanting the house to sell; Natasha wanting her hands on that juicy commission, not to mention the bonus Carole dangles in front of her agents every few months.

Natasha pulls a face at the porcelain shepherdess on the mantelpiece. It's like something her nan would have on a crocheted doily. Hardly The Hill vibes . . . She reaches for it.

'Ta da!' Emmy comes in with the cocktails on a silver tray.

'Amaz— Oh fuck!' Natasha clasps her hand to her mouth as the shepherdess hits the corner of the fireguard, then bounces on the carpet. 'Emmy, I'm so sorry. I think it's broken.' She crouches to pick up the figurine, which comes apart in her hand. 'What's this?'

Emmy isn't looking. 'Isn't it ghastly? Cara Jefferson at Hollies bought three of them from a yard sale on The Hill, donkey's years ago, and gave one each to Camilla and me. We dared each other to have them on display. First one to take it down loses.' Emmy sets down the silver tray. 'Guess I'm buying the champagne for our next girls' night.'

'Did you know this was inside?' Natasha unwraps the napkin that had been stuffed inside the shepherdess. 'Oh, wow, that's gorgeous.'

'Let me see.' Emmy holds up the locket, which sparkles in the sunlight from the windows. 'No, I've never seen it before.'

'Could Warren have put it there? Maybe it was a surprise for you . . .' Natasha tails off. Of course he wouldn't have bought it for Emmy. They hated each other; that's why she is selling their house. He must have bought it for someone else. Awkward . . . She tastes her cocktail. 'Mmm, you make the best martinis.'

'It must have been in there all these years.' Emmy is still admiring the locket. 'This will be like that time I hid our silverware in the washing machine when we went on holiday. Totally forgot about it till I went to wash the towels.' She clasps the locket in her fist. 'Finders keepers!'

Natasha carries on rearranging the drawing room, while Emmy looks on with mild indifference. 'Are you up to much at the weekend?' she says.

'Away with work.' Natasha karate-chops a cushion, then stands back to assess its impact. 'We're rafting, somewhere in North Wales. I can't remember what it's called. Luke's been there. He says it's a laugh, but I seriously doubt that.' She chops another cushion. 'How about you?'

'I have to sort jumble for this hideous yard sale I've agreed to organise.' Emmy rolls her eyes dramatically. 'I've co-opted some desperate woman from the next street to help me, and I can't decide whether enduring her company is worse than just sorting it all myself!'

Emmy is seriously bitchy. Natasha laughs because Emmy expects it, but she feels sorry for the 'desperate' woman, who's probably perfectly nice and not desperate at all. Emmy's the one Natasha always thinks is a bit desperate. Desperate for people to laugh at her jokes and enjoy her company; for everyone to side with her instead of her husband. Frankly, Natasha can see why Warren's divorcing her. Or trying to.

Upstairs, Natasha moves a vase from Emmy's bedside table to the dresser – she'll bring some flowers for it when she comes for the next viewing – and plumps up the pillows in the guest bedrooms. 'If you don't mind leaving it like this for viewings, it would be brilliant,' she says, when she's back with Emmy.

'Sure, sure.' Emmy's distracted, tapping on her phone.

'I'll be off, then. Thanks for the drink.'

Emmy doesn't acknowledge her. Money doesn't buy you manners, that's for sure.

Natasha's halfway home when she realises she's left her phone at Emmy's house. She put it down when she moved the vase in the bedroom, and . . . 'Fuck it!' she says out loud, squeezing her brakes hard. She can't leave it, not when she's going away tomorrow morning.

By the time she's got back to Tattenbrook and is pushing her bike up The Hill, Natasha is sweating. Thank God she doesn't have another client to see today.

There's no answer at the front door, but Emmy's left the back unlocked, and Natasha steps inside and calls out, 'Hello?' She walks into the kitchen, but there's no sign of Emmy. She must have popped over to one of the neighbours. Natasha will just run upstairs and grab her phone, and Emmy will be none the wiser.

Natasha's first thought on entering the master bedroom is one of immense frustration. If Emmy can't even keep the house straight for an hour, what hope is there that it'll be ready for viewings? Then she realises that what she'd taken for a messed-up duvet is moving. And it's moving because there are two people underneath it.

'Fuck,' she says.

'Fuck!' says Emmy, sitting bolt upright.

'Fuck!' says some bloke Natasha's never seen before, but who is most definitely not Warren Irvine.

Natasha snatches up her phone from the dresser and legs it down the stairs and out of the house.

At the bottom of The Hill, she stops to catch her breath. Ridiculous to think that Emmy might have chased her out, but Natasha had looked over her shoulder all the way, just in case. Emmy had looked so angry!

It's only later, at home, that Natasha realises she could use this to her advantage. Luke has gone downstairs to sleep on the sofa, in a huff about Russell being on the team-building weekend (as if Natasha would ever make *that* mistake again!), which means Natasha has the bed to herself. She stretches out and contemplates the opportunities presented by Emmy's infidelity.

A few weeks ago, over a couple of martinis, Emmy had opened up to Natasha about her husband's shortcomings. Actually, 'opened up' isn't quite right. Emmy had spent an hour slagging off Warren for everything from the way he leaves the toilet seat up, to the pre-nup he'd made her sign.

The pre-nup that would leave Emmy with nothing, should she ever be caught cheating.

Natasha sends Warren an email, cc'ing Emmy. She says she has some prospective buyers lined up, then adds an extra line. *The buyers are particularly keen to see the romantic master bedroom, which is a priority for them.* Natasha smirks at this. Emmy will want to make sure Natasha doesn't say anything to Warren, which means she might be open to a little . . . financial lubrication.

Natasha sighs happily, puts on an episode of *Without Conviction*, and snuggles into her duvet. When she next sees Emmy, Natasha is going to have some *fun*.

FORTY-SEVEN

SUNDAY | LEO

Having a stand-up row with a colleague is not the ideal way to prepare for a suspect interview. Having a stand-up row with a colleague who also happens to be your girlfriend is even less ideal.

'I was the one who put the final pieces together!' Ffion's eyes blaze. 'And now you pull rank and—'

'It's not down to me.' Leo is trying to stay calm. 'As soon as Sturrock heard Emmy had the locket, he told Boccacci Cheshire would take the lead.'

'And of course he's chosen two *male* detectives.'

It's remarkable, Leo thinks, how Ffion can make a perfectly neutral adjective sound like a swear word. 'John Evans heads up the cold case review team. He's the obvious choice to interview Emmy.'

'North Wales Police did all the groundwork on Natasha's murder,' Ffion says. 'She was an innocent young woman. Her murder shouldn't be the poor relation to the ten-year-old murder of a woman cheating on her husband!'

'That's a little simplistic, don't you think?'

'That's me. Too simple-minded to interview a suspect in my own case, apparently.'

'Oh, come on, Ffion. The Carmichael murders are high-profile.

The whole nation's talking about it, thanks to that podcast. Once John and I have finished, you can mop up what's left.'

The second the words leave Leo's lips he wishes he could take them back. Ffion glares at him. '*Mop up*? Well, thank you so much! Such a treat to be allowed the dregs, after all the real work's been done.'

'I didn't mean—'

'Yes, you did.' And Ffion walks away.

Leo sits opposite Emmy Irvine in the cramped, airless interview room, and tries not to dwell on his argument with Ffion.

'No comment.' Emmy answers John's latest question the same way she's answered all their questions so far. Her solicitor sits beside her, occasionally making notes on a laptop.

'Did you take the locket into We Buy Gold in Warrington, and attempt to sell it?' John says.

'No comment.'

'Who drove you to Warrington?'

'No comment.'

'Was it Ray Tinnion?'

'No comment.'

'Are you having an affair with Ray Tinnion?'

'No comment.'

Leo is getting tired of this. 'When we arrested you, you were wearing a belt identical to one I saw under Ray Tinnion's bed. As we speak, Ray is being arrested on suspicion of conspiracy to commit murder, and if you think he'll protect your reputation when his own's on the line you're deluded. Your fingerprints will be compared with prints lifted from the scene of Natasha's murder and the kayak in which she was placed. Although I'm not a betting man, I'd put money on us finding yours.'

'Is there a question coming any time soon, Detective Sergeant?' the solicitor says.

Leo ignores him. 'In addition to Natasha's murder, you are in possession of a critical piece of evidence from a historic double murder, and currently offering no explanation for it. In short, you're in a heap of trouble and not making the situation any better for yourself.'

'My client has the right not to answer your questions.'

Leo looks Emmy directly in the eye. 'This is your opportunity to give your side of the story. You won't get another one.'

Emmy glances at her solicitor, then back at Leo. She pulls at the inside of her lower lip with her teeth. 'If I were to give you information about the locket,' she says slowly, 'would it go in my favour?'

'We would certainly let the courts know about your co-operation,' John says.

There's a long silence.

'Warren got a text message,' Emmy says eventually. 'From Natasha.'

FORTY-EIGHT

EIGHT DAYS AGO | SATURDAY | EMMY

Emmy has had enough of being married. She would love to be able to sign the divorce papers Warren keeps shoving under her nose, but she needs to drag it out a little longer. Squirrelling money away from their joint finances in a way that avoids detection is a slow process, but she's damned if she's going to let Warren walk away with the lion's share. Also, she wants the house, and that means staying put. Warren will tire of Emmy's delaying tactics soon, and give her what she wants, simply to put an end to things.

And in the meantime, there's Ray.

Emmy adores Ray. She could never actually *be* with him, obviously, but she enjoys his company, and he is literal dynamite in bed. He's such a contrast to Warren, with his private school education and privileged upbringing. My *bit of rough*, Emmy always thinks, with a delicious shudder. When she'd found out Ray had been in prison, she had practically come on the spot. And, of course, the secrecy has made the whole thing so much more exciting, not to mention that it protected Emmy's finances.

Except that now Natasha knows Emmy's having an affair.

In itself, this wouldn't be such a problem. Having an affair isn't illegal, and Natasha takes a fairly liberal view on morals herself. Over cocktails one afternoon, Natasha had told Emmy how furious her boyfriend Luke had been when Natasha had shagged her colleague, Russell. The problem is that, during this same cosy chat, Emmy had told Natasha about the pre-nuptial agreement Warren had made her sign.

On Saturday morning, Warren comes into the kitchen as Emmy is making a cup of herbal tea. They have divided the house into zones, giving each of them two reception rooms downstairs, but there is, sadly, only one kitchen.

Warren's eye immediately goes to the draining board, on which there are two upturned martini glasses. 'Who did you have cocktails with yesterday?'

'Natasha.' Emmy had actually re-used the glasses for a round of post-coital drinks with Ray (she'd needed something to steady her nerves), but she's glad to have a more acceptable explanation to hand. 'Not that it's any of your business.'

'You're far too familiar with her,' Warren snaps. 'One can't be *mates* with contractors; it's important to maintain one's position.'

Emmy has a sudden mental image of the position she'd been maintaining with Ray before they'd been so rudely interrupted.

'Did you see the email she sent, by the way?' Warren pours granola into a bowl. 'About the viewing? These people are proceedable, so for God's sake make the house presentable.'

'I saw it.' Saw it, panicked about it. Emmy knows exactly what Natasha was playing at with that *romantic master bedroom* line. She's showing Emmy who has the upper hand. The question is, is Natasha just messing, or is there more to come?

The answer to that question comes faster than Emmy had expected.

'Huh.' Warren looks at his phone. 'Speak of the devil. Natasha wants to meet me on Monday to discuss "something of interest".'

Emmy freezes.

'Probably pissed off with her viewings being sabotaged by your slutty housekeeping.' Warren glares at her, then takes his breakfast into his study.

Fuck, fuck, fuck, fuck, fuck!

Emmy calls Natasha, but she doesn't pick up. Emmy spends the day catastrophising, eventually becoming so worked up that she needs a beta-blocker to stop her hands from shaking. She can't let Natasha tell Warren about Ray, it will ruin everything. Emmy will lose the house, the divorce settlement . . . She might even have to get a *job*.

As the evening draws in, Emmy tortures herself by looking at Natasha's Instagram feed, as though the girl's posts might give some insight into her thinking, or perhaps a glimpse of where she's staying: Emmy could go there in person and plead with Natasha not to tell Warren about Ray. But there's nothing.

Emmy keeps scrolling, wound up by Natasha's smug selfies in luxury houses, and on holiday with her older (and very ordinary-looking) boyfriend. Natasha has tagged him, and Emmy clicks through to Luke's profile, which mostly features pints of beer in pub gardens. There are lots of photos of Natasha too, unfiltered now and often unflattering. Here they are in Luke's car; there they are in front of a small terraced house. When she says yes to moving in! reads the caption.

Emmy knows the development: a new-build on the outskirts of Chester. She imagines Luke pacing the living room, tormenting himself with the thought of Natasha and Russell together. Emmy gives a hollow laugh. Who knew she'd have something in common with – she checks Luke's bio – a warehouse manager who studied at the *university of life*?

Emmy pauses as a thought strikes her.

She doesn't know where Natasha's staying . . . but Luke does.

It takes a while to locate Luke's house – all the houses look the same – but thanks to an Instagram post from Natasha of a summer wreath she'd bought for the front door, and several from Luke of his car from a variety of angles, Emmy eventually finds it and parks nearby, glad to be in Warren's car, which is less conspicuous than her own red convertible. She messages Luke from a brand-new Instagram account.

> I thought you should know that Natasha isn't away with work. She and Russell are there on their own. If you're quick, you'll catch them together . . .

Emmy signs it, A concerned friend, and presses send.

She sits in the car and waits. And waits . . .

It's a gamble, Emmy knows. Luke might not check his DMs. Even if he does read Emmy's message, he might call Natasha and talk to her boss, or—

Emmy smiles as the front door opens and Luke gets into his car.

—or he might lead Emmy straight to her.

When Luke turns on to a bumpy track leading to what looks like a converted barn, Emmy hangs back and then drives past the turning and parks. She can't follow him up there; it'll be obvious.

It seems like a lifetime before she sees Luke's car coming back down the track. She waits, then carefully turns the car and drives up. The holiday let is in darkness. What if Natasha's in bed now?

But as Emmy gets out of the car and walks the remaining hundred metres towards the barn, she sees Natasha making her way towards a small outbuilding in the garden. She's barefoot and wearing a cutaway swimsuit, with a towel slung around her shoulders, and, judging by the way she's walking, she's had a skinful.

By the time Emmy reaches the outbuilding, Natasha is lying in a hot tub, her eyes closed.

'Hello, Natasha.'

She imagines she'll make the girl jump, but Natasha simply opens one eye, and squints blearily at Emmy.

'Alright?' she says. 'Sh'lovely in here, you should join me.' The words slide into each other, a hiccup providing the full stop.

Emmy gets straight to the point. 'Please don't tell Warren you saw me with another man.'

Natasha looks momentarily confused, then her expression clears, and she giggles. She points at Emmy. 'You're a naughty girl!'

'It's very important. He mustn't find out.'

'Whashiworth?' Natasha looks sly, and Emmy feels the heat rising inside her once again. Who does she think she is?

'Not the only one with a shecret, though.' Natasha puts a finger to her lips. 'Shhhh!' She slips off her seat and disappears under the water, before emerging with a gasp. 'Oopssh.' She giggles again. 'Warrensh gotta shecret too.'

'What are you talking about?'

'Ashk him what he wash doing on Valentine'sh Day in 2014.' Natasha puts her hands to her open mouth. 'Oooh! I lishtened to the podcasht. I know what he did!'

'Christ, how much have you had to drink?' Emmy puts both her hands on the edge of the hot tub. Between them, Natasha's perfect pink toenails poke out of the water. 'Listen to me. *Do not tell Warren*, do you hear me?'

Natasha just smiles.

'Do you hear me?' Emmy is apoplectic with rage.

'Maybe I will, maybe I won't,' Natasha says in a sing-song voice. She giggles and slips off the seat again, disappearing under the froth of bubbles. Her feet shoot upwards, and Emmy grabs her ankles to teach her a lesson. Bloody millennials! They're so entitled, so fucking *smug*. Natasha kicks out and Emmy grips tighter, because now she's starting to panic. It's not a joke any more, and, if she lets Natasha go, Emmy will have to deal with the consequences, and she can't decide what to do, she can't decide, she can't . . .

So she just holds on.

Emmy holds on until Natasha stops moving, and then she drops the girl's ankles as if they're on fire and backs away from the hot tub. She presses her hands to her mouth. A low moan escapes. What has she done? Natasha stays beneath the water.

Emmy should leave. Natasha was drunk; they'll think she drowned by accident.

Will they?

Emmy thinks of the way she gripped Natasha's ankles. There might be a bruise. They might be able to tell someone pulled her under.

Emmy thinks fast. She needs to get rid of the body. She thinks of the white-water rafting centre she passed on the way here, which she sees now at the bottom of the field, the river snaking through the valley. White water means rocks; rocks mean bruises. If she could just get Natasha into the river . . .

Lying on the grass in the field, close to the hot tub, is a kayak. Emmy makes a plan.

She's glad of the boots and waterproofs Warren keeps in his car 'in case he needs them', as though tramping through snow or mud is a likely scenario for a man who only uses his car to drive to the railway station and back. Nevertheless, it's hard work getting Natasha's small body out of the hot tub and into the kayak, all the while looking anxiously at the holiday let in case someone should come looking for her.

*   *   *

Driving home, Emmy can't stop shaking. As she's putting the car back in the garage, she sees Bianca Dixon's dad out for a late-night walk and prays he hasn't seen her. She gets in the shower and scrubs herself from top to toe.

When the police come to Ormindale the next day, Emmy almost vomits on the spot. But they're here because of the burglary at Sunnyside, and the relief is exquisite. She dares to think she's got away with it. She wipes Natasha's phone and pushes it to the bottom of a jumble box, then she forces herself to mentally walk through every minute of last night, checking she's covered her tracks.

Warren's got a secret too.

Emmy keeps hearing it in her head, Natasha's slurred taunts that made no sense.

Ask him what he was doing on Valentine's Day in 2014.

Had she been implying that Warren, too, has had affairs? Even if he had, that doesn't help Emmy's cause: the pre-nuptial agreement only works one way.

On Monday afternoon, Ray drives Emmy to Warrington.

'What do you need in Warrington?' he asks, one hand resting on her thigh.

'I just have some errands to run,' Emmy says, as airily as she can manage on no sleep and a chest full of dread. The police are practically *living* on The Hill at the moment; it's not helping her nerves. She's decided to sell the locket Natasha found in the Royal Worcester shepherdess. It's a shame, really, it's terribly pretty, but Emmy feels more than ever that she needs ready cash. There's always the possibility she might need to disappear abroad for a while. Ray takes back his hand to change gear, and Emmy googles which countries no longer have extradition treaties with the UK.

She's standing in We Buy Gold, waiting for the man behind the counter to fetch his eyeglass, when she sees a poster on the wall. Is that . . .

Emmy snatches the locket off the counter and closes her fist around it. The locket's *stolen?* The last thing she needs is the police asking awkward questions, even if Emmy did come by the locket innocently. The poster says the locket went missing after the murders of Peter and Stephanie Carmichael on February 14th, 2014.

Valentine's Day, 2014.

Emmy leaves the shop as fast as she can.

'Just drive,' she tells Ray.

'You've not just done an armed robbery, have you?' He chuckles.

God, Emmy thinks, if only he knew.

Later, Emmy searches online for details of the Carmichael murders. Had Natasha seriously suspected Warren of being involved? *Had* he been involved? Emmy blanches at the idea that she might have been married to a murderer for all these years. She glosses over the fact that, technically, Warren is also married to a murderer.

Emmy clicks on a gossip site thread about the Carmichael case and scrolls through the posts. There are *thousands.* She reads speculation about a mystery lover, theatre tickets, a sticky note from a car showroom. And the locket. She bookmarks the site and checks it every day throughout the following week, finds other sites, a podcast called *Without Conviction*, a Facebook fan group discussing the case, which she joins. On Friday afternoon there is a breathless post on the Facebook site about the locket. It contains a photograph of the Carmichaels' wedding, Emmy learns, and then she finds herself rapt as she reads on and discovers there's a second photograph behind the first. A photograph of the lover!

Emmy opens the locket. She uses her fingernail to lift the edges of the first picture, her heart beating wildly. Will she find a photo of Warren behind it? The wedding photo releases and pings out, and Emmy stares at the man's face behind it.

It's not Warren.

But she does know him.

FORTY-NINE

SUNDAY | ALLIE

Allie rings the bell at the Coach House. Bianca would never remove her from the WhatsApp group intentionally, especially when there's so much happening on The Hill right now. Emmy's been widowed, for heaven's sake; she needs her friends around her. Allie can only assume there's been a mistake, and, rather than send a message, she thinks it's best to speak to Bianca about it face-to-face.

'Come away from that car,' she tells Harris. He's obsessed with Bianca's pink Mercedes.

'It's got leather seats.'

'Harris, come here.'

'You don't even need a key to drive it. Just your phone. It's so cool.' Reluctantly, Harris joins Allie on the doorstep. 'Can we get a Mercedes?'

'We'll see.'

'Not pink, though.'

Through the rippled glass door, Allie sees the shadow of someone approaching. Earlier, she had practised a smile that says *I'm really very relaxed about having been removed from the group*, and she adopts it now.

But it's Grandad Dixon who opens the door.

'Is Bianca around?' Allie hopes she sounds casual enough. She'd hate to appear *needy*.

'Sorry, love, she's gone for a run. Can I help?'

'It's just that she's accidentally removed me from the residents' group on WhatsApp, and—' To Allie's shame, her voice breaks and her eyes fill with tears. Harris looks at her, confused. 'Sorry.' She coughs into cupped hands, dipping her head and trying to wipe her eyes without Dennis seeing. 'I think I've got that cold that's been going around.'

'I'll get Bianca to give you a ring, shall I?'

'It's not important, obviously.' Allie forces a laugh. 'I hardly even look at the group, I don't even know when she removed me, that's how little I look at it. But I'm working on this yard sale, I mean, I've literally put *hours* of my own time into it, and—'

'Oh, love.' Dennis tilts his head. 'I'm sure she wouldn't have deleted you if she'd known what it meant to you.'

'It doesn't . . . I mean, I'm not . . .' Allie laughs again, but it sounds squeaky and hysterical, and she falls silent.

'You'll have to speak to Bianca about it. I'm sure she had a good reason for it.'

'It's useful to know what's going on in the neighbourhood, you see.' Allie has her voice under control again. 'And of course it means I can help out, too.'

'Of course. Like I said, Bianca—'

'That's how you got my number when you went to hospital and needed me to pick Scarlett up,' Allie says pointedly.

There's a pause. 'Why don't I just pop you back in the group?' Dennis says.

Allie's eyes widen. 'Can you do that?'

'To be honest, I don't know.' Dennis laughs. 'But I know Bianca has WhatsApp on her iPad, and as soon as Scarlett's finished playing Fruit Ninja I'll take a look. I'm sure between the two of us, we can figure out how to do it.'

'If you're an admin, it's in the group info,' Harris says. Both adults stare at him. 'Dominic's the admin for my football club,' he explains. 'You go to group info, then add member. If you know their number, you can add them like that, or you can send them a link.'

'Sounds like you're quite the expert,' Dennis says. He smiles. 'Tell you what, why don't you hang out with Scarlett and me for a bit? You can teach me how to use WhatsApp, and maybe Mum can go and have a coffee, or put her feet up for half an hour.'

'Sure,' Harris says.

'You don't have to do that,' Allie says. 'I'm fine, really.'

'You'll be doing me a favour. The kids will entertain each other, and I can get on with the ironing.' He gives Allie a kind smile. 'Go and have some you-time.'

'Thank you.' Allie kisses the top of Harris's head. 'Be good for Grandad Dixon.'

She's barely halfway down the hill when her phone buzzes. **Bianca Dixon (The Coach House) added you to a group**. Allie lets out a long sigh. Everything will be okay now.

FIFTY

SUNDAY | LEO

'Whose photo was in the locket?' Leo says. A faint hum comes from the recording equipment beside him.

'Bianca's dad,' Emmy says. 'Dennis Dixon. Younger by a decade or so, but unmistakably him. I remembered how I'd seen him on Saturday night when I got home. He'd been by JP and Camilla Lennox's house and I'd assumed he was out for a walk – maybe he couldn't sleep; to be honest, I'd been in too much of a state to give it head space – but I realised then it must have been him who broke into Sunnyside. That he must have been looking for the locket.' She looks first at Leo, then John. 'Now that I've told you, will it go in my favour for . . .' She hesitates. 'The other matter?'

Neither of them answers her. *The other matter*, Leo thinks, as though Emmy were trying to negotiate her way out of a parking ticket, rather than murder. 'Why didn't you bring this information – and the locket – to the police?' he asks.

'And be questioned about what I was doing in the street at that time of night?' Emmy shakes her head. 'Where I'd been all evening? I couldn't!'

'If you'd gone to the police as soon as you saw the photo,' Leo says, 'your husband wouldn't have been killed. In fact, if you'd brought it in right away on Monday once you knew it was connected to the Carmichaels, Dennis would have heard we had it and Alec Jefferson might not be in hospital.'

Emmy swallows. 'I wasn't to know that would happen.'

'You knew he'd already murdered two people!' Leo raises his voice, frustrated by Emmy's selfishness, and struggling to get his head around Dennis Dixon – Scarlett's fun-loving, energetic grandad – being a cold-blooded killer. Leo thinks of Harris hanging out with Scarlett at Bianca's house and feels sick at the thought of what could have happened. He needs to call Allie.

'There's no photo of Dennis Dixon in the locket now,' Leo says. 'Where is it?' He had looked as soon as Emmy had been taken to the cells, using the blade of a pair of scissors to lift up the photo of the Carmichaels on their wedding day.

'In my jewellery box, under the ring cushion. I separated the photo and the locket so that if I lost one – or it was taken – I could still use the other.'

'Use it?' Leo says.

Emmy colours slightly. 'After I realised it was Dennis who had broken into Sunnyside and Hollies, and hurt Alec Jefferson so badly, I realised he would stop at nothing to get the locket back.' She lifts her chin defiantly. 'I figured he might pay.'

'So you *told* Dennis Dixon you had it?' John says incredulously.

'I sent him a WhatsApp message when I was at the charity auction. I said I had something he'd been looking for, and that, if we could come to a financial arrangement, he could have it back.' She glances at her solicitor, who is typing notes with a stony expression on his face. The interview has clearly not gone the way they had agreed. 'I was panicking about what had happened to Natasha,' Emmy says. 'I thought I might need to leave the country, and I knew I'd need cash. Lots of it.'

'You tried to blackmail him,' Leo clarifies.

'It wasn't blackmail! It was . . . a reward for finding something lost.'

Leo gives a short laugh. 'Let's see what the judge thinks, shall we?'

'But you said we could do a deal!' Emmy cries. 'I'd give you information, and you—'

'Would let the courts know you'd been co-operative,' Leo says. 'That's the extent of it. No deals. You're on your own, Emmy.' He gets up. 'For the benefit of the recording, DS Brady is leaving the room. Excuse me,' he says to John. 'I have to make an urgent phone call.'

FIFTY-ONE

TWO DAYS AGO | FRIDAY | RONNIE

Ronnie isn't surprised to get a message from Emmy on Friday night. He's only surprised it has taken her so long.

Ronnie Kingsbridge was what his old man Dennis used to call 'a bit of a player'. In his late teens and twenties, he'd always had a girl on his arm, plus one or two on ice to keep the first on her toes. At his wedding to Sheryl, the best man had joked about how Sheryl had finally pinned Ronnie down; five minutes earlier, Ronnie had been shagging one of the bridesmaids against the bins.

Ironically, it had been Sheryl who had given him the idea of turning his charms into a business. 'I'm worried about Mum,' she'd said. 'She's lost her head over this new bloke. Expensive tastes, Mum says he's got, and, as far as I can tell, all on Mum's pension. She won't listen to me, mind.'

Ronnie had expensive tastes too. He had his heart set on a big house somewhere fancy like The Hill, and they didn't come cheap.

His first few marks had been picked up in bars. Ronnie would hang out in posh hotels, keeping his eye out for the right kind of woman. No wedding ring (but plenty of quality jewellery), a designer handbag, classy clothes . . . His hit rate was poor to begin with – women who dressed fancy but didn't have a pot to piss in; women who were loaded, but tight as a nun's fanny – but slowly Ronnie got his eye in.

Dating apps had been a game-changer. Suddenly, Ronnie could filter his targets into more lucrative categories. Lonely widows in big houses? A dead cert. Neglected wives who hadn't orgasmed in a decade? Show me the money. Soon, Ronnie was raking it in, managing his many women with the logistical expertise of a travelling salesman, which was precisely what Sheryl thought he was.

It didn't always work, of course. Sometimes Ronnie would walk away with nothing to show for months of hard graft. Occasionally the mark would get suspicious, or their family would show up and interrogate Ronnie about his intentions. And a handful of times, there had been pregnancies. Ronnie hadn't stuck around to find out whether there'd been babies at the end of them.

When Bianca had tracked him down two years ago, over twenty-five years after he had scammed her mother out of twenty grand, Ronnie had bricked it. But it turned out Bianca's mum (by then departed) had maintained a somewhat rose-tinted view of her relationship with the man she'd known as Dennis. Bianca was a firm believer in second chances, and now that she was a single mum herself, she was keen to rebuild her family.

'Mum said you had to take a job abroad,' Bianca said. 'She never got the chance to tell you she was pregnant.'

Ronnie's announcement of his compulsory relocation to Germany had come immediately after he'd seen a positive pregnancy test in the bathroom bin, but he was happy to stick with Bianca's account. Nevertheless, had Bianca turned up alone, Ronnie might have denied all knowledge. But she hadn't.

She had brought with her five-year-old Scarlett, who turned big blue eyes on Ronnie and said, 'Are you my grandad?'

Ronnie had melted. He'd crouched down, his face split in a smile. 'I believe I am, sweetheart.'

Scarlett had changed everything. In an instant, Ronnie had become Grandad Dennis (admitting to Bianca he had given her mum a false name would have undermined the romantic story with which she'd grown up), and Scarlett's best mate. When nursery staff had addressed him with Scarlett's surname instead of his own, Ronnie hadn't corrected them. He couldn't have explained it, but being part of a family unit gave him a feeling he'd never had before. Besides, even Bianca had taken to writing Christmas and birthday cards *from Bianca, Scarlett and Dennis Dixon.*

Ronnie hardly thought about his old life; about the crimes he'd committed. He separated his life into *before Scarlett* and *after Scarlett*, and preferred not to dwell on *before*. Occasionally he would think about Stephanie Carmichael, and the messed-up night when her husband had arrived home unexpectedly, but he always pushed the thought to one side. He had got away with it, and okay, another bloke had copped for it, but that was the way life went.

That bloody locket, though.

Ronnie had taken it out of instinct; the only thing of value he could lay his hands on in the precious seconds he had to make himself scarce. He would have sold it right away, only the family kicked up a stink about it being missing, and Ronnie decided he'd better wait until the heat had died down. He stashed it behind the water tank inside a porcelain shepherdess; part of a set he'd once given Sheryl for their anniversary. She'd made out she loved them, but they'd somehow found their way to the loft along with the rest of their unwanted junk.

If only he'd chucked it in the river, he wouldn't be in this mess now.

Ronnie had worried about DNA; had thought that if he was going to get rid of the locket he'd snatched so abruptly from Stephanie's neck, he would need to research how to properly rid it of all traces of him. The locket was intricately engraved and the thought of a tiny speck of DNA lingering in one of those scrolls gave him palpitations. It was safer hidden in the shepherdess, safely in the loft at home, where Ronnie could make sure no one ever found it.

Only then Sheryl had thrown him out and refused to let him back in the house, no matter how many times he insisted he still had stuff inside.

'What stuff?' she'd said, her hands on her hips.

Ronnie could hardly say *one of your Royal Worcester shepherdesses*, could he? He had to leave the locket, and as time passed, he would occasionally wake up in a cold sweat, thinking about his and Stephanie's DNA nestling in those intricate engraved scrolls.

He never imagined it would be the *contents* of the locket that would cause him trouble.

Ronnie had been strict about the need to keep their relationship a secret. 'Imagine if Peter finds out before we're ready to start our new life,' he'd said, when Stephanie had whipped out her new iPhone 5 and taken a photo of him as he lay in her marital bed.

'I don't care any more,' Stephanie said. 'I just want to be with you. I'm ready, Ronald.'

'Delete it.' Ronnie had not been ready. The money tap was still flowing, and he wasn't about to turn it off. Stephanie had protested, but she'd deleted the photo.

Or so Ronnie had thought.

Sometimes, when Ronnie said goodbye to Stephanie ahead of a few days apart, Stephanie would press a hand to her chest and say *I'll always have you close by, my love*. In her heart, Ronnie had assumed she meant, although he was always more focused on getting away and having a break from the woman's doe-eyed swooning.

Afterwards, though – after Stephanie was dead and buried, and Sheryl had kicked Ronnie out of Fairhaven – Ronnie kept coming back to it. Kept seeing Stephanie's hand pressed, not to her chest, but on that locket, and a cold dread had crept over him. What if she hadn't deleted that photo?

And then the shit really hit the fan.

Munson was posthumously pardoned, and the police reopened the Carmichael murder investigation. Suddenly Ronnie couldn't move without reading an appeal for information, or hearing radio and podcast hosts discuss the murders, or seeing photos of the locket.

He had to get it back.

Ronnie had a sizeable nest egg stashed away, thanks to thirty-odd years of breaking hearts, so he had called Simmonds estate agents, pretending to live in Spain and asking them to approach the owners of Fairhaven on his behalf. They wouldn't sell.

'Where's this, Dad?' Bianca had been looking at the photo of The Hill on his iPad.

'The Hill, in Tattenbrook.'

'What are the schools like?' Bianca had already gone on to Rightmove, seeing what was available in the area.

'Pretty good, I reckon.'

'How gorgeous is this one?' Bianca had showed him the Coach House. 'Bit out of my price range, though.' She'd laughed.

Ronnie had looked at the garden, which already had a playhouse and swing set for Scarlett and an office for Bianca. 'I reckon I could help you out with that,' he'd said.

* * *

Getting back the locket had become even more pressing when Philip and Suki Makepeace had applied for planning permission to convert the loft at Fairhaven into a painting studio. It was possible the shepherdess might not give up her secret, but it was equally possible she would be broken, and the locket would be revealed. Ronnie had never burgled a house before, but he'd crept in – and out – of numerous marital bedrooms, and the skill set was surely similar.

Discovering the shepherdesses weren't in Fairhaven was a blow, not least because it meant Ronnie had to track down his ex-wife. Sheryl had been predictably aggrieved to see him, but he had at least established that the trio of shepherdesses had been sold, and to someone on The Hill. For months he kept an eye out, led Bianca's friends into casual chats about home decoration and ornaments that bored him rigid, and then finally, from some teasing messages on the WhatsApp group on Bianca's phone, he found that they'd been split up and were now residing in Sunnyside, Hollies and Ormindale respectively.

Just as Ronnie had left Sunnyside last Saturday – without the locket, but with a bin bag of nicked goods to throw the police off the scent – Emmy Irvine had been closing up her garage. Ronnie had been twitchy for a few days, but nothing was said, so he concluded she hadn't seen him.

On Thursday night, Ronnie had accompanied Bianca and Scarlett to the barbecue at Ormindale. He'd watched Emmy carefully and caught her throwing a few glances in his direction, but she'd seemed generally to be out of sorts and a little erratic, so he'd told himself she couldn't know about the locket.

Only then Ronnie had gone to the garage to get a beer and had seen the broken shepherdess in the recycling bin. He'd left the party early, on the pretext of it being a school night. As he was tucking Scarlett into bed, he'd wondered if he should do a runner, but dismissed the thought almost before it took shape. It would devastate Scarlett. It would devastate *him*.

He would have to get the locket back.

So when Ronnie gets a message from Emmy on Friday night, his overriding feeling is one of relief.

How much do you want? he types back.

How much is it worth? comes the response.

She's home alone, Ronnie knows, thanks to Warren's airing of the couple's dirty laundry on the residents' WhatsApp chat. Warren has gone to some charity do with the Lennoxes, which gives Ronnie the perfect opportunity to have a little 'chat' with Emmy.

Except it isn't Emmy he finds at Ormindale.

Warren seems pleased to have company. 'I was just about to open a bottle of brandy,' he says, showing Ronnie into the kitchen. 'Can I tempt you?'

Killing him isn't part of the plan. But the locket is somewhere in the house, and Emmy is miles away, and what if Ronnie doesn't get another opportunity to search the place? The Irvines' domestic staff haven't been recruited through Bianca, which means Ronnie doesn't have ready access to their personal files. It might prove impossible to get the alarm code.

There is a poetic symmetry to taking a steak knife from the draining board, just as Ronnie had snatched one from the table so lovingly laid by Stephanie Carmichael a decade previously. It's less satisfying to turn the house upside down and still not find the locket.

Where is it?

Ronnie puts the bloodied knife in the dishwasher and leaves. He'll deal with Emmy Irvine another time.

FIFTY-TWO

SUNDAY | ALLIE

Allie feels particularly grateful to Dennis for having Harris, because Dominic is away this weekend, and Allie has some important phone calls to make. Firstly, she needs to tell PC Sam Taylor she's changed her mind about pressing charges over Ffion's dog, because although it rankles to give in to the woman, Allie knows when she's beaten.

Secondly, she needs to call Mike Foster. Allie will miss the income her 'side hustle' brings her, but Ffion's visit has rattled her. It sounds as though Simmonds could be facing some drama, and Allie doesn't want to be anywhere near it.

She's contemplating which of these calls to make first when her phone rings and Leo's name appears on the screen. She presses accept.

'Harris can't play with Scarlett Dixon any more,' Leo says, without so much as a hello.

'I beg your pardon.'

'They can hang out at school, and at yours, I suppose, but he's not to go back to her house.'

'How dare you tell me who Harris can or can't play with! Scarlett's a lovely little girl.'

'It's not Scarlett I'm worried about, it's her grandfather. Look, I can't explain now, please just—'

'This is about you thinking he's too old, isn't it?' Allie shakes her head. 'You're so *ageist*, Leo. Dennis Dixon is really fit. I've seen him playing football in the garden with the kids – he'd give you a run for your money, I reckon.'

'Allie, for God's sake!'

'Don't shout at me!' Allie raises her voice too, because why shouldn't she, if Leo's going to have a go at her? 'I know Bianca's dad far better than you, and if I'm happy to leave Harris in his care, you should be too.'

'He's not a responsible person to look after a child.'

'I've had enough of this. I've literally just left Harris at the Coach House. He's teaching Dennis how to use WhatsApp, believe it or—'

'Are you telling me Harris is there right now?'

'If you shout at me one more time, Leo, I'm hanging up.' Allie can't remember Leo ever losing his temper like this, not even when things were really bad between them. It'll be Ffion's influence, no doubt. Well, if Leo thinks he can bully her by shouting at her, he's got another think coming.

'Go and get him. Now, Allie!'

Allie ends the call.

FIFTY-THREE

SUNDAY | FFION

'I can't talk right now,' Leo says, when Ffion rings him to see how things are going in custody. 'I need to call Allie back.'

'What's Emmy saying?' Ffion says, but the line's gone quiet and when she looks at her phone she realises the call's dropped out. She calls him back. The phone rings twice, then goes to voicemail. Ffion tries again and this time the phone rings just once before the recorded message kicks in. *Sorry, I can't get to the phone right now. Leave a message . . .*

'Can't? Or won't?' mutters Ffion.

'You alright?' George glances up from her computer.

'Are you going to be much longer?' It's snappier than Ffion had intended.

George raises an eyebrow. 'I promised the property ombudsman I'd send everything through by the end of the weekend, and I remain hopeful – although perhaps I'm being naïve – that we'll get Emmy Irvine squared away by the end of the day, and actually get a day off tomorrow.' She types a covering email. 'I would have thought you'd be delighted by the thought of Carole Simmonds and Co. getting their comeuppance.'

Ffion is still smarting from being sidelined from the job she practically solved single-handedly. Leo hasn't bothered to text

347

her to let her know how it's going, and now he's screening her calls.

'Richard reckons there's easily enough to get Simmonds struck off,' George says. 'He thinks there'll be criminal charges too, once he's had a chance to look at the evidence Natasha put together on the mortgage fraud.' George presses send, then spins her chair to face Ffion. 'Seriously, mate, who took the jam out of your doughnut?'

'Leo just sent me to voicemail. Twice.'

'He'll be in the middle of something.'

'He said he had to call Allie.'

'So?' George laughs, but her eyes are concerned. 'Ffi, I really do think you need some time off. This isn't like you.'

'I know.' Ffion shakes her head hard, trying to shift her mood. George is right, she's not feeling herself. She's had low-level anxiety for weeks, a constant sick feeling in the pit of her stomach. Now the stress of the house move and the collapsed chain has tipped her over the edge. 'When I finally buy a house, I'm never moving again.'

'I thought you were getting a van?'

'I hadn't factored in Dave's flatulence,' Ffion says. 'I nearly suffocated last night, but at least I could leave the room.'

'Come on.' George stands. 'I'll make you a *paned*, and then we'll go to Chester nick and see what Emmy said, and you can speak to Leo and see that everything's absolutely fine.'

'Alright, but I'll make the tea. You never make it strong enough.' Ffion follows George towards the kitchen. She wants George to be right, but she can't shake the feeling that something truly terrible is about to happen.

FIFTY-FOUR

SUNDAY | LEO

Leo leans on the horn but is rewarded by nothing more than the same sound in return. The car in front jerks forward by less than half a metre and Leo follows, leaning forward in the seat as though that alone will help him make progress.

'Call Allie,' he tells his phone. A second later, a ringing tone fills the car.

Hi, this is Allison Green, I can't get to the phone right now, leave a—

'End call,' Leo says. 'Call Allie.' A white van slams on the brakes as Leo cuts in front of him, the driver leaning out of the window in case Leo can't quite see his wanker sign.

Allie's phone rings three times, then cuts off.

'Come on, Allie,' Leo says to the empty car, 'you can see it's me – pick up!'

She can see it's you. And she's ignoring you.

'Call Allie!'

This time, the phone goes straight to voicemail.

'You have to pick up Harris,' Leo says. 'Right now. Take him home and keep him there till I get there – I'll explain everything when I get to you.' Leo's pulse thrums in his ears. What if Allie won't even listen to his message? Leo needs to get to the Coach House, get Harris out and—

'You fucking moron!' A man's voice pierces Leo's thoughts. He doesn't look round to see who he's cut up now; doesn't care if he's speeding or if he's run a red light. He just wants to get to his son. He's leaving the city centre now and the roads are starting to free up, thank God, but what has always seemed like a quick drive to The Hill feels like eternity.

Should he have sent a marked car? Could he do that now? Radio up and ask uniform to . . .

To what? Send a frontline officer to collect his son from a play date? He imagines them turning up at Bianca's. Imagines them being met by 'Grandad Dixon' wearing dog ears and being bossed about by his seven-year-old granddaughter. Harris looking on, utterly bemused as to why the police have come to get him. Kingsbridge might even panic when he sees the uniformed officers and do something reckless.

Harris isn't in danger.

Leo repeats it to himself. Ronnie Kingsbridge doesn't know that Harris's dad is the detective who knocked on Bianca's door, asking questions about the burglaries. To Kingsbridge, Harris is just the kid his granddaughter plays with, the kid whose mum lives at the bottom of The Hill. He'll make the connection when Leo rocks up to collect Harris, but by then it won't matter: Leo can play it cool. He'll take Harris back to Allie's, tell her to keep Harris indoors, then he'll return to Bianca's and nick Kingsbridge.

He's so focused on his plan, he overshoots the turn-off for The Hill, screeching to a halt ten metres past the turning. He reverses, then drives more sedately – although it kills him to do so – up The Hill towards the Coach House.

Parked outside Bianca's house are the same two cars Leo saw previously: a Toyota Yaris and Bianca's hot pink Mercedes with personalised plate, *B14 NCA*.

Leo rings the doorbell. Maybe it'll be Bianca who answers. Maybe Leo won't have to see Ronnie Kingsbridge at all. And even if it is Kingsbridge, he might not even recognise—

'Ah, Detective Sergeant Brady.' Kingsbridge smiles. 'Not another burglary, I hope.'

'Fortunately not.' Leo's acting out scenarios in his head, fast-forwarding through each option to establish the safest way to play this. Neither of the kids has come to the door with Kingsbridge. Leo could make the arrest now, but what if Kingsbridge resists and the resulting noise brings the kids running? Leo has cuffs with him, and a radio, but does he really want Harris to see him fighting with his friend's grandad?

'How can I help you?' Kingsbridge is wearing a polka-dot apron. There's a dusting of flour on his hands.

'I'm here to collect Harris,' Leo says. His priority is his son. Ronnie Kingsbridge will keep.

Kingsbridge frowns, then his expression clears. 'Of course. He did tell me his dad was a police officer – I just assumed uniform.'

'CID.' Leo's palms are prickling. He wants to push past Kingsbridge and get Harris.

'You're the ex-husband, then.' A small smile plays on the older man's face. 'It all makes sense now. Allie's mentioned you a few times.'

'I can imagine.'

'I said I'd drop Harris back a bit later – we're making brownies.'

'Change of plan,' Leo says tightly. 'I need him now.'

There's a pause, then: 'Sure.' Kingsbridge takes a step towards the kitchen and raises his voice. 'Harris! Your dad's here!'

The two men wait. Leo realises that although Kingsbridge's hair is grey and thinning, there are well-formed muscles under the man's shirt. As on every other occasion Leo has seen him, Kingsbridge is wearing a long-sleeved top, but right now the sleeves are pushed up from his floury hands. Leo's eyes flick to Kingsbridge's forearms, remembering the tattoo Alec Jefferson saw. There's something there; a dark, reddish-brown, imperfect circle. Not a tattoo, but a birthmark.

Harris skids into the hall. 'How come you're here, Dad?' He's closely followed by Scarlett, who is laughing hysterically.

'Grandad, Bella jumped on to the counter and she's eating the brownie mixture!'

'Get her off, sweetheart – we don't want her getting sick.'

Scarlett runs back to the kitchen and Leo hears her shouting, 'Shoo! Shoo!'

'Dad, please can I stay a bit longer?' Harris says. 'Grandad Dixon said we can go for a ride in Scarlett's mum's Mercedes later.'

'Sorry, mate, we've got to go.'

'But—'

'I said no,' Leo snaps. He hands Harris his keys. 'Get in the car. Now.'

'Hey, go easy on him,' Kingsbridge says. 'The kid didn't do anything wrong.'

Leo stares at him. 'Are you telling me how to parent my son?'

Kingsbridge holds up his hands. 'Just saying.'

'Well, don't.' Leo backs away from the house.

Harris is lingering on the drive, walking slowly towards Leo's car, no doubt hoping Leo will change his mind before he gets there. Emboldened by 'Grandad Dixon', he scowls at his dad. 'It does nought to sixty in 4.4 seconds!' He almost shouts it, furious with Leo for spoiling his day. He touches the pearlescent paintwork on Bianca's Mercedes reverently.

'Get. In. The. Car,' Leo says.

'I don't want to go in your stupid car. I want to go in the Mercedes. Grandad Dixon said I can press—'

'Harris, don't make me tell you again. Get in the—'

'Leave the kid alone.' Kingsbridge steps out of the house, wincing as his bare feet hit the gravelled drive. 'It's my fault; I promised them a ride.'

Leo whips around, white anger exploding out of him. 'Back off, Kingsbri—' He stops before it's out, but it's too late, it's too late.

Everything moves fast. Too fast.

Kingsbridge: cornered, looking back at the house and then out towards the road, a mix of fury and panic in his eyes. Harris: hiding around the back of Bianca's car, knowing that Dad's cross, and not wanting to face the music.

There's a sudden *beep* as the Mercedes unlocks, and Leo realises what's happening and hurls himself across the drive, but Kingsbridge is already there and he's pulling Harris into the car, and Harris is half-screaming and half-laughing, because maybe this is some kind of game, but Leo knows it isn't a game, it isn't a game—

'No!' Leo gets hold of the passenger door handle, but the car's locked, and it's moving, and now Harris understands why his dad is shouting and he starts screaming for real, pounding at the window as the car picks up speed and Leo is thrown to the ground, rolling on to the gravel. He picks himself up and runs to his own car, but as the Mercedes races down The Hill, then screeches around the corner at the bottom, realisation hits Leo with a jolt.

Harris still has his car keys.

FIFTY-FIVE

SUNDAY | FFION

While George drives, Ffion distracts herself on her phone. She messages Leo to say they're on their way to Chester nick. She emails DI Malik to cancel the leave she booked to move house, then scrolls through Rightmove in the vain hope that something new will have appeared in the last hour. 'You're not looking for a flatmate, are you?' she asks George.

George snorts. 'We'd kill each other within the week. Anyway, I thought Leo was desperate for you to move in with him?'

'He is.'

'So?'

Ffion doesn't answer.

George glances at her. 'What's wrong?'

'Nothing. It's just . . .' Ffion shakes her head. 'I'm being paranoid, that's all.'

'You know what they say: you're not paranoid if they're really out to get you.'

Ffion lets out a half-laugh. 'Do you think . . .' She tails off.

'What?'

'Do you think Leo would ever cheat on me?'

'I don't think he'd dare.'

'Be serious.'

'I was being serious.' George laughs, relenting. 'Of course he wouldn't, Ffi, he adores you. Why are you even thinking that?'

'Allie said he would.'

'That's rich, given she cheated on him.'

'He's been funny about his phone lately,' Ffion says. 'He takes it into the toilet with him, which he never used to, and when I looked at it the other day, he practically snatched it out of my hand.' She rolls her eyes. 'God, it's such a cliché.'

'Maybe he's planning a surprise.'

'I hate surprises. Leo knows that.'

'Then it'll be a work thing . . . something he's preoccupied by. It'll pass.'

'Yeah, maybe.' Ffion chews on the inside of her cheek. 'Or maybe it's time to call it a day. Let's face it, his son doesn't even want to be in the same room as me, so—'

'Don't do this.'

'Do what?'

'Self-sabotage.'

'I'm not—'

'Just because something's hard, that doesn't make it broken.' George glances at her. 'Have you tried talking to him about it?'

Ffion shakes her head.

'You are hopeless.'

'Thanks.'

'Any time.' George grins.

The car radio crackles into life. 'All units, all units, observations please for a pink Mercedes S class. B14 NCA, registered to the Coach House, The Hill.' George reaches for the volume, but Ffion stops her.

'The Hill. That's where Emmy Irvine lives.'

'If I were choosing a getaway car,' George says, 'I think I'd go for something more discreet than a pink Merc.'

'The vehicle is being driven by Ronnie Kingsbridge, who has warnings for violence and firearms. He is believed to have with him the son of a serving police officer.'

Ffion and George stare at each other.

'It won't be,' George says firmly, but then Ffion's phone rings and it's Leo, and Ffion knows before he's even got a word out that it is.

'Harris,' Leo finally manages.

'I'm listening now.' Ffion's throat feels tight. 'Everyone's looking for him, Leo. They'll find him.'

'Oh, Ffion—' He breaks off.

'They'll find him,' she says fiercely.

'Roads Policing bloody lost him. They picked him up on the A55, and they were getting set up to intercept, but he pulled off at Northup, right at the last second. Our lot overshot. By the time they got off the A55, Kingsbridge had disappeared. We don't know if he's carried on into Wales, or doubled back, or—' Leo chokes back a sob. 'If anything happens to Harris, I'll never forgive—'

'Nothing's going to happen to him.' Ffion sees George's knuckles grip the steering wheel tighter; feels the car moving faster. 'Call me if you hear anything, okay?'

'Okay.'

'And Leo?'

'Yes?'

'I love you.'

'I love you too.'

George looks at her. 'Which way?'

'All units, all units,' comes the operator's voice over the radio. 'Further to my last, report of a pink Mercedes driving at speed through Llan Mawr. Direction of travel, Bryndare.'

'Left,' Ffion says, but George is already turning, her foot pressed as hard on the accelerator as is possible on a busy Friday evening.

'Get Maps up,' George says, but Ffion doesn't need a map, she just needs to get the route straight in her head.

'If Kingsbridge went from Northup to Llyn Mawr,' she says, 'he must be deliberately avoiding the main roads, but he won't want to decamp in the middle of nowhere, which means he's probably trying to get to a bigger town . . .'

The radio is alive with updates, units making from across North Wales Police area. Control Room cuts in with a report from a member of the public about a pink Mercedes shooting a red light, so now they know the road he's on, and Ffion's urging George to drive faster, to turn down *here*, to look out for that lorry . . .

'The helicopter is currently committed,' the operator is saying, 'but they'll make as soon as they come free.'

'Making from Bryndare,' comes the update from a Roads Policing unit, and a split second later a marked car shoots past Ffion and George. They've left the town now, driving on open roads with the mountains high on either side of them.

Ffion finally has the route clear in her head, and she calls up to control. 'If he's heading towards Penderw, there's a fork in the road just after Tref Y Nant. We'll need units stationed on both routes.'

'Roger that.'

Ffion points as they approach a bend. 'Left here,' she tells George.

'Where are we going?'

'As close to Tref Y Nant as we can get.'

'This isn't—' George winces as they bounce along a dirt track. 'This isn't a proper road.'

'It's the back entrance to Brynheulog Farm. It comes out just before Tref Y Nant.'

'I wouldn't fancy getting a sheep trailer up here,' George says, her knuckles tight around the steering wheel. The track is narrow, with no passing places, and they hug the left-hand side, which is flanked by moorland flooded by bright yellow gorse. To their right, the road drops into the valley, the earth barren and ignored by the few sheep that have made it this far up.

'You get used to it, I sup—' Ffion doesn't finish, because coming towards them, at a speed that leaves no time for thought, is a bright pink Mercedes. The driver, a white man with grey hair, is hunched over the steering wheel, and beside him, small and frightened, is a child.

Harris.

'Look out!' Ffion cries, and George yanks the wheel hard and pulls them into the dense gorse with an impact that forces the remaining breath from Ffion's body. She ignores the pain and twists in her seat, reaching for the car radio. She needs to tell Control Room that Kingsbridge is heading towards Bryndare, that he'll emerge on the farm track on the bend by the bus stop, so can they have a unit ready—

Ffion's finger freezes above the button. Because the Mercedes is careering into a corner so fast the back end swings wide, and then suddenly it's spinning and there's air between the tyres and the road, and then it's flying . . .

Off the road, spinning and rolling into the valley.

Gone.

FIFTY-SIX

SUNDAY | LEO

When Leo and Allie were married, they had lived in a small house with a long, thin garden, shaded by trees that made the grass scrubby and worn. One summer, when Harris was around three years old, he had climbed the biggest one, then called out to Leo.

'Look!'

It had taken Leo a moment to find him, far down the end of the garden, up in an apple tree that had never yet borne fruit. Leo had begun walking towards him. 'That's a bit high, mate.'

Harris had stretched out one leg, feeling for a branch below him.

'Don't move. I'm coming.' Leo had broken into a jog, but before he was even halfway down the garden, Harris lost his grip. Beyond a few bumps and bruises, there had been no damage done, but for years, Leo had relived those few seconds in his nightmares, experiencing all over again the impotency of watching his son fall and being unable to save him.

Leo listens to George's voice over the radio waves, her calm commentary belying the horror of what she is describing. *Vehicle has left the road*, she says, and at once Leo's chest is in a vice, lungs lacking breath, heart devoid of blood. He calls Ffion, but it rings and rings, and now George is saying *confirmed sighting of the suspect and the child.* Black dots swirl across Leo's vision, and he blinks them away. Someone reaches across Leo to turn off the radio, but not before he hears George's request to Control Room.

Air ambulance. We need the air ambulance – fast.

FIFTY-SEVEN

SUNDAY | FFION

Ffion yanks at her door handle and pushes the door, but the passenger side of their car is buried in dense gorse, and it won't give more than a few centimetres. George is out and running, and Ffion scrambles over the gearstick and runs too, back along the track to the corner where she saw the Mercedes disappear.

'Urgent assistance needed,' George is saying. She gives directions and Ffion hears her asking for an ETA on the air ambulance as Ffion starts slip-sliding her way towards the Mercedes. The car is on its roof, caught against a tree halfway down the mountain, and a stream of ominous smoke billows from beneath the bonnet. The air is still, and aside from Ffion's own ragged breathing there's no sound of life.

'Harris!' Another twenty metres and she'll be there. Ffion doesn't have her personal radio – didn't think to take it when they left the station – and although George's voice floats down towards her, she can't make out what's being said. Is the helicopter on its way? How long before back-up gets here?

The slope is so steep, Ffion has to use her hands to guide her way down, the shale slipping beneath her fingers. Her left foot hits a tree root and jolts her from toe to skull, sending a shooting pain up one side. She inhales sharply. Ten metres.

Keep going.

'Harris! Can you hear me?'

Nothing.

Five metres.

'Harris?'

Ffion's wary of touching the car. Its rapid progress down the mountain has been halted by a tree, but there's no way of knowing how precariously it's balanced. The windscreen is still intact, but a crazed mass of cracks stops Ffion from seeing inside, and instead she throws herself on the ground. All the side windows have smashed and a halo of broken glass glints from the grass around the car. Her palms sting.

At first Ffion thinks the driver's seat is empty, but as her eyes adjust to the dark space in the upside-down car, she realises Kingsbridge is crumpled against the roof of the vehicle. She can't see his face, and besides, he's not her priority right now, because even if Harris weren't Leo's, he's still a child.

Harris is hanging from the seatbelt in the passenger seat next to Kingsbridge. He's not moving. Ffion can hear sirens – thank God! – but there's no time to waste. There's no way the door will open, but most of the window is broken and Ffion kicks out the remaining glass and kneels beside the car. She puts a finger to his neck and it's warm, but there's no pulse – where's his pulse?

All Ffion can feel is her own panicked heartbeat in her own bleeding fingertips, and she moves them again, frantically searching for a sign that Harris is still alive. There's a terrifying pallor to his face, and his lips are ringed with purple.

There!

Weak. Slow. But there.

She looks for a rise and fall in his chest, but there's nothing;

holds her hand in front of his mouth but feels no reassuring breath. Ffion knows Harris could have hit his head or injured his back; she knows she's supposed to keep his spine stable and avoid moving his neck, but he's not breathing and if she leaves him here, he'll die.

She reaches for him, wriggling as much of her upper body as she can into the car, so that when she releases Harris's seatbelt, she's there to break his fall. Although she's braced for it, it knocks the wind from her, and she fights a sense of panic when for a split second, it feels as though she's trapped too.

She squeezes out from under him, so she can pull him out too, simultaneously hoping she's not hurting him and wishing he'd cry out. The sirens are louder now and there's another sound too; the faint whir of the helicopter coming closer. Ffion hooks a finger into Harris's mouth; tips back his chin and checks his airway is clear. She pinches his nose and leans over him, forming a tight seal between her mouth and his, and she breathes.

She counts to three.

Breathes again.

Another count of three. Another breath.

She's supposed to do this for a minute, she thinks, but she's already lost count, and the sirens are right on top of her, and the whir of the helicopter is now a deafening *whomp* which comes with a fierce wind that whips tears from her eyes.

'Come on, Harris,' she whispers, as she tips her head to the side. Her eyes are swimming, and she blinks them clear, but the boy's chest doesn't move. 'You can do it.' She breathes again, and again, and she doesn't know how many breaths she's given him, but her head is spinning. And now someone is kneeling beside her, pushing her aside. Someone else is squeezing her shoulder, helping her stand.

'No more,' they say. 'You've done everything you could.'

Ffion fights to get back to him, but the stranger leads her gently but firmly away. Ffion takes one look back at Harris's motionless body, and bursts into tears.

FIFTY-EIGHT

SUNDAY | LEO

Allie's face is swollen and blotchy, her eyes red from crying. Leo reaches a tentative hand towards her, and to his surprise she takes it. It's the first physical contact they've had since they separated – long before that, in all honesty – and it feels at once strange and familiar.

'I'm so sorry,' he says. It's not enough. It could never be enough.

Allie doesn't turn her head. 'He must have been so frightened.' The words release a fresh bout of tears.

Leo's insides hollow. For as long as he lives, he will never forget the sight of Harris's terrified face looking back at him as the Mercedes sped away from Bianca's house.

For as long as he lives, he will never forgive himself.

A low vibration comes from the depths of Allie's handbag. She pulls out her phone, glances at the screen, then switches it off. 'It's the gate people,' she says dully.

'Do you need to speak to them?' Leo says. 'I can wait here.'

'It doesn't matter.' Allie looks at the glass pane that runs the length of the room. 'None of it matters, does it?' The glass is opaque enough to afford privacy; translucent enough to let through the light from the hospital corridor on the other side. A constant stream of blurred blue scrubs moves from one side to the other.

Every now and then, the figures break into a run, and Leo's heart races after them.

'I'm not sure I even like them,' Allie is saying. She turns to Leo. 'The gates. Those stupid lions. They're a bit . . .' She frowns, searching for the right word. Leo knows better than to suggest one. 'When you rang to tell me what had happened, I looked at all the wallpaper I'd bought, all the ornaments and rugs. All the dupes I've found. They all seemed so pointless.'

'They are,' Leo says gently. 'Do your house up however you like, Allie, but do it because *you* like it, not because the idiots on The Hill do it that way.'

Allie takes back her hand. 'They're not idiots.'

'Okay, perhaps not all of them.' Leo pauses, then decides to risk it. 'It's nice not to be arguing.'

'We don't argue.'

'We do.'

'We don—' Allie bites her bottom lip. The corners of her mouth curve. 'Well, maybe a bit.'

'Can we try to get on?' Leo says. 'No bickering?' He holds her gaze. 'For Harris?'

'Agreed,' she says eventually. 'For Harris.'

The door opens and a nurse pops her head round. 'Sorry to keep you. Ward round's all finished; you can come back in. Also, there's a guy called Dominic here, says he's Harris's stepfather. Okay to bring him through?'

Allie glances at Leo, who doesn't hesitate.

'Of course.' He stands. 'In fact, why don't I give the three of you some time together? I need to pay someone a visit.' He hesitates, then gives Allie a brief hug. 'Tell Harris I won't be long.'

*   *   *

Leo crosses the car park towards A&E and shows his warrant card to a woman on the desk. 'My partner was involved in an incident earlier – I'm told she was brought in here to be checked over.'

'She might still be waiting,' the woman says. 'It's been mayhem here tonight.'

'Her name's Ffion Morgan. She's a police officer.'

The woman traces a finger down a list. 'She's been through triage . . .' She looks up. 'Down there and it's the last bay on your left. Don't go in if the curtain's drawn.'

When the update had come over the radio, Leo had almost missed it, so intent had he been on reaching the hospital.

He had turned to the officer driving him there. 'What did they just say?'

'The woman doing mouth-to-mouth.' The lad was young, a uniformed officer who had no idea who Ffion was. 'They said she's passed out. Unconscious but breathing, they said.'

Leo had called George. 'What the hell happened?' He knew the Mercedes had gone over the side of the mountain; he knew Ffion had gone after it. 'Did she hit her head?'

'I don't know. I don't think so.' Disquiet had bubbled beneath George's habitual calm. 'One of the medics took over resus and the other helped Ffion up and all of a sudden she just keeled over.'

As Leo reaches the last bay, he hears Ffion's voice. In his enthusiasm to see her, he pulls the curtain to one side, forgetting the instruction to wait.

'I'd like to do a scan, just to make sure.' A man in green scrubs is standing by Ffion's bed. He turns to look at Leo. 'Can I help you?'

'How's Harris?' Ffion's fully dressed, her shirt untucked and with the top two buttons undone. She's sitting up, her knees pulled to her chest, and when Leo bends to kiss her, she leans into him.

'I'll leave you to it,' the doctor says.

'You're having a scan?' Leo says, when he's gone. There had been something in Ffion's expression when he pulled back the curtain – a look he'd never seen before. Had it been . . . fear? Whatever it had been was so swiftly replaced by concern for Harris that Leo wondered if he'd been mistaken.

Ffion searches Leo's face. 'Is he okay?'

'Yes.' Tears spring to Leo's eyes. He sits on the side of the bed. 'He's awake and talking and he's going to be okay.' Ffion wraps her arms around him, and Leo cries all the tears he wanted to cry when he thought his son was going to die. It's several minutes before he pulls away, smoothing back her hair and holding her face between his hands. 'They said you saved his life. That if you hadn't started mouth-to-mouth when you did—'

'It was only a few minutes—'

'If he'd been without oxygen for even a few minutes, he could have been permanently brain-damaged – or worse.' Leo feels cold at the thought of how close they'd come to losing him. 'You saved his life, Ffi.'

She pulls away, embarrassed by his intensity. 'I'm just glad they arrived when they did – I got head rush and passed out.' She slaps her head with an open palm. 'What an idiot.'

'But you're okay?'

'Totally fine. My head's banging and they've got a couple of checks to do, but they'll boot me out after that.' Her eyes soften and she rests her forehead against his for a moment. 'Thank you for coming to find me. Go back to Harris – I'll let you know when they discharge me.'

Leo has one more visit to make before he goes back to Harris.

Ronnie Kingsbridge is easy to find, thanks to the armed police officer sitting outside his room, who stands as Leo walks towards him. Shrewd eyes assess the potential threat level, then relax when Leo pulls out his warrant card.

'How's the patient?' Leo says, nodding towards the room.

'Head injury, broken pelvis, shattered kneecap, ruptured spleen . . .' the armed officer rattles off a shopping list of injuries.

'Good,' Leo says tersely. His skin is prickling, as though the anger he feels towards Kingsbridge might split it open. He shouldn't be here – he is far too close to the investigation now to be objective – but he needs the closure. He needs to look Ronnie Kingsbridge in the eye.

Leo opens the door.

If you didn't know that the man in the bed was a hardened criminal, responsible in his prime for multiple romance frauds, and currently under investigation for murder, burglary, grievous bodily harm and abduction, you would never believe it. Ronnie Kingsbridge lies on his back with his eyes closed and his mouth open, an oxygen mask strapped to his face. His cheeks are sunken and his skin sallow, mottled with bruises. An angry wound dissects his forehead. He looks, Leo thinks, like a mugged pensioner.

Kingsbridge opens his eyes. There's no hint of recognition when he sees Leo. He tries to lift his hand, but the effort exhausts him. 'Pillow,' he manages. His eyes flick to a pillow lying on the chair by the side of his bed. Leo thinks of Alec Jefferson, now on the road to recovery, but who just a few days ago was similarly incapacitated. They will find Kingsbridge's DNA on that piece of cotton wool retrieved from Alec's throat. Leo's certain of it.

There's a roaring in Leo's ears. He's never felt like this before: as though his body doesn't belong to him, as though he has no control over what it does. He takes a step back because if he doesn't, he thinks he might step forward and go on stepping forward until he's standing right by the bed. Leo can picture his fingers grasping the crisp linen; can feel the tension of a pillow held between his fists.

He takes a deep breath, tries to slow his heart rate, because what's trying to pull him forward feels stronger than he is. A strange vibration takes over his body and he realises he's trembling.

'Pillow,' Kingsbridge says again.

Leo turns away. He does not trust himself to stay, is horrified by how much he wants to rip the oxygen mask from Kingsbridge and press that pillow against his face. He can see it vividly in his head: the older man barely able to struggle; the sudden limpness as he slips away. Retribution served.

Leo's shoes echo down the corridor.

No.

Leo is not that man. He is not like Kingsbridge, not like any of the scumbags he hauls into custody on a regular basis. Leo will not lose his own life by taking someone else's.

Besides, he has seen Kingsbridge with Scarlett. He knows how much Kingsbridge loves his granddaughter; knows from Bianca how much her father values their time together. Ronnie Kingsbridge killed Warren and put Alec in hospital because he was desperate to avoid being arrested for Peter and Stephanie Carmichael's murders. The greatest retribution of all will be sending him to jail.

FIFTY-NINE

ONE WEEK LATER | SUNDAY | FFION

Ffion closes her eyes and lets the early evening sun warm her face. Dave lies beside her, his heavy head resting on her stomach.

'So this is what you do when you tell Malik you're "working from home"?' Next to Ffion, George leans against a gnarled oak tree. In front of them, the lake is mirror-calm.

'I deeply resent that slur on my character,' Ffion says. 'I don't spend the entire time chilling by the lake, you know.' She props herself up on her elbows to admire the view. 'Sometimes I swim too. Anyway, we've worked two weeks on the bounce, and I'm in court tomorrow. Knocking off an hour early is the least we're owed.' She looks at George. 'Fancy a couple of drinks? You could stay at mine?'

'Can't – I've promised to see Luke Parks when he gets back from work.'

'How did you find your first FLO job, in the end?'

'Are you asking because you're interested, or because Malik told you to check on me?'

'Both.'

George shields her eyes and looks out to the lake, where a trio of paddleboarders are scudding across the still waters. 'I won't say I've enjoyed it – that feels disrespectful – but it's felt *right*, if that makes sense? As though I was in the right place, making the right sort of difference.'

Ffion makes a noise intended to sound like agreement, although she doesn't relate to what George is saying. Ffion wants to make a difference, sure – isn't that why they all joined the police? – but *making a difference* is investigating crime. Making a difference is gathering evidence, narrowing down suspects, locking up the bad guys. Not holding someone's hand.

'My husband hanged himself,' George says, still watching the paddleboarders. 'He never told me he was struggling with anything, and he didn't leave a note, and almost two years on, I still have no idea why he did it.'

'Christ, George, I'm so sorry.' Ffion doesn't know how George can talk so calmly about something so horrific. She imagines losing Leo to suicide, and her heart stops for a beat too long.

'You know what Luke kept saying to me?' George turns to her. '*I just want to know why. I just want answers.* And I knew exactly how he felt because that was all I wanted too. All I still want, although nowadays I've accepted I won't get them.' She plucks a handful of grass from the ground, then lets it tumble through her fingers. 'When I told Luke that Emmy had admitted to killing Natasha, it was awful, but it felt good too. I had an answer for him.'

'Closure,' Ffion says. She pulls herself to a seated position, so she can face George. 'I think you're amazing.' Dave, thinking they're on the move, leaps up and tugs at his lead.

'I don't know about that,' George says, but there's a pink flush to her cheeks. 'I'm just glad Emmy entered a guilty plea and Luke doesn't have to go through a trial.'

'Not that sparing Luke was Emmy's primary motivation.' Ffion rests her chin on her knees. 'As soon as forensics had her prints to compare with the crime scene, she knew she'd be fucked. Pleading guilty is her attempt to show good character. It won't work.'

Ffion has known judges look leniently on defendants who were provoked, or who lost their temper and bitterly regret their actions. No judge looks leniently on a woman who drives fifty miles to commit murder, then attempts to frame her own husband for the crime.

'God, it's beautiful here.' George gazes across the lake, where the paddleboarders are now tiny specks in the distance. The sky is the same colour as the water, the horizon a blurred line beneath the steep slopes of Pen y Ddraig. 'I can see why you live here.'

'I might not for much longer.'

George looks back in surprise. 'Have you given up on finding a house around here?' Abandoning the idea of a walk, Dave flops back down. 'Wait – are you moving in with Leo?'

Ffion is studying the ground intently. 'It's complicated,' she says eventually. 'Leo and I . . . we need to talk.'

'That sounds ominous.'

Ffion says nothing. Ominous is one way to describe it.

SIXTY

SUNDAY | ALLIE

Allie stands in her grey-carpeted hall and contemplates her console table. It is too big for the space, and leaves no room for coats or shoes, which instead have to be tided away into the wardrobes in the bedrooms. Every day, Dominic drops his car keys on the table, and every day Allie picks them up and puts them in the kitchen to avoid spoiling her display.

She reads the spines on the stack of fabric-bound books she bought as a job lot from a car boot sale. *The Collected Essays of Jeffrey R. Picklebooth. Tables of Logarithms. Fire-Hydrant Design: Volume V.* Allie was at the boot sale searching for a stack of novels – Jane Austen, perhaps, or Virginia Woolf – but none of the fiction she found had yellow covers. Allie doesn't love yellow, but she has been committed to including 'pops' of it ever since seeing a similar aesthetic in Camilla's living room. She can't imagine ever wanting to read Jeffrey R. Picklebooth's essays.

Next to the books is a squat vase covered in textured semi-spheres that catch the dust. The cleaner has wiped a cloth over it, and now the dust is damp and clings in the crevices. The sprigs of eucalyptus refuse to stay upright, falling over every time someone walks past too quickly. No one but Allie rearranges them, and she has grown to hate them.

She picks up the vase, stands still for a moment, then dumps it – eucalyptus and all – into the empty cardboard box she had once intended to take up to Emmy's. She does the same with the books, and with the gilt artichoke – why an *artichoke?* – then with the horrible dog with the bulging eyes she found in Home Bargains.

On the wall behind the console table is the Crittall-style mirror Allie had been so proud of. It comprises nine IKEA reflective tiles glued on to a black-painted square, and from a distance it could look impressive, but Allie's hall is only three metres wide. The tiles are plastic, and looking in them is like being in the funhouse at the fair. She works one fingernail under the corner of one of the tiles. It holds fast for a few seconds, but then it pings off so satisfyingly that Allie moves straight on to the next.

'What are you doing?' Harris says, appearing in the kitchen doorway.

The next tile takes with it a flake of paint. 'Changing the hall around.'

'Again?'

Harris has had a week at home to recover from his ordeal. He has proved to be remarkably resilient, which Allie reluctantly recognises as a trait inherited from his father, rather than from her. While Harris has spent the week playing computer games and kicking a ball around in the garden, Allie has struggled to let him out of her sight, getting up several times in the night to check he's still sleeping soundly.

'I want to get rid of this big table,' Allie says, even though Harris is no longer listening. He's looking in the cardboard box, his face falling when he sees it isn't something exciting from Amazon. 'I've found a bench with storage underneath for shoes,' she tells him, 'and a shelf for Dominic's keys. I'll put up some coat hooks, shall I?'

'Dad has hooks too.'

'That's very organised of him.' Allie can hear it now: the sharpness she no longer intends, but which has become such a habit.

'One for his coat, one for my coat, and one for Ffion's coat.'

Allie is learning that if she smiles, even if she doesn't always feel like doing so, the sharpness disappears completely. So she smiles now. 'That's a good idea. I expect Ffion stays at Dad's house a lot, so she needs somewhere to hang her coat.'

'Yeah.' Harris looks at the wall. 'We could have a hook for Ffion too.'

'I don't think that will be necessary,' Allie says. Harris has already wandered back into the kitchen, thankfully, because it turns out Allie's smile method isn't as foolproof as she thought. A coat hook for Ffion, indeed. There are limits.

SIXTY-ONE

MONDAY | LEO

'Ah, just the man!' the station duty officer calls after Leo as he's about to nip out for a sandwich. 'There's a woman at the front desk wants to speak to you. Bianca something.'

'Can you call up to the incident room?' Leo says. 'I've been moved on to another case. Conflict of interest.'

'Seriously? I'm up to my eyeballs here. She's in room one. It'll be a two-minute job.'

'It's never a two-minute job,' Leo says, but he heads to room one, because he knows that the station duty officer will today be dealing with everything from lost property and missing children to sex offenders and impatient solicitors, and it's not a job Leo would willingly do.

Bianca Dixon is wearing pink capri pants with white trainers and a tight vest top that shows off tanned, toned arms.

'So . . .' She looks him up and down. 'You're Harris's dad, then?'

'Indeed.'

'How is he?'

'He's home and he'll be fine. Thank goodness for seatbelts.'

'Good on him for having the sense to put one on.' Bianca says meaningfully, and Leo knows she's thinking about Kingsbridge,

377

whose injuries will keep him in hospital for weeks, if not months. 'I wondered . . .' Bianca hesitates. 'I quite understand if you don't want to, but . . . I'd like to say sorry to Harris. When he's ready.'

'I'll see how he feels,' Leo says, although the idea of taking Harris back to the Coach House makes him tense up. 'How's your father doing?'

'I have absolutely no idea.'

'You've not been to see him?'

'No. He called me – full of apologies – but it will be the last time we speak.' Bianca's jaw tightens. 'If it were only the burglaries, I might be able to forgive him. I understand why he couldn't risk the locket linking him to a former crime, and I genuinely believe people can change – that's why I set up my agency. But he hasn't changed at all. Killing Warren in cold blood . . . and leaving poor Alec for dead . . .' She shakes her head. 'It's unforgivable.'

'How is Scarlett?' Leo says.

'Upset. Confused. I told her that her grandfather has done some terrible things that mean he has to go away. I can't tell her the truth. Not yet.'

'While Ronnie's on remand, he's allowed three visits a week,' Leo says. 'They have a family room if—'

'DS Brady, two years ago I didn't even know Ronnie Kingsbridge existed.' Bianca stands. 'I hope to one day reach a point where I forget he ever did.'

SIXTY-TWO

MONDAY | FFION

Ffion regrets having been quite so ruthless with the packing.

'Which idiot thought it was a good idea to only leave out one of everything?' She drops the lone teaspoon on the draining board, then dries the only remaining glass for Leo.

'That would be you.' Leo fills the glass with wine and offers it to her.

'You have that one. I'll use the mug.' Ffion turns to open the cupboard, knowing she's putting off the inevitable, but not knowing where to start. 'How's Harris?'

'Playing football, believe it or not.' Leo grins. 'The kid's robust.' His phone pings with a notification, and he turns it screen-down with practised fluidity.

'What was that?' Ffion says.

'Hmm?'

'The notification. Is someone trying to get hold of you?'

'I don't think so.' Leo gives a careless shrug, but he doesn't meet her eyes.

'Show me.'

There's a long pause.

Leo gives a sort of laugh. 'Ffion, it's nothing—'

'Then show me.' She pushes back her hair in frustration, fingers catching in it. 'I'm not stupid, Leo. I know you've been keeping something from me. And if we're going to have any kind of future – if you want me to commit, like you're always saying you do – then we have to have complete honesty.'

He pauses. Then he hands her the phone.

Ffion frowns at the notification, still on the screen. 'But this is . . . Duolingo.'

'It pings when I haven't done my Welsh lesson. Or if I'm about to lose my place in the league.' Leo looks abashed. 'I'm a bit addicted.'

'You've been learning Welsh?'

'*Dw i isio siarad Cymraeg efo dy fam*,' he says falteringly.

'You want to speak Welsh . . . with my mam?' Ffion is filled with more love for Leo at that moment than she thought she could ever have for him. '*Diolch, cariad*,' she says. '*Diolch o galon*.'

'*Croeso*,' Leo says. 'I should warn you though, my topics are limited. I can talk about my hobbies, discuss our favourite foods, and have a surprisingly in-depth conversation about parsnips.'

Ffion laughs. 'I'll let Mam know.' She hesitates. 'There's something I need to tell you,' she says, but Leo is already talking.

'I spoke to Allie today—' He stops. 'Sorry, you first.'

'No, you go.'

'So . . .' Leo takes a big sip of his wine. 'I didn't tell Harris it was you who saved his—'

Ffion covers her face with her hands. 'Enough! I didn't save his life.'

'Okay, okay. Whatever you say. I didn't tell him. I didn't know how he felt about you, after . . . well, that time, and I didn't want him to feel under any pressure.'

'Sure,' Ffion says, as airily as she can manage. 'It doesn't matter.'

380

'But Allie told him.'

Ffion stares at him. 'Allie did?'

'And he'd like to say thank you.' Leo pauses. 'In person.'

'Right.' Ffion tries to sound nonchalant, but a small smile tugs at her lips.

'That's not all. Allie wants us to go over for coffee with her and Dominic.'

'Both of us?' Ffion narrows her eyes. 'What does she want?'

'That's what I wondered. But I honestly think it's an olive branch.'

'Poked in my eye?'

Leo laughs. 'We'll go next weekend, if you're free?'

'I can be free.'

'Great!' He laces his fingers through hers. 'What were you going to say?'

'It doesn't matter.'

'Sure it does.'

'Well, I've booked a storage unit for all my stuff,' Ffion says. 'And Mam says Dave and I can move back in with her.'

'Okay.' Leo's expression is neutral. Ffion's throat feels tight. She's not good at asking for things. If only he'd offer again, then she could—

'Although the offer still stands,' Leo says. 'If you want to move in with—'

'Yes.' Ffion says it quickly, before she changes her mind, and the surprise on Leo's face makes her heart soar. 'I mean, it's a long way from work, so I might have to sleep at Mam's sometimes, but I would like . . . I mean, living with you would be . . .' She catches her top lip between her teeth. 'I'd like it, is what I'm trying to say.'

'I'd like it too,' Leo says softly. 'And yes, it's too far from work for you, so maybe I could put my house on the market, and we can look for somewhere that works for us both. Close enough to Cwm Coed for you to see your mum, and swim in the lake, right? And so it's easy to see Seren when she's back from university. We'll find somewhere, I'm sure. There's no rush.'

'Right.' Ffion's smiling properly now, although her stomach's full of butterflies and she knows they won't calm unless she says what she needs to say. 'The thing is—'

'Two bedrooms,' Leo says, 'obviously. Harris needs to know he has his own space, no matter which house—'

'Three.' It's not quite how Ffion planned, but what the hell.

'Sure, three would be great, if we can make the budget work. Handy to have a spare room for when—'

'One for you and me . . .' Ffion reaches into her back pocket for the square of paper for a fortnight. 'One for Harris.' She hands it to Leo. 'And one for him.' Ffion watches as Leo makes sense of the black and white image. 'Or her.'

Leo looks up, his eyes shining.

'Yes. Her, I think.' Ffion moves a hand to her stomach.

'Another Ffion?' Leo says, with a smile so broad it almost reaches his ears. 'I don't know if the world's ready for that.'

ACKNOWLEDGEMENTS

It has been such a joy to spend more time with Ffion and Leo (not to mention Dave, who is secretly my favourite). I hope you've loved it, too. A book doesn't reach readers without a huge amount of work from a great number of people, and I am indebted to the team at Sphere for publishing the DC Ffion Morgan series so beautifully. My thanks to Tilda Key and Frances Rooney in Editorial, to Gemma Shelley and Brionee Fenlon in Marketing, to Laura Sherlock and Becky Hunter in Publicity, to the Rights team at Little, Brown Book Group, and to everyone else involved in this book, from cover design, typesetting and proof-reading to sales and distribution. Special thanks to Linda McQueen, whose copy-editing prowess has once again saved me from public humiliation.

Above all, though, my eternal thanks to my editor and publisher, Lucy Malagoni. Ten years ago, Lucy saw something special in the *very* rough-around-the-edges draft of my debut novel, *I Let You Go*, and took me on when no-one else would. She has been my biggest champion ever since, and I will always be grateful she said yes. Thank you for everything, Lucy.

Thank you to my agent Sheila Crowley, and the brilliant team at Curtis Brown Literary and Talent Agency, including my screen agent Camilla Young.

Writing a novel is not always easy and when the words won't come, a dog walk or a swim often does the trick. How lucky I am, then, to live in north Wales, where the mountains and lakes are always waiting. Thank you to the wonderful people of Bala (and beyond!) for making me feel so at home here. *Diolch o galon.* Including the Welsh language in the DC Ffion Morgan books is my small way of reminding readers around the world that Welsh is a living language, used daily by half a million people and spoken by many more. I'm grateful to Tracy Ellis for making sure the Welsh in *Other People's Houses* is correct. Any lingering mistakes are mine.

The crime writing community is extraordinarily supportive and there is not space here to individually thank everyone who deserves it. Thank you for the laughs, the festival drinks and the tax form discussions. Special thanks to Colin Scott, for bringing so many of us together.

As for my readers . . . where to start? Thank you for buying, borrowing and reviewing my books. Thank you for recommending me to your friends, for posting on social media, for taking the time to tell me who your favourite character is. Thank you for the fun we have in the Clare Mackintosh Book Club on Facebook, and for replying to my newsletters with your own chatty updates. Thank you for coming to my events.

Thank you to my friends, both near and far. And last, but by no means least, thank you to Rob, Josh, Evie and George, who continue to put up with me.